PRAISE FOR KAGE BAKER

"She's an edgy, funny, complex, ambitious writer with the mysterious, true gift of story-telling."
—Ursula K. Le Guin, author of *A Wizard of Earthsea*

"Her style is infused with a subtle humor that had me chuckling... She kept turning me in directions that I hadn't expected."
—Anne McCaffrey, author of *Dragonsinger and Dragonsong*

"Eccentric and often very funny.... Baker piles on such delights for anyone who wants more from fantasy than an epic journey to battle evil."
—*Denver Post*

PRAISE FOR THE COMPANY SERIES

"If there's a better time-travel series out there, go find it."
—*Kirkus*, starred review

"Ms. Baker is the best thing to happen to modern science fiction since Connie Willis or Dan Simmons. She mixes adventure, history and societal concerns in just the right amount, creating an action-packed but thoughtful read."
—*Dallas News*

"Historical detail and fast-paced action with a good dose of ironic wit and a dollop of bittersweet romance."
—*Library Journal*

"Another entry in Baker's superlative series about Dr. Zeus.... An astonishing and thoroughly satisfying installment. What's more, Baker's overall concept and rationale, flawlessly sustained through five books, grows ever more spellbinding and impressive."
—*Kirkus*, starred review

"Listen closely, and perhaps you will hear the collective sigh of delight from intelligent lovers of fantasy the world over."
—*Booklist*

If you're reading something by Kage Baker, fasten your seat belt—you're in for a wild ride."
—Gardner Dozois, editor of *The Year's Best Science Fiction*

PRAISE FOR *THE HOTEL UNDER THE SAND*

"It wouldn't surprise me if it turned out to be a classic and went on down the ages along with Alice and Oz and the very few others that have become immortal."
—Diana Wynne Jones, author of *Howl's Moving Castle*

"Charming...Baker's first book for younger readers is a delight."
—*Denver Post*

"Skillfully written..."
—*Publishers Weekly*

"There are few books that I immediately want to press into the hands of other readers the instant I turn the last page. My copy of *Hotel* will be one that I hand to my daughter in a few years. First, however, I'm going to force it on everybody I know."
—*Locus*

KAGE BAKER
IN THE COMPANY OF THIEVES

Tachyon Publications
1459 18th Street #139
San Francisco, CA 94107
www.tachyonpublications.com
tachyon@tachyonpublications.com

Series Editor: Jacob Weisman
Project Editor: Jill Roberts

Printed in the United States by Worzalla
First Edition: 2013
9 8 7 6 5 4 3 2 1

KAGE BAKER

IN THE
COMPANY OF THIEVES

TACHYON | SAN FRANCISCO

This volume is dedicated to Dr. Temple Grandin, Peter Bergman, Jason Sinclair, Dame Agatha Christie, Dr. Harry Turtledove, and the Spider Poolies. Each of these indefatigable scholars lit a light that sparked part of one of these stories in Kage Baker's mind. My thanks are most respectfully tendered.

—Kathleen Bartholomew

Table of Contents

THE CARPET BEDS OF SUTRO PARK

This bittersweet and very strange story was written on demand for a small East Coast literary magazine. They wanted something from a science fiction pro for their annual all-fiction edition. What Kage composed was an idea she'd been carrying around for some years—she was fascinated with the conflict between the emotional needs of someone on the autism spectrum, who nonetheless was an avid watcher of the human condition. In addition, Kage herself was enchanted with the remains of the Sutro Estate out on the ocean edge of San Francisco. The real irony of this story, she observed some years later, was that she wrote the heroine dying of cancer— to give finality to her ultimate fate. And then, of course, Kage died of it too. But it never entered her mind when she wrote this story in 2007.

—Kathleen Bartholomew

I had been watching her for years.

Her mother used to bring her, when she was a child. Thin, irritable woman dragging her offspring by the hand. "Kristy *Ann!* For God's sake, come *on!*" The mother would stop to light a cigarette or chat with a neighbor encountered on the paths, and the little girl would sidle away to stare at the old well house, or pet the stone lions.

Later she came alone, a tall adolescent with a sketch pad under her arm. She'd spend hours wandering under the big cypress trees, or leaning on the battlements where the statues used to be, staring out to sea. Her sweater was thin. She'd shiver in the fog.

I remember when the statues used to be there. Spring and Winter and Prometheus and all the rest of them, and Sutro's house that rose behind them on the parapet. I sat here then and I could see his observatory tower lifting above the trees. Turning my head I could see the spire of the Flower Conservatory. All gone now. Doesn't matter. I recorded them. As I record everything. My memory goes back a long way...

I remember my parents fighting. He wanted to go off to the gold fields. She screamed at him to go, then. He left, swearing. I think she must have died not long after. I remember being a little older and playing among the deserted ships, where they sat abandoned on the waterfront by crews who had gone hunting for gold. Sometimes people fed me. A lady noticed that I was alone and invited me to come live with her.

She took me into her house and there were strange things in it, things that shouldn't have been there in 1851: boxes that spoke and flameless lamps. She told me she was from the future. Her job was saving things from Time. She said she was immortal, and asked me if I'd like to be immortal too. I said I guessed I would.

I was taken to a hospital and they did a lot of surgery on me to make me like them. Had it worked, I'd have been an immortal genius.

The immortal part worked but the Cognitive Enhancement Procedure was a disaster. I woke up and couldn't talk to anyone, was frightened to death of people talking to me, because I could see all possible outcomes to any conversation and couldn't process any of them and it was too much, too much. I had to avoid looking into their eyes. I focused on anything else to calm myself: books, music, pictures.

My new guardians were very disappointed. They put me through years of therapy, without results. They spoke over my head.

What the fuck do we do with him now? He can't function as an operative.

Should we put him in storage?

2

No; the Company spent too much money on him.

Gentlemen, please; Ezra's intelligent, he can hear you, you know, he understands—

You could always send him out as a camera. Let him wander around recording the city. There'll be a lot of demand for historic images after 2125.

He could do that! My therapist sounded eager. *Give him a structured schedule, exact routes to take, a case officer willing to work with his limitations—*

So I was put to work. I crossed and recrossed the city with open eyes, watching everything. I was a bee collecting the pollen of my time, bringing it back to be stored away as future honey. The sounds and images went straight from my sensory receptors to a receiver at Company HQ. I had a room in the basement at the Company HQ, to which I came back every night. I had Gleason, my case officer. I had my routes. I had my rules.

I must never allow myself to look like a street vagrant. I must wash myself and wear clean clothing daily. I must never draw attention to myself in any way.

If approached by a mortal, I was to Avoid.

If I could not avoid, Evaluate: Was the mortal a policeman?

If so I was to Present him with my card. In the early days the card said I was a deaf mute, and any questions should be directed to my keeper, Dr. Gleason, residing on Kearney Street. In later years the card said I was a mentally disabled person under the care of the Gleason Sanatorium on Chestnut Street.

The one I carry now says I have an autiform disorder and directs the concerned reader to the Gleason Outpatient Clinic on Geary.

For the first sixty years I used to get sent out with an Augmented Equine Companion. I liked that. Norton was a big bay gelding, Edwin was a dapple gray and Andy was a palomino. They weren't immortal— the Company never made animals immortal—but they had human intelligence, and nobody ever bothered me when I was perched up on an impressive-looking steed. I liked animals; they were aware of details and pattern changes in the same way I was. They took care of remembering my routes. They could transmit cues to me.

We're approaching three females. Tip your hat.

Don't dismount here. We're going up to get footage of Nob Hill.

Hold on. I'm going to kick this dog.

Ezra, the fog's coming in. We won't be able to see Fort Point from here today. I'll take you back to HQ.

I was riding Edwin the first time I saw Sutro Park. That was in 1885, when it had just been opened to the public. He took me up over the hills through the sand dunes, far out of the city, toward Cliff House. The park had been built on the bluff high above.

I recorded it all, brand new: the many statues and flower urns gleaming white, the green lawns carefully tended, the neat paths and gracious Palm Avenue straight and well-kept. There was a beautiful decorative gate then, arching above the main entrance where the stone lions sit. The Conservatory, with its inlaid tile floor, housed exotic plants. The fountains jetted. The little millionaire Sutro ambled through, looking like the Monopoly man in his high silk hat, nodding to visitors and pointing out especially nice sights with his walking stick.

He was proudest of the carpet beds, the elaborate living tapestries of flowers along Palm Avenue. It took a boarding-house full of gardeners to manicure them, keeping the patterns perfect. Parterres like brocade, swag and wreath designs, a lyre, floral Grecian urns. Clipped boxwood edging, blue-green aloes and silver sempervivum; red and pink petunias, marigolds, pansies, alyssum in violet and white, blue lobelia. The colors sang out so bright they almost hurt my eyes.

They were an unnatural miracle, as lovely as the far more unnatural and miraculous phenomenon responsible for them: that a rich man should open his private garden to the public.

The mortals didn't appreciate it. They never do.

The years passed. The little millionaire built other gifts for San Francisco, his immense public baths and towering Cliff House. The little millionaire died and faded from memory, though not mine.

The Great Earthquake barely affected Sutro Park, isolated as it was beyond the sand dunes; a few statues toppled from their plinths, but the flowers still sang at the sky for a while. Sutro's Cliff House went up in smoke. After automobiles came, horses vanished from the streets. I had to walk everywhere now by myself.

So I watched Kristy Ann and I don't think she ever saw me once, over the years, though I was always on that same bench. But I watched the little girl discovering the remnant of the Conservatory's tiled floor, watched her get down on her hands and knees and dig furtively, hoping to uncover more of the lost city before her mother could call her away.

I watched the older Kristy Ann bringing her boyfriends there, the tall one with red hair and then the black one with dreadlocks. There were furtive kisses in amongst the trees and, at least once, furtive sex. There were long afternoons while they grew bored watching her paint the cypress trees. At last she came alone, and there were no more boys after that.

She walked there every afternoon, after work I suppose. She must have lived nearby. Weekends she came with her paints and did endless impressions of the view from the empty battlements, or the statue of Diana that had survived, back among the trees. Once or twice I wandered past her to look at her canvases. I wouldn't have said she had talent, but she had passion.

———— ✦ ————

I didn't like the twentieth century, but it finally went away. Everything went into my eyes: the Pan Pacific Exhibition, Dashiell Hammett lurching out of John's Grill, the building of the Golden Gate Bridge. Soldiers and sailors. Sutro's Baths destroyed. Mortals in bright rags, their bare feet dirty, carrying guitars. Workmen digging a pit to lay the foundations of the Transamerica Building and finding the old buried waterfront, the abandoned ships of my mortal childhood still down there in the mud. The Embarcadero Freeway rising, and falling; the Marina District burning, and coming back with fresh white paint.

My costume changed to fit the times. Now and again I caught a glimpse of myself, impartial observer, in a shop window reflection. I was hard to recognize, though I saw the same blank and eternally smooth face every time under the sideburns, or the mustache, or the glasses.

The new world was loud and hard. It didn't matter. I had all the literature and music of past ages to give me human contact, if second-hand through Dickens or Austen. And I had kept copies of the times I'd liked, out of what I sent into the Company storage banks. I could close my eyes at night and replay the old city as I'd known it, in holo.

Everything time had taken away was still there, in my city. Sutro was still there, in his silk hat. I could walk the paths of his park beside him, as I'd never done in his time, and imagine a conversation, though of course I'd never spoken to him or anyone. I didn't want to tell him about his house being torn down, or his park being "reduced" as the San Francisco Park Department put it, for easier maintenance, the Conservatory gone, the statues almost all gone, the carpet beds mown over.

Kristy Ann in her twenties became grim and intense, a thin girl who dressed carelessly. Sometimes she brought books of photographs to the park with her and stalked along the paths, holding up the old images to compare them with the bare modern reality. One day she came with a crowd of young mortals from her college class, and talked knowledgeably about the park. The term *urban archaeology* was used a number of times.

Now, when she painted the park, she worked with the old photographs beside her, imposing the light and colors of the present day on representations of the past. I knew what she was doing. I'd done it myself, hadn't I?

Kristy Ann in her thirties grew thinner, seldom smiled. She took to patrolling the park for trash, muttering savagely to herself as she picked up empty pop cans or discarded snack wrappers.

She came once to the park with two other women and a news crew from KQED. They were filmed in front of the statue of Diana, talking about a Park Preservation Society they'd founded. There was talk of budget cuts. A petition. One of the cameramen made a joke about the statue and I could see the rage flaring in Kristy Ann's eyes. She began to rant about the importance of restoring Sutro Park, replacing the statues, replanting the parterres.

Her two companions exchanged glances and tactfully cut her off, changing the focus of the interview to the increasing deterioration of Golden Gate Park and the need for native, drought-resistant plantings.

A year later a big smiling man with a microphone did a segment of his California history series there in the park, and Kristy Ann was on hand to be interviewed as "a local historian." She took his arm and pulled him to the bare slopes where the carpet beds had bloomed. She showed him her photocopies of the old photographs, which were growing tattered nowadays.

She talked and talked and talked about how the beds must be restored. The big man was too polite to interrupt her, but I could see the cameraman and assistant director rolling their eyes. Finally the assistant director led her away by the arm and gave her a handful of twenty dollar bills.

A couple of months after that she stopped coming to the park. Kristy Ann was gone, for most of a year. I wondered if she'd gone mad or gone to jail or one of those other places mortals go.

The Company had less and less for me to film, as the years rolled on. Evidently archivists weren't as interested in twenty-first century San Francisco. I was sent out for newsworthy events, but more and more of my time was my own. Gleason structured it for me, or I couldn't have managed.

I had a list: Shower, Breakfast, Walk, Park Time, Lunch at Park, Park Time, Walk, Dinner, Shower, Bed. I needed patterns. Gleason said I was like a train, where other people were like automobiles: they went anywhere, I had iron wheels and had to stay on my iron track. But a train carries more than an automobile. I carried the freight of Time. I carried the fiery colors of Sutro's design, the patterns of his flower beds.

I had a route worked out, from HQ to Sutro Park, and I carried my lunch in a paper bag, the same meal every day: wheat bread and butter sandwich, apple, bottle of water. I didn't want anything else. I was safe on my track. I was happy.

I sat in the park and watched the fog drifting through the cypress trees. I knew, after so many years, how to be invisible: never bothered anyone, never did anything to make a mortal notice I was there. There weren't many mortals, anyway. People only cut through Sutro Park on their way from 48th Avenue to Point Lobos Road. They didn't promenade there anymore.

When Kristy Ann wandered back into the park, she was rail-thin and all her hair was gone. She wore shapeless, stained sweat clothes and a stocking cap pulled down over her bare skull. She found a bench, quite near mine, that got the sunlight most of the day except when the fog rolled in, and she stayed there. All day, every day. Most days she had a cup of coffee with her, and always a laptop.

I found I could tune into her broadband connection, as she worked. She spent most of her day posting on various forums for San Francisco historical societies. I followed the forum discussions with interest.

At first she'd be welcomed into the groups, and complimented on her erudition. Gradually her humorlessness, her obsession came to the fore. Flame wars erupted when forum members wanted to discuss something other than the restoration of Sutro Park. She was always asked to leave, in the end, when she didn't storm out of her own accord. Once or twice she reregistered under a different name, but almost immediately was recognized. The forum exchanges degenerated into mutual name-calling.

After that Kristy Ann spent her days blogging, on a site decorated with gifs of her old photographs and scans of her lovingly colored re-creations of the park. Her entries were mostly bitter reflections on her failed efforts to restore the carpet beds. They became less and less coherent. A couple of months later, she disappeared again. I assumed her cancer had metastasized.

Ezra? Gleason was uncomfortable about something. *Ezra, we need to talk. The Company has been going over its profit and loss statements. They're spending more on your upkeep than they're making from your recordings. It's been suggested that we retrain you. Or relocate you. This may be difficult, Ezra...*

I don't think anyone but me would have recognized Kristy Ann, when she came creeping back. She moved like an old woman. She seemed to have shrunken away. There was no sign of the laptop; I don't think she was strong enough to carry it, now. She had a purse with her meds in it. She had a water bottle.

She found her bench in the sunlight and sat there, looking around her with bewildered eyes, all their anger gone.

Her electromagnetic field, the drifting halo of electricity that all mortals generate around their bodies, had begun to fluctuate around Kristy Ann. It happens, when mortals begin to die.

I wondered if I could do it.

I did; I got to my feet and walked toward her, cautious, keeping my eyes on the ground. I came to her bench and sat down beside her. My heart was pounding. I risked a glance sideways. She was looking at me with utter apathy. She wouldn't have cared if I'd grabbed her purse, slapped her, or pulled off her clothes. Her eyes tracked off to my left.

I turned and followed her stare. She was looking at an old stone basin on its pedestal, the last of Sutro's fountains, its sculpted water-works long since gone.

I edged closer. I reached into her electromagnetic field. I touched her hand—she was cold as ice—and tuned into the electrical patterns of her brain, as I had tuned into her broadband signal. I downloaded her.

I didn't hurt her. She saw the fountain restored, wirework shooting up to outline its second tier, its dolphins, its cherubs. Then it was solid and real. Clear water jetted upward into a lost sky. The green lawn spread out, flawless.

White statues rose from the earth: the Dancing Girls. The Dreaming Satyr. Venus de Milo. Antinous. The Boy with Bird. Hebe.

The Griffin. All the Gilded Age's conception of what was artistic, copied and brought out to the western edge of the world to refine and educate its uncultured masses.

Sutro's house lifted into its place again; the man himself rose up through the path and stood, in his black silk hat. Brass glinted on the bandstand. Music began to play. Before us the Conservatory took shape, for a moment a skeletal frame and then a paned bubble of glass flashing in the sun. Orchids and aspidistras steamed its windows from inside. And below it—

The colors exploded into being like fireworks, red and blue and gold, variegated tropical greens, purples, the carpet beds in all their precise glory. Managed Nature, in the nineteenth century's confident belief that unruly Nature *should* be managed to pleasing aesthetic effect. The intricate floral designs glowed, surreal grace notes, defying entropy and chaos.

She was struggling to stand, gasping, staring at it. The tether broke and she was pulled into the image. I gave her back her hair, with a straw hat for the sun. I gave her a long flounced skirt that swept the gravel, a suitable blouse and jacket. I gave her buttoned boots and a parasol. I gave her the body of young Kristy Ann, who had wandered alone with her sketchbook. Now she was part of the picture, not the dead thing cooling on the bench beside me.

She walked forward, her eyes fixed on the carpet beds, her lips parted. Color came into her face.

The fog came in, grayed the twenty-first century world. I heard crunching footsteps. A pair of women were coming up the path from the Point Lobos Road entrance. I got to my feet. I approached them, head turned aside, and managed to point at what was sitting on the park bench. One of the women said something horrified in Russian, the other put her hands to her white face and screamed.

They drew back from me. I pulled out my card and thrust it at them. Finally, suspicious, one of them took it and spelled out its message. I stared at my shoes while she put two and two together, and then I heard her pulling out her cell phone and calling the police.

I wasn't arrested. Once the police were able to look at the body and see its emaciation, the hospital band on its wrist, once they read the labels on the pill bottles in the purse, they knew. They called the morgue and then they called Gleason. He came and talked to them a while. Then he took me back to HQ.

They don't send me out much, anymore. I sleep a lot, in the place where the Company keeps me. I don't mind; at least I don't have to deal with strangers, and after all I have my memory.

I ride there on Edwin and the weather is always fine, the fog far out on the edge of the blue sea. The green park is always full of people, the poor of San Francisco out for a day of fresh air, sunlight and as much beauty as a rich man's money can provide for them. Pipefitters and laundresses sit together on the benches. Children run and scream happily. Courting couples sit on little iron folding chairs and listen to the band play favorites by Sir Arthur Sullivan. The intricate patterns blaze.

She will always be there, sometimes chatting with Mr. Sutro. Sometimes bustling from one carpet bed to the next with a watering can or gardening tools. I tip my hat and say the only words I can say, have ever said: "Good morning, Kristy Ann."

She smiles and nods. Perhaps she recognizes me, in a vague kind of way. But I never dismount to attempt conversation, and in any case she is too busy, weeding, watering, clipping to maintain the place she loves.

THE UNFORTUNATE GYTT

An early story of the Gentlemen's Speculative Society, featuring Edward Alton Bell-Fairfax, secret agent. It includes cameos by an infant Robert Louis Stevenson (and posits an extremely odd source for his great villain, Long John Silver); a dear friend who dabbles in world domination when not busy raising his twin toddlers; and the otherworldly Rosslyn Chapel, home of Templar ghosts and the Holy Grail. This story was one of Kage's first dabblings in steampunk, a genre she loved at first sight and eventually explored in much more detail and three subsequent tales.

—K. B.

4 SEPTEMBER 1855

Marsh had been blindfolded and led to the place where he now sat. The air was still, cold; he shivered in his thin white garment, breathing hard, and shook with an occasional ropy cough. He was suffering from intractable bronchitis.

Rough hands tore away his blindfold, but he opened his eyes to unrelieved blackness. A floating apparition formed, and swam toward him. It was a spectre draped all in luminous green, its skeletal face turned to him, its skeletal hand outstretched and pointing to his right.

Marsh peered in that direction, and saw the faintly glowing outline of a door. All manner of luminous phantoms appeared, circling the portal: other shrouded spirits, veiled and winged figures bearing wreaths, a monstrous demonic countenance and even—weirdly— what appeared to be Mr. Punch and a small dog.

The light cast by these apparitions was such that Marsh could make out the faint forms of the other initiates, seated in a row beside him. There were fewer than he had expected. He congratulated himself on surviving thus far.

A voice shouted behind them in the darkness. "Rise!"

He obeyed instantly, as did the others. The door opened, revealing the chamber beyond.

"Enter the Place of Judgment," commanded the unseen voice.

Marsh's fellow initiates shuffled forward, and he followed them.

The Place of Judgment was a long, low room of stone, from whose vaulted ceiling was suspended here and there a bronze lamp on a chain, providing unsteady illumination and fleeting shadows. Marsh recognized none of his fellow initiates, though he supposed they must all have frequented the same clubs and scientific institutions, must all have received the same mysterious offer from this most secret of societies.

Three figures were seated at the far end of the room, on golden thrones, before a scarlet curtain. Two were robed in blood-red, and wore golden masks of fearful aspect, grinning caricatures of humanity. The third was robed and hooded in black, apparently faceless, though something in the upper folds of its hood suggested the glint of watch- ful eyes.

One of the red-robed ones inclined its golden mask forward.

"What a puling little collection of creatures," it said, in a high harsh voice. "What human slugs, what snails, what maggots! Can *these* have aspired to our Society? Too, too unworthy."

"And yet, they dare to bring us gifts," said the other one in red. "Let them be put to the test."

"Yes. Let us winnow them quickly. My gorge rises at the sight of them!" said the first speaker. "Bring forth your offerings."

The initiates looked at one another uncertainly. Marsh, deciding he might as well take the initiative, came forward and laid his offering tray on the topmost step. His fellows rushed after him, setting down their trays beside his. They stood back then, heads bowed respectfully.

"It would appear they have followed the Sacred Plans," said the second speaker.

"Appearances can be deceiving," said the first speaker. It leaned forward, crossing its arms. "Supplicants! Rotate Lever Six exactly ninety degrees."

The initiates shuffled forward again to their trays. Marsh peered down at the thing he had made with such care, of copper wire and spools and bright brass. He had no idea what its function might be, nor to what possible use it might be put; but he had followed meticulously the detailed diagrams he had been sent, working long nights through into gray morning. He remembered exactly which part had been designated Lever Six.

He found it now, and slowly turned it, as he had been bid. Beside him, the other initiates were likewise fumbling with their offerings.

There was a faint noise from his offering, a hiss, and then a peculiar shrieking warble. Startled, he drew his hand back. He glanced over at the other trays, and saw that they contained offerings nearly identical to his own. But not quite; had he been the only one to follow the Plans exactly? Marsh felt a guilty thrill of superiority. A voice spoke from amid the gleaming wires of his offering, a male voice sounding faintly bored as it said:

"Testing, testing, testing. This supplicant has been found worthy."

"Only one?" said the first speaker. "Hear me, you failures! Leave your trash and depart this place. If we are feeling particularly magnanimous, you may hear from us again."

The door into darkness opened. The rejected initiates cowered. The figure in black, that had been silent all this while, rose to its feet. It towered over them, a veritable giant. One by one, the rejects were taken by the shoulders and ushered into obscurity.

The door shut; the figure returned to its place, and sat.

Marsh coughed into his fist. His eyes gleamed with fever and triumph.

"Worthy one," said the second speaker. "You are about to ascend to a new plane of existence. But, be warned! Your former self must die. Sacrifices are always required before any great enterprise. Are you prepared?"

"I am," said Marsh, not without certain qualms. His unease mounted as the black-robed giant stood again, and drew from the depths of its robe a short sword. It approached him, looming over him, and set one hand on his shoulder.

Marsh watched the blade glint in the lamplight as the blow came; somehow he managed not to flinch, and at the last possible second the giant feinted and sent the blade under Marsh's arm. He felt cold steel against his skin, and, to his mortification, a hot spurt of terror.

The giant stepped back. The more unpleasant of the red-robed ones spoke.

"Yes, you have been spared. But hear me: if you ever breathe so much as a word, if you ever hint or insinuate to any outsider about what has passed here, we will know. And knives will find you in the dark, and dogs will find your corpse before morning. Do you understand?"

"Yes," said Marsh, a little sullenly, feeling the yellow stain spread on the front of his robe.

"Then I think we can dispense with all this nonsense," said the first speaker, as he stood with the other masked figure. The black giant mounted the dais and, with one violent blow, swept the thrones to the floor. They fell with a crash. Marsh saw that they were only painted wood.

"So do thrones topple," said the first speaker.

"So are illusions dispelled," said the other speaker.

"And we are everywhere," they said together.

The black giant pulled the curtain to one side, revealing a rather ordinary-looking door.

"You are free to enter, sir," said the first speaker.

He opened the door and passed through. The first speaker followed him. Marsh started up the steps after them. Just inside, the black figure leaned down and laid a hand on his arm.

"There is a washroom just to your left," it advised, in a friendly voice.

Marsh found not only a lavatory but his clothing, neatly laid out. He washed and dressed hurriedly. He studied himself in the mirror as he tied his cravat: a nondescript man of about thirty, drab as a junior clerk. A disappointment, to himself and all the world, until tonight!

He found his way down a paneled corridor to a lamplit room. It appeared to be a library in one of the better clubs. The walls were lined with books; a coal-fire burned brightly in the hearth. On a central table was a tray with decanters and glasses, as well as a match stand and what promised to be a humidor, to judge from the wreaths of fragrant smoke drifting above three men sprawled at their ease in comfortable-looking armchairs.

"Here he is at last," drawled he who must have been the more unpleasant of the interrogators. He was a dark fellow, slightly rakish in appearance but dressed well. The red robe and mask lay discarded at his feet. "Welcome, brother. Well done!"

"You grasp the symbolism?" inquired the other interrogator, who resembled the bank manager a drab clerk must serve: portly, in early middle age, all benevolent self-importance. "Darkness and ritual, giving way to light! Here you see walls lined with the fruit of human knowledge and thought, instead of nursery bogeymen. Here you see medieval robes cast aside for modern dress."

"Here you see damned good brandy and decent tobacco," added the other. "Have a seat, won't you? Edward, fetch him a drink."

"Happy to oblige," said the third man, and rose from his chair. And rose, and rose; he had clearly worn the black robe. Marsh frowned at him, wondering what the hulking fellow's status was. Called by his Christian name; a servant? Told to fetch, and yet he sat as an equal with the other two men.

"Welcome, brother," he said, leaning down to offer Marsh a snifter of brandy. "Cigar?"

Seen close to, he had a long and rather horselike countenance, with eyes of quite a pale blue. He smiled in a good-natured way and offered the humidor.

"Yes, thank you, I believe I will indulge," said Marsh, wondering when anyone was going to perform introductions. He puffed appreciatively when his cigar was lit for him, and sipped his brandy, which sent him into a humiliating fit of coughing.

"I believe, sir, that we can offer you something you'll find more congenial than brandy," said the tall man. He poured a glass of colorless cordial from a decanter on the table, and offered it to Marsh, who took it with a certain ill-humor. He sipped it and immediately shuddered. However, after another cautious sip:

"You know," he said, "I think—yes, that's certainly doing me good! Thank you, sir."

"Not at all." Edward inclined in a half-bow.

"You will feel its full effect presently," said the benevolent gentleman, in a rather arch manner. "Miraculous cures are the least of our accomplishments. You will learn that there are many compensations for your labor in our service."

He cleared his throat and struck a pose before the fire. "And now, friend, to the matter at hand.

"You have been admitted to our ancient and noble Society. Your climb to the stars has only begun. But you will climb in secret, brother. Your name will be unknown. The bauble Fame is not for us!

"Consider: throughout the ages, who has borne the light of Reason above the mire of ignorance and superstition? It has not been the King, nor the Priest, nor the Poet, nor even the Philosopher. No! It has been the Scientist alone who has worked consistently and, I may say, practically, to elevate suffering Mankind above the pit. It is his patient labor that fills the coffers of Empire, though the Adventurer may win brief glory. Industry and Prosperity are the gifts of the Scientist.

"Yet, who is so unjustly slandered as he? The Church condemns him; Government grows fat on his accomplishments while declining to support him. Thanks to Mrs. Shelley's book, the popular imagination sees in him a madman, a heretic, a second Lucifer for pride!

"He struggles no less now than he did when the fires of the Inquisition raged.

"For this reason we conceal ourselves, we brother Technicians. For this reason we conceal our most vital work from ungrateful Mankind, until the world is sufficiently civilized to appreciate what we do. And for this reason, we in the higher ranks bear *assumed* names, even amongst ourselves. You shall know me as Hieron; and our august brother, here, is Daedalus." He indicated the dark gentleman, who had amused himself by blowing smoke rings through the speech.

Edward stepped forward and, with another half-bow, presented to Marsh a black velvet case. When opened, it proved to contain a set of calipers made of gold. Marsh, having decided that Edward was certainly a mere servant, nodded curt thanks and rose to bow fully to the benevolent gentleman.

The evening thereafter took on an informal tone, as Daedalus told amusing anecdotes and Hieron chit-chatted about certain members of Parliament in a manner that suggested he kept them in his vest pocket. The brandy went round freely; Marsh quite relaxed, laughing inwardly at what a fool he'd been, to be so frightened.

Edward took little part in any of the conversation, only answering when addressed, which seemed to confirm Marsh's impression of him. He merely leaned back in his chair, sipping brandy, smiling at the jokes and exhaling clouds of cigar smoke through his long nose.

Toward the end of the evening, Daedalus gave him a significant look across the room, though his voice had lost none of its nonchalance as he said:

"By the way, Edward, the Gytt affair's on again."

"Is it really?" Edward said. "Much for me to do?"

"Perhaps. Perhaps young Marsh here ought to follow along at your heel. Test his mettle. Ha! Ha!" Daedalus smacked the arm of his chair, chortling at wit Marsh found inexplicable until he realized that Daedalus was referring to the fact that he, Marsh, was a metallurgist. He promptly chuckled in appreciation.

Marsh heard the curtains flung open in his room, and pulled a pillow over his face to block the flood of morning light. He had just time to remember that he no longer lived with his mother before a voice said, in tones courteous yet firm, "Come along, Marsh, get up. We have half an hour to get to King's Cross Station."

Marsh sat bolt upright. Edward was standing beside his wardrobe, packing a traveling-bag for him.

"How the deuce did you get into my rooms?" demanded Marsh, feeling his head throb.

"With a key," said Edward coolly, closing the bag. "I've arranged for a hansom to arrive at half past seven promptly; we can breakfast on the way."

"But—"

"Quickly, please," said Edward, hauling Marsh out of bed by the back of his nightshirt and setting him on his feet. Shocked, not least by the man's strength, Marsh said:

"How dare you, sir!"

Edward bent down to look him in the eye. "You had a great deal of brandy last night. Perhaps you may be excused if you can't recall the particular business to which we are to attend. You do remember that you serve new masters, Marsh?"

"Oh!" Guiltily, Marsh grabbed up his trousers and put them on.

He waited for further explanation in the cab, but none was provided; nor did Edward bring up the matter at the station, where they boarded a train for Edinburgh. Nor, after the cold repast of meat pies and oranges Edward had purchased from a railway vendor, did he seem inclined to speak of the reason for their haste; merely opened a sporting paper and stretched out at considerable length on his side of the railway carriage, where he proceeded to amuse himself with an account of the latest prize-fight.

Marsh studied him resentfully. In the cold light of day, Edward's long, plain face had a certain unsettling quality. His cheekbones were very high and broad, his pale eyes rather small; Marsh wondered if he belonged to one of the Slavic races. There had been no trace of foreign accent in his speech, however.

"Look here, I really must insist you tell me where we're going," said Marsh at last.

"Why, I should have thought that was obvious. We're going to Edinburgh. More than that, I'm not at liberty to say at the present time. Rest assured, however, that you will receive all necessary information when you need to know it."

Marsh listened closely to his pronunciation, and grudgingly conceded that Edward must have attended one of the better schools. "Very well," he said, "but can you at least advise me whether we'll be back by Monday morning? I hold, after all, a respectable position in the firm of—"

"You *held*," said Edward. "I sent your letter of resignation this morning. Don't concern yourself, old fellow! They scarcely paid you what you were worth, did they? The Society will manage all your expenses."

"This is outrageous," Marsh sputtered. Edward smiled again, placing a hand on his shoulder.

"You have begun a new life, Marsh. Surely you understand that? Nothing is so important as the work you are henceforth to do. Come now; perhaps a look at some of your field equipment will cheer you up."

He pulled over a leather traveling-case and opened it, displaying its contents. There were tools Marsh recognized, and tools at whose function he could not guess.

"Permit me—" Edward reached in and removed what appeared to be a pair of absurdly thick spectacles in massive frames. He presented them to Marsh, who stared at them in incomprehension.

"And these would be—?"

"You are undoubtedly familiar with Masson's spark emission spectrometer," prompted Edward. "At least, I should hope—"

"Of course I am," said Marsh irritably.

"We have improved on it," said Edward, with only a trace of smugness. "This device may be used to determine the identity of all elements in any particular composition. Here—" he pointed within the case, "you will also find superior field assaying tools." He withdrew a pamphlet from an inner coat pocket, printed in an absurd violet ink on tissue-thin paper, and held it out to Marsh. "I suggest you study this; operating instructions for the Improved Spectrometer. It ought to occupy your attention until we arrive."

And it did, though Marsh spent the first few minutes fuming over Edward's demeanor, which was not that of an insolent servant so much as a patronizing older brother.

They arrived at Haymarket Station in late afternoon, under quite the widest and windiest heaven Marsh had ever seen. Smoke streamed sidelong from a thousand chimneys in stark crenellation, on a sky like blued steel.

Marsh stared up at it openmouthed, as he stumbled after Edward. The instrument case was much heavier than it looked, and he fell farther and farther behind. At last Edward turned back, and without a word took the case from Marsh. He hoisted it to his shoulder, before resuming his long-legged stride.

He led Marsh to a decidedly second-rate hotel, where they signed in as a pair of commercial travelers. The journey continued up a narrow and twisting flight of stairs, to a room wherein was scarcely space between the beds and the walls.

Here Marsh dropped his bag and flung himself down on the bed, panting. He watched with dull eyes as Edward sidestepped back and forth, unpacking his own valise and setting out shaving things with meticulous neatness.

"I believe I'll take a rest before dinner," said Marsh, groaning as he sat up to pull off his boots.

"No-oo," Edward said, as he set a stack of folded shirts in the wardrobe. "I'm afraid that won't be possible."

"Why the hell not?" demanded Marsh.

"We're going sightseeing," Edward replied.

At some point Marsh's sense of umbrage annealed into apathy. He slouched in the corner of the open cab, clutching the instrument case Edward had insisted on bringing, only anxious that the lap robe should not be twitched from under his chin. He ignored sweeping vistas of Auld Reekie and the Water of Leith. Edward was leaning forward, engaged in an animated conversation with the driver about Scotland's romantic scenery. His customary affability heightened into a faintly idiotic enthusiasm as he prattled on; Marsh could see the driver's eyes narrow with smiling calculation.

"O'course," said the driver, far too casually, "if it's high romance ye're after, Rosslyn Chapel is the *ne plus ultra*. Bare ruined choirs, gheestie knights an' a'. Mind ye, it's a' o' twelve mile awa', and the fare's nae modest sum; so I reckon ye'll wait that for another time..."

"Hang the expense, sir," cried Edward. "Can we get there before dark?"

"*Hang the expense,* is it?" The driver grinned and cracked his whip. "Bid yer friend hold tight, noo!"

Marsh held on tightly indeed, and cursed Edward in silence as the cab racketed over hill and dale for all of twelve miles. When they arrived under the Pentlands, however, even he was moved to sit up and stare.

Rosslyn Chapel was a ruin of parti-colored stone. Its windows had been smashed long since, and gaped black to the open air, save where they had been blocked with planking. Behind a shapeless broad front, seemingly the abandoned façade of a much more imposing building, a sort of cathedral in miniature rose instead, spiked buttresses projecting like ribs from a carcass. A profusion of carving drew the eye, a swarming complication of detail in its design; the longer one gazed, the greater was the sense of an endless receding pattern, an illusion done with mirrors.

Marsh blinked and drew his hand over his eyes. He turned and looked instead at the Chapel's situation, which was, as promised, romantic, at least if one found wooded glens and the view of a fairly prosaic-looking ruined castle so. But all in all there was a rather gloomy air about the place, the more so as the shadows were growing long and the air was distinctly chilly. He wondered if there might be a decent chop-house near their hotel, and whether it would be still serving meals by the time they got back. He was about to say something politely complimentary about Rosslyn Chapel when, to his horror, he realized that Edward was leaping down from the carriage.

"Charming!" Edward brayed. "Simply charming! Is there a way to view the interior?"

"Och, to be sure, dear sir; Wullie I' th' hut yonder's got the keys, and for a smallish gratuity I'm sure he'd oblige," the driver replied.

"Oh, but the hour—" protested Marsh. "Perhaps we can come back tomorrow—"

"Nonsense! You know you'll enjoy this, Marsh," said Edward, and reaching into the cab he gripped Marsh by the collar and extracted him. Marsh was obliged to follow Edward through a wet misery of thistles and rank grass to the aforesaid hut, where "Wullie" (a red-nosed ancient in a long coat and felt slippers) was roused after patient knocking and bribed, with sovereigns, to unlock the Chapel for them. Marsh noted the gleaming look that passed between Wullie and their driver, who laid a finger beside his nose and winked so vigorously it was a wonder his face uncreased afterward.

Within the Chapel, Wullie droned on at great length in nearly unintelligible Scots about the remarkable carvings within; indeed they extended floor to ceiling, swarming in chipped stone floral ornamentation of dizzying complexity, in biblical scenes of every description, and in the occasional scowling gargoyle's face.

Marsh thought it all rather second-rate, but he put on the nearest possible approximation of an expression of polite interest as he stumbled around in the shadows after Edward and Wullie, lugging the instrument case the whiles. He listened to the genealogy of the Sinclair family, who had built the place in the dim reaches of the past, and to a great deal of superstitious claptrap about Knights Templar, the Holy Grail, and the ghost of a Black Knight.

He waited an interminable length of time before one particularly torturously worked column, described by Wullie as the "Apprentice Pillar" and supposedly a marvel of craftsmanship. At last Marsh ventured the opinion that he thought a modern casting process could probably mass-produce the damned thing, and earned himself equally offended stares from the other two men.

Not until their breath had begun to vapor in the cold did they leave, and Wullie followed them back to their cab with many a bow and scrape. Edward took the hint and produced more sovereigns. As he doled them out into Wullie's palm, he asked casually:

"Would you know of any other notable antiquities hereabouts? Roman ruins, perhaps?"

Wullie counted the coins into his sporran before replying. "Och, sir, there's birkies fra' some University air other digging about the auld stones on yon brae; but ye won't get nae joy fra' the likes o' them, nae, sir. No' gentlemen at a', sir. Hosteel tae a friendly inquiry, like."

"I see," said Edward. He lifted his gaze to the hill the old man had referenced, where some manner of temporary camp had been erected. There were wagons drawn up, and two or three men who looked very like armed guards patrolling the boundaries. Marsh, watching, was a little taken aback to see Edward's mask of well-bred idiocy drop for a moment, revealing something coldly feral. As Edward turned his face back, however, he smiled, and the illusion returned smoothly.

"Well, I shouldn't think I'd care to watch a lot of fellows grubbing about in the mud! Thank you, sir, for a most memorable visit."

"I may as well tell you that I can't fathom any earthly reason for all this," grumbled Marsh, when they were once again in the cab and bounding through the gloaming.

"Driver!" said Edward, ignoring Marsh. "Is that Roslin Village, there?"

"So it is, sir," replied the driver, braking somewhat. "Wi' a splendid public hoose and a first-rate hotel, too, I might add."

"Let us out here, please. I believe we'll spend the night," said Edward decisively.

"What?" said Marsh, ready to burst into tears.

"Yes. It's rather later than I had realized. Thank you, driver."

Five minutes later, Marsh was trailing along behind Edward, hating him passionately, for they had gone nowhere near the comparatively cheery-looking high street of Roslin but doubled back instead in the direction of the chapel.

"I should really be grateful for any answers at all, you know," said Marsh, with the heaviest sarcasm he could muster.

"I expect you should," said Edward, peering ahead through the darkness. "Do you see the cottage there, amongst the trees?"

"I see a light," Marsh replied.

"Very well; that is our destination," said Edward, and strode on without another word. Marsh, infuriated to the point of rashness, drew on all his strength and sprinted forward, intent on seizing Edward's arm to demand more information; but as he did so, there appeared in the path before them two dark figures. A beam of red light, thin as a pencil, danced across the track. Edward stopped immediately and Marsh ran into him. It was like colliding with a wall.

"So do thrones topple," he heard Edward saying, in quite a calm voice.

"So are illusions dispelled," someone replied from the shadows.

"And we are everywhere."

Without another word they proceeded forward, all four, and Marsh saw clearly now the house, situated in a dark grove at the far end of a stretch of greensward. There had been some disturbance of the turf, apparently, for in the light from the single window Marsh glimpsed what seemed to be irregular clumps of earth and weed, scattered broadcast here and there. They called to his mind engravings of the battlefields in the Crimea; but that was all he was able to make out before they arrived at the door and he was hurried within.

Marsh blinked in the lamplight. He had expected at least a cozy, if poorly furnished, interior. He saw instead mounds of earth heaped everywhere, for the flagged floor had been covered with tarpaulins, and dirt and stones piled thereon to a height of four feet.

"I suspected they'd send *you*," said one of their hosts, to Edward. He was a middle-aged man, somewhat disheveled and unshaven, though his speaking manner indicated that he was an educated gentleman. He turned a grim visage on Marsh. "Who is this, may I ask?"

"May I present Marsh?" Edward indicated him with a nod, as he doffed his hat. "We thought it might be useful if you had a metallurgist on-site. Marsh, may I present Johnson and Williams? They are, respectively, your Project Administrator and Chief Engineer."

"Charmed, sir," said Johnson briefly, and turned back to Edward. "Look here, the whole business has become an absolute damned shambles—two men lost—"

"How unfortunate," said Edward. "I should very much like a cup of tea, as would my associate; I'm afraid I've rather run him off his legs to get him here. Perhaps you might brief us in the kitchen?"

They repaired to a grubby antechamber where a youth introduced as Wilson prepared tea and a fry-up of sausages, for which Marsh was profoundly grateful. Johnson lit a pipe with shaking hands, settled back and exhaled, and said:

"They found out about us, somehow, and they've begun a dig of their own."

"Ah! That would be the 'University' expedition on the hill across the way?" said Edward, who had produced a pistol from within his coat and begun cleaning it.

"Gytt's murderers, yes," said Johnson.

"Murderers?" Marsh said, horrified.

"Marsh hasn't been fully briefed," said Edward, not looking up from the pistol as he loaded it. "You'll explain as time permits, I'm certain? Just at present, what do *I* need to know?"

"That they're doing their best to close down our operation here," said Johnson bitterly. "They chose a dreadful place to dig—we think they've run into bedrock, and of course they can't blast. They tried to frighten us out first; the most absurd ghost-pantomime you can imagine! He lurked around the cottage the first few evenings, but we sat in here and laughed at him.

"Two nights ago, we stopped laughing. He galloped through and hurled some sort of detonating device, just over our tunnel. Flash, bang, and the roof collapsed in three places. We got our fellows out, but too late to revive them, and we've shored up the roof again—but he came back last night. This time the charge failed to go off, thank heaven—we found it this morning, where it had bounced into a ditch."

"And you expect him back tonight," said Edward, who was modifying his pistol with a pair of cylindrical attachments. "I expect I'd better wait for him, then."

"Then, this is a mining operation?" Marsh ventured.

Johnson considered him sourly. "No briefing at all? Very well. Blow out the light; we'll sit here by the window and watch for the beggar. How much do you know about Rosslyn Chapel?"

"Planned as a collegiate chapel and never finished," Marsh said uncomfortably, berating himself for not paying better attention to Wullie. "Smashed up during the Reformation. Lot of nonsense about Freemasons to do with that, er, pillar thing. And ghosts; Sir Walter Scott wrote about a crypt full of knights in armor, glowing with phantom lights. And there is talk of a treasure hidden there."

"Just so," said Johnson. "Treasure. Some claim the Holy Grail's down amid the bones in rusting armor. Some say it's loot from Jerusalem, brought back by crusaders. The Sinclairs sealed off the crypt in question long ago, which makes it difficult to see for oneself.

"Yet someone appears to have done just that," he added, and drew a case from an inner pocket of his coat. He opened it and passed it to Marsh. It was a daguerreotype, depicting a young man seated before a painted backdrop. He was a slightly made fellow, prematurely bald as an egg, regarding the camera with a smirk; he had posed with his finger pointing toward his rather large head, as though to call attention to its cranial magnificence.

"Jerome Gytt," said Johnson. "A self-styled criminal mastermind and a Sinclair in an irregular sort of way, if you take my meaning. As near as we've been able to piece it together, he used his family connection to get hold of old documents pertaining to Rosslyn Chapel. Became obsessed with finding a way into the hidden crypt. *Did* find a way, evidently. Then the family caught him out, and he was given a remittance and banished to the continent.

"Well, it seems he had a certain talent for invention, and offered his services to an organized network of criminals based in Paris. They're known to the gendarmerie as the Vespertile gang. Gytt amassed a fortune in their service, before breaking with them and returning to Edinburgh.

"There he built a house in Inverleith Terrace, fitted out a veritable alchemist's laboratory, and settled down to work. That was what brought him to our attention, you see; we have agents planted in wholesale chemists' firms, who monitor the sales of certain substances.

When a suspiciously large amount of one thing or another is ordered, we're informed; and so it was with Gytt, and we stationed a man to watch the house, to see if we could determine what he was up to.

"Unfortunately, he sent out letters of solicitation to investors, promising to demonstrate the remarkable properties of a substance he referred to as *Gyttite*. This alerted our people, of course, but also drew the attention of his former associates in crime.

"In brief, they called on him; he went out drinking with them; next morning our man found him dead in an alley with an expression of profound surprise on his face, and discovered the house has been ransacked.

"Had they taken the, er, Gyttite?" Marsh inquired.

"Had they?" Johnson raised his eyebrows in an ironical way. "It appeared that way; we couldn't find a trace of anything likely when we searched the house ourselves. What we did find, amongst what had been left of his effects, was half a notebook journal kept in code. We decrypted enough of it to know we must have the rest of the journal. Edward got it for us."

Marsh turned his head to question Edward, but he was no longer in the room.

"Yes," said Johnson, with a dour smile. "Edward's a very Robert-Houdin when it comes to vanishing and reappearing. Never mind; he's about his useful business.

"What we learned from Gytt's journal was that he had found the Gyttite—whatever it may be—*in the Rosslyn crypt*. That, moreover, he had discovered a tunnel enabling him to go in and out of the crypt as he pleased, to get samples for his experiments.

"What we didn't learn from Gytt's journal was where the damned tunnel was."

"Well, couldn't you bribe the watchman to let you in?" asked Marsh.

"We could," said Johnson, rising in the darkness to crouch before the stove. There was a faint red glow as he relit his pipe, and a ghostly cloud of smoke. "A failure; for the old crypt entrance was sealed with a block of stone so immense we might have removed it by blasting the Chapel into fragments, but not otherwise. Even our discreet efforts at digging were enough to call attention to ourselves. The Sinclairs descended in wrath and the watchman was summarily sacked.

"We took a different tack then: digging our own tunnel. This cottage became available for lease; one of our people engaged it. We took up the flagstones in the cellar and proceeded with a fair amount of success, smuggling the spoil-earth out in barrels under cover of darkness. I'd estimate we're within no more than a day or so of connecting with the crypt, after three years of work!

"But now it seems Gytt's associates were on the same track all along. God only knows what they were able to learn from the plundered pages, before Edward retrieved them, or from Gytt's own bibulous chatter; but a month ago they appeared over yonder. They seem to have realized they'll never outpace us—"

At that moment they heard the sound of hoofbeats approaching along the lane.

"Here he comes!" said Wilson, who had been sitting in silence by the window. There was a muttered commotion from the next room, and Marsh heard Williams ordering:

"Come up, for God's sake, men!"

Marsh heard a clatter of boots, and two more men swarmed through the kitchen door like ants fleeing a nest. His attention was drawn and held, however, by the fearful apparition beyond the window glass. A mounted rider, an armored knight as it seemed, and both black horse and black rider shimmered with some livid effulgence. The rider drew up on the lawn, fumbling with something; there was a tiny flame. The horseman lifted the object he had lit, as though to fling it toward the house.

He never completed the gesture, however, for there was a queer hollow *pop*, and with a cry he fell from the saddle. Before he had landed, a gray blur rushed from the darkness and wrestled with him. Marsh heard a clank, and a splash; the guttering flame was extinguished.

There was confusion, then, as one of the men ran out through the front room and flung open the door. Marsh heard sounds of a struggle, and growled oaths; a feeble cry of pain, then, and the sharp order: "Leave it!"

"We've caught him, by God," said Johnson. He drew the curtains and, leaning forward to the stove again, lit a candle. Light bloomed in the room to reveal Edward, bearing a man across his shoulders and stooping under the doorframe as he carried him within. To either side and behind followed the other two men. Though they wore spectacles and had the appearance of scholars rather than brute laborers, their faces were savage with anger.

"Your chair, Marsh, if you please," said Edward, and Marsh leaped up hastily as Edward dropped his burden into the seat. The Black Knight of Rosslyn groaned, and lifted his head in the candlelight.

"Got you at last, you bastard," said Johnson, tearing off the helmet—a thing of so much buckram and pasteboard, crudely daubed with paint containing phosphorous. The pale face it had concealed was undistinguished, grimacing, turning away from the flame, and blood flowed freely from the trench Edward's bullet had cut in its scalp.

"'So are illusions dispelled,'" quoted Edward. Johnson leaned forward and aimed a blow at the prisoner, before Edward seized his wrist.

"Self-control is called for, gentlemen," he said quietly, and scarcely audibly over the general mutters of "Shoot the murdering hound!" and "Break his arms!"

"I don't believe we want to do any of those things until we've learned what he knows, do we?" said Edward.

"Do your worst," said the Black Knight. "I ain't talking."

"You aren't, eh?" said Johnson, fetching a hammer. "Jenkins, bring me a pair of sixpenny nails."

Marsh, sweating, backed away from the table, and the Black Knight used that opportunity to lunge for the opening he had made thereby; but Edward caught him and threw him down again.

"Don't be a fool," he said. "Look at me, man; there's no point making this any more unpleasant for yourself than necessary."

The prisoner raised his defiant face. He looked Edward in the eye, about to utter some coarse refusal; but as he stared, some vital spark seemed to go out of him. He closed his mouth, tried to lower his head. Edward held his gaze.

"You're not an idiot," said Edward, almost gently. "You know what's at stake here, don't you? What has your chief decided to do?"

The man twitched violently, and the words came as though they were being forced from him: "We'll take the house, if this don't drive you out. We knows there's only a handful of you. There's fifteen of us, see, hard men all. Nobody crosses the Vespertile gang! We'll get the tunnel—and then we'll get the jewels and—"

"Jewels?" Edward smiled. "You've been told there are jewels down there?"

"Well—o' course..." said the man, looking bewildered. "We was told it'd be easy...Why'm I telling you all this?"

"Did you make the bombs yourself?" Edward inquired. "Or is there an armory up there?"

"No! All my own work," said the man, smiling as though he were among friends. "You won't find a better fuse-man, mate. I was in the army, you know. The rest of 'em ain't good for nothing except knife-play. Lot of frogs..."

"Really? Have they no firearms?"

"Oh, boxes full, mate," said the man, quite unconcerned now. "Colt revolvers and the like. We'll pick off them Society lads like they was clay pigeons!"

Johnson uttered an oath, looking at the others.

"Thank you," said Edward. He walked behind the prisoner's chair. "Look up there, at that pitcher on the shelf. Have you ever seen that china pattern before?"

The prisoner looked where he was bid and pursed his lips, trying to remember whether he had seen the pattern before or not, as Edward drew the pistol from within his coat and shot him in the back of the neck.

"Good God!" Marsh staggered back to avoid the body as it fell forward. "You've murdered him!"

"Necessary," said Edward with a cold opaque look, putting his gun away. "And only justice, after all."

"Black Knight indeed!" said Johnson. "It's worse than I feared. They'll be down on us now like a pack of wolves, I daresay. We'll have to clear out—but we'll set a pair of explosive charges in the tunnel before we go. I'm damned if they'll profit by our labor."

"I beg your pardon?" Edward lifted his head. "Retreat, after three years of work?"

"I don't see what else we can do," said Johnson, scowling at the floor. "We can scarcely fight a war here. Slaughter fifteen armed men? I should think that's a little much even for a man of your ability."

"I urge you to persevere, gentlemen," said Edward, and Marsh recognized the same tone of voice, the unnatural mildness he had used on the prisoner. "We are so close to our goal! Consider the disservice you do Civilization, if you fail here!"

Is he some kind of mesmerist? wondered Marsh, looking up into Edward's eyes, as the other men were doing. Their pale light held him; his fear of the man faded and he felt suddenly that it *was* a damned shame to give up, so near to success! Whatever that success might be—

"He's right, by God," said Williams. "There's too much at stake."

"We're so close!" cried Wilson.

"Yes!" said Edward, his voice rising. "You know we must finish, and will. Just a little farther!"

"Very well," said Johnson with a sigh, though he avoided Edward's intent gaze. "Down we go. I hope you can wield a shovel to as much effect as a pistol."

In answer, Edward pulled off his coat and rolled up his sleeves. He strode into the next room. Marsh hurried after him, still fired with enthusiasm, and saw the gaping excavation in the middle of the floor, surrounded by veritable mountains of earth. Edward seized a shovel and leaped into the tunnel, closely followed by the other men; and Marsh had just time to ask himself, *What am I doing?* before grabbing his equipment-case and leaping too.

The next hour was a closer approximation of Hell than any initiation rite dreamed up by the most perverse of Grand Masters. Afterward Marsh remembered running back and forth through darkness relieved here and there by mining lamps, running until he swam in his clothes for sweat, until his sides were ready to split and his heart hammered in his chest. Now and then he caught a glimpse of Edward and Williams, flailing away like demons with pick and mattock. Now and then he had a breath of cooler air and a glimpse of Johnson's stern face, as he handed him a bucket of earth to be passed up. Now and then he collided with one of the others, on their way with their own bucket.

And, ever as he ran, Edward's pale eyes were before his own, somehow, Edward's voice was ringing in his ears and driving out any sense of weariness or antipathy. They *must* succeed!

The nightmare came to an end in a confusion of noises. A sudden ring of steel on stone, a crack and hollow crash: Marsh came to himself in time to see Edward hurling himself at a wall of muddy mortar, that gave way and opened into Stygian darkness. Hard on its muffled thunder sounded an echoing volley of shots, and cries from back down the tunnel.

Disoriented, Marsh dropped his bucket and ran until he fell over something. It was square, and painfully solid; his instrument case? Before he could wonder further, it was snatched away, and he himself had been grabbed up and was being dragged along the tunnel at astonishing speed until the black gulf yawned before him.

Edward leaned down and shouted into his face. "In!" He thrust the case into Marsh's arms and propelled him into the void.

Marsh stumbled forward and fell again, rolling aside just in time to avoid the hurtling bodies of his fellows, who were scrambling through the entrance as fast as they might go. Johnson emerged, bearing one of the miner's lamps, but its circle of yellow light did little to relieve the palpable dark. More shots, and a cry of pain from someone; the whine and ping of bullets, a confused clattering.

Edward himself bounded through the gap, gripping his pistol. His white teeth were bared. He turned and fired again up the tunnel, and there was a scream and a sudden silence. It filled, gradually, with the strangled gasps of someone dying at the far end of the tunnel.

Marsh rose on his elbow, obscurely proud of himself for being alive.

A voice called down to them, too distorted by distance and echoes to be understood, but its tone of menace was unmistakable. There followed a thump, a crackling hiss and a flare of yellow light in the tunnel-mouth.

"What've they—" began Johnson. "Good God! Don't—"

This was directed at Edward, who had drawn something resembling a thin brass cylinder from his waistcoat. He paid no heed to Johnson, but twisted the thing and, leaning in swiftly, threw it far up the tunnel. Marsh heard it strike and bounce, and then—

"Down!" Edward said, and dropped, covering his ears. Marsh covered his own ears just ahead of the impact, which came before the sound, and the spatter of gravel and sand hitting him like stinging flies.

Even after the percussive roar had died away, it was a long moment before Marsh dared open his eyes. He sat up, peering about him. The others were getting slowly to their feet. The tunnel mouth had collapsed behind the broken wall, into a mass of earth and rock.

"Was that necessary?" said Johnson.

"Yes," said Edward, rising and brushing dirt from his trousers. "They'd thrown down a gas canister. Another thirty seconds and you'd have asphyxiated."

"But now we're buried!" said Jenkins.

"Ah! But we're buried in the Sinclair crypt," said Edward in satisfaction. "And I hope I need hardly remind you that there is another tunnel here, somewhere?"

Johnson stood and lifted high the miner's lamp. "Good lord," he said. Marsh looked up, and caught his breath. They must indeed have come out beneath Rosslyn Chapel. All around rose columns of the same intricate carving; this chamber had never known defacement, however.

All the angels, all the saints and greenmen stood out sharply, clean-edged as the day they had been cut, their paint bright, even inlaid with twined patterns of wrought metal. A riot of ornament, from the arched ceiling to the floor... Marsh lowered his gaze and shuddered, for here before him was a defunct Sinclair, brown bones moldering away in rusting armor, stretched out uncoffined on its catafalque. Beyond it was another, and still another, a long row of dead men as far as the light disclosed, with glimpses of yet more in the cold gloom beyond.

But there were no chests of gold, no piled heaps of altar-plate.

"Right," said Johnson. "What's your name, Marsh, you're a metallurgist? There'll be Gyttite here somewhere. Find it. Likely an alloy of some kind. Perhaps in the armor, or one of the swords."

"But—" Marsh's protest died unspoken as Edward bent beside him, opening the instrument case. He brought out the Improved Spectrometer and handed it to Marsh without a word. Marsh, summoning what he could recall of the instructions for use, pressed a switch and held the lenses up to his eyes.

He blinked in amazement. Through the Spectrometer, he beheld the world in outline—like an artist's preliminary sketch in charcoal on a white canvas, innocent of color. As he stared, each outline gradually filled with a cryptic scribble that resolved into lists of elements and percentage figures. They told him the precise chemical composition of the oxidized steel the skeleton wore, even of its dry bones. If he turned his head to focus on something else, the notations vanished as though blown away, only to re-form on the new object of his attention like birds returning to a roost.

Fascinated, Marsh held up his hand before his eyes and waited as the list formed, detailing to the last ounce that whereof he himself was made. "This is impossible," he murmured.

"Not for our people," said a voice close to his ear. He looked up to see Edward, a living illustration rendered even more subtly monstrous by the instrument's analysis of him, for its list of constituent chemicals was far more complex than Marsh's own. What *was* the man, if he was even a man? And who had made such an instrument, capable of such miraculous analysis? Marsh felt fear in his heart, swiftly transmuting to unholy joy.

"The recruiter hinted—but I never imagined it was true!" he whispered. "Why, we must have found the Philosopher's Stone!"

"Long ago," said Edward. "But there are more precious metals than gold. Your duty is to locate one, now. You had better commence."

Marsh wandered forth into the world of the Spectrometer, where the whole of the vault resembled a newspaper engraving come to life. He became so absorbed in his analysis of sword-hilts and shield-bosses that he scarcely noticed the others, feeling about like blind men in their search for another exit from the crypt.

"Bugger this," said Jenkins. "Didn't the silly bastard mention where it was in his notes?"

Johnson set down the lamp on the edge of the nearest catafalque and pulled a sheaf of papers from his coat. Holding the foremost page in the light, he cleared his throat and read aloud:

> "16 January, 1850. At last! The peace I require for un-
> interrupted work. Some trepidation at first as to whether
> I would be able to find the door from this side, or whether
> the passage of years might have rendered it impassible
> even should I recognise the egress; but my fears proved
> groundless.

"Before securing the alloy samples, I indulged myself so far as to satisfy a curiosity that has dogged me since I was so unfairly forbidden access to the vaults. I had brought with me a pair of calipers, and took pains to measure those of the skulls of my forebears not yet crumbled to fragments. Imagine my gratification on discovering that it was indeed as I had suspected—my cranial capacity far exceeds theirs. If ever I had required proof that I am, in fact, a criminal mastermind, this would have assured me that intellectually I so far exceed these dabblers in arcane geometry as ordinary men outstrip the ourang-outan in cognitive process."

"Less vanity, more information," requested Edward. Johnson read on hastily.

"He never says how he got out! Just, *'Having procured the Gyttite, I slid my ladder back into its place of concealment and returned here through the tunnel. How the wind howls! I really must do something about these draughts—'"*

"Ladder?" said Edward. Taking the papers, he held them up and read closely. Then he raised his head to peer at the distant ceiling.

"It's up there," he said.

"The tunnel?" said Marsh in dismay.

"No. The Gyttite." Edward walked to the nearest wall and jumped, catching hold of a projecting cornice. He braced his other hand on the wall, meaning no doubt to swing himself up; but as he did so the others exclaimed. Marsh pulled the Spectrometer off in some haste, and beheld another marvel.

The whole of the vaulted crypt was now brilliantly illuminated. The dead grinned up at an incandescent fairyland, where every arch and figure of ornamental tracery was outlined in pencil-strokes of flame. Nor did it flicker, rather glowing steadily.

Edward, momentarily frozen as he gaped at the spectacle,

recovered his composure and let go the cornice, dropping to the floor. Instantly the light went out. Only gradually did they regain their vision, by the comparatively dim beam of Johnson's lamp.

"The spectral lights of Rosslyn," said Johnson quietly. "The legends were true."

"Spectral!" said Edward. "I doubt it. Let us see, shall we?"

He stepped close to the wall again and tilted his head back, looking with attention at a dark band that ran just above the cornice, at a height of eight feet, the whole length of the wall and in fact along all adjoining walls. Edward reached up and set his hand there.

The uncanny light returned at once. Marsh, watching closely this time, observed that it originated at the point at which Edward's hand was in contact with the band, and spread so rapidly therefrom in all directions that it appeared nearly simultaneous.

"This doesn't half beat the Strand," said Wilson, with a tremulous giggle. Edward took his hand down. The light extinguished itself once more—and seemed, in doing so, to vanish at the outermost vaults of the crypt first, fleeing as it were to the point of its origin. Indeed, as it disappeared, its last manifestation took the phantom outline of a hand.

Johnson held the lamp as high as he could, peering at the ceiling. "It's some sort of wire, threaded amidst the carvings," he said.

"And the band is a panel of metal," said Edward. They exchanged a significant look. "Gyttite," he said. He set his hand to the panel again. As the light bloomed once more, they studied the remarkable care with which each floral pattern or hieratic emblem had been set with light. Yet it was possible to see where a few tiny areas had gone dark. A floret here, a bossed rosette there seemed to have been broken away; and these were all in the lower sections of the design. Johnson pointed.

"That's where he was getting his samples," he said. "The bloody little vandal."

"We must follow his example, I fear," said Edward. "Look sharp! Do any of you spy a ladder?"

He waited patiently, but diligent search on the part of the others failed to disclose where Gytt had hidden his ladder, even though the crypt was bright as a cathedral's worth of lit candles. He looked up and fixed his gaze on a large terminal pendant, in the (appropriate) shape of a fleur-de-luce, some twelve feet above the floor.

"We'll take that," he said. "Who's tallest after me? Jenkins? Come, please."

Wondering, Jenkins stepped forward. He was seized and hoisted into the air above Edward's head as though he weighed no more than a child. Edward shifted the young man to a standing position on his own shoulders.

Jenkins, struggling to keep his balance, reached up into the darkness and groped desperately for the fleur-de-luce. When his hand closed on it at last, the crypt lit once more; although it was altogether less bright than on the previous occasions. He wrenched and twisted at the ornament until it snapped off, whereupon the crypt darkened again; but the fleur-de-luce shone on in Jenkins's hand. It flashed in an unsteady arc as Edward crouched to set him down.

The others crowded close to stare.

"Doesn't it burn your hand?"

"It doesn't appear to be phosphorus—"

"Let the new man see!"

Jenkins offered the ornament to Marsh, who took it gingerly—it did not burn at all, though the metal was distinctly warm. He put on the Spectrometer. Once more, the world became a steel engraving, and the fleur-de-luce was a graceful basketwork of...of...

"Copper," he said, "tungsten, lead...but...what's this? That can't be right! Why would anyone alloy—"

There came a muffled thunder from the direction of the collapsed tunnel, just as Williams (who had been searching diligently for Gytt's exit, and gone far down one of the side aisles) called out:

"Here! This must be it!" He pointed to footprints in the dust, that led up to a blind wall and vanished.

"I believe a hasty departure is called for," said Edward. He led the others to the spot, and scowled at the wall. "More light! Pass the lamp this way, if you please." Johnson brought it close and, for good measure, Edward took the fleur-de-luce from Marsh. It flamed into brilliance in his hand.

"Here! Why's it light up like that for *him?*" demanded Wilson.

"His hands are hotter?" Johnson suggested. "Edward's closer to Hell than the rest of us, after all."

Edward narrowed his eyes at him, but said only: "I should imagine my body generates a superior electrical current."

"It may be..." said Marsh. They all turned to look at him, and he flushed. "It seems to be some sort of superior conductor. If its properties allow it to incandesce at relatively low temperatures..."

"It'd put the lamplighters out of business," said Wilson, grinning. "And the whalers and the tallow-makers too! New lamps of Gyttite!"

"Let us concentrate on the issue at hand, gentlemen," said Edward, thumping on the wall. "There has to be a lever, or a knob—"

"Like this?" Johnson pointed to the figure of a seraph, which had been carved with one arm extended, as though greeting someone. Was there an imperfectly concealed join at the figure's shoulder?

"Ah." Edward took the figure by the hand and pushed. There was no sound, but the stone wall promptly swung inward, perfectly balanced on an unseen pivot to move as though it weighed no more than a bubble. Beyond was a smooth stone passageway, leading down into darkness.

Edward waved the others across the threshold. It gave Marsh a queer feeling to look at the footprints that tracked off into the gloom, knowing that they had been made by a murdered man. When they were all safely in and the wall shut behind them, Edward led them forward, following the prints and necessarily obliterating the last traces of Jerome Gytt.

Marsh stumbled through a nasty place of dampness and fallen rock. He was hustled on, past great baulks of mining-timber gone black and nearly turned to stone with age. Once he caught a glimpse of what he was certain was an ancient pick, eaten to a mere crescent of rust; once he was sure he saw a Latin inscription scratched on the wall. Horrid white roots hung down from the ceiling here and there, below which Edward must stoop as he hurried on, holding aloft the fleur-de-luce. Hour after weary hour they must follow him, mile after mile.

"You realize where we're likely to come out," said Johnson to Edward, at some point in the long flight.

"Yes," said Edward, and touched briefly his pistol, which he carried in its leather holster under his arm. Nothing more was said, and Marsh wondered what the significance of their remarks was, until he recollected that Gytt had owned a house in Edinburgh. Would the tunnel stretch so far?

It seemed to; and now an ancient spillage of coal impeded their way, scattered lumps crunching and sliding under their boots. A mile further on they were obliged to splash ankle-deep through icy water for several hundred yards. Marsh might have been sleepwalking when at last he caromed into Wilson, who had stopped moving. He looked up and saw Edward peering at a rope ladder, holding the fleur-de-luce close. It was common rope, swinging loose from some point high above, and Marsh wondered fearfully if it would still bear weight.

Edward handed the light off to Johnson and ascended with the ease of a sailor. Staring after him, they saw the plain trap door at the top of the shaft; he reached it, listened warily a moment, and then set his shoulders against it and pushed upward.

Darkness above. He remained there a long, long moment in silence; at last he lowered himself so far as to look down at the others.

"The house has been let again," he said, in a low voice. "There are people asleep in the upper chambers. No dogs, thank heaven; but we shall have to be utterly silent."

"What about the Vespertiles?" said Johnson.

"An excellent question," said Edward, frowning. "Wait."

He climbed the rest of the way up, and they watched his long legs vanishing through the trap. Perhaps five minutes went by. Marsh had just put the instrument case down, and was wondering whether he could lower himself to sit on it comfortably, when Edward's face appeared in the trap once more.

"They've got three men posted across the street," he said. "Armed, I've no doubt. I suspect they've got a man watching the back door as well. You may as well come up; perhaps I can draw them off."

Marsh was closest to the ladder, and set his uneasy foot on the lowest rung. Swaying like a pendulum, he made an awkward progression to the point where Edward was able to simply lean down and haul him up through the trap, into what appeared to be someone's pantry. Marsh was leaning down for the instrument case, which Johnson was endeavoring to pass up to him, when he heard a voice exclaim in wordless surprise. He scrambled to his feet, on the defensive, and shut the trap.

A tiny boy stood on the threshold of the room, clutching to his chest a stone jar. His fingers, mouth and nightshirt were sticky with jam.

"Whae's there?" the child piped.

Marsh felt a disagreeable prickle of sweat. Edward, however, spoke calmly, and with a moral authority that would have done credit to a headmaster:

"We are policemen. Have you been stealing jam?"

The child looked down with wide eyes at the evidence.

"Och, nae," he said, after a moment's hesitation. "It was that other boy ate the jam."

"What other boy?" Edward demanded, looming above him.

"Er—Smout. Smout's a hateful, waeful, wicked sinner, sir. Ye wouldna believe the things he gets up tae. I was just putting the jam awa' so he couldna eat more an' risk the eternal damnation of his immortal soul," the child explained.

"Then you had better put it away, hadn't you?" said Edward sternly. The child nodded and edged toward a stool that had been pushed up to a high pantry shelf. Edward lifted him up, and assisted him in putting the jar back. Marsh winced, expecting to see child-brains spattering the wall at any minute; but Edward merely turned the boy by his little shoulders and looked into his eyes.

"I'm happy to hear you're not a thief, lad," said Edward, and now his voice was smooth and pleasant as sunlight. "Tell me, are you brave?"

"Sometimes," said the child, staring fascinated into Edward's eyes.

"I knew you were brave. I could see that straight away," said Edward, smiling. "Do you have the courage to help us defeat a fearsome enemy?"

"Aye!" said the child.

"Very good. There are certain wicked men, hiding in the shadows across the street. Their design is to break into this house and steal treasure."

"Like the spoons an' candlesticks an' a'?" asked the child, breathless with excitement.

"Exactly so. The worst of them have already crept into your back garden; my friend and I will deal with them. But you must run upstairs and tell your Papa and servants about the villains across the street, that they may drive them away."

"Might I see the villains, please?"

"Of course," said Edward, and, lifting the child in his arms, bore him silently from the room. Marsh tiptoed after them, fearing for the child's safety. Peering around the doorframe into what was evidently a solidly middle-class parlor, he saw the two of them standing at a window, peeking through a parted curtain into the moonlit street without.

"You see their leader, lurking in that doorway?" Edward was saying.

"Och, what a wee hideous devil!" the child whispered. "He has a stick! Does he beat people wi' it?"

"I shouldn't be surprised if he did," Edward whispered back.

"I shall run an' tell Papa," said the child soberly, and turned and ran for the stairs. Edward and Marsh ran for the pantry, where Edward pulled up the trap once more.

"Come up now! We have our diversion," he said in a low voice. "Not a sound, any of you. Where is the Gyttite?"

One after another the rest scrambled through the trap, and Edward seized the Gyttite. It promptly flared into unwelcome brightness, and was hastily wrapped into someone's coat. As they bunched together in the darkness, Marsh heard the boy's shrill voice somewhere above, raised in dramatic declaration. There followed deep grumbling response, remonstrations, and screams of temper; at last other voices raised, followed shortly thereafter by the sound of heavy boots descending the stairs.

Edward herded the others to the back door, drawing his gun as he did so. Moonlight streamed through the white curtain over a narrow window. The tumult reached the front of the house; they heard a door flung open, and the outraged bawl of "HA! WHUT D'YE FANCY YE'RE DOING, LURKING THEER?"

A shadow fled past the window, and they heard the sound of running footsteps diminishing with distance. Edward tucked the Gyttite, wrapped as it was in the coat, under his arm like a football.

"Scatter, gentlemen," he said, "as fast as your legs will carry you. Report to London Central in forty-eight hours." He threw the door wide and they bolted, all.

Marsh had a confused impression of scaling a wall, of someone throwing him the instrument case, and of being in a good deal of pain when he caught it. Thereafter he ran through the moonlit streets, terrified but with a certain exhilaration, in what he supposed was the general direction of the hotel.

The boyish glee faded, as he became conscious of his peril; there were men who would stop at nothing somewhere nearby. And was he any safer with his new friends? Ever before his mind's eye was the dead face of the Black Knight, when that unfortunate had collapsed forward...

As he staggered up an unfamiliar street, quite lost now, Edward stepped out of black shadow before him. Only a supreme effort of will kept him from turning and running away.

"Come along, Marsh," said Edward shortly, and said not another word to him all the way back to their hotel.

They neither bathed nor slept there. After a change of clothing they went straight back to the railway station, with the Gyttite safely packed in Edward's valise, and boarded the train to London.

Edward, for the first time, seemed weary. He sat with the valise in his lap, leaning into the corner of their carriage; after a while his eyes closed and his head nodded forward, though his body did not otherwise relax.

Marsh, propped in the other corner and observing him through half-closed eyes, was struck by the change in the man when he slept. With the pale eyes shut, all their persuasion ceased; with the golden voice silent, all its charm was dispelled. He seemed like a lamp whose flame had gone out, leaving a dull, inanimate and inexplicably fearsome thing of clay.

Mrs. Shelley's book...Frae Ghoules, gheesties an' long-leggety beasties, Guid Lord deliver us!

Marsh shook himself awake, unwilling to sleep yet.

A thought had been waiting, patiently, at the back of his mind for a time when it might have his full attention.

Now it stepped forward, and begged him to consider the technological marvels he had just observed. The Improved Spectrometer was a far more complex achievement than the Gyttite, which was, after all, merely an alloy of base metal that conducted supremely well. If the Society to which he now belonged had such working wonders... why were none of them already in evidence in the world?

He realized that it was entirely likely that the Gyttite, and all the other treasures of invention sought by the Society, were being sought not to "elevate suffering Mankind above the pit," but for private gain. Perhaps to amass power...*So do thrones topple.*

But if that were the case...well, when all was said and done, wasn't it better to be on the side that held the most power?

Jerome Gytt had somehow entered the compartment and was sitting across from him, shaking his head.

"You think you'll use them to mount to the stars," he told Marsh. "I thought so. I was so clever; yet I could no more extricate myself from the trap than a fly can win free out of a cobweb. I was only safe so long as I was useful, you see. I was so clever...but a bullet is cleverer."

"Don't be ridiculous!" Marsh was affronted. "The Vespertiles are merely professional criminals, whereas I have joined an ancient and honorable Society intent on the pursuit of knowledge. They're entirely different!"

Gytt's faintly mocking smile widened. He began to laugh, as though that had been quite the best joke he had heard in a while. He rocked to and fro, he held his sides and pointed at Marsh. Marsh was insulted, and sought to protest further; but felt his heart fail him as blood began spilling from Gytt's laughing mouth. The blood got everywhere. It ran all over Gytt's clothing, it stained the seat, it spattered even Edward's gray exhausted face, and Marsh tried to rise—

He jolted awake and stared about wildly. Edward slept on, oblivious.

Marsh turned up his collar and leaned back, blinking. No use to fight sleep any more; nature could only be resisted so long, after all, and the rocking of the carriage on its iron track was irresistibly soothing, and in any case the train had increased its speed and was going far too fast for him to jump off now.

THE WOMEN OF NELL GWYNNE'S

This was the second of Kage's novel-length steampunk series of stories—well, almost a novel. Nell Gwynne's, a brothel that houses the Ladies Auxiliary of the Gentlemen's Speculative Society, was originally introduced as a small side plot in *Not Less Than Gods*, which is the story of Edward Bell Fairfax's introduction to a life of eccentrically accoutered espionage. The Ladies as presented in that book simply would not be still—their voices, especially the cool and well-bred voice of Lady Beatrice—would not be silenced. Kage wanted to show the world how women can be heroes even when driven to what has always been regarded as a fate worse than death...by mere men, anyway. Hence this bedroom adventure, complete with subterranean labyrinths, unearthly hybrids, antigravity, dastardly industrial spies and the professional rigors of the lives of some unusually resourceful demimondaines.

—K. B.

ONE: IN WHICH IT IS ESTABLISHED THAT

In the city of Westminster, in the vicinity of Birdcage Walk, in the year of our Lord 1844...

There was once a private residence with a view of St. James's Park. It was generally known, among the London tradesmen, that a respectable widow resided there, upon whom it was never necessary to call for overdue payment. Beggars knew she could be relied upon for charity, if they weren't too importunate, and they were careful never to be so;

for she was one of their own, in a manner of speaking, being as she was blind.

Now and again Mrs. Corvey could be observed, with her smoked goggles and walking-stick, on the arm of her adolescent son Herbert, taking the pleasant air in the park. It was known that she had several daughters also, though the precise number was unclear, and that her younger sister was in residence there as well. There may even have been a pair of younger sisters, or perhaps there was an unmarried sister-in-law, and though the daughters had certainly left the schoolroom their governess seemed to have been retained.

In any other neighborhood, perhaps, there would have been some uncouth speculation about the inordinate number of females under one roof. The lady of the house by Birdcage Walk, however, retained her reputation for spotless respectability, largely because no gentlemen visitors were ever seen arriving or departing the premises, at any hour of the day or night whatsoever.

Gentlemen were unseen because they never went to the house near Birdcage Walk. They went instead to a certain private establishment known as Nell Gwynne's, two streets away, which connected to Mrs. Corvey's cellar by an underground passage and which was in the basement of a fairly exclusive dining establishment. The tradesmen never came near *that* place, needless to say. Had any one of them ever done so, he'd have been astonished to meet there Mrs. Corvey and her entire household, including Herbert, who under this separate roof was transformed, Harlequin-like, into Herbertina. The other ladies resident were likewise transformed from Ladies into Women, brandishing riding crops, birch rods and other instruments of their profession.

Nell Gwynne's clientele were often statesmen, who found the place convenient to Whitehall. They were not infrequently members of other exclusive clubs. Some were journalists. Some were notable persons in the sciences or the arts. All were desperately grateful to have been accorded membership at Nell Gwynne's, for it was known— among the sort of gentlemen who know such things—that there was no use whining for a sponsor. Membership was by invitation only, and entirely at the discretion of the lady whose establishment it was.

Now and again, in the hushed and circumspect atmosphere of the Athenaeum (or the Carlton Club, or the Traveller's Club), someone might imbibe enough port to wonder aloud just what it took to get an invitation from Mrs. Corvey.

The answer, though quite simple, was never guessed.

One had to know secrets.

Secrets were, in fact, the principal item retailed at Nell Gwynne's, with entertainments of the flesh coming in a distant second. Secrets were teased out of sodden members of Parliament, coaxed from lustful cabinet ministers, extracted from talkative industrialists, and finessed from members of the Royal Society as well as the British Association for the Advancement of Science.

Information so acquired was not, as you might expect, sold to the highest bidder. It went directly across Whitehall and up past Scotland Yard, to an unimposing-looking brick edifice in Craig's Court, wherein was housed Redking's Club. Membership at Redking's was composed equally of other MPs, ministers, industrialists and Royal Society members, and a great many other clever fellows besides. However, there were many more clever fellows beneath Redking's, for *its* secret cellars went down several storeys, and housed an organization known publicly—but to very few—as the Gentlemen's Speculative Society.

In return for the secrets sent their way by Mrs. Corvey, the GSS underwrote her establishment, enabling all ladies present to live pleasantly when they were not engaged in the business of gathering intelligence. Indeed, once a year Nell Gwynne's closed its premises when its residents went on holiday. The more poetical of the ladies preferred the Lake District, but Mrs. Corvey liked nothing better than a month at the seaside, so they generally ended up going to Torbay.

Life for the ladies of Nell Gwynne's was, placed in the proper historical, societal and economic context, quite tolerably nice.

Now and then it did have its challenges, however.

Two: In which our heroine is a Witness to History

We will call her Lady Beatrice, since that was the name she chose for herself later.

Lady Beatrice's Papa was a military man, shrewd and sober. Lady Beatrice's Mamma was a gently bred primrose of a woman, demure, proper, perfectly genteel. She was somewhat pained to discover that the daughter she bore was rather more bold and direct than became a little girl.

Lady Beatrice, encountering a horrid great spider in the garden, would not scream and run. She would stamp on it. Lady Beatrice, on having her doll snatched away by a bullying cousin, would not weep and plead; she would take back her doll, even at the cost of pulled hair and torn lace. Lady Beatrice, upon falling down, would never lie there sobbing, waiting for an adult to comfort her. She would pick herself up and inspect her knees for damage. Only when the damage amounted to bloody painful scrapes would she perhaps cry, as she limped off to the ayah to be scolded and bandaged.

Lady Beatrice's Mamma fretted, saying such brashness ill became a little lady. Lady Beatrice's Papa said he was damned glad to have a child who never wept unless she was really hurt.

"My girl's true as steel, ain't she?" he said fondly. Whereupon Lady Beatrice's Mamma would purse her lips and narrow her eyes.

Presently Lady Beatrice's Mamma had another focus for her

attention, however, for walking out in the cabbage patch one day she found a pair of twin baby girls, as like her and each other as it was possible to be. Lady Beatrice hadn't thought there was a cabbage patch in the garden. She went out and searched diligently, and found not so much as a Brussels sprout, which fact she announced loudly at dinner that evening. Lady Beatrice's Mamma turned scarlet. Lady Beatrice's Papa roared with laughter.

Thereafter Lady Beatrice was allowed a most agreeable childhood, by her standards, Mamma being preoccupied with little Charlotte and Louise. She was given a pony, and was taught to ride by their Punjabi groom. She was given a bow and arrows and taught archery. She was taught her letters, and read as many books as she liked. When she asked for her own regimental uniform, Mamma told her such a thing was wicked, and retired with a fainting fit, but Papa gave her a little red coat on her next birthday.

The birthdays came and went. Just after Lady Beatrice turned seventeen, Lady Beatrice's Grandmamma was taken ill, and so Lady Beatrice's Mamma took the twins and went back to England for a visit. Lady Beatrice was uninterested in going, having several handsome young officers swooning for her at the time, and Mamma was quite content to leave her in India with Papa.

Grandmamma had been expected to die rather soon, but for some reason lingered, and Lady Beatrice's Mamma found one reason after another to postpone returning. Lady Beatrice relished running Papa's house by herself, especially presiding over dinners, where she bantered with all the handsome young officers and not a few of the old ones. One of them wrote poetry in praise of her gray eyes. Two others dueled on her account.

Then Papa's regiment was ordered to Kabul.

Lady Beatrice was left alone with the servants for some months, bored beyond anything she had believed possible. One day word came that all the wives and children of the married officers were to be allowed to go to Kabul as well, as a way to keep up the troops' morale.

Lady Beatrice heard nothing directly from Papa, as it happened, but she went with all the other families. After two months of miserably difficult travel through all the red dust in the world, Lady Beatrice arrived in Kabul.

Papa was not pleased to see her. Papa was horrified. He sat her down and in few words explained how dangerous their situation was, how unlikely it was that the Afghanis would accept the British-backed ruler. He told her that rebellion was likely to break out any moment, and that the order to send for wives and children had been perfectly insane folly.

Lady Beatrice had proudly told Papa that she wasn't afraid to stay in Kabul; after all, all her handsome suitors were there! Papa had given a bitter laugh and replied that he didn't think it was safe now to send her home alone in any case.

So Lady Beatrice had stayed in Kabul, hosting Papa's dinners for increasingly glum and uninterested young suitors. She remained there until the end, when Elphinstone negotiated the retreat of the British garrison, and was one of the doomed sixteen thousand who set off from Kabul for the Khyber Pass.

Lady Beatrice watched them die, one after another after another. They died of the January cold; they died when Ghilzai snipers picked them off, or rode down in bands and skirmished with the increasingly desperate army. Papa died in the Khoord Kabul gorge, during one such skirmish, and Lady Beatrice was carried away screaming by a Ghilzai tribesman.

Lady Beatrice was beaten and raped. She was left tied among the horses. In the night she tore through the rope with her teeth and crawled into the shelter where her captors slept. She took a knife and cut their throats, and did worse to the last one, because he woke and attempted to break her wrist. She swathed herself in their garments, stole a pair of their boots. She stole their food. She took their horses, riding one and leading the others, and went down to find Papa's body.

He was frozen stiff when she found him, so she had to give up any idea of tying him across the saddle and taking him away. Instead she buried him under a cairn of stones, and scratched his name and regiment on the topmost rock with the knife with which she had killed her rapists. Then Lady Beatrice rode away, weeping; but she felt no shame weeping, because she was really hurt.

All along the Khyber Pass she counted the British and Indian dead. On three separate occasions she rode across the body of one and then another and then another of her handsome young suitors. Lady Beatrice looked like a gray-eyed specter, all her tears wept out, by the time she rode into Jellalabad.

No one quite knew what to do with her there. No one wanted to speak of what had happened, for, as one of the officers who had known her family explained, her father's good name was at stake. Lady Beatrice remained with the garrison all through the siege of Jellalabad that followed, cooking for them and washing clothes. In April, just after the siege had been raised, she miscarried.

Her father's friends saw to it that Lady Beatrice was escorted back to India. There she sold off the furniture, dismissed the servants, closed up the house and bought herself passage to England.

Once she had arrived, it took Lady Beatrice several weeks to find Mamma and the twins. Grandmamma had died at last, and upon receiving word of the massacre in Afghanistan, Mamma had bought mourning and thrown herself upon the mercy of her older brother, a successful merchant. She and the twins were now living as dependents in his household.

Lady Beatrice arrived on their doorstep and was greeted by shrieks of horror. Apparently Lady Beatrice's letters had gone astray in the mail. Her mother fainted dead away. Uncle Frederick's wife came in and fainted dead away as well. Charlotte and Louise came running down to see what had happened and, while they did not faint, they screamed shrilly. Uncle Frederick came in and stared at her as though his eyes would burst from his face.

Once Mamma and Aunt Harriet had been revived, to cling to each other weeping on the settee, Lady Beatrice explained what had happened to her.

A lengthy and painful discussion followed. It lasted through tea and dinner. It was revealed to Lady Beatrice that, though she had been sincerely mourned when Mamma had been under the impression she was dead, her unexpected return to life was something more than inconvenient. Had she never considered the disgrace she would inflict upon her family by returning, after all that had happened to her? What were all Aunt Harriet's neighbors to think?

Uncle Frederick as good as told her to her face that she must have whored herself to the men of the 13th Foot, during all those months in Jellalabad; and if she hadn't, she might just as well have, for all that anyone would believe otherwise.

At this point Mamma fainted again. While they were attempting to revive her, Charlotte and Louise reproached Lady Beatrice in bluntest terms for her selfishness. Had she never thought for a moment of what the scandalous news would do to *their* marriage prospects? Mamma, sitting up at this point, tearfully begged Lady Beatrice to enter a convent. Lady Beatrice replied that she no longer believed in God.

Whereupon Uncle Frederick, his face black with rage, rose from the table (the servants were in the act of serving the fish course) and told Lady Beatrice that she would be permitted to spend the night under his roof, for her Mamma's sake, but in the morning he was personally taking her to the nearest convent.

At this point Aunt Harriet pointed out that the nearest convent was in France, and he would be obliged to drive all day and hire passage on a boat, which hardly seemed respectable. Uncle Frederick shouted that he didn't give a damn. Mamma fainted once more.

Lady Beatrice excused herself and rose from the table. She went upstairs, found her mother's room, ransacked her jewel box, and left the house by the back door.

She caught the night coach in the village and went to London, where she pawned a necklace of her mother's and paid a quarter's rent on a small room in the Marylebone Road. Having done that, Lady Beatrice went to a dressmaker's and had an ensemble made in the most lurid scarlet silk the seamstress could find on her shelves. Afterward she went to a milliner's and had a hat made up to match.

The next day she went shopping for shoes and found a pair of ready-mades in her size that looked as though they would bear well with prolonged walking. Lady Beatrice purchased cosmetics also.

When her scarlet raiment was ready Lady Beatrice collected it. She took it back to her room, put it on, and stood before the cracked glass above her washstand. Holding her head high, she rimmed her gray eyes with blackest kohl.

What else was there to do, but die?

THREE: IN WHICH SHE GETS ON WITH HER LIFE

The work seemed by no means as dreadful as Lady Beatrice had heard tell. She realized, however, that her point of view was somewhat unusual. The act was never pleasurable for her but it was at least not painful, as it had been in the Khyber Pass. She took care to carry plenty of lambskin sheaths in her reticule. She worked her body like a draft horse. It obeyed her patiently and earned her decent meals and a clean place in which to sleep, and books. Lady Beatrice found that she still enjoyed books.

She felt nothing, neither for nor against, regarding the men who lay with her.

Lady Beatrice learned quickly where the best locations were for plying one's trade, if one didn't wish to be brutalized by drunken laborers: outside theaters, outside the better restaurants and wine bars. She discovered that her looks and her voice gave her an advantage over the other working women, who were for the most part desperate country girls or Cockneys. She watched them straggle through their nights, growing steadily drunker and more hoarse, sporting upper-arm bruises ever more purple.

They regarded her with disbelief and anger, especially when an old cove with a diamond stickpin could walk their importuning gauntlet unmoved, shaking off their hands, deaf to their filthiest enticements, but stop in his tracks when Lady Beatrice stepped out in front of him. "Oi! Milady's stole another one!" someone would cry. She liked the name.

One night three whores lay for her with clubs in an alley off the Strand. She pulled a knife—for she carried one—and held them at bay, and told them what she'd done to the Ghilzai tribesmen. They backed away, and fled. They spread the word that Milady was barking mad.

Lady Beatrice wasn't at all mad. It was true that the snows of the Khyber Pass seemed to have settled around her heart and left it incapable of much emotion, but her mind was sharp and clear as ice. It was difficult even to feel contempt for her fellow whores, though she saw plainly enough that many were ignorant, that they drank too much, that they habitually fell in love with men who beat them, that they wallowed in self-pity and festering resentments.

Lady Beatrice never drank. She lived thriftily. She opened a bank account and saved the money she made, reserving out enough to remain well-dressed and buy a novel now and again. She calculated how much she would need to save in order to retire and live quietly, and she worked toward that goal. She kept a resolute barrier between her body and her mind, only nominally resident in the one, only truly living in the other.

One evening she was strolling the pavement outside the British Museum (an excellent place to do business, judging from all the wealthy clientele she picked up there) when a previous customer recognized her and engaged her services for a gentlemen's party on the following night. Lady Beatrice dressed in her best evening scarlets for the occasion, and paid for a cab.

She recognized some of her better-dressed rivals at the party, at which some sporting victory was being celebrated, and they nodded to one another graciously. One by one, each portly financier or baronet paired off with a courtesan, and Lady Beatrice was just thinking that she could do with more of this sort of engagement when she heard her name called, in a low voice.

She turned and beheld an old friend of her father's, whom she had once charmed with an hour's sprightly conversation. Lady Beatrice stepped close to him, quickly.

"That is not the name I use now," she said.

"But—my dear child—how could you come to this?"

"Do you truly wish to hear the answer?"

He cast a furtive look around and, taking her by the wrist, led her into an antechamber and shut the door after them, to general laughter from those not too preoccupied to notice.

Lady Beatrice told him her story, in a matter-of-fact way, seated on a divan as he paced and smoked. When she had finished he sank into a chair opposite, shaking his head.

"You deserved better in life, my dear."

"No one deserves good or evil fortune," said Lady Beatrice. "Things simply happen, and one survives them the best one can."

"God! That's true; your father used to say that. He never flinched at unpleasantness. You are very like him, in that sense. He always said you were as true as steel."

Lady Beatrice heard the phrase with a sense of wonder, remembering that long-ago life. It seemed to her, now, as though it had happened to some other girl.

The old friend was regarding her with a strange mixture of compassion and a certain calculation. "For your father's sake, and for your own, I should like to assist you. May I know where you live?"

Lady Beatrice gave him her address readily enough. "Though I do not advise you to visit," she said. "And if you have any gallant ideas about rescuing me, think again. No lady in London would receive me, after what I endured, and you know that as well as I do."

"I know, my dear." He stood and bowed to her. "But women true as steel are found very rarely, after all. It would be shameful to waste your excellent qualities."

"How kind," said Lady Beatrice.

She expected nothing from the encounter, and so Lady Beatrice was rather surprised when someone knocked at the door of her lodging three days thereafter.

She was rather more surprised when, upon opening the door, she beheld a blind woman, who asked for her by her name.

"I am she," admitted Lady Beatrice.

"May I come in for a moment, miss, and have a few words with you?"

"As many as you wish," said Lady Beatrice. Swinging her cane before her, the blind woman entered the room. Seemingly quite by chance she encountered a chair and lowered herself into it. Despite her infirmity, she was not a beggar; indeed, she was well- dressed and well-groomed, resembling, if not a lady, certainly someone's respectable mother. Her accents indicated that she had come from the lower classes, but she spoke quietly, with precise diction. She drew off her gloves and bonnet, and held them in her lap, with her cane crooked over one arm.

"Thank you. I'll introduce myself, if I may: Mrs. Elizabeth Corvey. We have a friend in common." She uttered the name of the gentleman who had known Lady Beatrice in her former life.

"Ah," said Lady Beatrice. "And I expect you administer some sort of charity for fallen women?"

Mrs. Corvey chuckled. "I wouldn't say that, miss, no." She turned her goggled face toward Lady Beatrice. The smoked goggles were very black, and quite prominent. "None of the ladies in my establishment require charity. They're quite able to get on in the world. As you seem to be. Your friend told me the sort of things you've seen and done. What's done can't be undone, more's the pity, but there it is.

"That being the case, may I ask you whether you'd consider putting your charms to better use than streetwalking?"

"Do you keep a house of prostitution, madam?"

"I do and I don't," said Mrs. Corvey. "If it was a house of prostitution, you may be sure it would be of the very best sort, with girls as beautiful and clever as you, and some of them as well bred. I am not, myself; I was born in the workhouse.

"When I was five years old they sold me to a pin factory. Little hands are needed for the making of pins, you see, and little keen eyes. Little girls are preferred for the work; so much more painstaking than little boys, you know. We worked at a long table, cutting up the lengths of wire and filing the points, and hammering the heads flat. We worked by candlelight when it grew dark, and the shop-mistress read to us from the Bible as we worked. I was blind by the age of twelve, but I knew my Scripture, I can tell you.

"And then, of course, there was only one work I was fit for, wasn't there? So I was sold off into a sort of specialty house.

"You meet all kinds of odd ducks in a place like that. Sick fellows, and ugly fellows, and shy fellows. I was got with child twice, and poxed too. I do hope I'm not shocking you, am I? Both of us being women of the world, you see. I lost track of the years, but I think I was seventeen when I got out of there. Should you like to know how I got out?"

"Yes, madam, I should."

"There was this fellow came to see me. He paid specially to have me to himself a whole evening and I thought, *Oh, Lord, no,* because you get so weary of it, and the gentlemen don't generally like it if you seem as though you're not paying proper attention, do they? But all this fellow wanted to do was talk.

"He asked me all sorts of questions about myself—how old I was, where had I come from, did I have any family, how did I come to be blind. He told me he belonged to a club of scientific gentlemen. He said they thought they might have a way to cure blindness. If I was willing to let this Gentlemen's Speculative Society try it out on me, he'd buy me out of the house I was in and see that I was physicked for the pox as well, and found an honest living.

"He did warn me I'd lose my eyes. I said I didn't care—they weren't any use anyhow, were they? And he said I might find myself disfigured, and I said I didn't mind that—what had my looks ever gotten me?

"To be brief, I went with him and had it done. And I did lose my eyes, and I was disfigured, but I haven't regretted it a day since."

"You don't appear to be disfigured," said Lady Beatrice. "And clearly they were unable to cure your blindness."

Mrs. Corvey smiled. "Oh, no? The clock says half-past-twelve, and you're wearing such a lovely scarlet dressing-gown, miss, and you have such striking gray eyes—quite unlike mine. You're made of stern stuff, I know, so you won't scream now." Having said that, she slid her goggles up to reveal her eyes.

Lady Beatrice, who had been standing upright, took a step backward and clutched the edge of the table behind her.

"Dear me, you have gone quite pale," said Mrs. Corvey in amusement. "Sets off that scarlet mouth of yours a treat. House of Rimmel Red No. 3, isn't it? Not so pink as their No. 4. And, let me see, why, what a lot of books you have! *Sartor Resartus, Catherine, Falkner*— that's her last one, isn't it?—and, what's that on your bedside table?" The brass optics embedded in Mrs. Corvey's face actually protruded forward, with a faint whirring noise, and swiveled in the direction of Lady Beatrice's bed. "*Nicholas Nickleby*. Yes, I enjoyed that one, myself.

"I do hope I have proven my point now, miss."

"What a horror," said Lady Beatrice faintly.

"Oh, I shouldn't say that at all, miss! My condition is so much improved from my former state that I would go down on my knees and thank God morning and night, if I thought He ever took notice of the likes of me. I have my sight back, after all. I have my health—for I may say the Gentlemen's Speculative Society has an excellent remedy for the pox—and agreeable employment. I am here to offer you the same work."

"Would I pay for it with my eyes?" Lady Beatrice inquired.

"Oh, dear me, no. It would be a crime to spoil *your* looks, especially when they might be so useful. You were a soldier's daughter, as I understand it, miss. What would you think of turning your dishonor into a weapon, in a just cause?

"The Society's very old, you see. In the old days they had to work secretly, or folk would have burnt them for witchcraft, with all the astonishing things they invented. The secrecy was still useful even when times became more enlightened. There are all manner of devices that make our lives less wretched, that first came from the Society. They work to make the world better still.

"Now, it helps them in their work, miss, to have some sway with ministers and members of Parliament. And who better controls a man than a pretty girl, eh? A girl with sufficient charm can unlock a man's tongue and find out all sorts of things the Society needs to know. A girl with sufficient charm can persuade a man to do all sorts of things he'd never dream of doing, if he thought anyone else could see.

"And *I* can't see, of course, or so he thinks, for I never let my secret slip. When a man is a cabinet minister it reassures him to believe that the lady proprietress of his favorite brothel couldn't identify his face in a court of law. All the easier for us to trap him later. All the easier to persuade him to sign a law into being or vote a certain way, which benefits the Society.

"You and I both know how little it takes to ruin a girl, when a man can make the same mistakes and the world smiles indulgently at him. Wouldn't you like to make the world more just?

"You and I both know how little our bodies matter, for all the fuss men make over them. Wouldn't you like to put yours to good use? There are other girls like you—clever girls, well-bred girls. They did one unwise thing, or perhaps, like you, they were unlucky, and the world sent them down to the pavement. But they found they needn't stay there.

"You needn't stay there either, miss. We can offer you a clean, quiet room of your own, with a view of St. James's Park—I never tire of looking at it, myself—and a quiet life, except when working. We need never fear being beaten, or taking ill. We are paid very well. Shall you join us, miss?"

Lady Beatrice considered it.

"I believe I shall," said she.

And she did, to the great relief of the other streetwalkers.

Four: In which she Settles In and learns Useful Things

Lady Beatrice discovered that Mrs. Corvey had spoken perfect truth. The house near Birdcage Walk was indeed pleasant, commodious, and adjacent to St. James's Park. Her private room was full of the best air and light to be had in London. It had moreover ample shelves for her books, a capacious wardrobe, and a clean and comfortable bed.

She found her sister residents agreeable as well.

Mrs. Otley was, near Birdcage Walk, a rather studious young lady with fossils she had collected at Lyme Regis and a framed engraving of a scene in Pompeii in her room. At Nell Gwynne's, however, she generally dressed like a jockey, and had moreover a cabinet full of equestrian paraphernalia with which to pander to the tastes of gentlemen who enjoyed being struck with a riding crop while being forced to wear a bit between their teeth.

Miss Rendlesham, though quiet, bespectacled and an enthusiastic gardener, was likewise in the Discipline line, both general and (as needed) specialized. As a rule she dressed in a manner suggesting a schoolmistress, and was an expert at producing the sort of harsh interrogatory tones that made a member of Parliament regress to the age of the schoolroom, where he had been a very naughty boy indeed.

Herbertina Lovelock, on the other hand, was a very good boy, with the appearance of a cupid-faced lad fresh from a public school whereat a number of outré vices were practiced. She wore male attire exclusively, cropped hair pomaded sleek. She also smoked cigars, read the sporting papers with her feet on the fender, and occasionally went to the races. At Nell Gwynne's she had a wardrobe full of military uniforms both Army and Navy, all with very tight trousers with padding sewn into the knees.

The Misses Devere were three sisters, Jane, Dora and Maude, blonde, brunette and auburn-haired respectively. Their work at Nell Gwynne's consisted of unspecialized harlotry and also, when required, group engagements in which they worked as a team.

They alone were forthcoming to Lady Beatrice on the subject of their pasts: it seemed their Papa had been a gentleman, but ruined himself in the customary manner by drinking, gambling and speculating in a joint stock company. Depending on whether one heard the story from Jane, Dora or Maude, their Papa had then either blown his brains out, run away to the continent with a mistress, or become an opium-smoker in a den in Limehouse and fallen to depths of degradation too appalling to describe. Jane played the pianoforte, Dora played the concertina, and Maude sang. They were equally versatile in other matters.

All ladies resident at the house near Birdcage Walk proved good-natured upon further acquaintance. Lady Beatrice found it pleasant to sit in the common parlor after dinner on Sundays (for Nell Gwynne's did no business on the Sabbath) and attend to her mending while Herbertina read aloud to them all, or the Misses Devere performed a medley of popular songs, as Miss Rendlesham arranged a vase of flowers from the garden. It was agreed that Lady Beatrice ought not alter her scarlet costume in any respect, since it had such a galvanic effect on customers, but Mrs. Corvey and Herbertina went with her to the shops and the dressmaker's to have a few ensembles made up, in rather more respectable colors, for day wear. Mrs. Otley presented her with a small figure of the goddess Athena from her collection of antiquities, for, as she said, "You are so very like her, my dear, with those remarkable eyes!"

All in all, Lady Beatrice thought her new situation most agreeable.

"Oh, Major, sir, you wouldn't cane me, would you?" squeaked Herbertina. "Not for such a minor infraction?"

"I'll do worse than cane you, you young devil," leered the Major, or rather the Member of Parliament wearing a major's uniform. He grabbed Herbertina by the arm and dragged her protesting to a plush-upholstered settee. "Drop those breeches and bend over!"

"Oh, Major, sir, must I?"

"That's an order! By God, sir, I'll teach you what obedience means!"

"Look through this eyepiece and adjust the lens until the image comes into focus," said Mrs. Corvey in a low voice, from the adjacent darkened room. Lady Beatrice peered into the camera and beheld the slightly blurry Major gleefully dropping his own breeches.

"How does one adjust it?" Lady Beatrice inquired.

"This ring turns," explained Mrs. Corvey, pointing. Lady Beatrice turned it and immediately the Major came into focus, very much *in flagrante delicto*, with Herbertina looking rather bored as she cried out in boyish horror.

"Now squeeze the bulb," said Mrs. Corvey. Lady Beatrice did so. The gas-jets flared in the room for a moment, but the Major was far too busy to be distracted by the sudden intense brightness, or the faint *click*.

"Have we produced a daguerreotype?" inquired Lady Beatrice, rather intrigued, for she had just been reading about them in a scientific periodical to which Miss Rendlesham subscribed.

"Oh, no, dear; this is a much more advanced process. Something the Society gave us." Mrs. Corvey slid out the plate and slipped in another. "It produces an image that can be printed on paper. That shot was simply for our files. We'll have to wait until he's a bit quieter for an image we can really use. Herbertina will give you the signal."

Lady Beatrice watched carefully as the Major rode to his frenzy and at last collapsed over Herbertina. They ended up reclining on the settee, somewhat scantily clad.

"Now," said the Major, wheezing somewhat, "tell me how enormous I was, and how overpowered you were."

"Oh, Major sir, how could you do such a thing to a young man? I've never felt so helpless," said Herbertina tearfully, making a sign behind her back. Lady Beatrice saw it and squeezed the bulb again. Once more the lamps flared. The Major squinted irritably but paid no further heed, for Herbertina quite held his attention over the next five minutes with her imaginative account of how terrified and submissive the young soldier felt, and how gargantuan were the Major's personal dimensions.

Sadly, neither Mrs. Corvey nor Lady Beatrice heard her inspired improvisations, for they had both retreated to a small room, lit with red De la Rue's lamps and fitted up like a chemist's laboratory. There they had fastened cloth masks over their mouths and noses and were busily developing the plates.

"Oh, these are very good," said Mrs. Corvey approvingly. "Upon my soul, dear, you have a talent for photography."

"Are they to be used for blackmail?"

"Beg pardon? Oh, no; which is to say, only if it should become necessary. And if it should, this one—" she held up the second photograph, with the Major lying on the settee—" can be copied over onto a daguerreotype, and presented as an inducement to cooperate. For the present, the pictures will go into his file. We keep a file, you see, on each of the customers. So useful, when business is brisk, to have a record of each gentleman's likes and dislikes."

"I expect it is indeed. When does it become necessary to blackmail, if I may ask?"

"Why, when the Society requires it. I must say, it isn't necessary often. They're quite persuasive on their own account, and seldom have to resort to such extreme measures. Still, one never knows." Mrs. Corvey hung the prints up to dry. She turned the lever that switched off the De la Rue's lamp and they left the room, carefully shutting the door behind them. The two women walked out into the hidden corridor that ran between the private chambers. From the rooms to either side of the corridor could be heard roars of passion, or pleading cries, and now and again the rhythmic swish and crack of a birch rod over ardent confessions of wickedness.

"Are all of the customers men of rank?" Lady Beatrice inquired, raising her voice slightly to be heard over a baritone bawling, *Yes, yes, I did steal the pies!*

"Yes, as a rule; though now and again we treat members of the Society. The fellows whose business it is to go out and manage the Society's affairs, mostly; the rank and file, if you like. They want their pleasures as much as the next man, and most of them have to work a good deal harder to earn them, so we oblige. That is rather a different matter, however, from servicing statesmen and the like.

"In fact, there's rather a charming custom—at least I find it so— of treating the new fellows, before they're first sent on the Society's business. Give them a bit of joy before they go out traveling, poor things, because now and again they do fall in the line of duty. So sad."

"Is it dangerous work?"

"It can be." Mrs. Corvey gave a vague wave of her hand.

They entered the private chamber that served as Mrs. Corvey's office, stepping through the sliding panel and closing it just as Violet, the maid-of-all-work, entered from the reception area beyond.

"If you please, Mrs. Corvey, Mr. Felmouth's just stepped out of the Ascending Room this minute to pay a call. He's got his case with him."

"He'll want his tea, then. How nice! I was hoping we'd be allotted a few new toys." Mrs. Corvey lifted a device from her desk, a sort of speaking-tube of brass and black wax, and after a moment spoke into it: "Tea, please, with a tray of savories. The reception room. Thank you."

She set the device down. Lady Beatrice regarded it with quiet wonder. "And that would be another invention from the Society?"

"Only made by them; it was one of our own ladies invented it. Miss Gleason. Since retired to a nice little cottage in Scotland on the bonus, I am pleased to say. Sends us a dozen grouse every Christmas. Now, come with me, dear, and I'll introduce you to Mr. Felmouth. Such an obliging man!"

FIVE: IN WHICH INGENIOUS DEVICES ARE INTRODUCED

The reception room was rather larger than a private parlor, with fine old dark paneling on the walls and a thick carpet. It was lit by more De la Rue's lamps, glowing steadily behind tinted shades of glass. A middle-aged gentleman had already removed his coat and hat and hung them up, and rolled up his shirtsleeves; he was perched on the edge of a divan, leaning down to rummage in an open valise, but he jumped to his feet as they entered.

"Mr. Felmouth," said Mrs. Corvey, extending her hand.

"Mrs. Corvey!" Mr. Felmouth bowed and, taking her hand, kissed it.

"And may I introduce our latest sister? Lady Beatrice. Lady Beatrice, Mr. Felmouth, from the Society. Mr. Felmouth is one of the Society's artificers."

"How do you do, sir?"

"Enchanted to make your acquaintance, Ma'am," Mr. Felmouth said, stammering rather. He coughed, blushed, and tugged self-consciously at his rolled-up sleeves. "I do hope you'll excuse the liberty, my dear—one gets so caught up in one's work."

"Pray, be seated," said Mrs. Corvey, gliding to her own chair. At that moment a chime rang and a hitherto concealed door in the paneling opened. A pair of respectably clad parlormaids bore in the tea things and arranged them on a table by Mrs. Corvey's chair before exiting again through the same door. Tea was served, accompanied by polite conversation on trivial matters, though the whole time Mr. Felmouth's glance kept wandering from Lady Beatrice to the floor, and hence to his open valise, and then on to Mrs. Corvey.

At last he set his cup and saucer to one side. "Delightful refreshment. My compliments to your staff, Ma'am. Now, I must inquire—how are the present optics suiting you, my dear?"

"Very well," said Mrs. Corvey. "I particularly enjoy the telescoping feature. It's quite useful at the seaside, though of course one must take care not to be noticed."

"Of course. And the implant continues comfortable? No irritation?"

"None nowadays, Mr. Felmouth."

"Very good. Happy to hear it." Mr. Felmouth rubbed his hands together. "However, I have been experimenting with an improvement or two...may I demonstrate?"

"By all means, Mr. Felmouth."

At once he delved into his valise and brought up a leatherbound box about the size of a spectacle case. He opened it with a flourish. Lady Beatrice saw a set of optics very similar to those revealed when Mrs. Corvey had removed her goggles, as she did now. Lady Beatrice involuntarily looked away, then looked back as Mr. Felmouth presented the case to Mrs. Corvey.

"You will observe, Ma'am, that these are a good deal lighter. Mr. Stubblefield in Fabrication discovered a new alloy," said Mr. Felmouth, unrolling a case of small tools. Mrs. Corvey's optics extended outward with a whirr as she examined the new apparatus.

"Yes indeed, Mr. Felmouth, they are lighter. And seem more complicated."

"Ah! That is because...if I may..." Mr. Felmouth leaned forward and applied a tiny screwdriver to Mrs. Corvey's present set of optics, losing his train of thought for a moment as he worked carefully. Lady Beatrice found herself unable to watch as the optics were removed. "Because they are greatly improved, or at least that is my hope. Now then...my apologies, Ma'am, the blindness is entirely temporary...I will just fasten in the new set, and I think you will be pleased with the result."

Lady Beatrice made herself look up, and saw Mrs. Corvey patiently enduring having a new set of optics installed in her living face.

"There," said Mrs. Corvey, "I can see again."

"Splendid," said Mr. Felmouth, tightening the last screw. He sat back. "I trust you find them comfortable?"

"Quite," said Mrs. Corvey, turning her face from side to side. "Oh!" Her optics telescoped outward, a full two inches farther than the range of the previous set, and the whirring sound they produced was much quieter. "Oh, yes, greatly improved!"

"It was my thought that if you held your hands up to obscure them at full extension, you could give anyone observing you the impression that you are looking through a pair of opera glasses," said Mr. Felmouth. "However, permit me to demonstrate the *real* improvement."

He rose to his feet and, going to the nearest lamp, extinguished it by turning a key at its base. He did this with each of the lamps in turn. When he had extinguished the last lamp the room was plunged into Stygian blackness. His voice came out of the darkness:

"Now, Ma'am, if you will give the left-hand lens casing a three-quarter-turn..."

Lady Beatrice heard a faint *click,* and then a cry of delight from Mrs. Corvey.

"Why, the room is quite light! Though everything appears green. Ought it?"

"That is the effect of the filter," said Mr. Felmouth in satisfaction, as he switched on the lamp again. "But it was, I think, bright enough to read by? Yes, that was what I'd hoped for. We will improve it, of course, but from this moment I may confidently assert that you need never endure another moment of darkness, if you are not so inclined."

"How very useful this should prove," said Mrs. Corvey, in satisfaction. "My compliments, Mr. Felmouth! And please extend my thanks to the other kind gentlemen in Fabrication."

"Of course. As it happens, I do have one or two other small items," said Mr. Felmouth, as he went from one lamp to another, switching them back on. He sat down once more and, reaching into his bag, drew out what appeared to be a locket. "Here we are!"

He held it up for their inspection. "Now, ladies, wouldn't you say that was a perfectly ordinary ornament?" Lady Beatrice leaned close to see it; Mrs. Corvey merely extended her optics.

"I should have said so, yes," said Lady Beatrice. Mr. Felmouth raised his index finger, revealing the small hole in the locket's side, with a smaller protrusion a half-inch below.

"No indeed, ladies. This is, rather, positively the last word in miniaturization. Behold." He opened it to reveal a tiny portrait. "And—" Mr. Felmouth thumbed a catch and the portrait swung up, to display a compartment beyond, in which were a minute steel barrel and spring mechanism. "A pistol! The trigger is this knob just below the muzzle.

Hold it *so*—aim, and fire. Though for best results I recommend firing point-blank, if at all possible."

"Ingenious, I must say," said Mrs. Corvey. To Lady Beatrice she added, a little apologetically, "We do find ourselves in need of self-defense, now and then, you see."

"But surely the bullet must be too small to do much harm," said Lady Beatrice.

"You might think so," said Mr. Felmouth. He brought up an ammunition case, no bigger than a pillbox, and opened it to reveal a dozen tiny pin cartridges ranged in a rack, with a pair of tweezers for loading. "No bigger than flies, are they? However—one point three seconds after lodging in the target, they explode. Not with a quarter of the force of a Guy Fawkes squib, but should the bullet happen to be lodged in the brain or heart at the time, that would be quite enough to drop an assailant in his tracks."

"I would fire into my assailant's ear," said Lady Beatrice thoughtfully. "The entrance wound would be undetectable, and anyone looking at him would suppose the man had died of a stroke."

Mrs. Corvey and Mr. Felmouth stared at her. "I see you are not disposed to be squeamish, dear," said Mrs. Corvey at last. "You'll do very well."

The Misses Devere came wandering sadly into the reception area, dressed in costumes representing a doll, Puss in Boots and a harlequin respectively. "Our four o'clock gentleman sent word to say he is unavoidably detained and can't come until tomorrow," said Jane, "and we can't get the catch on the back of Dora's costume unfastened. Lady Beatrice, will you see what you can do? Oh! Hello, Mr. Felmouth!" Jane skipped across the room and sat on his knee. "Have you brought us any toys, Father Christmas?"

Mr. Felmouth, who had gone quite scarlet, sputtered a moment before managing to say, "Er—yes, as it happens, I do have one or two more items. H'em! If you'll permit me..." He pulled the bag up on his other knee and took out a couple of the pasteboard cards of buttons generally to be found at notions shops. There were approximately a dozen buttons on each card. One set resembled oystershell pearl buttons; the others appeared to be amber glass.

"The very thing for unruly customers," Mr. Felmouth said, waving the pearl buttons. "Sew them onto a garment, and they appear indistinguishable from ordinary buttons. They are, however, a profoundly strong sedative in a hard sugar shell. You have only to drop one of these in a glass of port wine, or indeed any beverage, and within seconds the button will dissolve. Any gentleman imbibing a wineglassful will fall into a profound sleep within minutes."

"And the amber buttons?" inquired Lady Beatrice, who had risen and was unworking the catch on the back of the Puss in Boots costume.

"Ah! *These* are really useful. One button, dissolved in a man's drink, will induce a state of talkative idiocy. Gently questioned, he will tell you anything, everything. Not all of it will be truthful, I suspect, but I am confident in your powers of discernment. When the drug wears off he will have absolutely no memory of the episode." Mr. Felmouth presented the cards to Mrs. Corvey.

"Splendid," said Mrs. Corvey.

"Oh, won't the amber ones look lovely on my yellow satin?" cried Dora, popping out of the top of her costume as Lady Beatrice freed her hair from the catch. Mr. Felmouth coughed and averted his eyes.

"They would, dear, but they really ought to go to Miss Rendlesham. She would make the best use of them, after all," said Mrs. Corvey. Dora pouted.

"Dear Mr. Felmouth, can't you make up some more in different colors? Miss Rendlesham never wears yellow." Dora leaned close and tickled Mr. Felmouth under his chin with her paw-gloved hand. "Please, Mr. Felmouth? Pussy will catch you a nice fish."

"It, er, ought to be quite easy," said Mr. Felmouth, breathing a little heavily. "Yes, I'm sure I should find nothing easier. Rely on me, ladies."

"As ever, Mr. Felmouth," said Mrs. Corvey.

Six: In which Disquieting Intelligence is conveyed

Sir Richard H. was of advanced years, quite stout, and so he preferred to lie on his back and engage the angels of bliss, as he called them, astraddle. He lay now groaning with happiness as Lady Beatrice rode away, her gray gaze fixed on the brass rail of the bed, her red mouth curved in a professional smile in which there was something faintly mocking. Her mind was some distance off, wondering how *The Luck of Barry Lyndon* was going to turn out, for she had not yet seen a copy of the latest *Fraser's Magazine*.

At some point her musings were interrupted by the realization that Sir Richard had stopped moving. Lady Beatrice's mind consented to return to the vicinity of her flesh long enough to determine that Sir Richard was, in fact, still alive, if drenched with sweat and puffing like a railway engine. "Are you quite all right, my dear?" she inquired. Sir Richard nodded feebly. She swung herself off him and down, lithe as though he were a particularly well-upholstered vaulting horse, and checked his pulse nevertheless. Having determined that he was unlikely to expire in the immediate future, Lady Beatrice gave him a brief, brisk sponging off with eau de cologne. He was snoring by the time she drew the blanket up over him and went off to bathe in the adjacent chamber.

Lady Beatrice tended her own body with the same businesslike impartiality. During her bout with Sir Richard, her nether regions might have been made of cotton batting like a doll's, for all the sensation she had derived from the act. Even now there was only a minor soreness from chafing. Applying lotion, she marveled once again at the absurd fuss everyone made, swooning over flesh, fearing it, dreading it, lusting after it, when none of it really mattered at all...

She knew there had been a time when the sight of Sir Richard's naked body with its purple tool would have caused her to scream in maidenly dismay; now the poor old thing seemed no more lewd or horrid than a broken-down cart horse. And what had her handsome suitors been but so many splendid racing animals, until they lay blue and stiff in a mountain gorge, when they were even less? They might have had shining souls that ascended to Heaven; it was certainly comforting to imagine so. *Bodies* in general, however, being so impermanent, were scarcely worth distressing oneself.

Lady Beatrice got dressed and returned to the boudoir, where she settled into an armchair and retrieved a copy of *Oliver Twist* from its depths. She read quietly until Sir Richard woke with a start, in the midst of a snore. Sitting up, he asked foggily where his trousers were. Lady Beatrice set her book aside and helped him dress himself, after which she took his arm and escorted him out to the reception area, where he toddled off into the ascending room without so much as a backward glance at her.

"He might have said 'thank you,'" observed Mrs. Corvey, from her chair by the tea-table.

"A little befuddled this evening, I think," said Lady Beatrice, leaning down to adjust her stocking. "Have I anyone else scheduled tonight?"

"No, dear. Mrs. Otley is entertaining his lordship until midnight; then we may all go home to our beds."

"Oh, good. May I ask a favor? Will you remind me to look for the latest number of *Fraser's* tomorrow? The last installment—" Lady Beatrice broke off, and Mrs. Corvey turned her head, for both had heard the distinct chime that indicated the ascending room was coming back down with a passenger.

"How curious," said Mrs. Corvey. "Generally the dining area closes at ten o'clock."

"I'll take him," said Lady Beatrice, assuming her professional smile and seating herself on the divan.

"Would you, dear? Miss Rendlesham had such a lot of cleaning up to do, after the duke left, that I gave her the rest of the evening off. You're very kind."

"It is no trouble," Lady Beatrice assured her. The panel slid open and a gentleman emerged. He was bespectacled and balding, with the look of a senior bank clerk, and in fact carried a file case under his arm. He swept his gaze past Lady Beatrice, with no more than a perfunctory nod, focusing his attention on Mrs. Corvey.

"Ma'am," he said.

"Mr. Greene?" Mrs. Corvey rose to her feet. "What an unexpected pleasure, sir. And what, may one ask, is *your* pleasure?"

"Not here on my own account," said Mr. Greene, going a little red. "Though, er, of course I should like to have the leisure to visit soon. Informally. You know. Hem. In any case, Ma'am, may we withdraw to your office? There is a matter I wish to discuss."

"Of course," said Mrs. Corvey.

"I don't mind sitting up. Shall I watch for any late guests?" Lady Beatrice inquired of Mrs. Corvey. Mr. Greene turned and looked at her again, more closely now.

"Ah. The new member. I knew your father, my dear. Please, join us. I think perhaps you ought to hear what I have to say as well."

Mr. Greene, having accepted a cup of cocoa in the inner office, drank, set it aside and cleared his throat.

"I don't suppose either of you has ever met Lord Basmond?"

"No indeed," said Mrs. Corvey.

"Nor have I," said Lady Beatrice.

"Quite an old family. Estate in Hertfordshire. Present Lord, Arthur Rawdon, is twenty-six. Last of the line. Unmarried, did nothing much at Cambridge, lived in town until two years ago, when he returned to the family home and proceeded to borrow immense sums of money.

Hasn't gambled; hasn't been spending it on a mistress; hasn't invested it. Has given out that he's making improvements on Basmond Hall, though why such inordinate amounts of rare earths should be required in home repair, to say nothing of such bulk quantities of some rather peculiar chemicals, is a mystery.

"There were workmen on the property, housed there, and they won't talk and they can't be bribed to. The old gardener does visit the local public house, and was overheard to make disgruntled remarks about his lordship destroying the yew maze, but on being approached, declined to speak further on the subject."

"What does it signify, Mr. Greene?" said Mrs. Corvey.

"What indeed? The whole business came to our attention when he purchased the rare earths and chemicals; for, you know, we have men who watch the traffic in certain sorts of goods. When an individual exceeds a certain amount in purchases, we want to know the reason why. Makes us uneasy.

"We set a man on it, of course. His reports indicate that Lord Basmond, despite his poor showing at university, nevertheless seems to have turned inventor. Seems to have made some sort of extraordinary discovery. Seems to have decided to keep it relatively secret. And most certainly *has* sent invitations to four millionaires, three of them foreign nationals I might add, inviting them to a private auction at Basmond Park."

"He intends to sell it, then," said Lady Beatrice. "Whatever it is. And imagines he can get a great deal of money for it."

"Indeed, miss," said Mr. Greene. "The latest report from our man is somewhat overdue; that, and the news of this auction (which came to us from another source) have us sufficiently alarmed to take steps. Fortunately, Lord Basmond has given us an opportunity. It will, however, require a certain amount of, ah, immoral behavior."

"And so you have come to us," said Mrs. Corvey, with a wry smile.

"It will also require bravery. And quick wits," Mr. Greene added, coloring slightly. "Lord Basmond sent out a request to a well-known establishment for a party of four, er, girls to supply entertainment for his guests. We intercepted the request. We require four volunteers from amongst your ladies here, Mrs. Corvey, to send to the affair."

"And what are we to do, other than service millionaires?" asked Lady Beatrice. Mr. Greene coughed.

"You understand, it is strictly voluntary—but we want to know what sort of invention could fetch a price only a millionaire could pay. Is it, for example, something that touches on our national security? And we need to know what has become of the man we got inside."

"We shall be happy to oblige," said Mrs. Corvey, with a graceful wave of her hand.

"We would be profoundly grateful, Ma'am." Mr. Greene stood and bowed, offering her the file case. "All particulars are here. Communication on the usual frequency. I shall leave the matter in your capable hands, Ma'am."

He turned to depart, and abruptly turned back. Very red in the face now, he took Lady Beatrice's hand and, after a fumbling moment of indecision, shook it awkwardly.

"God bless you, my dear," he blurted. "First to volunteer. You do your father credit." He fled for the reception chamber, and a moment later they heard him departing in the ascending room.

"Am I to assume there are certain dangers we may face?" said Lady Beatrice.

"Of course, dear," said Mrs. Corvey, who had opened the file case and was examining the documents within. "But then, what whore does not endure hazards?"

"And do we do this sort of work very often?"

"We do." Mrs. Corvey looked up at her, smiling slightly. "We are no *common* whores, dear."

Seven: In which visitors arrive at Basmond Hall

As the village of Little Basmond was some distance from the nearest railway line, they took a hired coach into Hertfordshire. Mrs. Corvey sat wedged into a corner of the coach, studying the papers in the file case, as the Devere sisters chattered about every conceivable subject. Lady Beatrice gazed out the window at the rolling hills, green even in winter, unlike any that she had ever known. The streets of London were a realm out of nature, easy to learn, since one city is in its essentials like any other; but the land was another matter. Lady Beatrice found it all lovely, in its greenness, in the vastness of the tracts of woodland with their austere gray branches; but her senses were still attuned to a hotter, dryer, brighter place. She wondered whether she would come in time to grow accustomed to—she very nearly said *Home* to herself, and then concluded that the word had lost any real meaning.

"...but it was only fifty-four inches wide, and so I was obliged to buy fifteen yards rather than what the pattern called for—" Jane was saying, when Mrs. Corvey cleared her throat. All fell silent at once, looking at her expectantly.

"Arthur Charles Fitzhugh Rawdon," she said, and drew out a slip of pasteboard the size of a playing card. Lady Beatrice leaned forward to peer at it. It appeared to be a copy of a daguerreotype. Its subject, holding his lapels and looking self-important, stood beside a Roman column against a painted backdrop of Pompeii. Lord Basmond was slender and pale, with small regular features and eyes of liquid brilliance; Lady Beatrice had thought him handsome, but for the fact that his eyes were set somewhat close together.

"Our host," said Mrs. Corvey. "Or our employer, if you like; one or all of you may be required to do him."

"What a pretty fellow!" said Maude.

"He looks bad-tempered, though," observed Dora.

"And I am quite sure all of you are practiced enough in the art of being agreeable to avoid provoking him," said Mrs. Corvey. "Your work will be to discover what, precisely, is being auctioned at this affair. We may be fortunate enough to have it spoken of in our presence, with no more thought of our understanding than if we were dogs. *He* may be more discreet, and in that case you will need to get it out of the guests. I suspect the lot of you will be handed around like bonbons, but if any one of them takes any one of you to his bedroom, then I strongly recommend the use of one of Mr. Felmouth's nostrums."

"Oh, jolly good," said Dora in a pleased voice, lifting the edge of her traveling cloak to admire the amber buttons on her yellow satin gown.

"Our other objective..." Mrs. Corvey sorted through the case and drew out a second photograph. "William Reginald Ludbridge." She held up the image. The subject of the portrait faced square ahead, staring into the camera's lens. He was a man of perhaps forty-five, with blunt pugnacious features rendered slightly diabolical by a moustache and goatee. His gaze was shrewd and leonine.

"One of our brothers in the Society," said Mrs. Corvey. "The gentleman sent to Basmond Park before us, in the guise of a laborer. He seems to have gone missing. We are to find him, if possible, and render any assistance we may. I expect that will be my primary concern, while you lot concentrate on the other gentlemen."

At that moment the coach slowed and, shortly, stopped. The coachman descended and opened the door. "The Basmond Arms, ladies," he informed them, offering his arm to Mrs. Corvey.

"Mamma, the kind man has put out his arm for you," said Maude. Mrs. Corvey pretended to grope, located the coachman's arm and allowed herself to be helped down from the coach.

"So very kind!" she murmured, and stood there feeling about in her purse while the other ladies were assisted into Basmond High Street, and their trunks lifted down. Temporarily anonymous and respectable, they stood all together outside the Basmond Arms, regarded with mild interest by passers-by. At length the publican ventured out and inquired whether he might be of service.

"Thank you, good man, but his lordship is sending a carriage to meet us," said Mrs. Corvey, just as Jane pointed and cried, "Oooh, look at the lovely barouche!" The publican, having by this time noticed their paint and the general style of their attire, narrowed his eyes and stepped back.

"Party for the Hall?" inquired the grinning driver. He pulled up before the public house. "Scramble up, girls!"

Muttering, the publican turned and went back indoors as the ladies climbed into the carriage. The driver jumped down, loaded on their trunks and sprang back into his seat. "How about the redhead sits beside me?" said the driver, with a leer.

"How about you give us a hand up like a gentleman, duckie?" retorted Maude.

"Say no more." The driver obliged by giving them each rather more than a hand up, after which Maude obligingly settled beside him and submitted herself to a kiss, a series of pinches and a brief covert exploration of her ankle. Lady Beatrice, observing this, fingered her pistol-locket thoughtfully, but Maude seemed equal to defending herself.

"Naughty boy!" said Maude, giving the driver an openly intimate fondle in return. The driver blushed and sat straight. He shook the reins and the carriage moved off along the high street, running a gauntlet of disgusted looks from such townsfolk as happened to be lounging on their front steps or leaning over their garden walls.

"My gracious, they ain't quite a friendly lot here, are they?" Maude inquired pertly, in rather coarser accents than was her wont. "Doesn't his lordship have working girls to call very often?"

"You're the first," said the driver, who had recovered a little of his composure. Looking over his shoulder to be certain they had passed the last of the houses, he slipped his arm around Maude's waist.

"The first! And here we thought he was a right sporting buck, didn't we, girls? What's your name, by-the-bye?"

"Ralph, miss—I mean—my dear."

"Well, you're a handsome chap, Ralph, and I'm sure we'll get on." Maude leaned into his arm. "So his lordship ain't a bit of an exquisite, I hope? Seems a bit funny him hiring us on if he is."

Ralph guffawed. "Not from what I heard. He ain't no sporting buck, but he did get a girl with child when he was at Cambridge. Sent her back here to wait it out, but the little thing died in any case."

"What, the girl?"

"No! The baby. It wasn't right. His lordship's been more careful since, I reckon."

"Well, what's he want with us, then?" Maude reached up and stroked Ralph's cheek, tracing a line with her fingertip down to his collar. "A big stout man like you, I know *you* know what to do with a girl. His lordship don't fancy funny games?"

"I reckon you're for his party," said Ralph, shivering. "For the guests."

"Oooh! We likes parties, girls, don't we?" Maude looked over her shoulder. As she looked back Ralph grabbed her chin and gave her a violent kiss of some length, until Jane was obliged to tell him rather sharply to mind the horse.

"It's all right," said Maude, surfacing for air with a gasp. "Look here, girls, I've taken such a fancy to our dear friend Ralph, would you ever mind very much if we pulled up a moment?"

"Please yourself," said Mrs. Corvey. The carriage happened to be proceeding down a long private drive along an aisle of trees at that moment, and Ralph steered the carriage to one side before taking Maude's hand and leaping down. They disappeared into the shrubbery. Lady Beatrice looked at Mrs. Corvey and raised an eyebrow in inquiry. Mrs. Corvey shrugged. "Helps to have friends and allies, doesn't it?" she said.

"Is that Basmond Hall?" Dora stood and peered up the aisle at a gray bulk of masonry just visible on a low hill beyond rhododendrons. Mrs. Corvey glanced once toward the shrubbery and, removing her goggles a moment, extended her optics for a closer look at the building.

"That would be it," she said, replacing her goggles. "Historic place. Dates back to the Normans and such."

"An old family, then," said Lady Beatrice.

"And his lordship the last of them," said Mrs. Corvey. "Interesting, isn't it? I do wonder what sort of fellow he is."

In due course Maude and Ralph emerged from the bushes, rather breathless. Ralph swept Maude up on the seat with markedly more gallantry than before, jumping up beside her bright-eyed.

"Had a nice rattle, did you?" inquired Mrs. Corvey. Ralph ducked his head sheepishly, but Maude patted his arm in a proprietary way.

"He's a jolly big chap, dear Ralph is. But we shan't mention our little tumble to his lordship, shall we? Wouldn't want you to lose your place, Ralph dear."

"No, ma'am," said Ralph. "Very kind of you, I'm sure."

They proceeded up the drive and beheld Basmond Hall in all its gloomy splendor. If Lord Basmond had given home improvement as his reason for borrowing money, it was certainly a plausible excuse; for the Hall was an ancient motte and bailey of flints, half-buried under a thick growth of ivy. No Tudor-era Rawdons had enlarged it with half-timbering and windows; no Georgian Rawdons had given it any Palladian grace or statues. Nor did it seem now that the Rawdon of the present age had any intention of making the place over into respectable Gothic Revival; there was no sign that so much as a few pounds had been spent to repoint the masonry.

Ralph drove the carriage up the slope, over the crumbling causeway that had replaced the drawbridge, and so under the portcullis into the courtyard.

"How positively medieval," observed Dora.

"And a bit awkward to get out of, if one had to," murmured Mrs. Corvey under her breath. "Caution is called for, ladies."

Lady Beatrice nodded. It all looked like an illustration from one of her schoolbooks, or perhaps *Ivanhoe*; the courtyard scattered with straw, the stables under the lowering wall, the covered well, the Hall with its steep-pitched roof and the squat castle behind it. All it wanted was a churl polishing armor on a bench.

Instead, a black-suited butler emerged from the great front door and gestured frantically at Ralph. "Take them to the trade entrance!"

Ralph shrugged and drove the wagon around to a small door at the rear of the Hall. Here he stopped and helped the ladies down as grandly as any knight-errant, while the butler popped out of the trade door and stood there wringing his hands in detestation.

"Here you go, Pilkins," said Ralph. "Fresh-delivered roses!"

Pilkins shooed them inside, and they found themselves in the back-entryway to the kitchens, amid crates of wines and delicacies ordered from some of the finest shops in London. Some two or three parlormaids were peering around a door frame at them, only to be ordered away in a hoarse bawl by the cook, who came and stared.

"I never thought I'd see the day," she said, shaking her head grimly. "Common whores in Lord Basmond's very house!"

"I beg your pardon," said Mrs. Corvey, tapping her cane sharply on the flagstones. "Very high-priced *and* quality whores, ordered special, and my girls would be obliged to you for a nice cup of tea after such a long journey, I'm sure."

"Fetch them something, Mrs. Duncan," said Pilkins. Pursing his mouth, he turned to Mrs. Corvey. "I assume you are their...proprietress, madam?"

"That's right," said Mrs. Corvey. "And am in charge of their finances as well. We was promised a goodly sum for this occasion, and I'm sure his lordship won't be so mean as to renege."

"His lordship will, in fact, be here presently to see whether your—your girls—are satisfactory," said Pilkins, his elocution a little hampered by the difficulty he had unpursing his lips.

"Of course they're satisfactory! Girls, drop your cloaks," said Mrs. Corvey.

They obeyed her. The plain gray traveling gear fell away to reveal the ladies in all their finery. Lady Beatrice wore her customary scarlet, and the Devere sisters had affected jewel tones: Maude in emerald green, Jane in royal blue, and Dora in golden yellow satin. The effect of such voluptuous color in such a drab chamber was breathtaking and a little barbaric. Pilkins, for one, found himself recalling certain verses of Scripture. To his horror, he became aware that his manhood was asserting itself.

"If that ain't what his lordship ordered, I'm sure I don't know what is," said Mrs. Corvey. Pilkins was unable to reply, for several reasons that need not be given here, and in the poignant silence that followed they heard footsteps hurrying down the stairs and along the corridor.

"Are those the whores?" cried an impatient voice. Arthur Rawdon, Lord Basmond, entered the room.

"None other," said Mrs. Corvey. Lord Basmond halted involuntarily, with a gasp of astonishment upon seeing them.

"By God! I'm getting my money's worth, at least!"

"I should hope so. My girls are very much in demand, you know," said Mrs. Corvey. "And they don't do the commoner sort of customer."

"Ah." Lord Basmond gawked at her. "Blind. And you would be their..."

"Procuress, my lord."

"Yes." Lord Basmond rubbed his hands together as he walked slowly round the ladies, who obligingly struck attitudes of refined invitation. "Yes, well. They're not poxed, I hope?"

"If you was at all familiar with my establishment, sir, you would know how baseless any allegations of the sort must be," said Mrs. Corvey. "Only look, my lord! Bloom of youth, pink of health, and not so much as a crablouse between the four of 'em."

"We'd be happy to give his lordship a closer look at the goods," said Dora, fingering her buttons suggestively. "What about a nice roll between the sheets before tea, dear, eh?" But Lord Basmond backed away from her.

"No! No thank you. Y-you must be fresh for my guests. Have they been told about the banquet?"

"Not yet, my lord," said Pilkins, blotting sweat from his face with a handkerchief.

"Well, tell them! Get them into their costumes and rehearse them! The business must proceed perfectly, do you understand?"

"Yes, my lord."

"And where are my girls to lodge, your lordship?" Mrs. Corvey inquired. Lord Basmond, who had turned as though to depart, halted with an air of astonishment.

"Lodge? Er—I assume they will lie with the guests."

"I ain't, however," said Mrs. Corvey. "And do require a decent place to sleep and wash, you know."

"I suppose so," said Lord Basmond. "Well then. Hem. We'll just have a bed made up for you in...erm..." He turned his back on the ladies and gestured wildly at Pilkins, mouthing in silence, *The closet behind the stables,* and pointed across the yard to be sure Pilkins got the point. "A nice little room below the coachman's, quite cozy."

"How very kind," said Mrs. Corvey.

But the window looks out on the—mouthed Pilkins, with an alarmed gesture. Lord Basmond grimaced and, with his index finger, drew Xs in the air before his eyes.

She won't see anything, you idiot, he mouthed. Pilkins looked affronted, but subsided.

"Certainly, my lord. I'll have Daisy see to it at once," he replied.

"See that you do." Lord Basmond turned and strode from the room.

EIGHT: IN WHICH PROPER HISTORICAL COSTUMING IS DISCUSSED

They were grudgingly served tea in the pantry, and then ushered into another low, dark room wherein were a great number of florist's boxes and a neatly folded stack of bedsheets.

"Those are your costumes," said Pilkins, with a sniff.

"Rather too modest, aren't they?" remarked Lady Beatrice. "Or not modest enough. What are we intended to do with them?"

Pilkins studied the floor. "His lordship wishes you to fashion them into, er, togas. The entertainment planned is to resemble, as closely as possible, a—hem—bacchanal of the ancient Romans. And he wishes you to resemble, ah, nymphs dressed in togas."

"But the toga was worn by men," Lady Beatrice informed him. Pilkins looked up, panic-stricken, and gently Lady Beatrice pressed on: "I suspect that what his lordship requires is the chiton, as worn by the ancient hetaerae."

"If you say so," stammered Pilkins. "With laurel wreaths and all."

"But the laurel wreath was rather worn by—"

"Bless your heart, dear, if his lordship wishes the girls to wear laurel wreaths on their heads, I'm sure they shall," said Mrs. Corvey. "And what must they do, besides the obvious? Dance, or something?"

"In fact, they are to bear in the dessert," said Pilkins, resorting to his handkerchief once more. "Rather a large and elaborate refreshment on a pallet between two poles. And if they could somehow contrive to dance whilst bringing it in, his lordship would prefer it."

"We'll do our best, ducks," said Maude dubiously.

"And there are some finger-cymbals in that red morocco case, and his lordship wishes that they might be played upon as you enter."

"In addition to dancing and carrying in the dessert," said Lady Beatrice.

"Perhaps you might practice," said Pilkins. "It is now half-past noon and the dinner will be served at eight o'clock precisely."

"Never you fear," said Mrs. Corvey. "My girls is nothing if not versatile."

At that moment they heard the sound of a coach entering the courtyard. "The first of the guests," exclaimed Pilkins, and bolted for the door, where he halted and called back, "Sort out the costumes for yourselves, please," before closing the door on them.

"Nice," said Mrs. Corvey. "Jane, dear, just open the window for us?"

Jane turned and obliged, exerting herself somewhat to pull the swollen wood of the casement free. The light so admitted was not much improved, for the window was tiny and blocked by a great deal of ivy. "Shall I try to pull a few leaves?" Jane asked.

"Not necessary, dear." Mrs. Corvey stepped close to the window and, removing her goggles, extended her optics through the cover of the vines.

"What do you see?"

"I expect this is the Russian," said Mrs. Corvey. "At least, that's a Russian crest on his coach. Prince Nakhimov, that was the name. Mother was Prussian; inherited businesses from her and invested, and it's made him very rich indeed. Well! And there he is."

"What's he look like?" asked Maude.

"He's quite large," said Mrs. Corvey. "Has a beard. Well-dressed. Footman, coachman, valet. There they go—he's been let off at the front door, I expect. Well, and who's this? Another carriage! Ah, now that must be the Turk. Ali Pasha."

"Oh! Has he got a turban on?"

"No, dear, one of those red sugar-loaf hats. And a military uniform with a lot of ornament. Some sort of official that's made a fortune in the Sultan's service."

"Has he got a carriage full of wives?"

"If he had, I should hardly think he'd bring them to a party of this sort. No, same as the other fellow: footman, driver, valet. And here's the next one! This would be the Frenchman, now. Count de Mortain, the brief said; I expect that's his coat-of-arms. Millionaire like the others, because his family did some favors for Bonaparte, but mostly the wealth's in his land. A bit cash-poor. Wonder if Lord Basmond knows?

"And here's the last one. Sir George Spiggott. No question *he's* a millionaire; pots of money from mills in the north. Bad-tempered-looking man, I must say. Well, ladies, one for each of you; and I doubt you'll get to choose."

"I suppose Lord Basmond is a bit of a fairy prince after all," said Maude.

"Might be, I suppose." Mrs. Corvey turned away from the window. "Notwithstanding, if he *does* require your services in the customary way, any one of you, be sure to oblige and see if you can't slip him something to make him talkative into the bargain."

Having been left to fend for themselves, the ladies spent an hour or two devising chitons out of the bed sheets. Fortunately Jane had a sewing kit in her reticule, and found moreover a spool of ten yards of peacock blue grosgrain ribbon in the bottom of her trunk, so a certain amount of tailoring was possible. The florist's boxes proved to contain laurel leaves indeed, but also maidenhair fern and pink rosebuds, and Lady Beatrice was therefore able to produce chaplets that better suited her sense of historical accuracy.

They were chatting pleasantly about the plot of Dickens's latest literary effort when Mrs. Duncan opened the door and peered in at them.

"I don't suppose one of you girls would consider doing a bit of honest work," she said.

"Really, madam, how much more honest could our profession be?" said Lady Beatrice. "We dissemble about nothing."

"What's the job?" inquired Mrs. Corvey.

Mrs. Duncan grimaced. "Churning the ice cream. The swan mold arrived by special post this morning, and it's three times the size we thought it was to be, and the girls and I have about broke our arms trying to make enough ice cream to fill the damned thing."

"As it's in aid of the general entertainment for which we was engaged, my girls will be happy to assist at no extra charge," said Mrs. Corvey. "Our Maude does a lot of heavy lifting and is quite strong, ain't you, dear?"

"Yes, Ma'am," replied Maude, dropping a curtsey. Mrs. Duncan, with hope dawning in her face, ventured further:

"And, er, if some of you wouldn't mind—there's some smallwork with the sugar paste, and the jellied Cupids want a steady hand in turning out..."

Aprons were found for them and the ladies ventured forth to assist with the Dessert.

A grain-sack carrier had been set across a pair of trestles, with a vast pewter tray fastened atop it, and a massive edifice of cake set atop that. One of the maids was on a stepladder, crouched over the cake with a piping-bag full of icing, attempting to decorate it with a frieze of scallop shells. As they entered, she dropped the bag and burst into tears.

"Oh! There's another one crooked! Oh, I'll lose my place for certain! Mrs. Duncan, I ain't no pastry cook, and my arm hurts like anything. Why don't I just go out and drown myself?"

"No need for theatrics," said Lady Beatrice, taking up the piping-bag. "Ladies? Forward!"

There was, it seemed, a great deal more to be done on the Dessert. There was sugar paste to press into pastillage forms to make all manner of decorations, including a miniature Roman temple, doves, a chariot, and bows and arrows. There were indeed Cupids of rose-flavored jelly to be turned out of their molds, resulting in rather horrible-looking little things like pinkly transparent babies. They wobbled, heads droop-ing disconcertingly as real infants, once mounted at the four corners of the cake. There were pots and pots of muscadine-flavored cream to be poured into the sorbetiere and churned, with grinding effort, before scraping it into the capacious hollow of an immense swan mold. When it was filled at last it took both Maude and Dora to lift it into the ice locker.

"And that goes on top of the cake?" Lady Beatrice asked.

"It's supposed to," said Mrs. Duncan plaintively, avoiding her gaze.

"And we're to carry that in and dance too, are we?" said Jane, pointing with her thumb at the main mass of the Dessert, which was now creaking on its supports with the weight of all the temples, Cupids, doves and other decorations, to say nothing of the roses and ferns trimming its bearer-poles.

"Well, that was what his lordship said," Mrs. Duncan replied. "And I'm sure you're all healthy young girls, ain't you? And it ain't like he ain't paying you handsome."

NINE: IN WHICH THE OBJECT OF PARTICULAR INTEREST APPEARS

Any further concerns were stilled, a half-hour into the dinner service, when Pilkins and Ralph entered the kitchen, bearing between them an object swathed in sacking. Ralph stopped short, gaping at the ladies in their chitons, and Pilkins swore as the object they carried fell to the kitchen flagstones with a clatter. Lady Beatrice glimpsed the corner of a long, flat box like a silverware case, before Pilkins hurriedly covered it over again with the sacking.

"You great oaf! Mind what you're about," said Pilkins. "And you, you—girls, clear out of here. You too, Cook. Go wait in the pantry until I call."

"Well, I like that! This ain't your kitchen, you know," cried Mrs. Duncan.

"Lordship's orders," said Pilkins. "And you can go with them, Ralph."

"Happy to oblige," said Ralph, sidling up to Maude.

"If you please," said Mrs. Corvey, "My rheumatism is painful, now that night's drawn on, and I find it troublesome to move. Mightn't I just bide here by the fire?"

Pilkins glanced at her. "I don't suppose *you'll* matter. Very well, stay there; but into the pantry with the rest of you, and be quick about it."

The ladies obeyed, with good grace, and Mrs. Duncan with markedly less enthusiasm. Ralph stepped after them and pulled the door shut.

"Heigh-ho! 'Here I stand like the Turk, with his doxies around,'" he chortled. "Saving your presence, Cook," he added, but she slapped him anyway.

Mrs. Corvey, meanwhile, watched with interest as Pilkins unwrapped the box—rather heavier, apparently, than its appearance indicated—and grunted with effort as he slid it across the floor to the creaking trestle that supported the Dessert. Mrs. Corvey saw what appeared to be a row of dials and levers along its nearer edge.

Pilkins pushed it underneath the trestle and fumbled with it a moment. Mrs. Corvey heard a faint humming sound, then saw the box rise abruptly through the air, as though it fell *upward*. It struck the underside of the tray with a crash and remained there, apparently, while Pilkins crouched on the flagstones and massaged his wrists, muttering to himself.

Then, almost imperceptively at first but with increasing violence, the Dessert began to tremble. The jellied Cupids shook their heads, as though in disbelief. As Mrs. Corvey watched in astonishment, the Dessert on its carrier lifted free of the trestles and rose jerkily through the air. It was within a hand's breadth of the ceiling when Pilkins, having exclaimed an oath and scrambled to his feet, reached up frantically and made some sort of adjustment with the dials and levers. One end of the carrier dipped, then the other; the whole affair leveled itself, like a new-launched ship, and settled gently down until it bobbed no more than an inch above its former resting place on the trestles. The flat box was so well screened by drooping ferns and flowers as to be quite invisible.

Pilkins sagged onto a stool and drew a flask from his pocket.

"Are you quite all right, Mr. Pilkins?" said Mrs. Corvey.

"Well enough," said Pilkins, taking a drink and tucking the flask away.

"I only wondered because I heard you lord mayoring there, in a temper."

"None of your concern if I was."

"I reckon his lordship must be a trial to work for, sometimes," said Mrs. Corvey, in the meekest possible voice. Pilkins glared at her sidelong.

"An old family, the Rawdons. If they've got strange ways about them, it's not my place to talk about 'em with folk from outside."

"Well, I'm sure I meant no harm—" began Mrs. Corvey, as Mrs. Duncan threw the pantry door open with a crash.

"I'll see you get your notice, Ralph, you mark my words!" she cried. "I ain't staying in there with him another minute. He's a fornicating disgrace!"

"Indeed, I think he does a very creditable job." Maude's voice drifted from the depths of the pantry. Ralph emerged from the pantry smirking, followed by the ladies. Upon seeing the floating Dessert, Ralph pointed and exclaimed:

"Hi! That's what it does, is it? I been going mad wondering—"

Mrs. Duncan, noticing the Dessert's new state, gave a little scream and backed away. "Marry! He's done it again, hasn't he? That unnatural—"

"Hold your noise!" Pilkins told her.

"Whatever's the matter?" said Mrs. Corvey.

"The Dessert appears to be levitating," Lady Beatrice said.

"Oh, stuff and nonsense! I'm sure it's just a conjuror's trick," said Mrs. Corvey. Pilkins gave her a shrewd look.

"That's it, to be sure; nothing but a stage trick, as his lordship likes to impress people."

"So the Dessert isn't really floating in midair?" Jane poked one of the Cupids with a fingertip, causing it to writhe. "Just as you say; I'm only grateful we shan't kill ourselves carrying it in."

A bell rang then. Pilkins jumped to his feet. "That's his lordship signaling for the next course! Get those finger cymbals on, you lot! Where's the bloody swan?"

The swan was heaved out in its mold and upended over the cake, and a screw turned to let air into its vacuum; the swan unmolded and plopped into its place on the cake with an audible thud, sending the Cupids into quivering agonies.

"Right! Pick the damned thing up! He wants you *smiling* and, and exercising your wiles when you go out there!" cried Pilkins.

"We strive to please, sir," said Lady Beatrice, taking her place on one of the carrier poles. The Devere sisters took their places as well. They found that the Dessert lifted quite easily, for it now seemed to weigh scarcely more than a few ounces. Lady Beatrice struck up a rhythm on the finger cymbals, the Devere sisters cut a few experimental capers, and Pilkins ran before them up the stairs and so to the vast banqueting table of Basmond Hall.

"I could do with a dram of gin, after all that," said Mrs. Duncan, collapsing into her chair.

"I could too," said Ralph.

"Well, you can just take yourself off to the stables!"

"Perhaps you'd be so kind as to guide me to my room?" asked Mrs. Corvey. "I'm rather tired."

TEN: In which a Proposition is Advanced

Lord Basmond had spared no expense in the pursuit of his chosen *motif*; an oilcloth had been laid down over the flagstones and painted with a design resembling a tiled mosaic on a villa floor. Hothouse palms had been carried about and placed in decorative profusion, as had an abundance of aspidistra. Five chaise-lounges had been set around the great central table on which Lady Beatrice spied the remains of the grand dishes that had preceded the Dessert from the kitchen: a roast suckling pig, a roast peacock with decorative tail, a dish of ortolans, a mullet in orange and lemon sauce.

On the chaise-lounges reclined Lord Basmond and his four guests. The gentlemen were flushed, all, with repletion. Lord Basmond, alone pale and sweating, sat up as the ladies entered and flung out an arm.

"*Now*, sirs! For your amusement, I present these lovely nymphs bearing a delectable and mysterious treat. The nymphs, being pagan spirits, have absolutely no morals whatsoever and will happily entertain your attentions in every respect. As for the other treat... you may have heard of a dish called 'Floating Island.' That is a mere metaphor. Behold the substance! Nymphs, free yourselves of your burden!"

Lady Beatrice let go her corner of the Dessert and essayed a Bacchic dance, drawing on her memories of India. She glimpsed Maude and Dora pirouetting and Jane performing something resembling a frenzied polka, finger-cymbals clanging madly. Alas, all terpsichorean efforts were going unnoticed, for the banqueters had riveted their stares on the Dessert, which drifted gently some four feet above the oilcloth. Lord Basmond, having assured himself that all was as he had intended, turned his gaze on the faces of his guests, and hungrily sought to interpret their expressions. Lady Beatrice considered them, one after the other.

Prince Nakhimov had lurched upright into a sitting position, gaping at the unexpected vision, and now began to laugh and applaud. Ali Pasha had glanced once at the Dessert, was distracted by Jane's breasts (which had emerged from the top of her chiton like rabbits bounding from a fox's den) and then, as what he had seen registered in his mind, turned his head back to the Dessert so sharply he was in danger of dislocating his neck.

Count de Mortain watched keenly and got to his feet, seemingly with the intention of going closer to the Dessert to see what the trick might be. He got as far as the end of his chaise-lounge before Dora leapt into his arms—her ribbons and securing stitches had all come unfastened, with results that had been catastrophic, were the party of another sort—and they plumped down together on the lounge. The count applied himself to an energetic appreciation of Dora's charms, but continued to steal glances at the Dessert. Sir George Spiggott's mouth was wide in an O of surprise, his eyes round too, but there was a scowl beginning to form.

"What d'you call this, then—" he exclaimed, ending in a *whoof* as Maude jumped astride him and emulated a few of Lady Beatrice's movements.

"What do I call it?" replied Lord Basmond, in rather a theatrical voice. "A demonstration, gentlemen. Here I come to the point and purpose of your presences here. All of you are men of means and influence; you would know whether your respective governments would be interested in a discovery so momentous it may grant ultimate power to its owner."

"What do you mean?" demanded Sir George, who had got his breath back, as he peered around Maude. Lord Basmond cleared his throat and struck an attitude.

"When I was at Cambridge, gentlemen, I studied the vanished civilization of Egypt. I chanced to be taking a holiday in France when I was approached by an elderly beggar, a former member of the late emperor's army and a veteran of the Egyptian campaign. In his destitution he was obliged to offer for sale certain papyrus scrolls he had looted, from what source he was unable to recall, in the land of the pharaohs.

"I purchased the scrolls and returned with them to England. When they yielded up their secrets to translation, I was astonished to discover therein the method by which the very pyramids themselves were built! The ancient priests had developed a means of circumventing the force of gravity itself, gentlemen, and not with charms or spells but by the application of sound scientific principles! Vast blocks of stone were made to float, as light as balloons. Sadly, the scrolls were later lost in a fire, but fortunately not before I had committed their texts to memory.

"Consider the confection floating before you. Do you see any wires? Any props? You do not, because there are none. I have been able to reproduce the device used by the Egyptians, and I intend to sell my secret to the highest bidder.

"Now, consider the applications! Any nation owning my device must swiftly outpace its rivals for dominance. Think of the speed and ease in public works, when a single workman may lift slabs of stone as though they were feathers. Think of the industrial uses to which this may be put, gentlemen. And—dare I say it—the uses for national defense? Envision cannons or supply wagons that might be floated with the ease of soap bubbles and the speed of sleds. Imagine floating platforms from which enemy positions may be spied out, or even fired upon.

"And he who offers the highest bid gains this splendid advantage, gentlemen!"

"What is your reserve?" inquired Prince Nakhimov.

"Two million pounds, sir," replied Lord Basmond, as Sir George uttered an oath.

"You ought to have offered it to your own countrymen first, you swine!"

"You were invited, weren't you? If you want it, you're free to outbid the others," said Lord Basmond coolly. "But, please! I perceive the ice cream is melting. Let us enjoy our treat, and hope that its effects will sweeten your temper. Pleasure before business, gentlemen; tomorrow you will be given a tour of my laboratory and witness further astonishing demonstrations of levitation. Bidding will commence at precisely two in the afternoon. Tonight, you will enjoy my hospitality and the ministrations of these charming females. Pilkins? Serve the sweet course, please."

"At once, sir," said Pilkins, climbing onto a chair.

An orgy commenced.

ELEVEN: In which our heroine and her benefactress
Make Discoveries

Having bid Ralph a civil good-night, Mrs. Corvey edged past her trunk and seated herself on the narrow bed that had been made up for her. Her hearing was rather acute, an advantage gained from the years of her darkness, and so she listened patiently as Ralph climbed the creaking stairs that led to his room above the stables. He undressed himself, he climbed into bed, he indulged in a prolonged episode of onanism (if Mrs. Corvey was any judge of the audible indicators of male solitary passion) and, finally, he snored.

When she was assured Ralph was unlikely to wake, Mrs. Corvey rose and walked to the end of her room, where a single small window admitted the light of the moon. She looked out and beheld a view down the steep slope to the gardens behind Basmond Hall. Perhaps *garden* was an ambitious term; there appeared to be an old orchard and a few rows of cabbages and herbs, on the near edge of a vast overgrown park. Directly below, however, was a modern structure of brick and slate, perhaps twice the size of a coachhouse, and in sharp contrast to the general air of picturesque ruin characteristic of Basmond Hall.

Mrs. Corvey regarded it thoughtfully a moment, before turning from the window and opening her trunk. She undressed quickly and drew forth a boy's clothing, simple dark trousers and a knitted jersey. Donning this attire, she opened a hidden panel in the trunk's lid and revealed a box containing a dozen brass shells, roughly the size of rifle ammunition. Taking her cane, she made certain alterations to it and loaded the shells into the chamber revealed thereby. So prepared, Mrs. Corvey crept from her room and into the courtyard, keeping to the shadows along its eastern edge.

It somewhat discomfited her to discover that the portcullis had been lowered. A moment's study of the grate, however, revealed that its iron gridwork had been constructed to block the entrance of great-thewed knights of old. Mrs. Corvey, by contrast, being female and considerably undernourished in her younger years, was sufficiently small enough to writhe through without much difficulty. She scrambled down the hillside and into the dry moat, and so made her way around to the gardens.

There she stepped out upon a short space of level lawn, somewhat ill-cared-for. Beyond it was the new structure, built close against the hillside. Mrs. Corvey wondered briefly whether it might be a hothouse, for the north face was almost entirely windows. Circling around it, she was surprised to note no door in evidence, nor did the windows appear to open.

Mrs. Corvey removed her goggles and extended her optics against the glass. Moonlight was illuminating the building's interior clearly. She saw no plants of any kind; rather, several tables upon which were glass vessels of the sort associated with chemists' laboratories. Upon other tables were tools and small machinery, at the purpose of which she could only speculate. The dark bulk of a steam engine crouched in one corner. In the other corner Mrs. Corvey spotted a door, and realized that the only entrance to the laboratory was from within; for the door was in the wall that backed up to the hill behind, and must communicate with a tunnel beyond that led upward into the tower above.

Nodding to herself, Mrs. Corvey proceeded to study the leading around the window panes. Near the ground she found a spot in which the pane had, apparently, been recently replaced, for the lead solder was brighter there. Drawing a long pin from her hair, she busied herself for a few minutes prizing down the lead, and after diligent work slipped out the glass and set it carefully to one side. Crawling through the gap thereby created was no more difficult than going through the portcullis had been; indeed, Mrs. Corvey mused to herself that she might have made a first-rate burglar, had fate decreed other than her present situation.

For the next while she examined the laboratory at some length, committing its details to memory and wishing that Mr. Felmouth would exert himself to build a camera small enough to be carried on such occasions. In vain she looked for any notes, papers or journals that might illuminate the purpose of the machines. At last Mrs. Corvey addressed the door with her hairpin, and a long moment later stood gazing into the utter darkness of the tunnel on the other side.

In retrospect, Lady Beatrice was obliged to admit that bedsheets made an admirably practical costume for the evening's festivities. In the course of her employment she had become liberally smeared with ice cream, sugar icing, cake crumbs, rose petals and spilled wine. The last item had fountained over her breasts, not in an excess of Bacchic enthusiasm, but when Prince Nakhimov had been startled into dropping his glass by the sight of Sir George swallowing one of the jellied Cupids whole. ("The damned press claim I eat workers' babies for breakfast," Sir George had said smugly. "Let's see if I can open my jaws wide enough!")

Lady Beatrice serviced each of the guests in turn during the amusements, for they were, one and all, inclined to share the ladies' favors. Lord Rawdon unbent so far as to permit himself to be fellatiated, when his guests insisted he partake of the carnal blisses available, but declined to retire with anyone when the long evening drew to its close. Rather, Lady Beatrice found herself claimed by Prince Nakhimov; Ali Pasha took Dora off to his bed. Jane was taken, in a brisk and businesslike manner, by Sir George Spiggott, and Maude retired on the arm of Count de Mortain.

In the privacy of the bedchamber Prince Nakhimov divested himself of his garments, and proved to be a veritable Russian Bear for hairiness and animal spirits. The sheer athleticism required left Lady Beatrice somewhat fatigued, and therefore she was more than a little discountenanced when, after two hours of his attentions, the prince pulled the blankets up, rolled away from her, and said: "Thank you. You may go now."

"But am I not to sleep here?"

"*Shto?*" The prince looked over his shoulder at her, surprised. "Sleep here? You? I never sleep with, please pardon my frankness, whores." He turned back toward his pillow and Lady Beatrice, profoundly irritated, picked up the sticky remnants of her costume and held it against herself as she left his room.

She faced now the choice of wandering downstairs in her present state of undress and searching for her trunk, there to change into a robe, and afterward to seek repose on one of the chaise-lounges in the dining room until morning, or simply opening one of the other bedroom doors and seeing if any of the other couples had room in bed for a third party. Being desirous of sleep, Lady Beatrice opted for the chaise-lounge.

She descended the stairs and made her way along the gallery that led to the grand staircase. Strong moonlight slanted in through the windows at this hour, throwing patches of brilliant illumination on several of the portraits that hung along the walls. Lady Beatrice slowed to examine them. It was plain that Lord Basmond was a true Rawdon; here in face after face were the same lustrous eyes and delicate features, to say nothing of a certain chilly hauteur common to all the portraits' subjects. Lady Beatrice remarked particularly one painting, upon which the moonlight fell directly. It was of a child, she supposed, a miniature beauty in Elizabethan costume. The wide lace collar framed the heart-shaped face. A silver net bound the hair, so fair as to appear white, and the contrast of the dark eyes with such ethereal pallor was striking indeed. *Hellspeth Rawdon, Lady Basmond,* read the brass plate on the lower frame.

Lady Beatrice, conscious of the cold, walked on. She had passed the last of the portraits when she spied a door ajar, through which the corner of a bed could be glimpsed. Hopeful of finding a warmer resting place for the night, Lady Beatrice opened the door and peered within.

The room was feebly lit by a single candle, much reduced in height, beside the bed. Lord Basmond lay across the bed, still fully dressed. His eyes were open and glistening in the candlelight. Lady Beatrice saw at once that he was dead. Nonetheless, she stepped across the threshold and had a closer look.

His mouth was open in a silent cry of protest. No wounds were in evidence; rather the unnatural angle of his neck told plainly what had effected Lord Basmond's dispatch. He could have been dead no more than two hours, and yet in that time seemed to have shrunken within his evening clothes. He looked frail and pathetic. Lady Beatrice thought of the ancestral portraits, all the centuries fallen down to this sad creature lying sprawled and broken, last of the long line.

Lady Beatrice swept the room with a glance, looking for obvious clues, but found none. She stepped back into the corridor and stood pensive a moment, considering what she ought to do next.

TWELVE: IN WHICH STILL MORE DISCOVERIES ARE MADE

Lady Beatrice decided fairly quickly that nothing much could be accomplished in her present state of undress, and therefore she went down to the kitchen. The fire there was banked, the range still radiating pleasant warmth, and so she pumped a few gallons of water and heated them sufficiently to bathe herself by the hearth.

Having located her trunk, she dressed herself in the firelight and went out by the side door, making her way across the courtyard to the stables. She found the room that had been assigned to Mrs. Corvey and knocked softly, intending to report her discovery. When no reply came to her knock she opened the door and saw the empty bed. Returning to the kitchens, Lady Beatrice encountered Dora, just coming down the stairs in a state of sticky nudity, trailing what remained of her costume.

"Oh, good, the fire's lit," Dora exclaimed, tossing aside her costume and going to the sink to pump water. "If I don't bathe I shall simply scream. Did yours snore too?"

"No; he pitched me out."

"Ah! They do, sometimes, don't they? My pasha went at it like a stoat in rut until he fell asleep, and then he snored so loud the bed curtains trembled."

"You never got a chance to drug him, then?"

"What, with my little buttons? No. In the first place he wouldn't drink any wine, and anyway, what would have been the point of drugging him? *We* know as much as *he* does. If we want to find out any more about the levitation device, the one to drug would be Lord Basmond."

"That would be rather difficult now, I'm afraid," said Lady Beatrice, and told what she had found on entering his lordship's bedchamber. Dora's eyes widened.

"No! You're sure?"

"I know a dead man when I see one," said Lady Beatrice.

"Damn and blast! *So* convenient to murder someone when there are whores about to blame for it. I suppose now we'll have to run all screaming and hysterical to the butler and report it. Jane and Maude will have firm alibis, at least. First, however, we'll need to report to the missus." Dora set a bucket of water on the fire.

"She isn't in her room," explained Lady Beatrice.

"No? I suppose it's possible *she* did for his lordship."

"Would she?"

"You never know; I should think it was a bit treasonous, wouldn't you, offering an invention like that to other empires? She may have made the decision to do for him and confiscate the thing for the Society. If she did, she may be out making arrangements to cover our tracks."

"Let's not go running to Pilkins yet, then," said Lady Beatrice. "What became of the rest of the Dessert?"

"That's a good question," said Dora. "Pantry?"

They left the silent kitchen and, following a trail of cake crumbs and blobs of crème anglaise, located the remaining Dessert in the pantry, as expected. Thoroughly ruined now, it lay spilt sideways on the flagstones, its grain carrier leaning against the wall.

"Once more, damn and blast," said Dora. "Where's the marvelous flying thing? The box or plank or whatever it was Pilkins carried in?"

"Not here, at any rate," said Lady Beatrice.

"You don't suppose the missus took it?"

"Might have, but—" Lady Beatrice began, as a prolonged bumping crash came from above. They looked at each other and ran upstairs, Lady Beatrice lifting her skirts to hurry. Dora, being nimbler in her present state of undress, arrived in the great hall first. Lady Beatrice heard her exclaim a fairly shocking oath, and upon joining her discovered why; for Arthur Fitzhugh Rawdon, Lord Basmond, lay in a crumpled heap at the foot of the great staircase.

The two ladies stood there considering his corpse for a long moment.

"Frightfully convenient accident," said Lady Beatrice at last.

"I think it will look better if you do the screaming," said Dora, with a gesture indicating her nudity.

"Very well," said Lady Beatrice. Dora retreated to the kitchen. Lady Beatrice cleared her throat and, drawing a deep breath, uttered the piercing shriek of a terrified female.

Mrs. Corvey paused only to switch on the night-vision feature of her optics before advancing down the tunnel. Instantly she beheld the tunnel walls and floor, stretching ahead into a green obscurity. She had expected the same neat brickwork that distinguished the laboratory building, but the tunnel appeared to be of some antiquity: haphazardly mortared with flints, here and there buttressed with timbers, and penetrated with roots throughout, threadlike white ones or gnarled and black subterranean limbs.

As she proceeded along the tunnel's length, Mrs. Corvey noted in several places the print of shoes. Most were small, not much bigger than her own, but twice she saw a much larger track, a man's certainly. Moreover she perceived strange and shifting currents of air in the tunnel. About a hundred yards in she spotted what must be their source, for a second tunnel opened where some of the flint and mortar had fallen in, creating a narrow gap in the wall.

Mrs. Corvey studied the tunnel floor in front of the gap. Someone had gone through in the recent past, to judge from the way the earth was disturbed. She turned and considered the main course of the tunnel, which ended a few yards ahead where a ladder ascended, doubtless to the tower above. Yielding to her intuition, however, she turned back and slipped through the gap into the second tunnel.

Here the walls seemed of greater antiquity still, indeed, scarcely as though shaped by human labors at all; rather burrowed by some great animal. There was an earthy damp smell and, distantly echoing, the sound of trickling water. Mrs. Corvey peered into the depths and spotted something scarlet ahead in the green gloom, an irregular mass against one wall.

She lifted her cane to her shoulder and went forward cautiously, five feet, ten feet, and then there was a sudden burst of hectic illumination and a blare of—sound? No, not sound; Mrs. Corvey was at a loss to say what sensation it was that affected her nerves so painfully. She swayed for a moment before regaining her balance. Two or three deep breaths restored her composure before she heard a groan in the darkness ahead. And then:

"You know," said a male voice, "If I'm to die here I'd much rather be shot. All this blinding me and chaining me to walls and so forth is becoming tedious."

THIRTEEN: IN WHICH MR. LUDBRIDGE TELLS A CURIOUS STORY

The scarlet mass had shifted, and resolved itself now into the shape of a man, slumped against the wall of the tunnel with one arm flung up awkwardly. As she neared him, Mrs. Corvey saw that he was in fact pinioned in place by a manacle whose chain had been passed about one of the ancient roots.

"Mr. Ludbridge?" she inquired.

His head came up sharply and he turned his face in her direction.

"Is that a lady?"

"I am, sir. William Reginald Ludbridge?"

"Might be," he said. She was within a few paces of him now and, opening a compartment in her cane, drew forth a lucifer and struck it for his benefit. The circle of dancing light so produced proved to her satisfaction that the prisoner was indeed the missing man Ludbridge. "Who's that?"

"I am Elizabeth Corvey, Mr. Ludbridge. From Nell Gwynne's."

"Are you? What becomes of illusions?"

"We dispel them," she replied, relieved to remember the counter-sign, for she was seldom required to give it.

"And we are everywhere. If you're wondering why your match isn't producing any light, it's because of that damned—excuse me—that device you tripped just now. It'll be at least an hour before we can see anything again."

"In fact, I can see now, Mr. Ludbridge." She blew out the tiny flame.

"I beg your pardon? Oh! Mrs. Corvey. You're the lady with the...do forgive me, madam, but I hardly expected the GSS to send the ladies' auxiliary to my aid. So the flash hasn't affected your, er, eyes?"

"It does not appear to have, sir."

"That's something, anyway. Er...I trust you weren't sent alone?"

"I was not, sir. Some of my girls are upstairs, I suppose you'd say, entertaining Lord Basmond and his guests."

"Ha! Ingenious. I don't suppose you happen to have a hacksaw with you, Mrs. Corvey?"

"No, sir, but let me try what I might do with a bullet." Mrs. Corvey set the end of her cane against the root where the manacle's chain passed over it, and pressed the triggering mechanism. With a *bang* the chain parted, and white flakes of root drifted down like snow. Ludbridge's arm fell, a dead weight.

"I am much obliged to you," said Ludbridge, gasping as he attempted to massage life back into the limb. "What have you found out?"

"We know about the levitation device."

"Good, but that isn't all. Not by a long way. There's this thing in the tunnel that makes such an effective burglar-catcher, and I suspect there's more still."

"What precisely is it, Mr. Ludbridge?"

"Damned if I know, beg your pardon. You saw the laboratory, did you?"

"Indeed, Mr. Ludbridge, I entered that way."

"So did I. Crawled through and had a good look round. Took notes and made sketches, which I still have here somewhere..." Ludbridge felt about inside his coat. "Yes, to be sure. Had started up the other tunnel when I heard the trap opening above and someone starting down the ladder. Put out my light in a hurry and ducked into what I'd assumed was an alcove in the wall, hoping to avoid notice. Bloody thing crumbled backward under my weight and I fell in here.

"I heard quick footsteps hurry past, in the main tunnel without. When I felt safe I lit my candle again and looked around me. This place is only the entrance to a great network of tunnels, you know, quite a warren; it's a wonder Basmond Hall hasn't sunk into the hill. I could hear water and felt the rush of air, so I thought I'd explore and see if I could find myself a discreet exit.

"That was two weeks ago, I think. I never found an exit, though I did find a great deal else, some of it very queer indeed. There's a spring-fed subterranean lake, ma'am, and what looks to be some of the ancestral tombs of the Rawdons—at least, I hope that's what they are. Midden heaps full of rather strange things. Someone lived in this place long before the Rawdons came with William the Conqueror, I can tell you that! I'm ashamed to admit I became lost more than once. If not for the spring and my field rations I'd have died down there.

"Having found my way back up at last, I was proceeding in triumph down this passageway when I ran slap into the—the whatever-it-is that makes such a flash-bang. I was knocked unconscious the first time. When I woke I discovered I'd been chained up as you found me. That was...yesterday? Not very clear on the passage of time, I'm afraid."

"Clearly Lord Basmond had noticed someone was trespassing," said Mrs. Corvey.

"Too right. Haven't seen him, though. He hasn't even come down to gloat, which honestly I'd have welcomed; always the chance I could persuade him to join the GSS, after all. Just as well it was you, perhaps."

"And what are we to do now, Mr. Ludbridge?"

"What indeed? I am entirely at your disposal, ma'am."

Mrs. Corvey turned and looked intently at the floor of the tunnel. She saw, now, the braided wire laid across their path, and the metal box to which it was anchored.

"I think we had better escape, Mr. Ludbridge."

Fourteen: In which Lord Basmond is mourned, with Apparent Sincerity

"He must have fallen," declared Sir George Spiggott.

"A lamentable accident," said Ali Pasha, looking very hard at Sir George. So did Jane, who had trailed after them clutching her chiton to herself.

"What becomes of the auction now, may I ask?" said Prince Nakhimov.

"He had bones like sugar-sticks," said Pilkins through his tears. He was on his knees beside Lord Basmond's body. "Always did. Broke his arm three times when he was a boy. Oh, Lord help us, what are we to do? He was the only one with...I mean to say..."

"The only one with the plans for the levitation device?" said Lady Beatrice. Pilkins looked up at her, startled, and then his face darkened with anger.

"That's enough of your bold tongue," he shouted. "I'm not having the constable see you lot here! I want you downstairs, all of you whores, now! Get down there and keep still, if you know what's good for you!" He turned to glare at Dora, who had just come up in a state of respectable dress from the kitchens.

"Suit yourself; we'll go," she said. Looking around, she added, "But where's Maude?"

"Where is the Count de Mortain? He cannot have slept through such screams," said Prince Nakhimov.

"Perhaps I'd better go fetch her," said Lady Beatrice, starting up the stairs.

"No! I said you were...were to...oh, damned fate," said Pilkins, drooping with fresh tears. "Go on, get up there and wake them up. And then I want to see the back of you all."

"Happy to oblige," said Jane, striding past him to go downstairs. Lady Beatrice, meanwhile, ran up the grand staircase and along the gallery, where the faces of Rawdons past watched her passage. The moonlight had shifted from her portrait, but Hellspeth Rawdon still seemed to glimmer with unearthly luminescence.

Lady Beatrice knocked twice at the door of the bedroom that had been allotted to the Count de Mortain, but received no response. At last, opening the door and peering in, she beheld one candle burning on the dresser and Maude alone in the bed, deeply asleep.

"Maude!" Lady Beatrice hurried in and shook Maude's shoulder. "Wake up! Where is the count?"

Maude remained unconscious, despite Lady Beatrice's best efforts. Lady Beatrice sniffed at the dregs remaining in the wine glass on the bedside table, and thought she detected some medicinal odor. There was no sign of Count de Mortain in the room.

When this fact was communicated to the parties downstairs, Sir George Spiggott exclaimed, "It's the damned frog! I'll wager a thousand pounds *he* pushed Lord Basmond down the stairs!"

"You had better send for your constabulary now, rather than wait for morning," Ali Pasha told Pilkins.

"In the meanwhile, perhaps someone would assist me in getting Maude downstairs?" Lady Beatrice inquired. Prince Nakhimov volunteered and brought Maude, limp as a washrag, down as far as the Great Hall; from there Lady Beatrice and Dora carried her between them down to the kitchen.

"How awfully embarrassing," said Jane, from the hearthrug where she was bathing. "*We* were supposed to be the ones administering drugs!"

"We ought to have expected this," said Lady Beatrice grimly. She went to the sink and pumped a bucketful of cold water. "I should think the count drugged her and then killed Lord Basmond, meaning to steal the device."

"What?" Jane looked up from soaping herself. "I thought his lord-ship fell down the stairs."

Dora explained that Lady Beatrice had found Lord Basmond dead in his bedroom before his body had been flung down the stairs. Jane's eyes narrowed.

"Don't be so sure the count was his murderer," she said. "Mine was in a towering temper—did me only once, quite rough and nasty, and kept telling me it was a damned good thing I was English. At last he got out of bed and left. I asked him where he was going and he told me to mind my own business. He wasn't gone above ten minutes. When he came back he looked a different man—white and shaking. I pretended to be asleep, because I was tired of his nonsense, but he didn't try to wake me for any more fun. He tossed and turned for about twenty more minutes and then leaped out of bed and ran from the room. He was only gone about five minutes this time, and very much out of breath when he came back. Jumped into bed and pulled the covers up. It seemed only a moment later we heard you screaming."

"Did he ever seem as though he paused to hide something in the bedroom?" asked Lady Beatrice, upending the bucket's contents over Maude, who groaned and tried to sit up.

"No, never."

"He might have killed his lordship, but that doesn't mean the device has been stolen," said Dora, crouching beside Maude and waving a bottle of smelling salts under her nose. Maude coughed feebly and opened her eyes.

"Damn and blast," she murmured.

"Wake up, dear."

"That bastard slipped me a powder!"

"Yes, dear, we'd guessed."

"And we'd had such a lovely time in bed." Maude leaned forward, massaging her temples. "Such a jolly and amusing man. He's got no money, though. Told me he was delighted to accept a night of free food and copulation, but isn't in any position to bid on the levitation device."

"Have you any idea where he's got to?"

"None. What's been going on?"

The other ladies gave her a brief summary of what had occurred. In the midst of it, Mrs. Duncan came shuffling downstairs in tears, clutching a candlestick.

"Oh, it's too cruel," she sobbed. "What'll become of us now? And the Basmonds! What of the Basmonds?"

"Bugger the Basmonds," said Maude, who was still feeling rather ill.

"How dare you, you chit! They're one of the oldest families in the land!" cried Mrs. Duncan. "Ruined now, ruined! And there he went and spent all the trust fund—What's to happen now?" She sank down on a stool and indulged in furious tears.

"Trust fund?" asked Lady Beatrice.

"None of your bloody business. It's the end of the Basmonds, that's all."

"There aren't any cousins to inherit?" inquired Dora sympathetically.

"No." Mrs. Duncan blew her nose. "And poor Master Arthur never married, on account of him being—well—"

"A fairy prince?" said Jane, toweling herself off. Lady Beatrice winced, for it was hardly a tactful remark, but Mrs. Duncan lifted her head sharply.

"You been reading in the library? You wasn't allowed in there!"

"No, I haven't read anything. I don't know what you mean," said Jane.

"That's in a book in the library," said Mrs. Duncan. "About the Rawdons having fairy blood. Old Sir Robert finding a girl sitting up there on the hill in the moonlight, and she putting a spell on him. And that was why, ever since..." She trailed off into tears again.

"What a charming story," said Lady Beatrice. "Now, if you'll pardon a change of subject, my dear: I notice the levitation device has been removed from under the cake. Do you happen to know where it was put?"

"Wasn't put anywhere," said Mrs. Duncan. "I pushed the nasty thing into the pantry like it was and left it for morning. You mean to say it's gone?"

FIFTEEN: IN WHICH OUR HEROINE IS OBLIGED TO EXERT HERSELF

Mrs. Corvey, upon inspecting the box on the passage floor, discovered a switch on one end. Cautiously, using her cane, she pushed the switch to its opposite position. A humming noise ceased, so faint it had been imperceptible until it stopped.

"I believe we may now pass safely, Mr. Ludbridge."

"Glad to hear it," Ludbridge said, wheezing as he tried to get to his feet. "Oh—ow—oh, bloody hell, I'm half crippled."

"You may lean on me," said Mrs. Corvey, taking his hand and pulling his arm around her shoulders. "Not to worry, dear; I'm a great deal stronger than I look."

"As yet I've no idea what you look like at all," replied Ludbridge. "Ha! The blind leading the blind, although in our case it makes excellent sense. Lead on, dear lady."

They made their way out again into the main tunnel, and hurriedly down it to the laboratory. Ludbridge was able to crawl through the hole in the window easily enough, but was obliged afterward to sit and catch his breath.

"It seems a lifetime ago I went in there," he said, gasping. "By God, the night air smells sweet! Rather odd nobody noticed the pane missing in all that time, though."

"In fact, someone did," said Mrs. Corvey. "It had been replaced when I found it this evening."

"Really? Well, that's enough to lend new vigor to my wasted limbs," said Ludbridge, getting up with a lurch. "Let's get the hell out of here, shall we?"

Mrs. Corvey led him out through the hedge and around the moat.

She had a moment of worry about getting through the portcullis, for Ludbridge was a man of respectable girth. However, just as they came to the causeway the portcullis came rattling up. Someone drove the carriage forth in great haste; the portcullis was left open behind them. Mrs. Corvey looked after the carriage in keen interest, thinking she recognized Ralph gripping the reins. She wondered what might have happened, to send him out at such speed.

"We had best hurry, Mr. Ludbridge," she said.

"Swiftly as I may, ma'am," he replied, crawling after her on hands and knees. When they reached the courtyard Mrs. Corvey was disconcerted to see lights blazing in the Great Hall. She endeavored to pull Ludbridge along after her, and was greatly relieved when they tumbled together through the door into her room.

"Forty years I've worked here," said Mrs. Duncan, somewhat indistinctly, for she was now on her third glass of gin. The scullery and parlormaids, all in their nightgowns, were huddled around her like chicks around a hen, in varying degrees of tearful distress.

"Well, consider: you are now at liberty to travel," said Jane helpfully. Mrs. Duncan gave her a dark look and two of the maids were provoked into fresh weeping.

"I've just remembered," said Lady Beatrice. "I left something in Prince Nakhimov's room. I wouldn't wish to be so indiscreet as to take the front stairs, when the constable may arrive any moment.... Are there back stairs, Mrs. Duncan?"

The cook pointed at a doorway beyond the pantry. "Mind you be quick about it."

"I shall endeavor to be," said Lady Beatrice. With a significant glance at the Devere sisters, she hastened up the back stairs.

"Lordship's good name at stake and all..." muttered Mrs. Duncan, and had another dram of gin.

———— ✦ ————

Lady Beatrice ran at her best speed, and arrived at last in the gallery. She paused a moment, catching her breath, listening. She heard Prince Nakhimov telling a long anecdote, to which Sir George, Pilkins, Ali Pasha and several valets were listening. Creeping to the edge of the grand staircase she beheld them through a fog of cigar smoke, seated around Lord Basmond's corpse.

Turning, she crossed the gallery and went up to the guests' rooms. She opened the count's door and stepped within. The candle still illuminated the room. By its light Lady Beatrice made a quick and thorough search for the levitation device. Opening the count's trunk, she dug through folded garments. Upon encountering a book she drew it forth and examined it. It was merely a popular novel, but stuck within were a number of papers. One in particular bore an official seal, and appeared to have been signed by Metternich. Lady Beatrice's grasp of French was imperfect, but sufficient for her to make out a phrase here and there. *You will attempt by any means possible to see if his lordship would be agreeable...do not need to remind you of the consequences if you fail...*

"I did not know that whores were fond of reading."

Lady Beatrice looked up. A man stood in the doorway of the antechamber connecting to Count de Mortain's room. His accent was harsh, Germanic; he appeared to be the count's valet. He was holding a knife. Lady Beatrice considered her options, which were few.

"We aren't," she replied. "I was looking for the count; did you know there's been an accident? Lord Basmond is dead."

The valet had started toward her, menace in his eyes, but at her news he stopped in astonishment. "Dead!"

She hurled herself at him and bore him backward. They fell across the bed. The valet stuck at her with the knife. Lady Beatrice experienced then an eerie sense of stepping away from herself, of watching as the patient draft animal of her body bared its teeth and fought for its life. The struggle was a vicious one, as any fight between animals must be. Lady Beatrice was pleased to observe that her flesh had not lost the strength it had drawn upon in the Khyber Pass. She was particularly pleased to see herself wrenching the knife from the valet's hand and stunning him with a sharp downward strike of the pommel. He sagged backward, momentarily unconscious.

So far sheer instinct had preserved her; now Lady Beatrice picked herself up, poured a glass of water from the carafe on the bedside table, and dropped into it a button torn from her blouse. The button dissolved with a gentle hiss. She lifted the valet's head, murmuring to him in a soothing voice, and held the glass to his lips. He drank without thinking, before opening his eyes.

"*Danke, mutter...*" he whispered. He opened his eyes, looked up at Lady Beatrice, and started. "Filthy bitch! I'll kill you—"

"Bitch, unfortunately, yes. Filthy? Certainly not." Lady Beatrice held him down without much effort, as the drug took its swift effect. "And certainly not the sort of bitch who allows herself to be killed by men like you. Yes, you do feel unaccountably sleepy now, don't you? You can barely move. Just close your eyes and go back to Dreamland, dear. It will be so much easier."

When he lay unconscious at last, and having verified by lifting his eyelid that he was, in fact, unconscious, Lady Beatrice rose and considered him coldly. She lifted his legs onto the bed, removed his shoes, and moreover made certain adjustments to his clothing in order to suggest the lewdest possible scenario to anyone discovering him later. Then Lady Beatrice retrieved the papers she had dropped from the floor and secreted them in her bodice.

She left the room and closed the door quietly.

Sixteen: In which a Curious Creature is introduced

"You know, I believe my sight has returned," said Ludbridge, blinking and rubbing his eyes. Mrs. Corvey, who had just finished changing her clothing while explaining how matters presently stood, turned to raise an eyebrow at him.

"My congratulations, Mr. Ludbridge. Lovely feeling, isn't it?"

"It is indeed, Mrs. Corvey."

"Now, Mr. Ludbridge, I believe I'll just go see how my ladies are getting on. Like to know why all the lights are burning at the Hall, as well. I suggest you avail yourself of the soap and the washbasin and polish yourself up a bit, eh? So you don't look quite so much as though you'd spent the last fortnight mucking about in caves. There's a hairbrush and a comb on the table you can use, too."

"Thank you, ma'am, I certainly shall."

Mrs. Corvey drew her shawl around her shoulders and stepped out into the courtyard. She walked briskly toward the Great Hall, watching the lit windows, and consequently was startled when she trod on something unexpected. She looked down. She stared for a long moment at what lay in the courtyard. Then Mrs. Corvey turned around and walked back to the room behind the stables. She opened the door and beheld Ludbridge in the act of washing his face. When, puffing and blowing like a walrus, he reached for a towel, she said:

"If you please, Mr. Ludbridge, there's a dead Frenchman outside. I wonder if you would be so kind as to come have a look at him?"

"Happy to oblige," said Ludbridge, and followed her out into the courtyard. When they reached the corpse he drew a small cylindrical object from his pocket and adjusted a switch on it. A thin beam of brilliant light shot from one end, occasioning a cry of admiration from Mrs. Corvey.

"Oh, I do hope Mr. Felmouth makes up a few of those for me!"

"We call them electric candles; very useful. Let's see the beggar..." Ludbridge shone the light on the dead man's face, and winced. Count de Mortain's features were still recognizable, for all that they were distorted and frozen in a grimace of fear; quite literally frozen too, blue with cold, glittering with frost. His arms were stretched above his head like a diver's, his fingers crooked as though clawing.

"What the deuce! This is Emile Frochard!"

"Not the Count de Mortain?"

"Not half. This fellow's a spy in the pay of the Austrians! But they've been blackmailing the real count. Shouldn't be surprised if they hadn't intercepted the invitation to this auction. Well, well. Damned odd. I wonder how he died?"

"I believe I have an idea," said Mrs. Corvey, glancing it the house. "I'll know more presently."

"Ought we to do anything with him?"

"No! Let him lie for now, Mr. Ludbridge."

Lady Beatrice stood still a moment in the corridor outside the bed-chambers, listening intently. Prince Nakhimov had apparently launched into another anecdote, something to do with hunting wolves. An icy gust of wind crossed the floor, so unexpected as to make Lady Beatrice start. Were she a less ruthlessly pragmatic woman, she had imagined some spectral origin to the chill. A moment's keen examination of the hallway revealed that a tapestry hung at the rear of the hall, moving as though stirred by a breeze. Lady Beatrice glimpsed the bottom of a door in the wall.

She approached it warily and drew the tapestry aside. The revealed door was ajar. Lady Beatrice saw beyond a short corridor, lit by moonlight through unglazed slit-windows, with another door at its end.

Venturing into the corridor, Lady Beatrice peered through one of the windows and saw that it was high in the air, in effect an enclosed bridge connecting the rear of the house with the tower atop the motte. She hurried across bare wooden planks and tried the door at the other end. It opened easily, for the lock was broken.

Lady Beatrice stood blinking a moment in the brilliant light of the room beyond. The light came not from candles or oil lamps, but from something very like an immense battery of De la Rue's vacuum lamps; and this astonished Lady Beatrice, for, as far as she had been aware, no one but the Gentlemen's Speculative Society had been able to build practical vacuum lamps.

Her astonishment was as nothing, however, compared to that of the room's occupant. He turned, saw her, and froze a moment. He might have been Lord Basmond's ghost, so like him he was; but smaller, paler, infinitely more fragile-looking. His hands and naked feet were white as chalk, and too long to seem graceful. In the way of clothing he wore only trousers with braces and a shirt, cuffs rolled up prodigiously, and a leather band about his nearly hairless head. Clipped to the band were several pairs of spectacles of different sorts, on swiveling brackets, and a tiny vacuum lamp that presently threw a flood of ghastly light upon his terrified face.

He screamed, shrill as a rabbit in a trap, and scuttled out of sight.

Lady Beatrice stepped forward into the circular chamber. Against the far wall was a small bed, a dresser and a washstand. In the midst of the room was a trap door, firmly shut and locked. Beside it was a sort of workbench, on which was what appeared to be a disassembled clock, and it was plain from the tools scattered about that the creature had been working on it when Lady Beatrice entered. The most remarkable thing about the room, however, was its decoration. All around the room's white plaster, reaching as high as ten to twelve feet, were charcoal drawings of machines: gears, pulleys, pistons, springs, wires. Here and there were what seemed to be explanatory notes in shorthand, quite illegible to Lady Beatrice. Nor was she able to discern any purpose or plan to the things depicted.

She walked around the workbench, searching for the room's inhabitant. He was nowhere in sight now, but there beyond the trap door was a chest roughly the size and shape of a blanket-press. Lady Beatrice knelt beside the chest.

"You needn't be afraid, Mr. Rawdon," she said.

From within the chest came a gibbering shriek, which cut off abruptly.

"Leave him alone," said another voice, seemingly out of midair. The illusion was so complete Lady Beatrice looked very hard at the wall, half-expecting to see a speaking tube. "Can't you see you can't talk to Hindley? Go talk to Arthur instead."

"I'm afraid Arthur is dead, Hindley."

"I'm not Hindley! I'm Jumbey. Arthur isn't dead. How ridiculous! Now, you run along and leave poor Hindley alone. He's far too busy to deal with distractions."

"May I speak with you, then, Jumbey? If I promise to leave Hindley alone?"

"You must promise. And keep your promise!"

"I do. I will. Tell me, Jumbey: Hindley builds things, doesn't he?"

"Of course he does! He's a genius."

"Yes, I can see that he must be. He built the levitation device, didn't he?"

"You saw it, did you? Yes. Arthur took it, but Hindley didn't mind. He can always make another."

"Did Arthur ask Hindley to make a levitation device for him?"

"Arthur? No! Arthur's the stupid one. He'd never have come up with such an idea on his own. Hindley was being kept in the little room with the wardrobe. His toys kept rolling under the wardrobe, and poor Hindley couldn't reach them, and nasty Pilkins wouldn't come fetch them for him anymore. So Hindley made something to make the wardrobe float, you see, and then he could always rescue his own toys.

"And then Arthur came home and the servants told on Hindley, and he was so frightened, poor thing, because he was sure it would be the little dark room and the cold water again. But Arthur told Hindley he'd give him a nice big room and a laboratory of his own, if Hindley would make things for him. And Hindley could have all the candy floss he wanted. And Arthur would keep all the strangers away. But he didn't!" The last words were spat out with remarkable venom.

"Didn't he, Jumbey?"

"No! Not a scrap nor a shred of candy floss has Hindley tasted. And there was a big blundering nosey-parker spying on Hindley, down in the tunnels. Hindley had to deal with him all by himself, which was so difficult for poor Hindley, because he can't be seen by people, you know."

"I am so sorry to hear it, Jumbey."

"Arthur is *supposed* to look after Hindley and protect him! Mummy said so. Always."

"Well, Jumbey dear, I'm afraid Arthur can't do that anymore. We will have to make some other arrangement for Hindley."

"Has Arthur gone away to school again?"

Lady Beatrice thought carefully before she spoke. "Yes. He has."

"A-and poor Hindley will be left with Pilkins again?" The confident voice wavered. "Hindley doesn't want that. Hindley doesn't like the little room and the cold water!"

"I believe we can help Hindley, Jumbey."

"How?"

Seventeen: In which the Ladies Triumph

"Bloody hell!" exclaimed Mrs. Corvey. Dora, who had just concluded explaining the events of the last two hours, reeled at her language. She glanced around, grateful that Mrs. Duncan had drunk herself into insensibility and the maids had all gone back to their beds, and said: "I'm sure we did our best, ma'am."

"I'm sure you did; but this is a complication, as now there'll be an inquiry. We ain't getting the levitating thing either; I rather suspect it's well on its way to the moon by this time. At least none of that lot upstairs will get it either. Dear, dear, what a puzzle. Where's Lady Beatrice?"

"Here," said she, hurrying down the back stairs swift as a cat. "I am so glad to see you well, ma'am. Did you discover anything?"

"I did, as it happens."

"So did I." Lady Beatrice drew up a kitchen chair and, leaning forward, told her a great deal in an admirably brief time. Mrs. Corvey then returned the favor. Jane, Dora and Maude listened intently, now and then exclaiming in amazement or dismay.

"Well!" said Mrs. Corvey at last. "I think I see a way through our difficulties. Jane, my dear, just go out to the room behind the stable and knock. Ask Mr. Ludbridge if he would be so kind as to step across, and bring the dead Frenchman with him."

Pilkins looked up with a scowl as Lady Beatrice entered the Great Hall.

"Didn't I tell you hussies to keep to your places belowstairs?" he cried. "The constable will be here any minute!"

"If you please, sir, there's a gentleman arrived in the courtyard, but it's not the constable," said Lady Beatrice. "And I was wondering, sir, if we mightn't just take ourselves off to London tonight, so as to avoid scandal?"

"For all I care you can go to—" said Pilkins, before a solemn knock sounded at the door. He rose to open it. Mr. Ludbridge stood there with a grave expression on his face.

"Good evening; Sir Charles Haversham, Special Investigator for Her Majesty's Office of Frauds and Impostures. I have a warrant for the arrest of Arthur Rawdon, Lord Basmond."

Pilkins gaped. "He—he's dead," he said.

"A likely story! I demand you produce him at once."

"No, he really is dead," said Prince Nakhimov, standing and lifting a corner of the blanket that had been thrown over Lord Basmond's corpse. Ludbridge, who had walked boldly into the Great Hall, peered down at the dead man.

"Dear, dear. How inconvenient. Oh, well; I do hope none of you gentlemen had paid him any considerable sums of money?"

"What d'you mean?" said Sir George Spiggott.

"I mean, sir, that my department has spent the last six months carefully building a case against his late lordship. We have the sworn testimony of no fewer than three conjurors, most notably one Dr. Marvello of the Theater Royal, Drury Lane, that his lordship paid them to teach him common tricks to produce the illusion of levitation. We also intercepted correspondence that led us to believe his lordship intended to use this knowledge to defraud a person or persons unknown."

"But—but—" said Pilkins.

"Good God!" cried Sir George. "A confidence trickster! I knew it! I told him to his face he was a damned un-English bounder—"

"Do you mean to say you quarreled with his lordship, sir?" inquired Lady Beatrice quietly.

"Er," said Sir George. "No! Not exactly. I implied it. I mean to say, I was going to tell him that. In the morning. Because I was, er, suspicious, yes, damned suspicious of his proposal. Yes. I know a liar when I see one!"

"So do I," said Ludbridge, giving him a stern look, at which he wilted somewhat. "And I take it his lordship has died as the result of misadventure?"

"We are waiting for your constabulary to arrive, but *it would appear* Lord Basmond fell down the stairs and broke his neck," said Ali Pasha, with a glance at Sir George.

"Shame," said Ludbridge. "Still, Providence has a way of administering its own justice. None of you were defrauded, I hope?"

"We had as yet not even bid," said Prince Nakhimov.

"Capital! You've had a narrow escape, then. I suspect that my work is done," said Ludbridge. "Much as I would have liked to bring the miscreant into a court of law, he is presently facing a far sterner tribunal."

"If you please, sir," said Pilkins, in a trembling voice. "My lordship wasn't no fraud—"

Ludbridge held up his hand in an imperious gesture. "To be sure; your loyalty to an old family fallen on evil times is commendable, but it won't do, my good man. We have proof that his lordship was heavily in debt. Do you deny it?"

"No, sir." Pilkins's shoulders sagged. The sound of wheels and hoofbeats came from the courtyard. "Oh; that'll be our Ralph bringing the constable, I reckon."

"Very good." Ludbridge surveyed them all. "Gentlemen, in view of the tragic circumstances of this evening, and considering the Rawdons' noble history—to say nothing of your own reputations as shrewd men of the world—I do think nothing is to be gained by bruiting this scandal abroad. Perhaps I ought to quietly withdraw."

"If you only would, sir—" said Pilkins, weeping afresh.

"The kitchens are down here, sir," said Lady Beatrice, leading the way. As they descended, they heard the constable's knock and Ali Pasha saying, "Should someone not go waken the count?"

"A splendid farrago of lies, sir," said Lady Beatrice, as they descended.

"Thank you. Perhaps we ought to quicken our pace," said Ludbridge. "I should like to be well clear of the house before anyone goes in search of the Frenchman."

"Where did you put him, sir, if I may ask?"

"In his bed, where else? And a nice job someone did on his partner, I must say. Let the Austrians clean that up!"

"Thank you, sir."

"Did anyone hear us?" asked Dora, as they entered the kitchen.

"I had to get Jane to help me lift it—not heavy, you know, but awkward."

"They didn't hear a thing," said Lady Beatrice, kneeling beside the chest. "Jumbey? Jumbey, dear, is poor Hindley all right?"

"He's frightened," said the eerie voice. "He can tell there are strangers about."

"Tell him he needn't worry. No one will disturb him, and soon he'll have a bigger and better laboratory to play in."

"Maude, just you go catch your Ralph before he puts the horses away," said Mrs. Corvey, and Maude went running out crying:

"Ralph, my love, would you oblige us ever so much? We just need a ride to the village."

The tragedy of Lord Basmond's death set tongues wagging in Little Basmond, but what really scandalized the village was the death of the French count at the hands of his Austrian valet; a crime of passion, apparently, though no one could quite determine how the valet had managed to break all the count's bones. The local magistrate was secretly grateful when an emissary of the Austrian government showed up with a writ of extradition and took the valet away in chains. More: in a handsome gesture, the Austrians paid to have the count's corpse shipped back to France.

Ali Pasha and Prince Nakhimov returned alive to their respective nations, wiser men. Sir George Spiggott returned to his vast estate in Northumberland, where he took to drink and made, in time, a bad end.

When Lord Basmond's solicitors looked through his papers and discovered the extent of his debts, they shook their heads sadly. The staff was paid off and dismissed; every stick of furniture was auctioned in an attempt to satisfy the creditors, and when even this proved inadequate, Basmond Park itself was forfeit. Here complications ensued, with the two most importunate creditors wrangling over whose claim took precedence. In the end the case was tied up in chancery for thirty years.

EIGHTEEN: IN WHICH IT IS SUMMED UP

"I say, ladies!" Herbertina tilted her chair back and rested her feet on the fender. "Here's a bit of news; Basmond Hall has collapsed."

"How awfully sad," said Jane, looking up from the pianoforte.

"Indeed," said Miss Otley. "It was a historic site of great interest."

"It says here it fell in owing to the collapse of several hitherto unsuspected mine shafts beneath the property," said Herbertina.

"I don't doubt it," remarked Mrs. Corvey, with a shudder. "I'm surprised the place didn't fall down with us in it."

"And soon, no doubt, shall be a moldering and moss-grown mound haunted by the spectres of unquiet Rawdons," said Lady Beatrice, snipping a thread of scarlet embroidery floss. "Speaking of whom, has there been any word of poor dear Jumbey?"

"Not officially," said Mrs. Corvey. "There wouldn't be, would there? But Mr. Felmouth has intimated that the present Lord Basmond is developing a number of useful items for Fabrication."

"Happily, I trust?"

"As long as he gets his candy floss regular, yes."

"Jolly good!" Maude played a few experimental notes on her concertina. "Who's for a song? Shall we have 'Begone, Dull Care,' ladies?"

MOTHER AEGYPT

Kage wrote this in a mood of high hilarity, just as surprised as any reader at what her impecunious anti-hero got up to in the course of the plot. On one level, it's a Company story of the evil Labienus and his Plague Cabal, and the Stupid Little People hybrids they use to plot their destruction of humanity. On another level, it's about the endless torment and grief of an immortal who longs to die—and cannot, ever. And on yet a third level, this is Zero Mostel in a Marx Brothers movie. Kage laughed out loud the whole time she was writing it. I hope you do too.

—K. B.

Speak sweetly to the Devil, until you're both over the bridge.
Transylvanian proverb

In a country of mad forests and night, there was an open plain, and pitiless sunlight.

A man dressed as a clown was running for his life across the plain.

A baked-clay track, the only road for miles, reflected the sun's heat and made the man sweat as he ran along it. He was staggering a little as he ran, for he had been running a long while and he was fat, and the silken drawers of his clown costume had begun to work their way down his thighs. It was a particularly humiliating costume, too. It made him look like a gigantic dairymaid.

His tears, of terror and despair, ran down with his sweat and streaked the clown-white, graying his big moustache; the lurid crimson circles on his cheeks had already run, trickling pink down his neck. His straw-stuffed bosom had begun to slip, too, working its way down his dirndl, and now it dropped from beneath his petticoat like a stillbirth. Gasping, he halted to snatch it up, and peered fearfully over his shoulder.

No sign of his pursuers yet; but they were mounted and must catch up with him soon, on this long straight empty plain. There was no cover anywhere, not so much as a single tree. He ran on, stuffing his bosom back in place, whimpering. Gnats whined in his ears.

Then, coming over a gentle swell of earth, he beheld a crossroads. There was his salvation!

A team of slow horses drew two wagons, like the vardas of the Romanies but higher, and narrower, nor were they gaily painted in any way. They were black as the robe of scythe-bearing Death. Only: low, small and ominous, in white paint in curious antiquated letters, they bore the words: *MOTHER AEGYPT.*

The man wouldn't have cared if Death himself held the reins. He aimed himself at the hindmost wagon, drawing on all his remaining strength, and pelted on until he caught up with it.

For a moment he ran desperate alongside, until he was able to gain the front and haul himself up, over the hitch that joined the two wagons. A moment he poised there, ponderous, watching drops of his sweat fall on hot iron. Then he crawled up to the door of the rear wagon, unbolted it, and fell inside.

The driver of the wagons, hooded under that glaring sky, was absorbed in a waking dream of a place lost for millennia. Therefore she did not notice that she had taken on a passenger.

The man lay flat on his back, puffing and blowing, too exhausted to take much note of his surroundings. At last he levered himself up on his elbows, looking about. After a moment he scooted into a sitting position and pulled off the ridiculous lace milkmaid's cap, with its braids of yellow yarn. Wiping his face with it, he muttered a curse.

In a perfect world, he reflected, there would have been a chest of clothing in this wagon, through which he might rummage to steal some less conspicuous apparel. There would, at least, have been a pantry with food and drink. But the fates had denied him yet again; this was nobody's cozy living quarters on wheels. This wagon was clearly used for storage, holding nothing but boxes and bulky objects wrapped in sacking.

Disgusted, the man dug in the front of his dress and pulled out his bosom. He shook it by his ear and smiled as he heard the *clink-clink*. The gold rings were still there, some of the loot with which he'd been able to escape.

The heat within the closed black box was stifling, so he took off all his costume but for the silken drawers. Methodically he began to search through the wagon, opening the boxes and unwrapping the parcels. He began to chuckle.

He knew stolen goods when he saw them.

Some of it had clearly been lifted from Turkish merchants and bureaucrats: rolled and tied carpets, tea services edged in gold. But there were painted ikons here too, and family portraits of Russians on wooden panels. Austrian crystal bowls. Chased silver ewers and platters. Painted urns. A whole umbrella-stand of cavalry sabers, some with ornate decoration, some plain and ancient, evident heirlooms. Nothing was small enough to slip into a pocket, even if he had had one, and nothing convenient to convert into ready cash.

Muttering, he lifted out a saber and drew it from its scabbard.

As he did so, he heard the sound of galloping hooves. The saber dropped from his suddenly-nerveless fingers. He flattened himself against the door, pointlessly, as the hoofbeats drew near and passed.

He heard the shouted questions. He almost—not quite—heard the reply, in a woman's voice pitched very low. His eyes rolled, searching the room for any possible hiding place. None at all; unless he were to wrap his bulk in a carpet, like Cleopatra.

Yet the riders passed on, galloped ahead and away. When he realized that he was, for the moment, safe, he collapsed into a sitting position on the floor.

After a moment of listening to his heart thunder, he picked up the saber again.

It was night before the wagon halted at last, rumbling over rough ground as it left the road. He was still crouched within, cold and cramped now. Evidently the horses were unhitched, and led down to drink at a stream; he could hear splashing. Dry sticks were broken, a fire was lit. He thought of warmth and food. A light footfall approached, followed by the sound of someone climbing up on the hitch. The man tensed.

The door opened.

There, silhouetted against the light of the moon, was a small, pale, spindly looking person with a large head. A wizened child? It peered into the wagon, uncertainty in its big rabbitlike eyes. There was a roll of something—another carpet?—under its arm.

"Hah!" The man lunged, caught the other by the wrist, hauling him in across the wagon's threshold. Promptly the other began to scream, and he screamed like a rabbit too, shrill and unhuman. He did not struggle, though; in fact, the man had the unsettling feeling he'd grabbed a ventriloquist's dummy, limp and insubstantial within its mildewed clothes.

"Shut your mouth!" the man said, in the most terrifying voice he could muster. "I want two things!"

But his captive appeared to have fainted. As the man registered this, he also became aware that a woman was standing outside the wagon, seeming to have materialized from nowhere, and she was staring at him.

"Don't kill him," she said, in a flat quiet voice.

"Uh—I want two things!" the man repeated, holding the saber to his captive's throat. "Or I'll kill him, you understand?"

"Yes," said the woman. "What do you want?"

The man blinked, licked his lips. Something about the woman's matter-of-fact voice disturbed him.

"I want food, and a suit of clothes!"

The woman's gaze did not shift. She was tall, and dark as a shadow, even standing in the full light of the moon, and simply dressed in black.

"I'll give you food," she replied. "But I haven't any clothing that would fit you."

"Then you'd better get me some, hadn't you?" said the man. He made jabbing motions with the saber. "Or I'll kill your little...your little..." He tried to imagine what possible relationship the creature under his arm might have with the woman. Husband? Child?

"Slave," said the woman. "I can buy you a suit in the next village, but you'll have to wait until morning. Don't kill my slave, or I'll make you sorry you were ever born."

"Oh, you will, will you?" said the man, waving the saber again. "Do you think I believe in Gypsy spells? You're not dealing with a village simpleton, here!"

"No," said the woman, in the same quiet voice. "But I know the police are hunting you. Cut Emil's throat, and you'll see how quickly I can make them appear."

The man realized it might be a good idea to change strategies. He put his head on one side, grinning at her in what he hoped was a charmingly roguish way.

"Now, now, no need for things to get nasty," he said. "After all, we're in the same trade, aren't we? I had a good look around in here."

He indicated the interior of the wagon with a jerk of his head. "Nice racket you've got, fencing the big stuff. You don't want me to tell the police about it, while I'm being led away, do you?"

"No," said the woman.

"No, of course not. Let's be friends!" The man edged forward, dragging his captive—Emil, had she called him?—along. "Barbu Golescu, at your service. And you'd be Madame...?"

"Amaunet," she said.

"Charmed," said Golescu. "Sure your husband hasn't a spare pair of trousers he can loan me, Madame Amaunet?"

"I have no husband," she replied.

"Astonishing!" Golescu said, smirking. "Well then, dear madame, what about loaning a blanket until we can find me a suit? I'd hate to offend your modesty."

"I'll get one," she said, and walked away.

He stared after her, momentarily disconcerted, and then put down the saber and flexed his hand. Emil remained motionless under his other arm.

"Don't you get any ideas, little turnip-head," muttered Golescu. "Hey! Don't get any ideas, I said. Are you deaf, eh?"

He hauled Emil up by his collar and looked at him critically. Emil whimpered and turned his face away. It was a weak face. His head had been shaved at one time, and the hair grown back in scanty and irregular clumps.

"Maybe you *are* deaf," conceded Golescu. "But your black mummy loves you, eh? What a useful thing for me." He groped about and found a piece of cord that had bound one of the carpets. "Hold still or I'll wring your wry neck, understand?"

"You smell bad," said Emil, in a tiny voice.

"Bah! You stink like carpet-mold, yourself," said Golescu, looping the cord about Emil's wrist. He looped the other end about his own wrist and pulled it snug. "There, so you can't go running away. We're going to be friends, you see? You'll get used to me soon enough."

He ventured out on the hitch and dropped to the ground. His legs were unsteady and he attempted to lean on Emil's shoulder, but the little man collapsed under him like so much cardboard.

"She doesn't use you for cutting wood or drawing water much, does she?" muttered Golescu, hitching at his drawers. Amaunet came around the side of the wagon and handed him the blanket, without comment.

"He's a flimsy one, your slave," Golescu told her. "What you need is a man to help with the business, if you'll pardon my saying so." He wrapped his vast nakedness in the blanket and grinned at her.

Amaunet turned and walked away from him.

"There's bread and tomatoes by the fire," she said, over her shoulder.

Clutching the blanket around him with one hand and dragging Emil with the other, Golescu made his way to the fire. Amaunet was sitting perfectly still, watching the flames dance, and only glanced up at them as they approached.

"That's better," said Golescu, settling himself down and reaching for the loaf of bread. He tore off a hunk, sopped it in the saucepan of stewed tomatoes and ate ravenously. Emil, still bound to his wrist and pulled back and forth when he moved, had gone as limp and unresponsive as a straw figure.

"So," said Golescu, through a full mouth, "no husband. Are you sure you don't need help? I'm not talking of bedroom matters, madame, you understand; perish the thought. I'm talking about security. So many thieves and murderers in this wicked old world! Now, by an astounding coincidence, *I* need a way to get as far as I can from the Danube, and *you* are headed north. Let's be partners for the time being, what do you say?"

Amaunet's lip curled. Contempt? But it might have been a smile.

"Since you mention it," she said, "Emil's no good at speaking to people. I don't care to deal with them, much, myself. The police said you were with a circus; do you know how to get exhibition permits from petty clerks?"

"Of course I do," said Golescu, with a dismissive gesture. "The term you're looking for is *advance man*. Rely on me."

"Good." Amaunet turned her gaze back to the fire. "I can't pay you, but I'll lie for you. You'll have room and board."

"And a suit of clothes," he reminded her.

She shrugged, in an affirmative kind of way.

"It's settled, then," said Golescu, leaning back. "What business are we in? Officially, I mean?"

"I tell people their futures," said Amaunet.

"Ah! But you don't look like a Gypsy."

"I'm not a Gypsy," she said, perhaps a little wearily. "I'm from Egypt."

"Just so," he said, laying his finger beside his nose. "The mystic wisdom of the mysterious east, eh? Handed down to you from the ancient pharaohs. Very good, madame, that's the way to impress the peasants."

"You know a lot of big words, for a clown," said Amaunet. Golescu winced, and discreetly lifted a corner of the blanket to scrub at his greasepaint.

"I am obviously not a real clown, madame," he protested. "I am a victim of circumstances, calumny and political intrigue. If I could tell you my full story, you'd weep for me."

She grinned, a brief white grin so startling in her dark, still face that he nearly screamed.

"I doubt it," was all she said.

He kept Emil bound to him that night, reasoning that he couldn't completely trust Amaunet until he had a pair of trousers. Golescu made himself comfortable on the hard floor of the wagon by using the little man as a sort of bolster, and though Emil made plaintive noises now and then and did in fact smell quite a lot like moldy carpet, it was nothing that couldn't be ignored by a determined sleeper.

Only once Golescu woke in the darkness. Someone was singing, out there in the night; a woman was singing, full-throated under the white moon. There was such throbbing melancholy in her voice Golescu felt tears stinging his eyes; yet there was an indefinable menace too, in the harsh and unknown syllables of her lament. It might have been a lioness out there, on the prowl. He thought briefly of opening the door to see if she wanted comforting, but the idea sent inexplicable chills down his spine. He snorted, rolled on his back and slept again.

Golescu woke when the wagons lurched back into motion, and stared around through the dissipating fog of vaguely lewd dreams. Sunlight was streaming in through cracks in the plank walls. Though his dreams receded, certain sensations remained. He sat upright with a grunt of outrage and looked over his own shoulder at Emil, who had plastered himself against Golescu's backside.

"Hey!" Golescu hauled Emil out. "What are you, a filthy sodomite? You think because I wear silk, I'm some kind of Turkish fancy boy?"

Emil whimpered and hid his face in his hands. "The sun," he whispered.

"Yes, it's daylight! You're scared of the sun?" demanded Golescu.

"Sun hurts," said Emil.

"Don't be stupid, it can't hurt you," said Golescu. "See?" He thrust Emil's hand into the nearest wavering stripe of sunlight. Emil made rabbity noises again, turning his face away and squeezing his eyes shut, as though he expected his hand to blister and smoke.

"See?" Golescu repeated. But Emil refused to open his eyes, and Golescu released his hand in disgust. Taking up the saber, he sliced through the cord that bound them. Emil promptly curled into himself like an angleworm and lay still, covering his eyes once more. Golescu considered him, setting aside the saber and rubbing his own wrist.

"If you're a *vampyr*, you're the most pathetic one I've ever heard of," he said. "What's she keep you around for, eh?"

Emil did not reply.

Some time after midday, the wagons stopped; about an hour later, the door opened and Amaunet stood there with a bundle of clothing.

"Here," she said, thrusting it at Golescu. Her dead stare fell on Emil, who cringed and shrank even further into himself from the flood of daylight. She removed one of her shawls and threw it over him, covering him completely. Golescu, pulling on the trousers, watched her in amusement.

"I was just wondering, madame, whether I should maybe get myself a crucifix to wear around our little friend, here," he said. "Or some bulbs of garlic?"

"He likes the dark," she replied. "You owe me three piastres for that suit."

"It's not what I'm accustomed to, you know," he said, shrugging into the shirt. "Coarse-woven stuff. Where are we?"

"Twenty kilometers farther north than we were yesterday," she replied.

Not nearly far enough, Golescu considered uneasily. Amaunet had turned her back on him while he dressed. He found himself studying her body as he buttoned himself up. With her grim face turned away, it was possible to concede that the rest of her was lovely. Only in the very young could bodily mass defy gravity in such a pert and springy-looking manner. How old *was* she?

When he had finished pulling on his boots, he stood straight, twirled the ends of his moustaches and sucked in his gut. He drew one of the gold rings from his former bosom.

"Here. Accept this, my flower of the Nile," said Golescu, taking Amaunet's hand and slipping the ring on her finger. She pulled her hand away at once and turned so swiftly the air seemed to blur. For a moment there was fire in her eyes, and if it was more loathing than passion, still, he had gotten a reaction out of her.

"Don't touch me," she said.

"I'm merely paying my debt!" Golescu protested, pleased with himself. "Charming lady, that ring's worth far more than what you paid for the suit."

"It stinks," she said in disgust, snatching the ring off.

"Gold can afford to smell bad," he replied. His spirits were rising like a balloon.

Uninvited, he climbed up on the driver's seat beside her and the wagons rolled on, following a narrow river road through its winding gorge.

"You won't regret your kindness to me, dear madame," said Golescu. "A pillar of strength and a fountain of good advice, that's me. I won't ask about your other business in the wagon back there, as Discretion is my middle name, but tell me: what's your fortunetelling racket like? Do you earn as much as you could wish?"

"I cover my operating expenses," Amaunet replied.

"Pft!" Golescu waved his hand. "Then you're clearly not making what you deserve to make. What do you do? Cards? Crystal ball? Love potions?"

"I read palms," said Amaunet.

"Not much overhead in palm reading," said Golescu, "But on the other hand, not much to impress the customers either. Unless you paint them scintillating word-pictures of scarlet and crimson tomorrows, or warn them of terrifying calamity only *you* can help them avoid, yes? And, you'll excuse me, but you seem to be a woman of few words. Where's your glitter? Where's your flash?"

"I tell them the truth," said Amaunet.

"Ha! The old, 'I-am-under-an-ancient-curse-and-can-only-speak-the-truth' line? No, no, dear madame, that's been done to death. I propose a whole new approach!" said Golescu.

Amaunet just gave him a sidelong look, unreadable as a snake.

"Such as?"

"Such as I would need to observe your customary clientele before I could elaborate on," said Golescu.

"I see," she said.

"Though *Mother Aegypt* is a good name for your act," Golescu conceded. "Has a certain majesty. But it implies warmth. You might work on that. Where's your warmth, eh?"

"I haven't got any," said Amaunet. "And you're annoying me, now."

"Then, *taceo*, dear madame. That's Latin for 'I shall be quiet,' you know."

She curled her lip again.

Silent, he attempted to study her face, as they jolted along. She must be a young woman; her skin was smooth, there wasn't a trace of gray in her hair or a whisker on her lip. One could say of any ugly woman, *Her nose is hooked,* or *Her lips are thin,* or *Her eyes are too close together.* None of this could be said of Amaunet. It was indeed impossible to say anything much; for when Golescu looked closely at her he saw only shadow, and a certain sense of discord.

They came, by night, to a dismal little town whose slumped and rounded houses huddled with backs to the river, facing the dark forest. After threading a maze of crooked streets, they found the temporary camp for market fair vendors: two bare acres of open ground that had been a cattle pen most recently. It was still redolent of manure. Here other wagons were drawn up, and fires burned in iron baskets. The people who made their livings offering rides on painted ponies or challenging all comers to games of skill stood about the fires, drinking from bottles, exchanging news in weary voices.

Yet when Amaunet's wagons rolled by they looked up only briefly, and swiftly looked away. Some few made gestures to ward off evil.

"You've got quite a reputation, eh?" observed Golescu. Amaunet did not reply. She seemed to have barely noticed.

Golescu spent another chilly night on the floor in the rear wagon—alone this time, for Emil slept in a cupboard under Amaunet's narrow bunk when he was not being held hostage, and Amaunet steadfastly ignored all Golescu's hints and pleasantries about the value of shared body warmth. As a consequence, he was stiff and out of sorts by the time he emerged next morning.

Overnight, the fair had assumed half-existence. A blind man, muscled like a giant, cranked steadily at the carousel, and thin pale children rode round and round. A man with a barrel-organ cranked steadily too, and his little monkey sat on his shoulder and watched the children with a diffident eye. But many of the tents were still flat, in a welter of ropes and poles. A long line of bored vendors stood attendance before a town clerk, who had set up his permit office under a black parasol.

Golescu was staring at all this when Amaunet, who had come up behind him silent as a shadow, said:

"Here's your chance to be useful. Get in line for me."

"Holy Saints!" Golescu whirled around. "Do you want to frighten me into heart failure? Give a man some warning."

She gave him a leather envelope and a small purse instead. "Here are my papers. Pay the bureaucrat and get my permit. You won't eat tonight, otherwise."

"You wouldn't order me around like this if you knew my true identity," Golescu grumbled, but he got into line obediently.

The town clerk was reasonably honest, so the line took no more than an hour to wind its way through. At last the man ahead of Golescu got his permit to sell little red-blue-and-yellow paper flags, and Golescu stepped up to the table.

"Papers," said the clerk, yawning.

"Behold." Golescu opened them with a flourish. The clerk squinted at them.

"Amaunet Kematef," he recited. "Doing business as 'Mother Aegypt.' A Russian? And this says you're a woman."

"They're not my papers, they're—they're my wife's papers," said Golescu, summoning an outraged expression. "And she isn't Russian, my friend, she *is* a hot-blooded Egyptian, a former harem dancer if you must know, before an unfortunate accident that marred her exotic beauty. I found her starving in the gutters of Cairo, and succored her out of Christian charity. Shortly, however, I discovered her remarkable talent for predicting the future based on an ancient system of—"

"A fortune-teller? Two marks," said the clerk. Golescu paid, and as the clerk wrote out the permit he went on:

"The truth of the matter is that she was the only daughter of a Coptic nobleman, kidnapped at an early age by ferocious—"

"Three marks extra if this story goes on any longer," said the clerk, stamping the permit forcefully.

"You have my humble gratitude," said Golescu, bowing deeply. Pleased with himself, he took the permit and strutted away.

"Behold," he said, producing the permit for Amaunet with a flourish. She took it without comment and examined it. Seen in the strong morning light, the indefinable grimness of her features was much more pronounced. Golescu suppressed a shudder and inquired, "How else may a virile male be of use, my sweet?"

Amaunet turned her back on him, for which he was grateful. "Stay out of trouble until tonight. Then you can mind Emil. He wakes up after sundown."

She returned to the foremost black wagon. Golescu watched as she climbed up, and was struck once more by the drastically different effect her backside produced on the interested spectator.

"Don't you want me to beat a drum for you? Or rattle a tambourine or something? I can draw crowds for you like a sugarloaf draws flies!"

She looked at him, with her white grimace that might have been amusement. "I'm sure you can draw flies," she said. "But I don't need an advertiser for what I do."

Muttering, Golescu wandered away through the fair. He cheered up no end, however, when he discovered that he still had Amaunet's purse.

Tents were popping up now, bright banners were being unfurled, though they hung down spiritless in the heat and glare of the day. Golescu bought himself a cheap hat and stood around a while, squinting as he sized up the food vendors. Finally he bought a glass of tea and a fried pastry, stuffed with plums, cased in glazed sugar that tasted vaguely poisonous. He ate it contentedly and, licking the sugar off his fingers, wandered off the fairground to a clump of trees near the river's edge. There he stretched out in the shade and, tilting his hat over his face, went to sleep. If one had to babysit a *vampyr* one needed to get plenty of rest by day.

By night the fair was a different place. The children were gone, home in their beds, and the carousel raced round nearly empty but for spectral riders; the young men had come out instead. They roared with laughter and shoved one another, or stood gaping before the little plank stages where the exhibitions were cried by mountebanks. Within this tent were remarkable freaks of nature; within this one, an exotic dancer plied her trade; within another was a man who could handle hot iron without gloves. The lights were bright and fought with shadows. The air was full of music and raucous cries.

Golescu was unimpressed.

"What do you mean, it's too tough?" he demanded. "That cost fifteen groschen!"

"I can't eat it," whispered Emil, cringing away from the glare of the lanterns.

"Look." Golescu grabbed up the ear of roasted corn and bit into it. "Mm! Tender! Eat it, you little whiner."

"It has paprika on it. Too hot." Emil wrung his hands.

"Ridiculous," said Golescu through a full mouth, munching away. "It's the food of the gods. What the hell *will* you eat, eh? I know! You're a *vampyr*, so you want blood, right? Well, we're in a slightly public place at the moment, so you'll just have to make do with something else. Taffy apple, eh? Deep fried sarmale? Pierogi? Pommes Frites?"

Emil wept silently, tears coursing from his big rabbit-eyes, and Golescu sighed and tossed the corn cob away. "Come on," he said, and dragged the little man off by one hand.

They made a circuit of all the booths serving food before Emil finally consented to try a Vienna sausage impaled on a stick, dipped in corn batter and deep-fried. To Golescu's relief he seemed to like it, for he nibbled at it uncomplainingly as Golescu towed him along. Golescu glanced over at Amaunet's wagon, and noted a customer emerging, pale and shaken.

"Look over there," Golescu said in disgust. "One light. No banners, nobody calling attention to her, nobody enticing the crowds. And one miserable customer waiting, look! That's what she gets. Where's the sense of mystery? She's *Mother Aegypt!* Her other line of work must pay pretty well, eh?"

Emil made no reply, deeply preoccupied by his sausage-on-a-spike.

"Or maybe it doesn't, if she can't do any better for a servant than you. Where's all the money go?" Golescu wondered, pulling at his moustache. "Why's she so sour, your mistress? A broken heart or something?"

Emil gave a tiny shrug and kept eating.

"I could make her forget whoever it was in ten minutes, if I could just get her to take me seriously," said Golescu, gazing across at the wagon. "And the best way to do that, of course, is to impress her with money. We need a scheme, turnip-head."

"Four thousand and seventeen," said Emil.

"Huh?" Golescu turned to stare down at him. Emil said nothing else, but in his silence the cry of the nearest hawker came through loud and clear:

"Come on and take a chance, clever ones! Games of chance, guess the cards, throw the dice, spin the wheel! Or guess the number of millet-grains in the jar and win a cash prize! Only ten groschen a guess! *You* might be the winner! You, sir, with the little boy!"

Golescu realized the hawker was addressing him. He looked around indignantly.

"He is not my little boy!"

"So he's your uncle, what does it matter? Take a guess, why don't you?" bawled the hawker. "What have you got to lose?"

"Ten groschen," retorted Golescu, and then reflected that it was Amaunet's money. "What the hell."

He approached the gaming booth, pulling Emil after him. "What's the cash prize?"

"Twenty thousand lei," said the hawker. Golescu rolled his eyes.

"Oh, yes, I'd be able to retire on *that,* all right," he said, but dug in his pocket for ten groschen. He cast a grudging eye on the glass jar at the back of the counter, on its shelf festooned with the new national flag and swags of bunting. "You've undoubtedly got rocks hidden in there, to throw the volume off. Hm, hm, all right...how many grains of millet in there? I'd say..."

"Four thousand and seventeen," Emil repeated. The hawker's jaw dropped. Golescu looked from one to the other of them. His face lit up.

"That's the right answer, isn't it?" he said. "Holy saints and patriarchs!"

"No, it isn't," said the hawker, recovering himself with difficulty.

"It is so," said Golescu. "I can see it in your eyes!"

"No, it isn't," the hawker insisted.

"It is so! Shall we tip out the jar and count what's in there?"

"No, and anyway you hadn't paid me yet—and anyway it was your little boy, not you, so it wouldn't count anyway—and—"

144

"Cheat! Shall I scream it aloud? I've got very good lungs. Shall I tell the world how you've refused to give this poor child his prize, even when he guessed correctly? Do you really want—"

"Shut up! Shut up, I'll pay the damned twenty thousand lei!" The hawker leaned forward and clapped his hand over Golescu's mouth. Golescu smiled at him, the points of his moustaches rising like a cockroach's antennae.

Wandering back to Amaunet's wagon, Golescu jingled the purse at Emil.

"Not a bad night's work, eh? I defy her to look at this and fail to be impressed."

Emil did not respond, sucking meditatively on the stick, which was all that was left of his sausage.

"Of course, we're going to downplay your role in the comedy, for strategic reasons," Golescu continued, peering around a tent and scowling at the wagon. There was a line of customers waiting now, and while some were clearly lonely women who wanted their fortunes told, a few were rather nasty-looking men, in fact rather criminal-looking men, and Golescu had the uneasy feeling he might have met one or two of them in a professional context at some point in his past. As he was leaning back, he glanced down at Emil.

"I think we won't interrupt her while she's working just yet. Gives us more time to concoct a suitably heroic and clever origin for this fine fat purse, eh? Anyway, she'd never believe that *you*—" Golescu halted, staring at Emil. He slapped his forehead in a gesture of epiphany.

"Wait a minute, wait a minute! She *knows* about this talent of yours! That's why she keeps you around, is it? Ha!"

He was silent for a moment, but the intensity of his regard was such that it penetrated even Emil's self-absorption. Emil looked up timidly and beheld Golescu's countenance twisted into a smile of such ferocious benignity that the little man screamed, dropped his stick and covered his head with both hands.

"My dear shrinking genius!" bellowed Golescu, seizing Emil up and clasping him in his arms. "Puny friend, petite brother, sweetest of *vampyrs!* Come, my darling, will you have another sausage? No? Polenta? Milk punch? Hot chocolate? Golescu will see you have anything you want, pretty one. Let us go through the fair together."

The purse of twenty thousand lei was considerably lighter by the time Golescu retreated to the shadows under the rear wagon, pulling Emil after him. Emil was too stuffed with sausage and candy floss to be very alert, and he had a cheap doll and a pinwheel to occupy what could be mustered of his attention. Nonetheless, Golescu drew a new pack of cards from his pocket, broke the seal and shuffled them, looking at Emil with lovingly predatory eyes.

"I have heard of this, my limp miracle," crooned Golescu, making the cards snap and riffle through his fat fingers. "Fellows quite giftless as regards social graces, oh yes, in some cases so unworldly they must be fed and diapered like babies. And yet, they have a brilliance! An unbelievable grasp of systems and details! Let us see if you are one such prodigy, eh?"

An hour's worth of experimentation was enough to prove to Golescu's satisfaction that Emil was more than able to count cards accurately; if a deck was even fanned before his face for a second, he could correctly identify all the cards he had glimpsed.

"And now, dear boy, only one question remains," said Golescu, tossing the deck over his shoulder into the night. The cards scattered like dead leaves. "Why hasn't Madame Amaunet taken advantage of your fantastic abilities to grow rich beyond the dreams of avarice?"

Emil did not reply.

"Such a perfect setup. I can't understand it," persisted Golescu, leaning down to peer at the line stretching to the door of the forward wagon. A woman had just emerged, wringing her hands and sobbing. Though the fairground had begun to empty out now, there were still a few distinct thugs waiting their turn to...have their fortunes told? It seemed unlikely. Three of them seemed to be concealing bulky parcels about their persons.

"With a lucky mannikin like you, she could queen it at gambling houses from Monte Carlo to St. Petersburg," mused Golescu. "In fact, with a body like hers, she could be the richest whore in Rome, Vienna or Budapest. If she wore a mask, that is. Why, then, does she keep late hours fencing stolen spoons and watches for petty cutthroats? Where's the money in that? What does she want, Emil, my friend?"

"The Black Cup," said Emil.

When the last of the thugs had gone his way, Amaunet emerged from the wagon and looked straight at Golescu, where he lounged in the shadows. He had been intending to make an impressive entrance, but with the element of surprise gone he merely waved at her sheepishly.

"Where's Emil?" demanded Amaunet.

"Safe and sound, my queen," Golescu replied, producing Emil and holding him up by the scruff of his neck. Emil, startled by the light, yelled feebly and covered his eyes. "We had a lovely evening, thank you."

"Get to bed," Amaunet told Emil. He writhed from Golescu's grip and darted into the wagon. "Did you feed him?" she asked Golescu.

"Royally," said Golescu. "And how did I find the wherewithal to do that, you ask? Why, with *this.*" He held up the purse of somewhat less than twenty thousand lei and clinked it at her with his most seductive expression. To his intense annoyance, her eyes did not brighten in the least.

"Fetch the horses and hitch them in place. We're moving on tonight," she said.

Golescu was taken aback. "Don't you want to know where I got all this lovely money?"

"You stole it?" said Amaunet, taking down the lantern from its hook by the door and extinguishing it.

"I never!" cried Golescu, genuinely indignant. "I won it for you, if you must know. Guessing how many grains of millet were in a jar."

He had imagined her reaction to his gift several times that evening, with several variations on her range of emotion. He was nonetheless unprepared for her actual response of turning, swift as a snake, and grabbing him by the throat.

"How did you guess the right number?" she asked him, in a very low voice.

"I'm extraordinarily talented?" he croaked, his eyes standing out of his head.

Amaunet tightened her grip. "It was Emil's guess, wasn't it?"

Golescu merely nodded, unable to draw enough breath to speak.

"Were you enough of a fool to take him to the games of chance?"

Golescu shook his head. She pulled his face close to her own.

"If I ever catch you taking Emil to card-parlors or casinos, I'll kill you. Do you understand?"

She released him, hurling him back against the side of the wagon. Golescu straightened, gasped in air, pushed his hat up from his face and said:

"All right, so I discovered his secret. Does Madame have any objections to my asking why the hell she isn't using our little friend to grow stinking rich?"

"Because Emil doesn't have a secret," Amaunet hissed. "He *is* a secret."

"Oh, that explains everything," said Golescu, rubbing his throat.

"It had better," said Amaunet. "Now, bring the horses."

Golescu did as he was told, boiling with indignation and curiosity, and also with something he was barely able to admit to himself. It could not be said, by any stretch of the imagination, that Amaunet was beautiful in her wrath, and yet...

Something about the pressure of her fingers on his skin, and the amazing strength of her hands...and the scent of her breath up close like that, like some unnamable spice...

"What strange infatuation enslaves my foolish heart?" he inquired of the lead horse, as he hitched it to the wagon-tongue.

They traveled all the rest of the moonless night, along the dark river, and many times heard the howling of wolves, far off in the dark forest.

Golescu wove their cries into a fantasy of heroism, wherein he was possessed of an immense gun and discharged copious amounts of shot into a pack of ferocious wolves threatening Amaunet, who was so grateful for the timely rescue she...she threw off her disguise, and most of her clothing too, and it turned out that she'd been wearing a fearsome mask all along. She was actually beautiful, though he couldn't quite see how beautiful, because every time he tried to fling himself into her arms he kept tangling his feet in something, which seemed to be pink candy-floss someone had dropped on the fairground...

And then the pink strands became a spiderweb and Emil was a fly caught there, screaming and screaming in his high voice, which seemed odd considering Emil was a *vampyr*. "Aren't they usually the ones who do the biting?" he asked Amaunet, but she was sprinting away toward the dark river, which was the Nile, and he sprinted after her, pulling his clothing off as he went too, but the sun was rising behind the pyramids...

Golescu sat up with a snort, and shielded his eyes against the morning glare.

"We've stopped," he announced.

"Yes," said Amaunet, who was unhitching the horses. They seemed to have left the road in the night; they were now in a forest clearing, thickly screened on all sides by brush.

"You're camping here," Amaunet said. "I have an appointment to keep. You'll stay with the lead wagon and watch Emil. I should be gone no more than three days."

"But of course," said Golescu, stupid with sleep. He sat there rubbing his unshaven chin, watching her lead the horses out of sight through the bushes. He could hear water trickling somewhere near at hand. Perhaps Amaunet was going to bathe in a picturesque forest pool, as well as water the horses?

He clambered down from the seat and hurried after her, moving as silently as he could, but all that rewarded his stealthy approach was the sight of Amaunet standing by the horses with her arms crossed, watching them drink from a stream. Golescu shuddered. Strong morning light was really not her friend.

Sauntering close, he said:

"So what does the little darling eat, other than sausages and candy?"

"Root vegetables," said Amaunet, not bothering to look at him. "Potatoes and turnips, parsnips, carrots. He won't eat them unless they're boiled and mashed, no butter, no salt, no pepper. He'll eat any kind of bread if the crusts are cut off. Polenta, but again, no butter, no salt. He'll drink water."

"How obliging of him," said Golescu, making a face. "Where'd you find our tiny friend, anyway?"

Amaunet hesitated a moment before replying. "An asylum," she said.

"Ah! And they had no idea what he was, did they?" said Golescu. She turned on him, with a look that nearly made him wet himself.

"And *you* know what he is?" she demanded.

"Just—just a little idiot savant, isn't it so?" said Golescu. "Clever at doing sums. Why you're not using his big white brain to get rich, I can't imagine; but there it is. Is there anything else Nursie ought to know about his care and feeding?"

"Only that I'll hunt you down and kill you if you kidnap him while I'm gone," said Amaunet, without raising her voice in the slightest yet managing to convince Golescu that she was perfectly sincere. It gave him another vaguely disturbing thrill.

"I seek only to be worthy of your trust, my precious one," he said. "Where are you going, anyway?"

"That's none of your business."

"To be sure," he agreed, bowing and scraping. "And you're taking the rear wagon, are you? One can't help wondering, my black dove of the mysteries, whether this has anything to do with all the loot hidden back there. Perhaps you have a rendezvous with someone who'll take it off your hands, eh?"

Her look of contempt went through him like a knife, but he knew he'd guessed correctly.

The first thing Golescu did, when he was alone, was to go into Amaunet's wagon and explore.

Though his primary object was money, it has to be admitted he went first to what he supposed to be her underwear drawer. This disappointed him, for it contained instead what seemed to be alchemist's equipment: jars of powdered minerals and metals, bowls, alembics and retorts. All was so spotlessly clean it might never have been used. When he found her underwear at last, in a trunk, he was further disappointed. It was plain utilitarian stuff; evidently Amaunet didn't go in for frills. Nevertheless, he slipped a pair of her drawers into his breast pocket, like a handkerchief, and continued his search.

No money at all, nor any personal things that might give him any clue to her history. There were a few decorative items, obviously meant to give an Egyptian impression to her customers: a half-size mummy case of papier-mâché. A hanging scroll, hieroglyphs printed on cloth, of French manufacture.

No perfumes or cosmetics by the washbasin; merely a bar of yellow soap. Golescu sniffed it and recoiled; no fragrance but lye. Whence, then, that intoxicating whiff of not-quite-cinnamon on her skin?

No writing desk, no papers. There was something that might have been intended for writing, a polished box whose front opened out flat to reveal a dull mirror of green glass at its rear. It was empty. Golescu gave it no more than a cursory glance. After he'd closed it, he rubbed the fingertips of his hand together, for they tingled slightly.

Not much in the larder: dry bread, an onion, a few potatoes. Several cooking pots and a washing copper. Golescu looked at it thoughtfully, rubbing his chin.

"But no money," he said aloud.

He sat heavily on her bed, snorting in frustration. Hearing a faint squeak of protest, he rose to his feet again and looked down. "Yes, of course!" he said, and opened the drawer under the bed. Emil whimpered and rolled away from the light, covering his face with his hands.

"Hello, don't mind me," said Golescu, scooping him out. He got down on his hands and knees, ignoring Emil's cries, and peered into the space. "Where does your mistress keep her gold, my darling? Not in here, eh? Hell and Damnation."

He sat back. Emil attempted to scramble past him, back into the shadows, but he caught the little man by one leg.

"Emil, my jewel, you'll never amount to much in this world if you can't walk around in the daytime," he said. "And you won't be much use to me, either. What's your quarrel with the sun, anyway?"

"It burns my eyes," Emil wept.

"Does it?" Golescu dragged him close, prized down his hands and looked into his wet eyes. "Perhaps there's something we can do about that, eh? And once we've solved that problem..." His voice trailed off, as he began to smile. Emil wriggled free and vanished back into the drawer. Golescu slid it shut with his foot.

"Sleep, potato-boy," he said, hauling himself to his feet. "Don't go anyplace, and dear Uncle Barbu will be back with presents this afternoon."

Humming to himself, he mopped his face with Amaunet's drawers, replaced them in his pocket, and left the wagon. Pausing only to lock its door, he set off for the nearest road.

It took him a while to find a town, however, and what with one thing and another it was nearly sundown before Golescu came back to the wagon.

He set down his burdens—one large box and a full sack—and unlocked the door.

"Come out, little Emil," he said, and on receiving no reply he clambered in and pulled the drawer open. "Come out of there!"

"I'm hungry," said Emil, sounding accusatory, but he did not move.

"Come out and I'll boil you a nice potato, eh? It's safe; the sun's gone down. Don't you want to see what I got you, ungrateful thing?"

Emil came unwillingly, as Golescu backed out before him. He stepped down from the door, looking around, his tiny weak mouth pursed in suspicion. Catching sight of the low red sun, he let out a shrill cry and clapped his hands over his eyes.

"Yes, I lied," Golescu told him. "but just try *these*—" He drew from his pocket a pair of blue spectacles and, wrenching Emil's hands away, settled them on the bridge of his nose. They promptly fell off, as Emil's nose was far too small and thin to keep them up, and they only had one earpiece anyway.

Golescu dug hastily in the sack he had brought and drew out a long woolen scarf. He cut a pair of slits in it, as Emil wailed and jigged in front of him. Clapping the spectacles back on Emil's face and holding them in place a moment with his thumb, he tied the scarf about his head like a blindfold and widened the slits so the glass optics poked through.

"Look! Goggles!" he said. "So you're protected, see? Open your damned eyes, you baby!"

Emil must have obeyed, for he stood still suddenly, dropping his hands to his sides. His mouth hung open in an expression of feeble astonishment.

"But, wait!" said Golescu. "There's more!" He reached into the sack again and brought out a canvas coachman's duster, draping it around Emil's shoulders. It had been made for someone twice Emil's size, so it reached past his knees, indeed it trailed on the ground; and Golescu had a difficult three minutes' labor working Emil's limp arms through the sleeves and rolling the cuffs up. But, once it had been painstakingly buttoned, Emil stood as though in a tent.

"And the crowning touch—" Golescu brought from the sack a wide-brimmed felt hat and set it on Emil's head. Golescu sat back to admire the result.

"Now, don't you look nice?" he said. Emil in fact looked rather like a mushroom, but his mouth had closed. "You see? You're protected from the sun. The *vampyr* may walk abroad by day. Thanks are in order to good old Uncle Barbu, eh?

"I want my potato," said Emil.

"Pah! All right, let's feast. We've got a lot of work to do tonight," said Golescu, taking up the sack and shaking it meaningfully.

Fairly quickly he built a fire and set water to boil for Emil's potato. He fried himself a feast indeed from what he had brought: rabbit, bacon and onions, and a jug of wine red as bull's blood to wash it down. The wine outlasted the food by a comfortable margin. He set it aside and lit a fine big cigar as Emil dutifully carried the pans down to the stream to wash them.

"*Good* slave," said Golescu happily, and blew a smoke ring. "A man could get used to this kind of life. When you're done with those, bring out the laundry-copper. I'll help you fill it. And get some more wood for the fire!"

When Emil brought the copper forth they took it to the stream and filled it; then carried it back to the fire, staggering and slopping, and set it to heat. Golescu drew from the sack another of his purchases, a three-kilo paper bag with a chemist's seal on it. Emil had been gazing at the bright fire, his vacant face rendered more vacant by the goggles; but he turned his head to stare at the paper bag.

"Are we making the Black Cup?" he asked.

"No, my darling, we're making a golden cup," said Golescu. He opened the bag and dumped its contents into the copper, which had just begun to steam. "Good strong yellow dye, see? We'll let it boil good, and when it's mixed—" he reached behind him, dragging close the box he had brought. He opened it, and the firelight winked in the glass necks of one hundred and forty-four little bottles. "And when it's cooled, we'll funnel it into these. Then we'll sell them to the poultry farmers in the valley down there."

"Why?" said Emil.

"As medicine," Golescu explained. "We'll tell them it'll grow giant chickens, eh? That'll fill the purse of twenty thousand lei back up again in no time. This never fails, believe me. The dye makes the yolks more yellow, and the farmers think that means the eggs are richer. Ha! As long as you move on once you've sold all your bottles, you can pull this one anywhere."

"Medicine," said Emil.

"That's right," said Golescu. He took a final drag on his cigar, tossed it into the fire, and reached for the wine jug.

"What a lovely evening," he said, taking a drink. "What stars, eh? They make a man reflect, indeed they do. At times like this, I look back on my career and ponder the ironies of fate. I was not always a vagabond, you see.

"No, in fact, I had a splendid start in life. Born to a fine aristocratic family, you know. We had a castle. Armorial devices on our stained-glass windows. Servants just to walk the dog. None of that came to me, of course; I was a younger son. But I went to University, graduated with full honors, was brilliant in finance.

"I quickly became Manager of a big important bank in Bucharest. I had a fine gold watch on a chain, and a desk three meters long, and it was kept well polished, too. Every morning when I arrived at the bank, all the clerks would line up and prostrate themselves as I walked by, swinging my cane. My cane had a diamond set in its end, a diamond that shone in glory like the rising sun.

"But they say that abundance, like poverty, wrecks you; and so it was with me. My nature was too trusting, too innocent. Alas, how swiftly my downfall came! Would you like to hear the circumstances that reduced me to the present pitiable state in which you see me?"

"...What?" said Emil. Golescu had another long drink of wine.

"Well," he said, "My bank had a depositor named Ali Pasha. He had amassed a tremendous fortune. Millions. Millions in whatever kind of currency you could imagine. Pearls, rubies, emeralds too. You should have seen it just sitting there in the vault, winking like a dancing girl's...winky parts. Just the biggest fortune a corrupt bureaucrat could put together.

"And then, quite suddenly, he had to go abroad to avoid a scandal. And, bam! He was killed in a tragic accident when his coal-black stallion, startled by a pie wagon, threw him from its back and trampled him under its hooves.

"Being an honest man, I of course began searching for his next of kin, as soon as I heard the news of his demise. And you would think, wouldn't you, that he'd have a next of kin? The way those lustful fellows carry on with all their wives and concubines? But it was revealed that the late Ali Pasha had had an equally tragic accident in his youth, when he'd attracted the attention of the Grand Turk because of his sweet singing voice, and, well...he was enabled to keep that lovely soprano until the time of his completely unexpected death.

"So no wives, no children, a yawning void of interested posterity.

"And this meant, you see, that the millions that lay in our vault would, after the expiration of a certain date, become the property of the Ottoman Empire.

"What could I do? The more I reflected on the tyranny under which our great nation suffered for so long, the more my patriotic blood began to boil. I determined on a daring course of action.

"I consulted with my colleagues in the international banking community, and obtained the name of an investor who was known far and wide for his integrity. He was a Prussian, as it happened, with a handsome personal fortune. I contacted him, apologized for my presumption, explained the facts of the case, and laid before him a proposition. If he were willing to pose as the brother of the late Ali Pasha, I could facilitate his claim to the millions sitting there on deposit. He would receive forty per cent for his part in the ruse; the remaining sixty per cent I would, of course, donate to the Church.

"To make a long story short, he agreed to the plan. Indeed, he went so far as to express his enthusiastic and principled support for Romanian self-rule.

"Of course, it was a complicated matter. We had to bribe the law clerks and several petty officials, in order that they might vouch for Smedlitz (the Prussian) being a long-lost brother of Ali Pasha, his mother having been kidnapped by Barbary Coast pirates with her infant child and sold into a harem, though fortunately there had been a birthmark by which the unfortunate Ali Pasha could be posthumously identified by his sorrowing relation.

"And Smedlitz was obliged to provide a substantial deposit in order to open an account in a bank in Switzerland, into which the funds could be transferred once we had obtained their release. But he agreed to the expenditure readily—too readily, as I ought to have seen!" Golescu shook his head, drank again, wiped his moustache with the back of his hand and continued:

"How I trusted that Prussian! Alas, you stars, look down and see how an honest and credulous soul is victimized."

He drank again and went on:

"The fortune was transferred, and when I went to claim the agreed-upon sixty per cent for charity—imagine my horror on discovering that Smedlitz had withdrawn the entire amount, closed the account, and absconded! As I sought him, it soon became apparent that Smedlitz was more than a thief—he was an impostor, a lackey of the international banking community, who now closed ranks against me.

"To make matters worse, who should step forward but a new claimant! It developed that Ali Pasha had, in fact, a real brother who had only just learned of his death, having been rescued from a remote island where he had been stranded for seven years, a victim of shipwreck.

"My ruin was complete. I was obliged to flee by night, shaming my illustrious family, doomed to the life of an unjustly persecuted fugitive." Golescu wiped tears from his face and had another long drink. "Never again to sit behind a polished desk, like a gentleman! Never again to flourish my walking-stick over the heads of my clerks! And what has become of its diamond, that shone like the moon?" He sobbed for breath. "Adversity makes a man wise, not rich, as the saying goes; and wisdom is all I own now. Sometimes I think of self-destruction; but I have not yet sunk so low."

He drank again, belched, and said, in a completely altered voice:

"Ah, now it's beginning to boil! Fetch a long stick and give it a stir, Emil darling."

Golescu woke in broad daylight, grimacing as he lifted his face from the depths of his hat. Emil was still sitting where he had been when Golescu had drifted off to sleep, after some hours of hazily remembered conversation. The empty jug sat where Golescu had left it; but the hundred and forty-four little glass bottles were now full.

"What'd you..." Golescu sat up, staring at them. He couldn't recall filling the bottles with concentrated yellow dye, but there they were, all tidily sealed.

"The medicine is ready," said Emil.

Golescu rose unsteadily. The empty copper gleamed, clean as though it were new.

"No wonder she keeps you around," he remarked. "You must be part kitchen fairy, eh? Poke up the fire, then, and we'll boil you another potato. Maybe a parsnip too, since you've been such a good boy. And then, we'll have an adventure."

He picked up the sack and trudged off to attend to his toilet.

———— ✦ ————

Two hours later they were making their way slowly along a country lane, heading for a barred gate Golescu had spotted. He was sweating in the heat, dressed in the finest ensemble the rag shop had had to offer: a rusty black swallowtail coat, striped trousers, a black silk hat with a strong odor of corpse. On his left breast he had assembled an impressive-looking array of medals, mostly religious ones dressed up with bits of colored ribbon, and a couple of foil stickers off a packet of Genoa biscuits. In one hand he carried a heavy-looking satchel.

Emil wore his duster, goggles and hat, and was having to be led by the hand because he couldn't see very well.

When they came within a hundred yards of the gate, two immense dogs charged and collided with it, barking at them through the bars.

"Take the bag," said Golescu, handing it off to Emil

"It's heavy," Emil complained.

"Shut up. Good morning to you, my dear sir!" He raised his voice to address the farmer who came out to investigate the commotion.

"I'm too hot."

"Shut up, I said. May I have a moment of your time, sir?"

"Who the hell are you?" asked the farmer, seizing the dogs by their collars.

Golescu tipped his hat and bowed. "Dr. Milon Cretulescu, Assistant Minister of Agriculture to Prince Alexandru, may all the holy saints and angels grant him long life. And you are?"

"Buzdugan, Iuliu," muttered the farmer.

"Charmed. You no doubt have heard of the new edict?"

"Of course I have," said Farmer Buzdugan, looking slightly uneasy. "Which one?"

Golescu smiled at him. "Why, the one about increasing poultry pro-duction on the farms in this region. His highness is very concerned that our nation become one of the foremost chicken-raising centers of the world! Perhaps you ought to chain up your dogs, dear sir."

When the dogs had been confined and the gate unbarred, Golescu strode through, summoning Emil after him with a surreptitious shove as he passed. Emil paced forward blindly, with tiny careful steps, dragging the satchel. Golescu ignored him, putting a friendly hand on Buzdugan's shoulder.

"First, I'll need to inspect your poultry yard. I'm certain you passed the last inspection without any difficulties, but, you know, standards are being raised nowadays."

"To be sure," agreed Buzdugan, sweating slightly. In fact, there had never been any inspection of which he was aware. But he led Golescu back to the bare open poultry yard, an acre fenced around by high palings, visible through a wire-screen grate.

It was not a place that invited lingering. Poultry yards seldom are. The sun beat down on it mercilessly, so that Golescu felt the hard-packed earth burning through the thin soles of his shoes. A hundred chickens stood about listlessly, quite unbothered by the reek of their defecation or the smell of the predators impaled on the higher spikes of the fence: two foxes and something so shrunken and sun-dried its species was impossible to identify.

"*Hmmm,*" said Golescu, and drew from his pocket a small book and a pencil stub. He pretended to make notes, shaking his head.

"What's the matter?" asked Buzdugan.

"Well, I don't want to discourage you too much," said Golescu, looking up with a comradely wink. "Good pest control, I'll say that much for you. Make an example of them, eh? That's the only way foxes will ever learn. But, my friend! How spiritless your birds are! Not exactly fighting cocks, are they? Why aren't they strutting about and crowing? Clearly they are enervated and weak, the victims of diet."

"They get nothing but the best feed!" protested Buzdugan. Smiling, Golescu waved a finger under his nose.

"I'm certain they do, but is that enough? Undernourished fowl produce inferior eggs, which produce feeble offspring. Not only that, vapid and tasteless eggs can ruin your reputation as a first-class market supplier. No, no; inattention to proper poultry nutrition has been your downfall."

"But—"

"Fortunately, I can help you," said Golescu, tucking away the book and pencil stub.

"How much will I have to pay?" asked Buzdugan, sagging.

"Sir! Are you implying that a representative of his highness the prince can be bribed? That may have been how things were done in the past, but we're in a new age, after all! I was referring to Science," Golescu admonished.

"Science?"

"Boy!" Golescu waved peremptorily at Emil, who had just caught up with them. "This loyal subject requires a bottle of Golden Formula Q."

Emil did nothing, so Golescu grabbed the satchel from him. Opening it, he drew forth a bottle of the yellow dye. He held it up, cradling it between his two hands.

"This, dear sir, is a diet supplement produced by the Ministry of Agriculture. Our prince appointed none but university-trained men, ordering them to set their minds to the problem of improving poultry health. Utilizing the latest scientific discoveries, they have created a tonic of amazing efficacy! *Golden Formula Q*. Used regularly, it produces astonishing results."

Buzdugan peered at the bottle. "What does it do?"

"Do? Why, it provides the missing nourishment your birds so desperately crave," said Golescu. "Come, let me give you a demonstration. Have you a platter or dish?"

When a tin pan had been produced, Golescu adroitly let himself into the chicken yard, closely followed by Buzdugan. Within the yard it was, if possible, even hotter. "Now, observe the behavior of your birds, sir," said Golescu, uncorking the bottle and pouring its contents into the pan. "The poor things perceive instantly the restorative nature of Golden Formula Q. They hunger for it! Behold."

He set the pan down on the blistering earth. The nearest chicken to notice turned its head. Within its tiny brain flashed the concept: THIRST. It ran at once to the pan and drank greedily. One by one, other chickens had the same revelation, and came scrambling to partake of lukewarm yellow dye as though it were chilled champagne.

"You see?" said Golescu, shifting from one foot to the other. "Poor starved creatures. Within hours, you will begin to see the difference. No longer will your egg yolks be pallid and unwholesome, but rich and golden! All thanks to Golden Formula Q. Only two marks a bottle."

"They *are* drinking it up," said Buzdugan, watching in some surprise. "I suppose I could try a couple of bottles."

"Ah! Well, my friend, I regret to say that Golden Formula Q is in such limited supply, and in such extreme demand, that I must limit you to one bottle only," said Golescu.

"What? But you've got a whole satchel full," said Buzdugan. "I saw, when you opened it."

"That's true, but we must give your competitors a chance, after all," said Golescu. "It wouldn't be fair if you were the only man in the region with prize-winning birds, would it?"

The farmer looked at him with narrowed eyes. "Two marks a bottle? I'll give you twenty-five marks for the whole satchel full, what do you say to that?"

"Twenty-five marks?" Golescu stepped back, looking shocked. "But what will the other poultry producers do?"

Buzdugan told him what the other poultry producers could do, as he dug a greasy bag of coin from his waistband.

They trudged homeward that evening, having distributed several satchels' worth of Golden Formula Q across the valley. Golescu had a pleasant sense of self-satisfaction and pockets heavy with wildly assorted currency.

"You see, dear little friend?" he said to Emil. "This is the way to make something of yourself. Human nature flows along like a river, never changes; a wise man builds his mill on the banks of that river, lets foibles and vanities drive his wheel. Fear, greed and envy have never failed me."

Emil, panting with exhaustion, made what might have been a noise of agreement.

"Yes, and hasn't it been a red-letter day for you? You've braved the sunlight at last, and it's not so bad, is it? Mind the path," Golescu added, as Emil walked into a tree. He collared Emil and set his feet back on the trail. "Not far now. Yes, Emil, how lucky it was for you that I came into your life. We will continue our journey of discovery tomorrow, will we not?"

And so they did, ranging over to the other side of the valley, where a strong ammoniac breeze suggested the presence of more chicken farms. They had just turned from the road down a short drive, and the furious assault of a mastiff on the carved gate had just drawn the attention of a scowling farmer, when Emil murmured: "Horse."

"No, it's just a big dog," said Golescu, raising his hat to the farmer. "Good morning, dear sir! Allow me to introduce—"

That was when he heard the hoofbeats. He began to sweat, but merely smiled more widely and went on: "—myself. Dr. Milon Cretulescu, of the Ministry of Agriculture, and I—"

The hoofbeats came galloping up the road and past the drive, but just as Golescu's heart had resumed its normal rhythm, they clattered to a halt and started back.

"—have been sent at the express wish of Prince Alexandru himself to—"

"Hey!"

"Excuse me a moment, won't you?" said Golescu, turning to face the road. He beheld Farmer Buzdugan urging his horse forward, under the drooping branches that cast the drive into gloom.

"Dr. Cretulescu!" he said. "Do you have any more of that stuff?"

"I beg your pardon?"

"You know, the—" Buzdugan glanced over at the other farmer, lowered his voice. "That stuff that makes the golden eggs!"

"Ah!" Golescu half-turned, so the other farmer could see him, and raised his voice. "You mean, *Golden Formula Q*? The miracle elixir developed by his highness's own Ministry of Agriculture, to promote better poultry production?"

"Shush! Yes, that! Look, I'll pay—"

"*Golden eggs*, you say?" Golescu cried.

"What's that?" The other farmer leaned over his gate.

"None of your damn business!" said Buzdugan.

"But, dear sir, *Golden Formula Q* was intended to benefit everyone," said Golescu, uncertain just what had happened but determined to play his card. "If this good gentleman wishes to take advantage of its astonishing qualities, I cannot deny him—"

"A hundred marks for what you've got in that bag!" shouted Buzdugan.

"What's he got in the bag?" demanded the other farmer, opening his gate and stepping through.

"Golden Formula Q!" said Golescu, grabbing the satchel from Emil's nerveless hand and opening it. He drew out a bottle and thrust it up into the morning light. "Behold!"

"What was that about golden eggs?" said the other farmer, advancing on them.

"Nothing!" Buzdugan said. "Two hundred, Doctor. I'm not joking. Please."

"The worthy sir was merely indulging in hyperbole," said Golescu to the other farmer. "Golden eggs? Why, I would never make that claim for Golden Formula Q. You would take me for a mountebank! But it is, quite simply, the most amazing dietary supplement for poultry you will ever use."

"Then, I want a bottle," said the other farmer.

Buzdugan gnashed his teeth. "I'll buy the rest," he said, dismounting.

"Not so fast!" said the other farmer. "This must be pretty good medicine, eh? If you want it all to yourself? Maybe I'll just buy two bottles."

"Now, gentlemen, there's no need to quarrel," said Golescu. "I have plenty of Golden Formula Q here. Pray, good Farmer Buzdugan, as a satisfied customer, would you say that you observed instant and spectacular results with Golden Formula Q?"

"Yes," said Buzdugan, with reluctance. "Huge eggs, yellow as gold. And all the roosters who drank it went mad with lust, and this morning all the hens are sitting on clutches like little mountains of gold. Two hundred and fifty for the bag, Doctor, what do you say, now?"

Golescu carried the satchel on the way back to the clearing, for it weighed more than it had when they had set out that morning. Heavy as it was, he walked with an unaccustomed speed, fairly dragging Emil after him. When they got to the wagon, he thrust Emil inside, climbed in himself and closed the door after them. Immediately he began to undress, pausing only to look once into the satchel, as though to reassure himself. The fact that it was filled to the top with bright coin somehow failed to bring a smile to his face.

"What's going on, eh?" he demanded, shrugging out of his swallowtail coat. "I sold that man bottles of yellow dye and water. Not a *real* miracle elixir!"

Emil just stood there, blank behind his goggles, until Golescu leaned over and yanked them off.

"I said, we sold him fake medicine!" he said. "Didn't we?"

Emil blinked at him. "No," he said. "Medicine to make giant chickens."

"No, you silly ass, that's only what we *told* them it was!" said Golescu, pulling off his striped trousers. He wadded them up with the coat and set them aside. "We were lying, don't you understand?"

"No," said Emil.

Something in the toneless tone of his voice made Golescu, in the act of pulling up his plain trousers, freeze. He looked keenly at Emil.

"You don't understand lying?" he said. "Maybe you don't. And you're a horrible genius, aren't you? And I went to sleep while the stuff in the copper was cooking. Hmmm, hm hm." He fastened his trousers and put on his other coat, saying nothing for a long moment, though his gaze never left Emil's slack face.

"Tell me, my pretty child," he said at last. "Did you put other things in the brew, after I was asleep?"

"Yes," said Emil.

"What?"

In reply, Emil began to rattle off a string of names of ingredients, chemicals for the most part, or so Golescu assumed. He held up his hand at last.

"Enough, enough! The nearest chemist's is three hours' walk away. How'd you get all those things?"

"There," said Emil, pointing at the papier-mâché mummy case. "And some I got from the dirt. And some came out of leaves."

Golescu went at once to the mummy case and opened it. It appeared to be empty; but he detected the false bottom. Prizing back the lining he saw rows of compartments, packed with small jars and bags of various substances. A faint scent of spice rose from them.

"Aha," he said, closing it up. He set it aside and looked at Emil with narrowed eyes. He paced back and forth a couple of times, finally sitting down on the bed.

"How did you know," he said, in a voice some decibels below his customary bellow, "what goes into a medicine to make giant chickens?"

Emil looked back at him. Golescu beheld a strange expression in the rabbity eyes. Was that...scorn?

"I just know," said Emil, and there might have been scorn in his flat voice too.

"Like you just know how many beans are in a jar?"

"Yes."

Golescu rubbed his hands together, slowly. "Oh, my golden baby," he said. "Oh, my pearl, my plum, my good-luck token." A thought struck him. "Tell me something, precious," he said. "On several occasions, now, you have mentioned a Black Cup. What would that be, can you tell your Uncle Barbu?"

"I make the Black Cup for her every month," said Emil.

"You do, eh?" said Golescu. "Something to keep the babies away? But no, she's not interested in love. Yet. What happens when she drinks from the Black Cup, darling?"

"She doesn't die," said Emil, with just a trace of sadness.

Golescu leaned back, as though physically pushed. "Holy saints and angels in Heaven," he said. For a long moment ideas buzzed in his head like a hive of excited bees. At last he calmed himself to ask:

"How old is Madame Amaunet?"

"She is old," said Emil.

"Very old?"

"Yes."

"How old are you?"

"I don't know."

"I see." Golescu did not move, staring at Emil. "So that's why she doesn't want any attention drawn to you. You're her philosopher's stone, her source of the water of life. Yes? But if that's the case..." He shivered all over, drew himself up. "No, that's crazy. You've been in show business too long, Golescu. She must be sick with something, that's it, and she takes the medicine to preserve her health. Ugh! Let us hope she doesn't have anything catching. Is she sick, little Emil?"

"No," said Emil.

"No? Well. Golescu, my friend, don't forget that you're having a conversation with an idiot, here."

His imagination raced, though all the while he was tidying away the evidence of the chicken game, and all that afternoon as the slow hours passed. Several times he heard the sound of hoofbeats on the road, someone riding fast—searching, perhaps, for Dr. Cretulescu?

As the first shades of night fell, Golescu crept out and lit a campfire. He was sitting beside it when he heard the approach of a wagon on the road, and a moment later the crashing of branches that meant the wagon had turned off toward the clearing. Golescu composed an expression that he hoped would convey innocence, doglike fidelity and patience, and gave a quick turn to the skillet of bread and sausages he was frying.

"Welcome back, my queen," he called, as he caught sight of Amaunet. "You see? Not only have I not run off with Emil to a gambling den, I've fixed you a nice supper. Come and eat. I'll see to the horses."

Amaunet regarded him warily, but she climbed down from the wagon and approached the fire. "Where is Emil?"

"Why, safe in his little cupboard, just as he ought to be," said Golescu, rising to offer his seat. Seeing her again up close, he felt a shiver of disappointment; Amaunet looked tired and bad-tempered, not at all like an immortal being who had supped of some arcane nectar. He left her by the fire as he led the horses off to drink. Not until he had come back and settled down across from her did he feel the stirring of mundane lust.

"I trust all that unsightly clutter in the wagon has been unloaded on some discreet fence?" he inquired pleasantly.

"That's one way of putting it," said Amaunet, with a humorless laugh. "You'll have all the room you need back there, for a while."

"And did we get a good price?"

Amaunet just shrugged.

Golescu smiled to himself, noting that she carried no purse. He kept up a disarming flow of small talk until Amaunet told him that she was retiring. Bidding her a cheery good night without so much as one suggestive remark, he watched as she climbed into the wagon—her back view was as enthralling as ever—and waited a few more minutes before lighting a candle-lantern and hurrying off to the other wagon.

On climbing inside, Golescu held the lamp high and looked around.

"Beautifully empty," he remarked in satisfaction. Not a carpet, not a painting, not so much as a silver spoon anywhere to be seen. As it should be. But—

"Where is the money?" he wondered aloud. "Come out, little iron-bound strongbox. Come out, little exceptionally heavy purse. She must have made a fortune from the fence. So..."

Golescu proceeded to rummage in the cupboards and cabinets, hastily at first and then with greater care, rapping for hollow panels, testing for hidden drawers. At the end of half an hour he was baffled, panting with exasperation.

"It must be here somewhere!" he declared. "Unless she made so little off the bargain she was able to hide her miserable share of the loot in her cleavage!"

Muttering to himself, he went out and banked the fire. Then he retrieved his satchel of money and the new clothes he had bought, including Emil's daylight ensemble, from the bush where he had stashed them. Having re-secured them in a cupboard in the wagon, he stretched out on the floor and thought very hard.

"I've seen that dull and sullen look before," he announced to the darkness. "Hopeless. Apathetic. Ill-used. She might be sick, but also that's the way a whore looks, when she has a nasty brute of a pimp who works her hard and takes all her earnings away. I wonder...

"Perhaps she's the hapless victim of some big operator? Say, a criminal mastermind, with a network of thieves and fences and middlemen all funneling profits toward him? So that he sits alone on a pyramid of gold, receiving tribute from petty crooks everywhere?

"What a lovely idea!" Golescu sat up and clasped his hands.

He was wakened again that night by her singing. Amaunet's voice was like slow coals glowing in a dying fire, or like the undulation of smoke rising when the last glow has died. It was heartbreaking, but there was something horrible about it.

They rolled on. The mountains were always ahead of them, and to Golescu's relief the valley of his labors was far behind them. No one was ever hanged for selling a weak solution of yellow dye, but people have been hanged for being too successful; and in any case he preferred to keep a good distance between himself and any outcomes he couldn't predict.

The mountains came close at last and were easily crossed, by an obscure road Amaunet seemed to know well. Noon of the second day they came to a fair-sized city in the foothills, with grand houses and a domed church.

Here a fair was setting up, in a wide public square through which the wind gusted, driving yellow leaves before it over the cobbles. Golescu made his usual helpful suggestions for improving Amaunet's business and was ignored. Resigned, he stood in the permit line with other fair vendors, whom he was beginning to know by sight. They also ignored his attempts at small talk. The permit clerk was rude and obtuse.

By the time evening fell, when the fair came to life in a blaze of gaslight and calliope music, Golescu was not in the best of moods.

"Come on, pallid one," he said, dragging Emil forth from the wagon. "What are you shrinking from?"

"It's too bright," whimpered Emil, squeezing his eyes shut and trying to hide under Golescu's coat.

"We're in a big modern city, my boy," said Golescu, striding through the crowd and towing him along relentless. "Gaslight, the wonder of the civilized world. Soon we won't have Night at all, if we don't want it. Imagine that, eh? You'd have to live in a cellar. You'd probably like that, I expect."

"I want a sausage on a stick," said Emil.

"Patience," said Golescu, looking around for the food stalls. "Eating and scratching only want a beginning, eh? So scratch, and soon you'll be eating too. Where the hell is the sausage booth?"

He spotted a vendor he recognized and pushed through the crowd to the counter.

"Hey! Vienna sausage, please." He put down a coin.

"We're out of Vienna sausage," said the cashier. "We have sarmale on polenta, or tochitura on polenta. Take your pick."

Golescu's mouth watered. "The sarmale, and plenty of polenta."

He carried the paper cone to a relatively quiet corner and seated himself on a hay bale. "Come and eat. Emil dear. Polenta for you and nice spicy sarmale for me, eh?"

Emil opened his eyes long enough to look at it.

"I can't eat that. It has sauce on it."

"Just a little!" Golescu dug his thumb in amongst the meatballs and pulled up a glob of polenta. "See? Nice!"

Emil began to sob. "I don't want that. I want a sausage."

"Well, this is like sausage, only it's in grape leaves instead of pig guts, eh?" Golescu held up a nugget of sarmale. "Mmmm, tasty!"

But Emil wouldn't touch it. Golescu sighed, wolfed down the sarmale and polenta, and wiped his fingers on Emil's coat. He dragged Emil after him and searched the fairground from end to end, but nobody was selling Vienna sausage. The only thing he found that Emil would consent to eat was candy floss, so he bought him five big wads of it. Emil crouched furtively under a wagon and ate it all, as Golescu looked on and tried to slap some warmth into himself. The cold wind pierced straight through his coat, taking away all the nice residual warmth of the peppery sarmale.

"This is no life for a red-blooded man," he grumbled. "Wine, women and dance are what I need, and am I getting any? It is to laugh. Wet-nursing a miserable picky dwarf while the temptress of my dreams barely knows I exist. If I had any self-respect, I'd burst into that wagon and show her what I'm made of."

The last pink streamer of candy floss vanished into Emil's mouth. He belched.

"Then, of course, she'd hurt me," Golescu concluded. "Pretty badly, I think. Her fingers are like steel. And that excites me, Emil, isn't that a terrible thing? Yet another step downward in my long debasement."

Emil belched again.

The chilly hours passed. Emil rolled over on his side and began to wail to himself. As the fair grew quieter, as the lights went out one by one and the carousel slowed through its last revolution, Emil's whining grew louder. Amaunet's last customer departed; a moment later her door flew open and she emerged, turning her head this way and that, searching for the sound. Her gaze fell on Emil, prostrate under the wagon, and she bared her teeth at Golescu.

"What did you do to him?"

"Nothing!" said Golescu, backing up a pace or two. "His highness the turnip wouldn't eat anything but candy, and now he seems to be regretting it."

"Fool," said Amaunet. She pulled Emil out from the litter of paper cones and straw. He vomited pink syrup, and said, "I want a potato."

Amaunet gave Golescu a look that made his heart skip a beat, but in a reasonable voice he said: "I could take us all to dinner. What about it? My treat."

"It's nearly midnight, you ass," said Amaunet.

"That café is still open," said Golescu, pointing to a garishly lit place at the edge of the square. Amaunet stared at it. Finally she shrugged. "Bring him," she said.

Golescu picked up Emil by the scruff of his neck and stood him on his feet. "Your potato is calling, fastidious one. Let us answer it." Emil took his hand and they trudged off together across the square, with Amaunet slinking after.

They got a table by the door. For all that the hour was late, the café was densely crowded with people in evening dress, quite glittering and cosmopolitan in appearance. The air was full of their chatter, oddly echoing, with a shrill metallic quality. Amaunet gave the crowd one surly look, and paid them no attention thereafter. But she took off her black shawl and dropped it over Emil's head. He sat like an unprotesting ghost, shrouded in black, apparently quite content.

"And you're veiling him because...?" said Golescu.

"Better if he isn't seen," said Amaunet.

"What may we get for the little family?" inquired a waiter, appearing at Golescu's elbow with a speed and silence that suggested he had popped up through a trap door. Golescu started in his chair, unnerved. The waiter had wide glass-bright eyes, and a fixed smile under a straight bar of moustache like a strip of black fur.

"Are you still serving food?" Golescu asked. The waiter's smile never faltered; he produced a menu from thin air and presented it with a flourish.

"Your *carte de nuit*. We particularly recommend the black puddings. Something to drink?"

"Bring us the best you have," said Golescu grandly. The waiter bowed and vanished again.

"It says the Czernina Soup is divine," announced Golescu, reading from the menu. "Hey, he thought we were a family. Charming, eh? You're Mother Aegypt and I'm..."

"The Father of Lies," said Amaunet, yawning.

"I shall take that as a compliment," said Golescu. "Fancy French cuisine here, too: *Boudin Noir*. And, for the hearty diner, *Blutwurst*. So, who do you think will recognize our tiny prodigy, Madame? He wouldn't happen to be a royal heir you stole in infancy, would he?"

Amaunet gave him a sharp look. Golescu sat up, startled.

"You can't be serious!" he said. "Heaven knows, he's inbred enough to have the very bluest blood—"

The waiter materialized beside them, deftly uncorking a dusty bottle. "This is very old wine," he said, displaying the label.

"'Egri Bikaver,'" read Golescu. "Yes, all right. Have you got any Vienna sausage? We have a little prince here who'll hardly eat anything else."

"I want a potato." Emil's voice floated from beneath the black drape.

"We will see what can be done," said the waiter, unblinking, but his smile widened under his dreadful moustache. "And for Madame?"

Amaunet said something in a language with which Golescu was unfamiliar. The waiter chuckled, a disturbing sound, and jotted briefly on a notepad that appeared from nowhere in particular. "Very wise. And for Sir?"

"Blutwurst. I'm a hearty diner," said Golescu.

"To be sure," said the waiter, and vanished. Golescu leaned forward and hissed, "Hey, you can't mean you actually stole him from some—"

"Look, it's a gypsy!" cried a young woman, one of a pair of young lovers out for a late stroll. Her young man leaned in from the sidewalk and demanded, "What's our fortune, eh, gypsy? Will we love each other the rest of our lives?"

"You'll be dead in three days," said Amaunet. The girl squeaked, the boy went pale and muttered a curse. They fled into the night.

"What did you go and tell them that for?" demanded Golescu. Amaunet shrugged and poured herself a glass of wine.

"Why should I lie? Three days, three hours, three decades. Death always comes, for them. It's what I tell them all. Why not?"

"No wonder you don't do better business!" said Golescu. "You're supposed to tell them *good* fortunes!"

"Why should I lie?" repeated Amaunet.

Baffled, Golescu pulled at his moustaches. "What makes you say such things?" he said at last. "Why do you pretend to feel nothing? But you love little Emil, eh?"

She looked at him in flat astonishment. Then she smiled. It was a poisonous smile.

"Love *Emil?*" she said. "Who could love that thing? I could as soon love you."

As though to underscore her contempt, a woman at the bar shrieked with laughter.

Golescu turned his face away. Immediately he set about soothing his lacerated ego, revising what she'd said, changing her expression and intonation, and he had nearly rewritten the scene into an almost-declaration of tender feeling for himself when the waiter reappeared, bearing a tray.

"See what we have for the little man?" he said, whisking the cover off a dish. "Viennese on a stake!"

The dish held an artful arrangement of Vienna sausages on wooden skewers, stuck upright in a mound of mashed potato.

"Well, isn't that cute?" said Golescu. "Thank the nice man, Emil."

Emil said nothing, but reached for the plate. "He says Thank You," said Golescu, as smacking noises came from under the veil. The waiter set before Amaunet a dish containing skewered animal parts, flame-blackened to anonymity.

"Madame. And for Sir," said the waiter, setting a platter before Golescu. Golescu blinked and shuddered; for a moment he had the strongest conviction that the Blutwurst was pulsing and shivering, on its bed of grilled onions and eggplant that seethed like maggots. Resolutely, he told himself it was a trick of the greenish light and the late hour.

"Be sure to save room for cake," said the waiter.

"You'll be dead in three days, too," Amaunet told the waiter. The waiter laughed heartily.

They journeyed on to the next crossroads fair. Two days out they came to the outskirts of another town, where Amaunet pulled off the road onto waste ground. Drawing a small purse from her bosom, she handed it to Golescu.

"Go and buy groceries," she said. "We'll wait here."

Golescu scowled at the pouch, clinked it beside his ear. "Not a lot of money," he said. "But never mind, dearest. You have a man to provide for you now, you know."

"Get potatoes," Amaunet told him.

"Of course, my jewel," he replied, smiling as he climbed down. He went dutifully off to the main street.

"She is not heartless," he told himself. "She just needs to be wooed, that's all. Who can ever have been kind to her? It's time to drop the bucket into your well of charm, Golescu."

The first thing he did was look for a bathhouse. Having located one and paid the morose Turk at the door, he went in, disrobed, and submitted to being plunged, steamed, scraped, pummeled, and finally shaved. He declined the offer of orange flower water, however, preferring to retain a certain manly musk, and merely asked to be directed to the market square.

When he left it, an hour later, he was indeed carrying a sack of potatoes. He had also onions, flour, oil, sausages, a bottle of champagne, a box of Austrian chocolates, and a bouquet of asters.

He had the satisfaction of seeing Amaunet's eyes widen as he approached her.

"What's this?" she asked.

"For you," he said, thrusting the flowers into her arms. Golescu had never seen her taken aback before. She held them out in a gingerly sort of way, with a queer look of embarrassment.

"What am I supposed to do with these?" she said.

"Put them in water?" he said, grinning at her as he hefted his other purchases.

That night, when they had made their camp in a clearing less cob-
webbed and haunted than usual, when the white trail of stars made its
way down the sky, Golescu went into the wagon to retrieve his treats.
The asters had drooped to death, despite having been crammed in a
jar of water; but the champagne and chocolates had survived being at
the bottom of his sack. Humming to himself, he carried them, together
with a pair of chipped enamel mugs, out to the fireside.

Amaunet was gazing into the flames, apparently lost in gloomy
reverie. She ignored the popping of the champagne cork, though
Emil, beside her, twitched and started. When Golescu opened the
chocolates, however, she looked sharply round.

"Where did you get that?" she demanded.

"A little fairy brought it, flying on golden wings," said Golescu. "Out
of his purse of twenty thousand lei, I might add, so don't scowl at me
like that. Will you have a sweetmeat, my queen? A cherry cream? A bit
of enrobed ginger peel?"

Amaunet stared fixedly at the box a long moment, and then reached
for it. "What harm can it do?" she said, in a quiet voice. "Why not?"

"That's the spirit," said Golescu, pouring the champagne. "A little
pleasure now and again is good for you, wouldn't you agree? Especially
when one has the money."

Amaunet didn't answer, busy with prizing open the box. When he
handed her a mug full of champagne, she took it without looking up;
drained it as though it were so much water, and handed it back.

"Well quaffed!" said Golescu, as a tiny flutter of hope woke in his
flesh. He poured Amaunet another. She meanwhile had got the box
open at last, and bowed her head over the chocolates, breathing in
their scent as though they were the perfumes of Arabia.

"Oh," she groaned, and groped in the box. Bringing out three
chocolate creams, she held them up a moment in dim-eyed contem-

plation; then closed her fist on them, crushing them as though they were grapes. Closing her eyes, she licked the sweet mess from her hand, slowly, making ecstatic sounds.

Golescu stared, and in his inattention poured champagne in his lap. Amaunet did not notice.

"I had no idea you liked chocolates so much," said Golescu.

"Why should you?" said Amaunet through a full mouth. She lifted the box and inhaled again, then dipped in with her tongue and scooped a nut cluster straight out of its little paper cup.

"Good point," said Golescu. He edged a little closer on the fallen log that was their mutual seat, and offered her the champagne once more. She didn't seem to notice, absorbed as she was in crunching nuts. "Come, drink up; this stuff won't keep. Like youth and dreams, eh?"

To his astonishment, Amaunet threw back her head and laughed. It was not the dry and humorless syllable that had previously expressed her scorn. It was full-throated, rolling, deep, and so frightful a noise that Emil shrieked and put his hands over his head, and even the fire seemed to shrink down and cower. It echoed in the night forest, which suddenly was darker, more full of menace.

Golescu's heart beat faster. When Amaunet seized the mug from him and gulped down its contents once more, he moistened his lips and ventured to say:

"Just let all those cares wash away in the sparkling tide, eh? Let's be good to each other, dear lady. You need a man to lessen the burden on those poor frail shoulders. Golescu is here!"

That provoked another burst of laughter from Amaunet, ending in a growl as she threw down the mug, grabbed another handful of chocolates from the box and crammed them into her mouth, paper cups and all.

Scarcely able to believe his luck (*one drink and she's a shameless bacchante!*) Golescu edged his bottom a little closer to Amaunet's. "Come," he said, breathing heavily, "tell me about yourself, my Nile lily."

Amaunet just chuckled, looking at him sidelong as she munched chocolates. Her eyes had taken on a queer glow, more reflective of the flames perhaps than they had been. It terrified Golescu, and yet...

At last she swallowed, took the champagne bottle from his hand and had a drink.

"Hah!" She spat into the fire, which blazed up. "You want to hear my story? Listen, then, fat man."

"A thousand thousand years ago, there was a narrow green land by a river. At our backs was the desert, full of jackals and demons. But the man and the woman always told me that if I stayed inside at night, like a good little girl, nothing could hurt me. And if I was a very good little girl always, I would never die. I'd go down to the river, and a man would come in a reed boat and take me away to the Sun, and I'd live forever.

"One day, the Lean People came out of the desert. They had starved in the desert so long, they thought that was what the gods *meant* for people to do. So, when they saw our green fields, they said we were Abomination. They rode in and killed as many as they could. We were stronger people and we killed them all, threw their bodies in the river—no boats came for *them!* And that was when I looked on Him, and was afraid."

"Who was He, precious?" said Golescu.

"Death," said Amaunet, as the firelight played on her face. "The great Lord with long rows of ivory teeth. His scales shone under the moon. He walked without a shadow. I had never seen any boat taking good children to Heaven; but I saw His power. So I took clay from the riverbank and I made a little Death, and I worshipped it, and fed it with mice, with birds, anything I could catch and kill. *Take all these*, I said, *and not me; for You are very great.*

"Next season, more riders came out of the desert. More war, more food for Him, and I knew He truly ruled the world.

"Our people said: *We can't stay here. Not safe to farm these fields.* And many gave up and walked north. But the man and woman waited too long. They tried to take everything we owned, every bowl and dish in our house, and the woman found my little image of Him. She beat me and said I was wicked. She broke the image.

"And He punished her for it. As we ran along the path by the river, no Sun Lord came to our aid; only the desert people, and they rode down the man and the woman.

"I didn't help them. I ran, and ran beside the river, and I prayed for Him to save me." Amaunet's voice had dropped to a whisper. She sounded young, nearly human.

Golescu was disconcerted. It wasn't at all the mysterious past he had imagined for her; only sad. Some miserable tribal struggle, in some backwater village somewhere? No dusky princess, exiled daughter of pharaohs. Only a refugee, like any one of the hatchet-faced women he had seen along the roads, pushing barrows full of what they could salvage from the ashes of war.

"But at least, this was in Egypt, yes? How did you escape?" Golescu inquired, venturing to put his arm around her. His voice seemed to break some kind of spell; Amaunet turned to look at him, and smiled with all her teeth in black amusement. The smile made Golescu feel small and vulnerable.

"Why, a bright boat came up the river," she said. "There was the Sun Lord, putting out his hand to take me to safety. He didn't come for the man and woman, who had been good; He came for *me*, who had never believed in him. So I knew the world was all lies, even as I went with him and listened to his stories about how wonderful Heaven would be.

"And it turned out that I was right to suspect the Sun, fat man. The price I paid for eternal life was to become a slave in Heaven. For my cowardice in running from Death, they punished me by letting the sacred asps bite me. I was bitten every day, and by the end of fifteen years, I was so full of poison that nothing could ever hurt me. And by the end of a thousand years, I was so weary of my slavery that I prayed to Him again.

"I went out beside the river, under the light of the moon, and I tore my clothes and bared my breasts for Him, knelt down and begged Him to come for me. I wailed and pressed my lips to the mud. How I longed for His ivory teeth!

"But He will not come for me.

"And the Sun Lord has set me to traveling the world, doing business with thieves and murderers, telling foolish mortals their fortunes." Amaunet had another drink of champagne. "Because the Sun, as it turns out, is actually the Devil. He hasn't got horns or a tail, oh, no; he looks like a handsome priest. But he's the master of all lies.

"And I am so tired, fat man, so tired of working for him. Nothing matters; nothing changes. The sun rises each day, and I open my eyes and hate the sun for rising, and hate the wheels that turn and the beasts that pull me on my way. And Him I hate most of all, who takes the whole world but withholds His embrace from me."

She fell silent, looking beyond the fire into the night.

Golescu took a moment to register that her story was at an end, being still preoccupied with the mental image of Amaunet running bare-breasted beside the Nile. But he shook himself, now, and gathered his wits; filed the whole story under *Elaborate Metaphor* and sought to get back to business in the real world.

"About this Devil, my sweet," he said, as she crammed another fistful of chocolates into her mouth. "and these thieves and murderers. The ones who bring you all the stolen goods. You take their loot to the Devil?"

Amaunet didn't answer, chewing mechanically, watching the flames.

"What would happen if you didn't take the loot to him?" Golescu persisted. "Suppose you just took it somewhere and sold it yourself?"

"Why should I do that?" said Amaunet.

"So as to be rich!" said Golescu, beginning to regret that he'd gotten her so intoxicated. "So as not to live in wretchedness and misery!"

Amaunet laughed again, with a noise like ice splintering.

"Money won't change that," she said. "For me or you!"

"Where's he live, this metaphorical Devil of yours?" said Golescu. "Bucharest? Kronstadt? I could talk to him on your behalf, eh? Threaten him slightly? Renegotiate your contract? I'm good at that, my darling. Why don't I talk to him, man to man?"

That sent her into such gales of ugly laughter she dropped the chocolate box.

"Or, what about getting some real use out of dear Emil?" said Golescu. "What about a mentalist act? And perhaps we could do a sideline in love philtres, cures for baldness. A little bird tells me we could make our fortunes," he added craftily.

Amaunet's laugh stopped. Her lip curled back from her teeth.

"I told you," she said, "No. Emil's a secret."

"And from whom are we hiding him, madame?" Golescu inquired.

Amaunet just shook her head. She groped in the dust, found the chocolate box and picked out the last few cordials.

"*He'd* find out," she murmured, as though to herself. "And then he'd take him away from me. Not fair. *I* found him. Pompous fool; looking under hills. Waiting by fairy rings. As though the folk tales were real! When all along, he should have been looking in the lunatic asylums. The ward keeper said: here, madame, we have a little genius who thinks he's a *vampyr*. And I saw him and I knew, the big eyes, the big head, I knew what blood ran in his veins. Aegeus's holy grail, but *I* found one. Why should I give him up? If anybody could find a way, he could..."

More damned metaphors, thought Golescu. "Who's Aegeus?" he asked. "Is that the Devil's real name?"

"Ha! He wishes he were. The lesser of two devils..." Amaunet's voice trailed away into nonsense sounds. Or were they? Golescu, listening, made out syllables that slid and hissed, the pattern of words.

If I wait any longer, she'll pass out, he realized.

"Come, my sweet, the hour is late," he said, in the most seductive voice he could summon. "Why don't we go to bed?" He reached out to pull her close, fumbling for a way through her clothes.

Abruptly he was lying flat on his back, staring up at an apparition.

Eyes and teeth of flame, a black shadow like cloak or wings, claws raised to strike. He heard a high-pitched shriek before the blow came, and sparks flew up out of velvet blackness.

Golescu opened his eyes to the gloom before dawn, a neutral blue from which the stars had already fled. He sat up, squinting in pain. He was soaked with dew, his head pounded, and he couldn't seem to focus his eyes.

Beside him, a thin plume of smoke streamed upward from the ashes of the fire. Across the firepit, Emil still sat where he had been the night before. He was watching the east with an expression of dread, whimpering faintly.

"God and all His little angels," groaned Golescu, touching the lump on his forehead. "What happened last night, eh?"

Emil did not respond. Golescu sorted muzzily through his memory, which (given his concussion) was not at its best. He thought that the attempt at seduction had been going rather well. The goose egg above his eyes was clear indication *something* hadn't gone as planned, and yet...

Emil began to weep, wringing his hands.

"What the hell's the matter with you, anyway?" said Golescu, rolling over to get to his hands and knees.

"The sun," said Emil, not taking his eyes from the glow on the horizon.

"And you haven't got your shade-suit on, have you?" Golescu retorted, rising ponderously to his feet. He grimaced and clutched at his head. "Tell me, petite undead creature, was I so fortunate as to get laid last night? Any idea where black madame has gotten to?"

Emil just sobbed and covered his eyes.

"Oh, all right, let's get you back in your cozy warm coffin," said Golescu, brushing dust from his clothing. "Come on!"

Emil scuttled to his side. He opened the wagon door and Emil vaulted in, vanishing into the cupboard under Amaunet's bed. Emil pulled the cupboard door shut after himself with a bang. A bundle of rags on the bed stirred. Amaunet sat bolt upright, staring at Golescu.

Their eyes met. *She doesn't know what happened either!* thought Golescu, with such a rush of glee, his brain throbbed like a heart.

"If you please, madame," he said, just a shade reproachfully, "I was only putting poor Emil to bed. You left him out all night."

He reached up to doff his hat, but it wasn't on his head.

"Get out," said Amaunet.

"At once, madame," said Golescu, and backed away with all the dignity he could muster. He closed the door, spotting his hat in a thorn bush all of ten feet away from where he had been lying.

"What a time we must have had," he said to himself, beginning to grin. "Barbu, you seductive devil!"

And though his head felt as though it were splitting, he smiled to himself all the while he gathered wood and rebuilt the fire.

On the feast days of certain saints and at crossroad harvest fairs, they lined up their black wagons beside the brightly painted ones. Amaunet told fortunes. The rear wagon began to fill once more with stolen things, so that Golescu slept on rolls of carpet and tapestry, and holy saints gazed down from their painted panels to watch him sleep. They looked horrified.

Amaunet did not speak of that night by the fire. Still, Golescu fancied there was a change in her demeanor toward him, which fueled his self-esteem: an oddly unsettled look in her eyes, a hesitance, what in anybody less dour would have been *embarrassment*.

"She's dreaming of me," he told Emil one night, as he poked the fire. "What do you want to bet? She desires me, and yet her pride won't let her yield."

Emil said nothing, vacantly watching the water boil for his evening potato.

Amaunet emerged from the wagon. She approached Golescu and thrust a scrap of paper at him.

"We'll get to Kronstadt tomorrow," she said. "You'll go in. Buy what's on this list."

"Where am I to find this stuff?" Golescu complained, reading the list. "An alchemist's? I don't know what half of it is. Except for..." He looked up at her, trying not to smile. "Chocolate, eh? What'll you have, cream bonbons? Caramels? Nuts?"

"No," said Amaunet, turning her back. "I want a brick of the pure stuff. See if you can get a confectioner to sell you some of his stock."

"Heh heh heh," said Golescu meaningfully, but she ignored him.

Though Kronstadt was a big town, bursting its medieval walls, it took Golescu three trips, to three separate chemists' shops, to obtain all the items on the list but the chocolate. It took him the best part of an hour to get the chocolate, too, using all his guile and patience to convince the confectioner's assistant to sell him a block of raw material.

"You'd have thought I was trying to buy state secrets," Golescu said to himself, trudging away with a scant half-pound block wrapped in waxed paper. "Pfui! Such drudge work, Golescu, is a waste of your talents. What are you, a mere donkey to send on errands?"

And when he returned to the camp outside town, he got nothing like the welcome he felt he deserved. Amaunet seized the carry-sack from him and went through it hurriedly, as he stood before her with aching feet. She pulled out the block of chocolate and stared at it. She trembled slightly, her nostrils flared. Golescu thought it made her look uncommonly like a horse.

"I don't suppose you've cooked any supper for me?" he inquired.

Amaunet started, and turned to him as though he had just asked for a roasted baby in caper sauce.

"No! Go back into Kronstadt. Buy yourself something at a tavern. In fact, take a room. I don't want to see you back here for two days, understand? Come back at dawn on the third day."

"I see," said Golescu, affronted. "In that case I'll just go collect my purse and an overnight bag, shall I? Not that I don't trust you, of course."

Amaunet's reply was to turn her back and vanish into the wagon, bearing the sack clutched to her bosom.

Carrying his satchel, Golescu cheered up a little as he walked away. Cash, a change of clothes, and no authorities in pursuit!

He was not especially concerned that Amaunet would use his absence to move on. The people of the road had a limited number of places they could ply their diverse trades, and he had been one of their number long enough to know the network of market fairs and circuses that made up their itinerary. He had only to follow the route of the vardas, and sooner or later he must find Amaunet again. Unless, of course, she left the road and settled down; then she would be harder to locate than an egg in a snowstorm. Or an ink bottle in a coal cellar. Or...he amused himself for at least a mile composing unlikely similes.

Having returned to Kronstadt just as dusk fell, Golescu paused outside a low, dark door. There was no sign to tell him a tavern lay within, but the fume of wine and brandy breathing out spoke eloquently to him. He went in, ducking his head, and as soon as his eyes had adjusted to the dark he made out the bar, the barrels, the tables in dark corners he had expected to see.

"A glass of schnapps, please," he said to the sad-faced publican. There were silent drinkers at the tables, some watching him with a certain amount of suspicion, some ignoring him. One or two appeared to be dead, collapsed over their drinks. Only a pair of cattle-herders standing near the bar were engaged in conversation. Golescu smiled cheerily at one and all, slapped down his coin, and withdrew with his glass to an empty table.

"...Hunting for him everywhere," one of the drovers was saying. "He was selling this stuff that was supposed to make chickens lay better eggs."

"Has anybody been killed?" said the other drover.

"I didn't hear enough to know, but they managed to shoot most of them—"

Golescu, quietly as he could, half-rose and turned his chair so he was facing away from the bar. Raising his glass to his lips, he looked over its rim and met the eyes of someone propped in a dark corner.

"To your very good health," he said, and drank.

"What's that you've got in the satchel?" said the person in the corner.

"Please, sir, my mummy sent me to the market to buy bread," said Golescu, smirking. The stranger arose and came near. Golescu drew back involuntarily. The stranger ignored his reaction and sat down at Golescu's table.

He was an old man in rusty black, thin to gauntness, his shabby coat buttoned high and tight. He was bald, with drawn and waxen features, and he smelled a bit; but the stare of his eyes was intimidating. They shone like pearls, milky as though he were blind.

"You travel with Mother Aegypt, eh?" said the old man.

"And who would that be?" inquired Golescu, setting his drink down. The old man looked scornful.

"I know her," he said. "Madame Amaunet. I travel, too. I saw you at the market fair in Arges, loafing outside her wagon. You do the talking for her, don't you, and run her errands? I've been following you."

"You must have me confused with some other handsome fellow," said Golescu.

"Pfft." The old man waved his hand dismissively. "I used to work for her, too. She's never without a slave to do her bidding."

"Friend, I don't do anyone's bidding," said Golescu, but he felt a curious pang of jealousy. "And she's only a poor weak woman, isn't she?"

The old man laughed. He creaked when he laughed.

"Tell me, is she still collecting trash for the Devil?"

"What Devil is that?" said Golescu, leaning back and trying to look amused.

"Her master. I saw him, once." The old man reached up absently and swatted a fly that had landed on his cheek. "Soldiers had looted a mosque, they stole a big golden lamp. She paid them cash for it. It wasn't so heavy, but it was, you know, awkward. And when we drove up to the Teufelberg to unload all the goods, she made me help her bring out the lamp, so as not to break off the fancy work. I saw him there, the Devil. Waiting beside his long wagons. He looked like a prosperous Saxon."

"Sorry, my friend, I don't know what you're talking about," said Golescu. He drew a deep breath and plunged on: "Though I *have* heard of a lord of thieves who is, perhaps, known in certain circles as the Devil. Am I correct? Just the sort of powerful fellow who has but to pull a string and corrupt officials rush to do his bidding? And he accumulates riches without lifting a finger?"

The old man creaked again.

"You think you've figured it out," he said. "And you think he has a place for a fast-talking fellow in his gang, don't you?"

Taken aback, Golescu just stared at him. He raised his drink again.

"Mind reader, are you?"

"I was a fool, too," said the old man, smacking the table for emphasis, though his hand made no more sound than an empty glove. "Thought I'd make a fortune. Use her to work my way up the ladder. I hadn't the slightest idea what she really was."

"What is she, grandfather?" said Golescu, winking broadly at the publican. The publican shuddered and looked away. The old man, ignoring or not noticing, leaned forward and said in a lowered voice:

"There are *stregoi* who walk this world. You don't believe it, you laugh, but it's true. They aren't interested in your soul. They crave beautiful things. Whenever there is a war, they hover around its edges like flies, stealing what they can when the armies loot. If a house is going to catch fire and burn to the ground, they know; you can see them lurking in the street beforehand, and how their eyes gleam! They're only waiting for night, when they can slip in and take away paintings, carvings, books, whatever is choice and rare, before the flames come. Sometimes they take children, too.

"*She's* one of them. But she's tired, she's lazy. She buys from thieves, instead of doing the work herself. The Devil doesn't care. He just takes what she brings him. Back she goes on her rounds, then, from fair to fair, and even the murderers cross themselves when her shadow falls on them, but still they bring her pretty things. Isn't it so?"

"What do you want, grandfather?" said Golescu.

"I want her secret," said the old man. "I'll tell you about it, and then you can steal it and bring it back here, and we'll share. How would you like eternal youth, eh?"

"I'd love it," said Golescu patiently. "But there's no such thing."

"Then you don't know Mother Aegypt very well!" said the old man, grinning like a skull. "I used to watch through the door when she'd mix her Black Cup. Does she still have the little mummy case, with the powders inside?"

"Yes," said Golescu, startled into truthfulness.

"That's how she does it!" said the old man. "She'd put in a little of this— little of that—she'd grind the powders together, and though I watched for years I could never see all that went in the cup, or what the right amounts were. Spirits of wine, yes, and some strange things— arsenic, and paint! And she'd drink it down, and weep, and scream as though she was dying. But instead, she'd live. My time slipped away, peering through that door, watching her live. I could have run away from her many times, but I stayed, I wasted my life, because I thought I could learn her secrets.

"And one night she caught me watching her, and she cursed me. I ran away. I hid for years. She's forgotten me, now. But when I saw her at Arges, and you with her, I thought—he can help me.

"So! You find out what's in that Black Cup of hers, and bring it back to me. I'll share it with you. We'll live forever and become rich as kings."

"Will I betray the woman I love?" said Golescu. "And I should believe such a story, because—?"

The old man, who had worked himself into a dry trembling passion, took a moment to register what Golescu had said. He looked at him with contempt.

"Love? *Mother Aegypt*? I see I have been wasting my breath on an idiot."

The old man rose to his feet. Golescu put out a conciliatory hand. "Now, now, grandfather, I didn't say I didn't believe you, but you'll have to admit that's quite a story. Where's your proof?"

"Up your ass," said the old man, sidling away from the table.

"How long were you with her?" said Golescu, half rising to follow him.

"She bought me from the orphan asylum in Timisoara," said the old man, turning with a baleful smile. "I was ten years old."

Golescu sat down abruptly, staring as the old man scuttled out into the night.

After a moment's rapid thought, he gulped the rest of his schnapps and rose to follow. When he got out into the street, he stared in both directions. A round moon had just lifted above the housetops, and by its light the streets were as visible as by day, though the shadows were black and fathomless. Somewhere, far off, a dog howled. At least, it sounded like a dog. There was no sign of the old man, as far as Golescu could see.

Golescu shivered, and went in search of a cheap hotel.

Cheapness notwithstanding, it gave Golescu a pleasant sense of status to sleep once again in a bed. Lingering over coffee and sweet rolls the next morning, he pretended he was a millionaire on holiday. It had long been his habit not to dwell on life's mysteries, even fairly big and ugly ones, and in broad daylight he found it easy to dismiss the old man as a raving lunatic. Amaunet clearly had a bad reputation amongst the people of the road, but why should he care?

He went forth from the hotel jingling coins in his pocket, and walked the streets of Kronstadt as though he owned it.

In the Council Square his attention was drawn by a platform that had been set up, crowded with racks, boxes and bins of the most unlikely looking objects. Some twenty citizens were pawing through them in a leisurely way. Several armed policemen stood guard over the lot, and over two miserable wretches in manacles.

Catching the not-unpleasant scent of somebody else's disaster, Golescu hurried to investigate.

"Am I correct in assuming this is a debtors' sale, sir?" he asked a police sergeant.

"That's right," said the sergeant. "A traveling opera company. These two bankrupts are the former managers. Isn't that so?" He prodded one of them with his stick.

"Unfortunately so," agreed the other gloomily. "Please go in, sir, and see if anything catches your fancy. Reduce our debt and be warned by our example. Remember, the Devil has a stake in Hell especially reserved for defaulting treasurers of touring companies."

"I weep for you," said Golescu, and stepped up on the platform with an eager expression.

The first thing he saw was a rack of costumes, bright with tinsel and marabou. He spent several minutes searching for anything elegant that might fit him, but the only ensemble in his size was a doublet and pair of trunk hose made of red velvet. Scowling, he pulled them out, and noticed the pointy-toed shoes of red leather, tied to the hanger by their laces. Here was a tag, on which was scrawled FAUST 1-2.

"The Devil, eh?" said Golescu. His eyes brightened as an idea began to come to him. He draped the red suit over his arm and looked further. This production of *Faust* had apparently employed a cast of lesser demons; there were three or four child-sized ensembles in black, leotards, tights and eared hoods. Golescu helped himself to the one least moth eaten.

In a bin he located the red tights and skullcap that went with the Mephistopheles costume. Groping through less savory articles and papier-mâché masks, he found a lyre strung with yarn. He added it to his pile. Finally, he spotted a stage coffin, propped on its side between two flats of scenery. Giggling to himself, he pulled it out, loaded his purchases into it, and shoved the whole thing across the platform to the cashier.

"I'll take these, dear sir," he said.

By the time Golescu had carried the coffin back to his hotel room, whistling a cheery tune as he went, the Act had begun to glow in his mind. He laid out his several purchases and studied them. He tried on the Mephistopheles costume (it fit admirably, except for the pointy shoes, which were a little tight) and preened before the room's one shaving mirror, though he had to back all the way to the far wall to be able to see his full length in it.

"She can't object to this," he said aloud. "Such splendor! Such classical erudition! Why, it would play in Vienna! And even if she does object...you can persuade her, Golescu, you handsome fellow."

Pleased with himself, he ordered extravagantly when he went down to dinner. Over cucumber salad, flekken and wine he composed speeches of such elegance that he was misty-eyed by the bottom of the second bottle. He rose at last, somewhat unsteady, and floated up the stairs from the dining room just as a party of men came in through the street door.

"In here! Sit down, poor fellow, you need a glass of brandy. Has the bleeding stopped?"

"Almost. Careful of my leg!"

"Did you kill them both?"

"We got one for certain. Three silver bullets, it took! The head's in the back of the wagon. You should have seen..."

Golescu heard no more, rounding the first turn of the stair at that point, and too intent on visions of the Act to pay attention in any case.

So confident was Golescu in his dream that he visited a printer's next day, and commissioned a stack of handbills. The results, cranked out while he loafed in a tavern across the street in the company of a bottle of slivovitz, were not as impressive as he'd hoped; but they were decorated with a great many exclamation points, and that cheered him.

The Act was all complete in his head by the time he left Kronstadt, just before dawn on the third day. Yawning mightily, he set down the coffin and his bag and pulled out his purse to settle with the tavern keeper.

"And a gratuity for your staff, kind sir," said Golescu, tossing down a handful of mixed brass and copper in small denominations. "The service was superb."

"May all the holy saints pray for you," said the tavern keeper, without enthusiasm. "Any forwarding address in case of messages?"

"Why, yes; if my friend the Archduke stops in, let him know that I've gone on to Paris," said Golescu. "I'm in show business, you know."

"In that case, may I hire a carriage for you?" inquired the tavern keeper. "One with golden wheels, perhaps?"

"I think not," Golescu replied. "I'm just walking on to Predeal. Meeting a friend with a private carriage, you know."

"Walking, are you?" The tavern keeper's sneer was replaced with a look of genuine interest. "You want to be careful, you know. They say there's a new monster roaming the countryside!"

"A monster? Really, my friend," Golescu waggled a reproving finger at him. "Would I ever have got where I am in life if I'd believed such stories?"

He shouldered the coffin once more, picked up his bag and walked out.

Though the morning was cool, he was sweating by the time he reached the outskirts of Kronstadt, and by the time he stepped off to the campsite track Golescu's airy mood had descended a little. Nonetheless, he grinned to see the wagons still there, the horses cropping placidly where they were tethered. He bellowed heartily as he pounded on Amaunet's door:

"Uncle Barbu's home, darlings!"

Not a sound.

"Hello?"

Perhaps a high, thin whining noise?

"It's *meeee*," he said, trying the door. It wasn't locked. Setting down the coffin, he opened the door cautiously.

A strong, strong smell: spice and sweetness, and blood perhaps. Golescu pulled out a handkerchief and clapped it over his nose. He leaned forward, peering into the gloom within the wagon.

Amaunet lay stretched out on her bed, fully dressed. Her arms were crossed on her bosom, like a corpse's. Her skin was the color of ashes and her eyes were closed. She looked so radiantly happy that Golescu was unsure, at first, who lay there. He edged in sideways, bent to peer down at her.

"Madame?" He reached down to take her hand. It was ice-cold. "Oh!"

She just lay there, transfigured by her condition, beautiful at last.

Golescu staggered backward, and something fell from the bed. A cup rolled at his feet, a chalice cut of black stone. It appeared at first to be empty; but as it rolled, a slow black drop oozed forth to the lip.

"The Black Cup," stated Golescu, feeling the impact of a metaphorical cream pie. He blinked rapidly, overwhelmed by conflicting emotions. It was a moment before he was able to realize that the whining noise was coming from the cabinet under Amaunet's bed. Sighing, he bent and hauled Emil forth.

"Come out, poor little maggot," he said.

"I'm hungry," said Emil.

"Is that all you have to say?" Golescu demanded. "The Queen of Sorrow is dead, and you're concerned for a lousy potato?"

Emil said nothing in reply.

"Did she kill herself?"

"The cup killed her," Emil said.

"Poison in the cup, yes, I can see that, you ninny! I meant— why?"

"She wanted to die," said Emil. "She was too old, but she couldn't die. She said, 'Make me a poison to take my life away.' I mixed the cup every month, but it never worked. Then she said, 'What if you tried Theobromine?' I tried it. It worked. She laughed."

Golescu stood there staring down at him a long moment, and finally collapsed backward onto a stool.

"Holy God, Holy mother of God," he murmured, with tears in his eyes. "It was true. She was an immortal thing."

"I'm hungry," Emil repeated.

"But how could anyone get tired of being alive? So many good things! Fresh bread with butter. Sleep. Making people believe you. Interesting possibilities," said Golescu. "She had good luck handed to her, how could she want to throw it away?"

"They don't have luck," said Emil.

"And what are you, exactly?" said Golescu, staring at him. "You, with all your magic potions? Hey, can you make the one that gives eternal life, too?"

"No," said Emil.

"You can't? You're sure?"

"Yes."

"But then, what do you know?" Golescu rubbed his chin. "You're an idiot. But then again..." He looked at Amaunet, whose fixed smile seemed more unsettling every time he saw it. "Maybe she did cut a deal with the Devil after all. Maybe eternal life isn't all it's cracked up to be, if she wanted so badly to be rid of it. What's that in her hand?"

Leaning forward, he opened her closed fist. Something black protruded there: the snout of a tiny figure, crudely sculpted in clay. A crocodile.

"I want a potato," said Emil.

Golescu shuddered.

"We have to dig a grave first," he said.

In the end he dug it himself, because Emil, when goggled and swathed against daylight, was incapable of using a shovel.

"Rest in peace, my fair unknown," grunted Golescu, crouching to lower Amaunet's shrouded body into the grave. "I'd have given you the coffin, but I have other uses for it, and the winding sheet's very flattering, really. Not that I suppose you care."

He stood up and removed his hat. Raising his eyes to Heaven, he added: "Holy angels, if this poor creature really sold her soul to the Devil, then please pay no attention to my humble interruption. But if there were by chance any loopholes she might take advantage of to avoid damnation, I hope you guide her soul through them to eternal rest. And, by the way, I'm going to live a much more virtuous life from now on. Amen."

He replaced his hat, picked up the shovel once more and filled in the grave.

That night Golescu wept a little for Amaunet, or at least for lost opportunity, and he dreamed of her when he slept. By the time the sun rose pale through the smoke of Kronstadt's chimneys, though, he had begun to smile.

"I possess four fine horses and two wagons now," he told Emil, as he poked up the fire under the potato-kettle. "Nothing to turn up one's nose at, eh? And I have you, you poor child of misfortune. Too long has your light been hidden from the world."

Emil just sat there, staring through his goggles at the kettle. Golescu smeared plum jam on a slab of bread and took an enormous bite.

"Bucharest," he said explosively, through a full mouth. "Constantinople, Vienna, Prague, Berlin. We will walk down streets of gold in all the great cities of the world! All the potatoes your tiny heart could wish for, served up on nice restaurant china. And for me..." Golescu swallowed. "The life I was meant to live. Fame and universal respect. Beautiful women. Financial embarrassment only a memory!

"We'll give the teeming masses what they desire, my friend. What scourges people through life, after all? Fear of old age. Fear of inadequacy. Loneliness and sterility, what terrible things! How well will people pay to be cured of them, eh? Ah, Emil, what a lot of work you have to do."

Emil turned his blank face.

"Work," he said.

"Yes," said Golescu, grinning at him. "With your pots and pans and chemicals, you genius. Chickens be damned! We will accomplish great things, you and I. Future generations will regard us as heroes. Like, er, the fellow who stole fire from Heaven. Procrustes, that was his name.

"But I have every consideration for *your* modest and retiring nature. I will mercifully shield you from the limelight, and take the full force of public acclaim myself. For I shall now become..." Golescu dropped his voice an octave, "Professor Hades!"

———— ✦ ————

It was on Market Day, a full week later, that the vardas rolled through Kronstadt. At the hour when the streets were most crowded, Golescu drove like a majestic snail. Those edged to the side of the road had plenty of time to regard the new paint job. The vardas were now decorated with suns, moons and stars, what perhaps might have been alchemical symbols, gold and scarlet on black, and the words:

PROFESSOR HADES
Master Of The Miseries

Some idle folk followed, and watched as Golescu drew the wagons up in a vacant field just outside the Merchants' Gate. They stared, but did not offer to help, as Golescu unhitched the horses and bustled about with planks and barrels, setting up a stage. They watched with interest as a policeman advanced on Golescu, but were disappointed when Golescu presented him with all necessary permits and a hand-some bribe. He left, tipping his helmet; Golescu climbed into the lead wagon and shut the door. Nothing else of interest happened, so the idlers wandered away after a while.

But when school let out, children came to stare. By that time, scarlet curtains had been set up, masking the stage itself on three sides, and handbills had been tacked along the edge of the stage planking. A shopkeeper's son ventured close and bent to read.

"'FREE ENTERTAINMENT,'" he recited aloud, for the benefit of his friends. "'Health and Potency can be Yours!! Professor Hades Knows All!!! See the Myrmidion Genius!!!!'"

"'*Myrmidion?*'" said the schoolmaster's son.

"'Amazing Feats of Instant Calculation,'" continued the shopkeeper's son. "'Whether Rice, Peas, Beans, Millet or Barley, The Myrmidion Genius will Instantly Name the CORRECT Number in YOUR JAR.

A Grand Prize will be Presented to Any Person who can Baffle the Myrmidion Genius!'"

"What's a Myrmidion?" wondered the blacksmith's son.

"What's a Feat of Instant Calculation?" wondered the barber's son. "Guessing the number of beans in a jar?"

"That's a cheat," said the policeman's son.

"No, it isn't!" a disembodied voice boomed from behind the curtain. "You will see, little boys. Run home and tell your friends about the free show, here, tonight. You'll see wonders, I promise you. Bring beans!"

The boys ran off, so eager to do the bidding of an unseen stranger that down in Hell the Devil smiled, and jotted down their names for future reference. Dutifully they spread the word. By the time they came trooping back at twilight, lugging jars and pots of beans, a great number of adults followed them. A crowd gathered before the wagons, expectant.

Torches were flaring at either side of the stage now, in a cold sweeping wind that made the stars flare too. The scarlet curtain flapped and swayed like the flames. As it moved, those closest to the stage glimpsed feet moving beneath, accompanied by a lot of grunting and thumping.

The barber cleared his throat and called, "Hey! We're freezing to death out here!"

"Then you shall be warmed!" cried a great voice, and the front curtain was flung aside. The wind promptly blew it back, but not before the crowd had glimpsed Golescu resplendent in his Mephistopheles costume. He caught the curtain again and stepped out in front of it. "Good people of Kronstadt, how lucky you are!"

There was some murmuring from the crowd. Golescu had applied makeup to give himself a sinister and mysterious appearance, or at least that had been his intention, but the result was that he looked rather like a fat raccoon in a red suit. Nevertheless, it could not be denied that he was frightening to behold.

"Professor Hades, at your service," he said, leering and twirling the ends of his moustache. "World traveler and delver-into of forbidden mysteries!"

"We brought the beans," shouted the barber's son.

"Good. Hear, now, the story of my remarkable—"

"What are you supposed to be, the Devil?" demanded someone in the audience.

"No indeed! Though you are surely wise enough to know that the Devil is not so black as he is painted, eh?" Golescu cried. "No, in fact I bring you happiness, my friends, and blessings for all mankind! Let me tell you how it was."

From under his cloak he drew the lyre, and pretended to twang its strings.

"It is true that in the days of my youth I studied the Dark Arts, at a curious school run by the famed Master Paracelsus. Imagine my horror, however, when I discovered that every seven years he offered up one of his seven students as a sacrifice to Hell! And I, I myself was seventh in my class! I therefore fled, as you would surely do. I used my great wealth to buy a ship, wherewith I meant to escape to Egypt, home of all the mysteries.

"Long I sailed, by devious routes, for I lived in terror that Master Paracelsus would discover my presence by arcane means. And so it happened that I grew desperately short of water, and was obliged to thread dangerous reefs and rocks to land on an island with a fair spring.

"Now, this was no ordinary island, friends! For on it was the holy shrine of the great Egyptian god Osiris, once guarded by the fierce race of ant-men, the Myrmidions!"

"Don't you mean the *Myrmidons?*" called the schoolmaster. "They were—"

"No, that was somebody else!" said Golescu. "These people I am talking about were terrors, understand? Giant, six-limbed men with fearsome jaws and superhuman strength, whom Osiris placed there to guard the secrets of his temple! Fangs dripping venom! Certain death for any who dared to set foot near the sacred precinct! All right?

"Fortunately for me, their race had almost completely died out over the thousands of years that had passed. In fact, as I approached the mysterious temple, who should feebly stagger forth to challenge me but the very last of the ant-men? And he himself such a degraded and degenerate specimen, that he was easily overcome by my least effort. In fact, as I stood there in the grandeur of the ancient moonlight, with my triumphant foot upon his neck, I found it in my heart to pity the poor defeated creature."

"Where do the beans come in?" called the policeman's son.

"I'm coming to that! Have patience, young sir. So I didn't kill him, which I might easily have done. Instead, I stepped over his pathetic form and entered the forbidden shrine of Osiris.

"Holding my lantern high, what should I see but a towering image of the fearsome god himself, but this was not the greatest wonder! No, on the walls of the shrine, floor to ceiling, wall to wall, were inscribed words! Yes, words in Ancient Egyptian, queer little pictures of birds and snakes and things. Fortunately I, with my great knowledge, was able to read them. Were they prayers? No. Were they ancient spells? No, good people. They were nothing more nor less than recipes for medicine! For, as you may know, Osiris was the Egyptians' principal god of healing. Here were the secret formulas to remedy every ill that might befall unhappy mankind!

"So, what did I do? I quickly pulled out my notebook and began to copy them down, intending to bring this blessing back for the good of all.

"Faster I wrote, and faster, but just as I had cast my eye on the last of the recipes—which, had I been able to copy it, would have banished the awful specter of Death himself—I heard an ominous rumbling. My lamp began to flicker. When I looked up, I beheld the idol of Osiris trembling on its very foundation. Unbeknownst to me, my unhallowed feet crossing the portal of the shrine had set off a dreadful curse. The shrine was about to destroy itself in a convulsive cataclysm!

"I fled, thoughtfully tucking my notebook into my pocket, and paused only to seize up the last of the Myrmidions where he lay groveling. With my great strength, I easily carried him to my ship, and cast off just before the shrine of Osiris collapsed upon itself, with a rumble like a hundred thousand milk wagons!

"And, not only that, the island itself broke into a hundred thousand pieces and sank forever beneath the engulfing waves!"

Golescu stepped back to gauge his effect on the audience. Satisfied that he had them enthralled, and delighted to see that more townfolk were hurrying to swell the crowd every minute, he twirled his moustache.

"And now, little children, you will find out about the beans. As we journeyed to a place of refuge, I turned my efforts to taming the last of the Myrmidions. With my superior education, it proved no difficulty. I discovered that, although he was weak and puny compared with his terrible ancestors, he nevertheless had kept some of the singular traits of the ant!

"Yes, especially their amazing ability to count beans and peas!"

"Wait a minute," shouted the schoolmaster. "Ants can't count."

"Dear sir, you're mistaken," said Golescu. "Who doesn't remember the story of Cupid and Psyche, eh? Any educated man would remember that the princess was punished for her nosiness by being locked in a room with a huge pile of beans and millet, and was supposed to count them all, right? And who came to her assistance? Why, the ants! Because she'd been thoughtful and avoided stepping on an anthill or something. So the little creatures sorted and tided the whole stack for her, and counted them too. And that's in classical literature, my friend. Aristotle wrote about it, and who are we to dispute him?"

"But—" said the schoolmaster.

"And NOW," said Golescu, hurrying to the back of the platform and pushing forward the coffin, which had been nailed into a frame that stood it nearly upright, "Here he is! Feast your astonished eyes on—*the last of the Myrmidions!*"

With a flourish, he threw back the lid.

Emil, dressed in the black imp costume that had been modified with an extra pair of straw-stuffed arms, and in a black hood to which two long antenna of wire had been attached, looked into the glare of the lights. He screamed in terror.

"Er—yes!" Golescu slammed the lid, in the process trapping one of the antennae outside. "Though you can only see him in his natural state in, er, the briefest of glimpses, because—because, even though weak, he still has the power of setting things on fire with the power of his gaze! Fortunately, I have devised a way to protect you all. One moment, please."

As the crowd murmured, Golescu drew the curtain back across the stage. Those in the front row could see his feet moving to and fro for a moment. They heard a brief mysterious thumping and a faint cry. The curtain was opened again.

"*Now,*" said Golescu. "Behold the last of the Myrmidions!"

He opened the lid once more. Emil, safely goggled, did not scream. After a moment of silence, various members of the audience began to snicker.

"Ah, you think he's weak? You think he looks harmless?" said Golescu, affecting an amused sneer. "Yet, consider his astonishing powers of calculation! You, boy, there." He lunged forward and caught the nearest youngster who was clutching a jar, and lifted him bodily to the stage. "Yes, you! Do you know—don't tell me, now!—do you know exactly how many beans are in your jar?"

"Yes," said the boy, blinking in the torchlight.

"Ah! Now tell me, good people, is this child one of your own?"

"That's my son!" cried the barber.

"Very good! Now, is there a policeman here?"

"I am," said the Captain of Police, stepping forward and grinning at Golescu in a fairly unpleasant way.

"Wonderful! Now, dear child, will you be so kind as to whisper to the good constable—whisper, I say—the correct number of beans in this jar?"

Obediently, the barber's son stepped to the edge of the planking and whispered into the Police Captain's ear.

"Excellent! And now, brave Policeman, will you be so good as to write down the number you have just been given?" said Golescu, sweating slightly.

"Delighted to," said the Police Captain, and pulling out a notebook he jotted it down. He winked at the audience, in a particularly cold and reptilian kind of way.

"Exquisite!" said Golescu. "And now, if you will permit—?" He took the jar of beans from the barber's son and held it up in the torchlight. Then he held it before Emil's face. "Oh, last of the Myrmidions! Behold this jar! *How many beans?*"

"Five hundred and six," said Emil, faint but clear in the breathless silence.

"How many?"

"Five hundred and six."

"And, sir, what is the figure you have written down?" demanded Golescu, whirling about to face the Police Captain.

"Five hundred and six," the Police Captain responded, narrowing his eyes.

"And so it is!" said Golescu, thrusting the jar back into the hands of the barber's son and more or less booting him off the stage. "Let's have more proof! Who's got another jar?"

Now a half-dozen jars were held up, and children cried shrilly to be the next on stage. Grunting with effort, Golescu hoisted another boy to the platform.

"And you are?" he said.

"That's *my* son!" said the Police Captain.

"Good! How many beans? Tell your papa!" cried Golescu, and as the boy was whispering in his father's ear, "Please write it down!"

He seized the jar from the boy and once more held it before Emil. "Oh last of the Myrmidions, *how many beans?*"

"Three hundred seventeen," said Emil.

"Are you certain? It's a much bigger jar!"

"Three hundred seventeen," said Emil.

"And the number you just wrote down, dear sir?"

"Three hundred seventeen," admitted the Police Captain.

"I hid an onion in the middle," said his son proudly, and was promptly cuffed by the Police Captain when Golescu had dropped him back into the crowd.

Now grown men began to push through the crowd, waving jars of varied legumes as well as barley and millet. Emil guessed correctly on each try, even the jar of rice that contained a pair of wadded socks! At last Golescu, beaming, held up his hands.

"So, you have seen one proof of my adventure with your own eyes," he cried. "But this has been a mere parlor entertainment, gentle audience. Now, you will be truly amazed! For we come to the true purpose of my visit here. *Behold the Gifts of Osiris!*"

He whisked a piece of sacking from the stacked boxes it had concealed. The necks of many medicine bottles winked in the torchlight.

"Yes! Compounded by me, according to the ancient secret formulas! Here, my friends, are remedies to cure human misery! A crown a bottle doesn't even cover the cost of its rare ingredients—I'm offering them to you practically as a charity!"

A flat silence fell at that, and then the Police Captain could be heard distinctly saying, "I thought it would come to this."

"A crown a bottle?" said somebody else, sounding outraged.

"You require persuasion," said Golescu. "*Free* persuasion. Very good! You, sir, step up here into the light. Yes, you, the one who doesn't want to part with his money."

The man in question climbed up on the planks and stood there looking defiant, as Golescu addressed the audience.

"Human misery!" he shouted. "What causes it, good people? Age. Inadequacy. Inability. Loneliness. All that does not kill you, but makes life not worth living! Isn't it so? Now you, good sir!" He turned to the man beside him. "Remove your hat, if you please. I see you suffer from baldness!"

The man turned red and looked as though he'd like to punch Golescu, but the audience laughed.

"Don't be ashamed!" Golescu told him. "How'd you like a full growth of luxurious hair, eh?"

"Well—"

"Behold," said Golescu, drawing a bottle from the stack. "The Potion of Ptolemy! See its amazing results."

He uncorked the bottle and tilted it carefully, so as to spill only a few drops on the man's scalp. Having done this, he grabbed the tail of his cloak and spread the potion around on the man's scalp.

"What are you doing to me?" cried the man. "It burns like Hell!"

"Courage! Nothing is got without a little pain. Count to sixty, now!"

The audience obliged, but long before they had got to forty they broke off in exclamations: for thick black hair had begun to grow on the man's scalp, everywhere the potion had been spread.

"Oh!" The man clutched his scalp, unbelieving.

"Yes!" said Golescu, turning to the audience. "You see? Immediately, this lucky fellow is restored to his previous appearance of youth and virility. And speaking of virility!" He smacked the man's back hard enough to send him flying off the platform. "What greater source of misery can there be than disappointing the fair ones? Who among you lacks that certain something he had as a young buck, eh?

"Nobody here, I'm sure, but just think: someday, you *may* find yourself attempting to pick a lock with a dead fish. When that day comes, do you truly want to be caught without a bracing bottle of the Pharaoh's Physic? One crown a bottle, gentlemen! I'm sure you can understand why no free demonstrations are available for this one."

There was a silence of perhaps five seconds before a veritable tidal wave of men rushed forward, waving fistfuls of coin.

"Here! One to a customer, sirs, one only. That's right! I only do this as a public service, you know, I love to make others happy. Drink it in good health, sir, but I'd suggest you eat your oysters first. Pray don't trample the children, there, even if you can always make more. And speaking of making more!" Golescu stuffed the last clutch of coins down his tights and retreated from the front of the stage, for he had sold all his bottles of Pharaoh's Physic and Potion of Ptolemy.

"What's the use of magnificent potency when your maiden is cold as ice, I ask you? Disinterest! Disdain! Diffidence! Is there any more terrible source of misery than the unloving spouse? Now, you may have heard of love philtres; you may have bought charms and spells from mere gypsies. But what your little doves require, my friends, is none other than the *Elixir of Isis!* Guaranteed to turn those chilly frowns to smiles of welcome!"

A second surge made its way to the front of the platform, slightly less desperate than the first but moneyed withal. Golescu doled out bottles of Elixir of Isis, dropped coins down his tights, and calculated. He had one case of bottles left. Lifting it to the top of the stack, he faced his audience and smiled.

"And now, good people, ask yourselves a question: What is it that makes long life a curse? Why, the answer is transparent: it is *pain.* Rending, searing, horrible agony! Dull aches that never go away! The throb of a rotten tooth! Misery, misery, misery, God have mercy on us! But! With a liberal application of Balm Bast, you will gain instant relief from unspeakable torment."

There was a general movement toward the stage, though not such a flood as Golescu had expected; some distraction was in the crowd, though he couldn't tell what it was. Ah! Surely, this was it: an injured man, with bandaged head and eye, was being helped forward on his crutches.

"Give way! Let this poor devil through!"

"Here, Professor Hades, here's one who could use your medicine!"

"What about a free sample for *him?*"

"What's this, a veteran of the wars?" said Golescu, in his most jovial voice. "Certainly he'll get a free sample! Here, for yo—" He ended on a high-pitched little squeak, for on leaning down he found himself gazing straight into Farmer Buzdugan's single remaining eye. Mutual recognition flashed.

"Yo—" began Farmer Buzdugan, but Golescu had uncorked the bottle and shoved it into his mouth quick as thought. He held the bottle there, as Buzdugan choked on indignation and Balm Bast.

"AH, YES, I RECOGNIZE THIS POOR FELLOW!" said Golescu, struggling to keep the bottle in place. "He's delusional as well! His family brought him to me to be cured of his madness, but unfortunately—"

Unfortunately the distraction in the crowd was on a larger scale than Golescu had supposed. It had started with a general restlessness, owing to the fact that all those who had purchased bottles of Pharaoh's Physic had opened the bottles and gulped their contents straight down. This had produced general and widespread priapism, at about the time Golescu had begun his spiel on the Elixir of Isis.

This was as nothing, however, to what was experienced by those who had purchased the Potion of Ptolemy and, most unwisely, decided to try it out before waiting to get it home. Several horrified individuals were now finding luxuriant hair growing, not only on their scalps but everywhere the potion had splashed or trickled in the course of its application, such as ears, eyelids, noses and wives. More appalled still were those who had elected to rub the potion well in with their bare hands.

Their case was as nothing, however, compared to the unfortunate who had decided that all medicines worked better if taken internally. He was now prostrate and shrieking, if somewhat muffledly, as a crowd of horrified onlookers stood well back from him.

Buzdugan threw himself back and managed to spit out the bottle.

"Son of a whore!" he said. "This is him! This is the one who sold us the—"

"MAD, WHAT DID I TELL YOU?" said Golescu.

"He sold us the stuff that created those—" Buzdugan said, before the Balm Bast worked and he abruptly lost all feeling in his body. Nerveless he fell from his crutches into the dark forest of feet and legs.

But he was scarcely noticed in the excitement caused by the man who had purchased both Pharaoh's Physic and Elixir of Isis, with the intention of maximizing domestic felicity, and in the darkness had opened and drunk off the contents of the wrong bottle. Overcome by a wave of heat, and then inexplicable and untoward passion, and then by a complete loss of higher cerebral function, he had dropped his trousers and was now offering himself to all comers, screaming like a chimpanzee. Several of those afflicted by the Pharaoh's Potion, unable to resist, were on the very point of availing themselves of his charms when—

"Holy saints defend us!" cried someone on the edge of the crowd. "Run for your lives! It's *another demon cock!*"

This confused all who heard it, understandably, but only until the demon in question strode into sight.

Golescu, who had been edging to the back of the platform with tiny little steps, smiling and sweating, saw it most clearly: a rooster, but no ordinary bird. Eight feet tall at the shoulder, tail like a fountain of fire, golden spurs, feathers like beaten gold, comb like blood-red coral, and a beak like a meat cleaver made of brass! Its eyes shone in the light of the torches with ferocious brilliance, but they were blank and mindless as any chicken's. It beat its wings with a sound like thunder. People fled in all directions, save those who were so crazed with lust they could not be distracted from what they were doing.

"Oh why, oh why do these things happen?" Golescu implored no one in particular. "I have *such* good intentions."

The great bird noticed the children crowded together at the front of the platform. Up until this point, they had been giggling at the behavior of their elders. Having caught sight of the monster, however, they dove under the platform and huddled there like so many mice. The bird saw them nonetheless, and advanced, turning its head to regard them with one eye and then the other. Terrified, they hurled jars of beans at it, which exploded like canisters of shot. Yet it came on, raking the ground as it came.

And Golescu became aware that there was another dreadful noise below the cries of the children, below Buzdugan's frenzied cursing where he lay, below the ever-more-distant yells of the retreating audience. Below, for it was low-pitched, the sort of noise that makes the teeth vibrate, deep as an earthquake, no less frightening.

Something, somewhere, was growling. And it was getting louder.

Golescu raised his head, and in a moment that would return to him in nightmares the rest of his life saw a pair of glowing eyes advancing through the night, eyes like coals above white, white teeth. The nearer they came, floating through the darkness toward the wagon, the louder grew the sound of growling. Nearer now, into the light of the torches, and Golescu saw clearly the outstretched arms, the clawing fingers caked with earth, the murderous expression, the trailing shroud.

"Good heavens, it's Amaunet," he observed, before reality hit him and he wet himself. The Black Cup had failed her again after all, and so—

"*rrrrrrrkillYOU!*" she roared, lunging for the platform. Golescu, sobbing, ran to and fro only a moment; then fear lent him wings and he made one heroic leap, launching himself from the platform to the back of the chicken of gold. Digging his knees in its fiery plumage, he smote it as though it were a horse.

With a squawk that shattered the night, his steed leaped in the air and came down running. Golescu clung for dear life, looking over his shoulder. He beheld Emil, antennae wobbling, scrambling frantically from the coffin.

"Uncle Barbu!" wailed Emil. But Amaunet had Emil by the ankle now. She pulled him close. He vanished into the folds of her shroud, still struggling. Golescu's last glimpse was of Amaunet lifting Emil to her bosom, clutching him possessively, horrific Madonna and limp Child.

Golescu hugged the neck of his golden steed and urged it on, on through the night and the forest. He wept for lost love, wept for sour misfortune, wept for beauty, and so he rode in terrible glory through water and fire and pitiless starlight. When bright day came he was riding still. Who knows where he ended up?

Though there is a remote village beyond the forests, so mazed about with bogs and streams no roads lead there, and every man has been obliged to marry his cousin. They have a legend that the Devil once appeared to them, riding on a golden cock, a fearful apparition before which they threw themselves flat. They offered to make him their prince, if only he would spare their lives.

And they say that the Devil stayed with them a while, and made a tolerably good prince, as princes go in that part of the world. But he looked always over his shoulder, for fear that his wife might be pursuing him. He said she was the Mother of Darkness. His terror was so great that at last it got the better of him and he rode on, rather than let her catch him.

The men of the village found this comforting, in an obscure kind of way. *Even the Devil fears his wife,* they said to one another. They said it so often that a man came from the Ministry of Culture at last, and wrote it down in a book of proverbs.

But if you travel to that country and look in that great book, you will look in vain; for unfortunately some vandal has torn out the relevant page.

RUDE MECHANICALS

Kage loved Shakespeare, and the Hollywood Hills where she grew up, and the Hollywood Bowl where we played all through our adolescence. When she learned that the MGM movie of *A Midsummer Night's Dream* had started out as a stage extravaganza in her beloved Bowl, she knew she had to write a story around it. Old (and real, by the way) tales of treasure in the Hills were incorporated into it. The crazy (and also real) story of Jack McDermott's Moorish Castle, plus some details from Hollywood parties in our mother's house, also add to the story. The rest of it seems to have arisen inevitably from the craziness that follows Joseph and Lewis around whenever they join forces. And Kage was able to explicate some weird old details of the original production for the Bowl's Historian, who had never climbed around in the Hills that Kage knew so intimately.

—K. B.

HOLLYWOOD, 1934

ONE: *FULL OF VEXATION COME I, WITH COMPLAINT...*

Lewis sat alone in his booth at Musso and Frank's, smiling down at a perfect martini. The booth was dark wood, above which there was just enough light to make out the restaurant's mural depicting a forest landscape. In this dim and cozy bower his drink shone out with a silvery light, its icy disk fragrant with aromatic gin, just a polite nod of vermouth.

As he fished out the small olive and popped it in his mouth, Lewis murmured a prayer of thanks to the goddess Athena, bestower of the olive tree on mortals. Lewis generally prayed to Apollo, having been left, as an infant, by the statue of that deity in the temple of Aquae Sulis in 130 A.D; but he liked to give credit where credit was due.

Little beams of light from the swirling gin danced on the table, subsided. All was calm. The universe was a rational and ordered place...

There came a reek of sweat, thinly masked by Burma-Shave Lotion. Lewis lifted his head, frowning, looking about; a second later he nodded in recognition as another immortal slid into the booth.

"Joseph, what on earth have you been doing?"

The other man sighed, loosening his tie. The two immortals presented a striking contrast to each other. Lewis was slight, fair-haired and immaculately groomed; Joseph was stocky, dark, sloppily shaven and had a coffee-stain on his right cuff. It was displayed as he waved for a waiter. Lewis recoiled from the fresh wave of sweat. "And when did you *bathe* last?"

"Yesterday morning. In the bus station," said Joseph. He noticed Lewis's martini and grabbed for it. Lewis raised it out of reach.

"Get your own! What were you doing in a bus station?"

"Tailing Wallace Beery," said Joseph, in a weary voice. "You don't want to know."

"Ohh." Lewis nodded sympathetically. In his twenty-thousand or so years Joseph had worked as an Egyptian priest, a Roman centurion, a Byzantine spy, a Spanish inquisitor and a number of other difficult occupations, but seldom for so demanding an employer as Louis B. Mayer. "Pancho Villa's on another rampage, is he?"

"Yeah, the son of a bitch. Waiter! Scotch on the rocks. Make it a double."

"It's not easy being a studio dick, I suppose," said Lewis.

"You can say that again," said Joseph, sagging back in the booth. His black eyes were sunk back in his head with exhaustion. "Goddam Hays Code. This week, I jumped through hoops so Gentleman Wally doesn't do five to ten on a manslaughter charge. Last week, I had to dig through Jean Harlow's garbage for a certain letter. The week before that, I was pulling Jack Barrymore out of a brothel in Ensenada at one AM to get him all the way back to a makeup chair in Culver City by five AM. Don't let anybody ever tell you a Model A can't do eighty-five. We outran five cops between Escondido and Culver City. And Garbo slapped my face. Again."

"'What? And leave show business?'" Lewis quoted, chuckling.

In silence Joseph transmitted: *And on top of everything else, the Company picks now, of all times, to throw me a job.*

Lewis raised his eyebrows. The Company to which Joseph referred was better known, in cyborg circles, as Dr. Zeus Incorporated. Joseph's orders came from an all-powerful cabal of research scientists and investors based in the twenty-fourth century, who had invented time travel and immortality. Having failed to find a way to make these inventions marketable, however, they had used them to create immortal cyborg servants based in the past, who could be used to retrieve precious objects lost in time and send them on to the future, there to command obscenely high prices from private collectors.

What sort of job? Lewis transmitted back.

Well, that was sort of what I wanted to talk to you about. Joseph straightened up and looked at Lewis with wide sincere eyes. *You're working with Max Reinhardt right now, aren't you? The German theater guy?*

Lewis took a fortifying sip of his martini before replying. *I've inveigled myself into a position as one of his assistants. He's producing* A Midsummer Night's Dream *at the Hollywood Bowl.*

Company job, right? What are you after?

Some billionaire up in 2342 wants Reinhardt's notes and promptbook. Why do you ask?

Can you get me a job on the crew?

Lewis, midway through another sip, nearly choked. He set the glass down hastily. "But—Joseph, that's Facilitator work! I'm only a Literature Preservation Specialist," he said aloud, so shocked he was.

"Hey, you're a smart guy. Improvise," said Joseph breezily. He looked up with a smile of gratitude at the waiter who brought his drink. "Thanks a million, pal. How about a menu?"

The waiter obliged in silence. Joseph took a fortifying gulp of Scotch and studied the menu, ignoring Lewis's expression of dismay. "Say, is the chicken pot pie any good?"

"Never mind the chicken pot pie! What could you possibly want with Mr. Reinhardt? He doesn't run in—" Lewis tried to find a tactful way to say it, and couldn't—"your sort of circles. No fisticuffs, no boozing, no gambling. No ladies of the evening. No mob connections."

"This has nothing to do with Reinhardt," said Joseph. "I just need a job on the construction crew. You can get me one, right?"

"Wrong," said Lewis. "Joseph, I'm not even an assistant director, for gods' sake! I'm a director's assistant and translator! I just explain things to Mr. Reinhardt and keep his production notes tidy."

"And I'm sure you do a swell job, too," said Joseph. "I'll bet he's never had such tidy notes in his whole life. Which is why he'll undoubtedly appreciate *your* valuable recommendation that he employ your dear friend who's the best set painter in Hollywood."

"But you aren't," said Lewis. "And anyway, there aren't any painters on this show. It's outdoors. He's even having the Bowl shell taken off. We're putting in trees instead. Moss and cobwebs and things. And a giant ramp for a procession onstage."

"Well, O.K., so I'm the best giant ramp builder in Hollywood."

"But you aren't!"

"I built goddam pyramids in Egypt, I can build a ramp at the Hollywood Bowl," said Joseph, exasperated. "For crying out loud, Lewis, use your imagination! *This is a Company job.* And what All-Seeing Zeus wants, he gets. Don't make me go to your case officer on this."

"You would, too, wouldn't you?" said Lewis waspishly. He drained his martini at a gulp. "Why don't you just use your awesome powers of persuasion on Mr. Reinhardt yourself? He's sitting right over there."

"No kidding?" Joseph leaned out of the booth to stare.

"*Discreetly*, for heaven's sake! He doesn't like being bothered," said Lewis. Joseph leaned back again but kept his gaze on the occupant of the table across the room. He saw a middle-aged man with stern, heavy features and blazing blue eyes. Max Reinhardt looked like a Beethoven symphony personified, all thunder and lightning, but at the moment he was placidly dawdling over the remains of a substantial dinner.

"Talk about lucky coincidences," said Joseph. He got to his feet, shot his cuffs, straightened his tie, and approached Reinhardt's table with his hand out and an ingratiating smile on his face.

"You'll be sorry," Lewis murmured, but was ignored.

"Say, Mr. Reinhardt, what a pleasure to run into you like this!" said Joseph, in his most captivating tones. "Joseph Denham. May I trouble you for a moment of your time?"

The great man looked up, disconcerted. "I beg your pardon?" he said, in German.

"I just wanted to say, Mr. Reinhardt, how happy we are to have you here in Hollywood, bringing your unique brand of showmanship to our shores," said Joseph, switching to perfectly accented Viennese with overtones of Berlin. He shook Reinhardt's hand. "And I just wondered whether you might have an opening in your show for a man of my talents. Maybe I should explain—"

"Please," said Reinhardt, with a shy smile that did not extend to his eyes. "I—er—" He fumbled in his coat. "One moment please—I have a card case." Further fumbling did not produce one. He glanced down at the remnants of his meal and said, "Would you have the kindness to excuse me one moment?"

"Of course!" Joseph stepped back. "Take all the time you want."

Reinhardt walked to the back of the restaurant and vanished around the corner of a booth. Five minutes passed. Ten more went after them.

"I ordered you the chicken pot pie," Lewis called. "You may as well come back, you know. He's halfway to his hotel by this time."

"No, he isn't," said Joseph, though with a sinking feeling. "I think he's looking for his card case. Maybe he dropped it in the john."

"Yes, of course," said Lewis. Joseph waited five more minutes and then returned to the booth, sighing.

"Hell. He took a powder, didn't he?"

"It's just possible," said Lewis, without a trace of sarcasm. "That's not the way to approach him, you know. Reinhardt can vanish in a puff of smoke when he's feeling pressured. Doesn't quite inhabit the same base terrestrial regions as you or I. He's a true artist. And you just might have given the impression you were a Nazi spy, with that accent. He's a Jewish refugee, in case you were unaware."

"But I used his own accent. Mortals like that. It relaxes them," said Joseph.

"I use British-accented schoolbook German," said Lewis. "It's what he expects. I'm afraid you came off a bit unnecessarily Mephistophelean."

"How are you going to get me on the crew, then?"

Lewis pursed his lips. "Let's just pretend for a moment that our masters did me the honor of programming me as a big-cheese Facilitator, like you, instead of as a humble Preserver. Of course I'll wave my magic wand and get you a job on the show, Joseph; nothing easier! Perhaps you ought to tell me why you need one."

"It's a long story." Joseph slumped over his drink. "You ever hear of the Lost Treasure of the Cahuenga Pass?"

"I beg your pardon?"

"I guess not, huh?"

"No," said Lewis. "No, I haven't. This is just going to get weirder, isn't it?"

"1865," said Joseph. "Maximilian ruling Mexico, as much as he was able. The rebellion happens. Mazatlan, big wealthy port city with a lot of European émigrés living there, declares for the rebels. But the rebels are running out of guns and ammo. Freedom-loving Mexicans pass the hat to raise money to buy more. Rich mortals donate gold and jewels.

"The treasure's sent north by ship, with two Mexican captains and a couple of English mercenaries who just happen to be there agitating against French rule. Imagine that, huh? The plan is to take the loot to San Francisco, buy arms with it and take them back to the heroic freedom fighters. But, en route, the Mexican who knew all the contacts dies, without getting the chance to pass the secret names to his fellow conspirators.

"So the three remaining mortals land in San Francisco with all this fairly heavy and obvious treasure. They don't know who they can trust. They decide to ride out into the hills and bury the treasure, then go back to Mazatlán to find out who they're supposed to contact. They do. They come back to San Francisco, but the treasure's gone. Doesn't make any difference in the long run; Maximilian goes down anyway, poor dope.

"One of the English guys passes the story of the treasure on in his family, and one of his descendants is one of the founders of Dr. Zeus. Or something like that. Anyway, the treasure got the Company's attention."

"Cahuenga Pass is a long way from San Francisco, Joseph," said Lewis, taking another sip of his martini.

"I'm coming to that, O.K.? What happens is, this shepherd is grazing his flocks in the hills above San Bruno and he sees the three guys burying the treasure. As soon as they go, he digs it up again.

"Then he loads it on two mules and a horse and decides to make tracks. He goes south and gets as far as—"

"The Cahuenga Pass," said Lewis, pointing over Joseph's shoulder in the direction of the Pass.

"Yeah. Where his nerve gives out. He stops at a stagecoach inn and tavern. Guess who runs it?"

"No idea," said Lewis. Then he winced. "Oh—wait—that was where—"

At that moment the waiter brought his veal cutlet and Joseph's chicken pot pie, and there was appreciative silence for a while before Joseph resumed, speaking through a full mouth:

"Stagecoach inn's a Company HQ. The mortal brings the loot straight to the arms of Dr. Zeus, can you beat it? The operative running the place is a Security Tech. He reports straight to the Company and is told to persuade the mortal that Los Angeles is really dangerous (which it was) and he really ought to hide anything valuable he might happen to be carrying nearby and rest up awhile.

"Which the mortal obligingly does. He goes up into what's now the Hollywood Bowl and buries the loot in six little caches around an ash tree. Goes back to the tavern and gets drunk. Keeps drinking. Drinks some more. The Security Tech sneaks out, finds where the loot is buried, contacts Dr. Zeus for further orders. Company tells him to leave it be, but make sure no mortals get a chance to get near it.

"So the Company op takes a subsonic generator up there, one of the old field models, and hides it in a bush by the ash tree and switches it on. It puts out its fourteen-cycle note at maybe sixty decibels, so any mortals coming close will panic if they walk into its range.

"Meanwhile, back at the tavern, the shepherd drinks himself into collapse. He has a local friend who comes and moves him to his house, so he can recover there. Only he doesn't. He gets worse and dies. But before he does—he tells his friend about the treasure, and where he buried it."

"And his friend goes to dig it up, but runs into the subsonic field and panics?" said Lewis.

"Has an anxiety attack so bad he has a stroke and dies," said Joseph. "Though not before the story gets out. *Madre de Dios, it's a Cursed Treasure!* So none of the local mortals ever dare come search for it again. And there it sits, until the 1880s. This was where I came in."

"Wait. The treasure's hidden in the Hollywood Bowl. You need to dig it up?" Lewis knit his brows. "But you could go up there anytime, Joseph. You needn't be employed there. The place is completely open."

"No, I don't need to dig it up. There's a complication," said Joseph. He held up his empty glass and waved it hopefully in the direction of a waiter. The waiter glided close, took the empty glass and returned a moment later with a full one.

"There would be a complication," said Lewis.

"1885," said Joseph. "First big real estate boom in L.A. County. The joint is filling up with mortals. Company decides the treasure needs to be moved to a place it'll stay hidden. I get orders to go to the Cahuenga Pass HQ. I report for duty and it's Palinurus in command there now, remember him? He sets me up with a cover as a Basque shepherd.

"So I go back in there and dig up the treasure, move the rest of it to a different location close by. One that'll have a famous landmark close to it pretty soon that's going to stay there for the rest of recorded history, so the Company *knows* it's going to be pretty much undisturbed. With a couple of brief exceptions."

"Oh," said Lewis. "Light dawneth."

"It doth, huh?" Joseph drained his drink and crunched ice.

"Why didn't the Company just have you retrieve the whole treasure right then?"

"It'd contradict the Temporal Concordance. More than that, you don't need to know."

"Oh."

"Anyway, I go back to HQ. Palinurus and I spread the word that some coins and jewelry have been found, up in that canyon. The local mortals remember the story from twenty years before and everyone tells me, *Señor, be careful, that's a Cursed Treasure!* And I say, *Ha! Don't be foolish, there's no such thing as a curse!* Then I leave, announcing I'm going home to my native Pyrenees, and six months later Palinurus spreads the word: *That Basque fell overboard on his way home and drowned! And what sunk him was...the Cursed Treasure, sewn into his coat!*"

"Unnecessarily theatrical, if you ask me," said Lewis.

"Yeah, well, it kept the mortals from snooping around up there," said Joseph. "And now the Company sends word it would like a

Company op on the spot to make sure Mr. Reinhardt's stupendous colossal earthworks don't disturb a Company cache. That's where I come in. All *you* have to do is get me on the work crew."

"I'll do my best," said Lewis. "I have my hands full with my own mission, though, I warn you. I won't be able to help you much."

Joseph grinned. "Relax! How many centuries of experience have I racked up, misdirecting mortals on account of Dr. Zeus didn't want them to see something? *'I will lead them up and down'!*"

"Fair enough. I may be able to get Mr. Girton to take you on. You won't bother Mr. Reinhardt again, though, will you?" said Lewis. "I don't think you made a favorable impression on him, somehow."

"Trust me!" said Joseph cheerily, and signaled the waiter for another drink.

TWO: *SO QUICK BRIGHT THINGS COME TO CONFUSION...*

Joseph was as good as his word, though Lewis (hurrying along in Reinhardt's wake clutching sketch pads and the promptbook) spotted him on the work crew a scant week later.

Joseph had taken some pains with his disguise as a mortal laborer, purchasing overalls, workboots and a battered felt hat from an old-clothes dealer. When he spotted Lewis, he lifted his hat with an ironical smile. Reinhardt didn't seem to recognize him, at least; but on those occasions when the great man floated through the set, his eyes seemed focused on the faery forest that didn't yet exist, rather than the acoustic shell that was in the process of being moved from its base by a horde of sweating workmen.

Sunlight poured down into the Bowl valley, soft and with a certain heaviness; it was easy to imagine the light falling like a blanket, muffling the noise of the crowbars and chains. Any time work stopped, a dreamlike silence descended. The immense half-cup of the shell inched its way along, surreal as a pyramid walking under timeless light, and finally vanished like a magician's trick.

Truckloads of earth were brought in, then, mountains of loam, to be shoveled and sculpted on the wide bare stage; then the base was built for the great trestle that was to bridge the ravine behind the stage. Reinhardt stalked out across the valley floor to watch, mopping his face with a handkerchief in the heat, barely noticing Lewis at his elbow. He frowned at the timber framework against the bright sky. Lewis squinted up at it hoping Reinhardt hadn't noticed Joseph, swaggering with a bucket of nails along an eight-inch catwalk three stories above.

"Es geschieht schnell, Herr Professor," said Lewis.

"Yes, but," said Reinhardt. He fell silent a moment, apparently forgetting Lewis was there. At last he scowled and waved his hand at the raw planks and beams. "Too *real*," he said, as though to himself. "It must be clouds and moonlight. Herr Thomas must build mist, and stars. Book—...?"

Hastily Lewis put the promptbook and a pencil in Reinhardt's hand. Reinhardt opened it, licked the end of the pencil and set to scribbling in a margin. He walked away, failing to look where he was going, and Lewis had to steer him around three ladders and a lumber pile before they got back to the stage. Behind them, Lewis heard Joseph whistling "The St. Louis Blues."

The way was cleared at last for the Wood Near Athens to rise.

Lewis followed like a shadow as Reinhardt stalked through the forests of Calabasas, hand-selecting live trees to be planted on the stage. No mere spindly little ornamentals, either; gigantic oaks, elms and aspen trees were dug up, loaded onto wagons and trucked into the Bowl. There Reinhardt sat at the top of the house like God with a megaphone, directing as each tree was moved into precisely the right spot. A few feet this way—a few feet that way—more forest, more shadows, more mystery!

Watching him, Lewis shook his head in sympathy. It would never be exactly as Reinhardt dreamed; nothing could. *How lucky mortals are,* thought Lewis, *that they never live long enough to learn it.*

LEWIS!!!!!

Lewis sat bolt upright in bed, convinced the telephone was ringing. It wasn't. A mortal might have looked next at his alarm clock, but Lewis did not require one. He stared around at his apartment, noting the predawn gloom beyond the windows. No desperate cyborg clinging to the fifth-story ledge; no one standing by his worktable, where his inks and papers were tidily arranged around the copies he was making of Reinhardt's papers. Tea makings laid out in the kitchenette, his solitary three-minute egg and slice of toast still inhabiting the realm of yet-to-be, his carefully pressed suit still over the chair where he had laid it out the night before. He was, as usual, alone. So who—

Lewis, where the heck are you?

Lewis scowled and pressed his fingertips to his temples. *You needn't transmit at that volume! And I'm in bed, where do you think? It's half past six.*

O.K., sorry. I've been signaling for five minutes. Some people have to get up early, you know? Joseph seemed to be struggling with his temper. *Look, I'm in a jam. Some goddam mortal wrecked my car. I need a lift to the Bowl. I'm late for work.*

Crumbs. I'm still in my pajamas. I'll be there as soon as I can. You're over on Morningside Court, aren't you?

Just throw on a bathrobe!

I can't walk through the lobby in my dressing gown! Why can't you take a streetcar?

It'll take too long. Come on, Lewis, be a pal!

Muttering to himself, Lewis scrambled out of bed and got dressed. It was ten minutes before he retrieved his Plymouth coupe from the Orchid Apartments garage, and drove straight into morning rush-hour traffic. There was a traffic accident at Highland; he lost more time casting about for Joseph's street. Altogether it was a full hour before he spotted Joseph, pacing back and forth on the sidewalk in front of a tiny apartment court and shouting at a cop who stood beside Joseph's Ford, which was now fenderless and doorless on its left side and displaying more of its undercarriage than was strictly proper.

"No, it was parked!" he was saying. "I'm up at five, I'm shaving, I hear this helluva crash, I go running out in my underwear and see this huge Oldsmobile backing out of my car with some idiot college kid at the wheel! He took off toward Vine! What are you going to do about it? *There* you are!" He turned to Lewis. "What kept you?"

He went to pull open the door of Lewis's car, but the cop put a hand on his shoulder.

"I'll tell you what I'm going to do about it, bub—I'm going to take an accident report while you cool down. Or would you like to go downtown?"

"He doesn't," said Lewis. "Joseph, talk to the nice policeman."

Joseph talked to the nice policeman for another twenty minutes, during which time a neighbor emerged from one of the other cottages in the court, inspected the damage, and offered to tow Joseph's car to his machine shop and do a repair estimate. It was eight-thirty by the time Lewis was able to pull away from the curb again, with Joseph fuming in the seat beside him.

"How the hell could you get *lost*?" Joseph demanded. "You're a cyborg."

"It might interest you to know that we're programmed with map coordinates taken in 1960," said Lewis. "It just so happens your address isn't on those maps. The whole block will be bulldozed for parking lots, as I discovered when I did an emergency access of the 1926 Sanborn survey, by which point I'd been around the block at Sunset and Vine six times."

"You...oh. Well, crap. What stupid data entry tech didn't catch that?" Joseph gnashed his teeth. He subsided and glared out the window. "You'd still have gotten there faster if you hadn't shaved before you left."

"I haven't shaved," said Lewis, with a certain edge in his voice.

"Really?" Joseph turned to peer at him. "Well, some guys have all the luck." He turned back and made an impatient gesture at a milk truck that had just pulled out in front of them. "Look at this! Where's he think he is, a dance floor? Jeez, if I'd gone ahead and taken the streetcar, I'd have been there by now. Son of a bitch. Serves me right. You know, I should have been warned about this! How come that cop's accident report doesn't make it into the Temporal Concordance? What are those guys up in 2334 *doing,* anyway, huh?"

"Failing to plot Event Shadows," said Lewis.

"You're telling me. Sometimes it *stinks,* being a cyborg!"

Lewis dropped him off in front of the Bowl with a sense of relief, and went home to shave.

Reinhardt was in a fine mood that morning, scarcely noticing when Lewis showed up late. He flung out his arm at the Wood Near Athens, his blue eyes shining.

"*Wunderbar,*" he said.

"Yes, sir," said Lewis, gazing down at the set with a certain amount of awe. "My, that's remarkable. It might have been growing there forever."

"It has," said Reinhardt. "I know every tree, every blade of grass in this wood. I have been here half my life. I have lost cities and castles and my home...but this I cannot lose, because this alone is real."

"It..." Lewis blinked, transposing the image of the stage as he had last seen it with its present appearance. "It looks as though it got bigger overnight."

"It needed more trees," said Reinhardt. "I had some dug up and moved."

"Ah," said Lewis. "Dug up. From...?"

Reinhardt made an expansive gesture that took in the surrounding valley. He strolled down the steps toward the stage, where the assistant director was engaged in heated conversation with the actor playing Bottom, as the other actors wandered to and fro along the apron. Lewis ran along behind Reinhardt, feeling curiously uneasy.

Reinhardt seated himself in the front row and, feeling for his reading glasses with one hand, put out the other for the playbook. Lewis handed it to him.

"Look, I have to do this big," argued the actor. "I'm the only one moving on the goddam stage at this point, aren't I?"

Weissberger, the assistant, threw up his hands in impatience. "Not *that* big! You look like you are having an epileptic seizure, Mr. Connolly."

"Baloney!" Connolly clenched his fists. "Look at the size of this house! I'm going to be lucky if anybody at the top even sees *me*, let alone how I play this scene."

"Hmm?" Reinhardt looked over his glasses. "What is their trouble?" he inquired of Lewis, never taking his eyes from the stage. Lewis explained, quickly. Reinhardt got up, leaving the playbook and glasses on the bench, and threaded his way between the lights to the stage. Lewis followed him at two paces' distance.

"Let's see the scene again. Where is the child?" said Reinhardt. Lewis translated, and Mickey Rooney stood up.

"Do we do it again?"

"Yes, please," said Lewis.

"O.K." Rooney walked upstage and hit his mark. With a snort of impatience, Connolly lay down under a tree and sprawled at length.

"And exit Oberon and Titania and..." said Weissberger. Rooney scrambled from behind the tree on hands and knees, and mimed pulling off Bottom's ass's head.

"'*Now-when-thou-wak'st-with-thine-own-fool's-eyes-peep,*'" he recited, and dove back behind the tree.

"Now," said Reinhardt softly, "you must realize that it will be night, you will be well lit, and the whole stage will be yours. They will all be looking at you. You are the last unresolved question." Lewis translated.

Connolly raised his arm, with a galvanic jerk, and waved away imaginary flies. He opened one eye, wide; he opened the other.

"Yes," said Reinhardt, with Lewis echoing him in English. "Yes, all right, you must reach the top of the house, but what then? Go on—"

Connolly sat bolt upright, and stared around wildly. "*Heigh ho!*" he shouted. "*Peter Quince? Flute the bellow-mender?*" He jumped to his feet, and ran to and fro. "*Snout the tinker? Starveling? God's my life! Stolen hence, and left me asleep!*"

"You see? That's—" said Weissberger.

"That's what you call *audible*," said Connolly. Lewis began to translate for Reinhardt, but he put out a hand for silence.

"You see, you are still asleep here," he said. "You are in a dream within a dream. You have only wakened out of the first layer. It is a good dream; you do not yet remember the nightmare. So, no need to jump; you only lean up on your elbow, like a man in his bed, until you come through the next shroud of the dream on *I have had a most rare vision*. Again, please, from the eyes opening."

Lewis translated. Connolly lay down again, opened his eyes, played the scene as requested.

"And *now* you wake a little more and get to your feet," coaxed Reinhardt, "and go on—"

"*I have had a most rare vision,*" said Connolly excitedly, jumping upright. He smacked his left fist into his right palm. "*I have had a dream, past the wit of man to say what dream it was.*" He stuck an index finger in the air. "*Man is but an ass if he go about to expound this dream!*"

"But you are not so awake even now," said Reinhardt. "There is still another layer to come through. You must say this slowly. Sleepily." Lewis translated, and Connolly rolled his eyes.

"Look, *Man is but an ass* is where I get the laugh," he protested. "It's funnier this way." Without waiting for Lewis to translate for him,

Reinhardt stepped forward and assumed Bottom's stance. He mimed stretching, murmured the lines in German, and at *past the wit of man to say what dream it was* he yawned elaborately, holding his hand far out as though before an ass's muzzle.

"O.K.," said Connolly, watching him closely. "O.K., that would get a laugh."

"You have been under an enchantment, you have drowned in moonlight, you have been sleeping in the arms of a mist-goddess," said Reinhardt. "And the spell is still on you and you remember now the pleasure, but then the horror sets in too, yes?"

"What'd he say?" Connolly looked at Lewis, who translated.

"Oh." Connolly turned to look at Reinhardt. "So...I get some drama?"

In answer, Reinhardt played the scene through in German. *Methought I was*—and the bewilderment came into his eyes, *there is no man can tell what.* Now he was frightened, feeling his face, feeling the air above his head in case he had ass-ears. *Methought I was, and methought I had*—Reinhardt delivered the lines giggling, weak with relief, and the giggle built to hysterical laughter that culminated in an ass's bray. He froze, as though appalled.

Hesitantly he went on with *But man is but a patched fool if he will offer to say...*and felt again at his face, and scratched his head—was that a tuft of hair, or an ass's ear?...*what methought I had.*

"Yeah!" said Connolly, clapping his hands.

Now Reinhardt mimed silent terror, doubt, confusion, dawning horror. His knees trembled. His frantic hands gripped two long hanks of hair, pulled them upright. Then he released them, stood straight, and swept back his hair. "So. You cannot awake from the nightmare. The audience will feel an echoing scream in their hearts. The wood is the source of all strange beauty, and all fear. The scene is not funny until you wake all the way and know it was only a dream, and then is the catharsis, and *then* you will caper like a fool and make them laugh."

All the actors were watching Reinhardt as though spellbound.

Lewis realized his heart was pounding. He swallowed hard and translated, as Reinhardt calmly put his hands in his pockets. Connolly looked from Lewis to Reinhardt, and clapped Lewis on the shoulder.

"Now, that's more like it! Boy, is that a scene." He looked around, triumphantly, at the assistant director. "No wonder they made *him* a professor!"

But as Reinhardt turned away and climbed back to his seat, his face was bleak. "I wanted Charlie Chaplin in that part," he murmured to Lewis. "Why couldn't I have had Charlie Chaplin?"

THREE: *THE NINE-MENS'-MORRIS IS FILL'D UP WITH MUD...*

When Lewis tucked his copywork under one arm and walked out to his car to drive home, he saw Joseph already in the passenger seat.

"Yes, of course I'll give you a ride home," said Lewis. "How silly of you to make such a fuss about asking, Joseph." He drew nearer, stopped and stared. "Are you all right?"

"No," said Joseph. "I'm screwed. And, much as I'd like to go on a bender at C.C. Brown's with about five hot fudge sundaes, that ain't going to happen. *'I must go seek some dewdrops here, and hang a pearl in every cowslip's ear.'* Can I borrow your car tonight?"

"Why?" Lewis looked anxiously at the Plymouth. "I just had it waxed—"

"I have to break into somebody's house."

"I see." Lewis got into the car. "Phew! I strongly suggest—"

"Yeah, yeah, I know, have a bath first or they'll track me by scent. I was sweating a little more than usual today, OK?"

Lewis started the car and pulled out onto Highland. "Perhaps you ought to tell me what happened."

"It wasn't my fault," said Joseph morosely. "I worked hard on this job, you know? Had this great character I'd made up. 'Joe Wilson.'

I had this whole history I'd invented for him. I had pictures of his wife and kids in my wallet. The mortals bought it hook, line and sinker. I made friends with the other guys on the crew. I traded them sandwiches from my dinner pail. We even talked baseball. Like: Is Dizzy Dean as good a pitcher as everybody thinks he is? That kind of thing." He grabbed for his hat as they accelerated. "Can we roll up the windows?"

"No. Go on," said Lewis, who had no idea who Dizzy Dean might be and no inclination to access records on twentieth-century baseball just at that moment in any case. Joseph sighed.

"And I might have painted myself green and worn a goddam ballet tutu, for all the good it did me. Did you ever hear of the Tavernier Violet?"

Lewis accessed rapidly. "A diamond? Yes. You're referring to the French Blue? Recut as the Hope Diamond."

"Ha! No, I'm not referring to the French Blue. How much of that story do you *really* know?"

Lewis focused in more detail. "Hmmm. 1668, India, one Jean-Baptiste Tavernier bought a crudely cut 110-carat stone described in color as *'a beautiful violet.'* Sold the stone to Louis XIV, along with several others. Stone recut in 1673, reduced to 69 carats—thereafter called the French Blue. Stolen from the Royal Treasury sometime in mid-September 1792, during the Revolution. Resurfaced twenty years and two days later (just as the Statute of Limitations time ran out) in London, in the possession of Daniel Eliason, recut to 44 carats. Mmmm...George IV acquired it somehow...turned up in the possession of Lord Hope, 1839...sold...sold...Turkish Sultan...Cartier sold it to Mrs. Evelyn Walsh of Washington, D.C. Well?"

"Anything strike you as funny in that little data stream?"

"Some mortal had remarkable self-control, holding on to it for twenty years," said Lewis, turning left onto Hollywood Boulevard.

"No, Lewis. More basic than that. Access the current description of the stone."

"Weight: 44.5 carats," said Lewis promptly. "Cut: Cushion antique brilliant with faceted girdle, extra facets on pavilion. Clarity: VS1. Color: Fancy Dark Steel Blue. Oh. That's not exactly Violet, is it?"

"You bet it isn't," said Joseph.

"So...the Hope diamond, formerly the French Blue, *isn't* the Tavernier Violet," said Lewis. "Well, isn't that fascinating?"

"See—what we have here is another Event Shadow. The blue rock got conflated with the violet one at some point. The blue rock moved on into history and became so famous, with its curse and everything, that it overshadowed the existence of the other stone. Even with the discrepancy in color staring everybody in the face."

"Maybe Tavernier was color-blind," said Lewis.

"He wasn't," said Joseph. "There was an error in the records. 110 carats cut down to 69, doesn't that seem a little drastic to you? And no trace of the remaining 41 carats' worth of violet diamond? Which there wasn't. No, it was recut, all right, but only down to 91 carats. Set in a necklace. Given by the Sun King to his favorite popsy of the moment, Madame de Montespan. And then he asked for it back. He tended to do that kind of thing."

"But she didn't give it back?"

"She didn't. Oh, she brought His Solarness the case, with a big purple fake in it; one that wouldn't have fooled anybody. *Madame,* says Louis, *this stone is paste!* She goes white and looks like she's about to faint. Athenais was a helluva good actress," Joseph added, taken for a moment by fond memories. He shook his head. "She yells, *I have been robbed! It must have been that dreadful man who repaired the broken clasp for me!* And there was a lot of smoke and mirrors about some mysterious guy who'd made off with the real stone. Never happened, though.

"Louis didn't believe her for a minute, but he wasn't going to push the matter, and she knew she was on the outs with him by that time anyway, so she didn't care. She kept the Tavernier Violet. She passed it on to one of her kids by Louis, so you could say it stayed in the family, the Orleans branch of it anyhow. Until 1866, by which time it'd found its way to Mexico."

"And you know all this because...?"

"Because I knew Athenais. And the family passed on the secret with the stone. And there's a Duke of Orleans who owns shares in Dr. Zeus."

"You mean they'll hang on into the twenty-fourth century?" Lewis was genuinely impressed. "My, that's tenacity."

"There's a Hapsburg who owns stock, too," said Joseph.

"No!" Lewis sat back. Then he made a face. "Oh, ugh, you don't suppose they've still got those awful—"

"Yeah, I'm afraid they do."

Lewis shuddered. "I don't want to think about how you know. But, go on."

"Well, remember where the Lost Treasure comes from in the first place? One of the jewels donated to the revolutionary cause, see, is the Tavernier Violet, which by this time is in a gold filigree setting.

"What I didn't mention before was the fact that when I got orders to dig the treasure up and move it, I was supposed to look for the Tavernier Violet and make sure it was near the top of the pile, because the Company's going to want it specially retrieved at some point in the near future. I found it; thing looked like a chunk of grape Popsicle.

"Well, I figured I'd make my job a little easier, right? So I stuck the rock in a Mason jar and buried it by itself, right under this one oak sapling, nice and deep."

"Oh, dear," said Lewis. "I have a feeling I know what's coming next." He turned right at Ivar and headed down past the library.

"So, you want to know what happened this morning, after you dropped me off?" said Joseph. "I go running up the canyon with my tail on fire, because I *know* something's gone wrong. You get to be a few thousand years old, you've been around the block a few times, you start to get an instinct for this kind of thing, you know what I'm saying? And here's Cookie's truck zooming down the road toward me, doing maybe forty miles an hour, and I'm thinking—"

"Cookie?"

"Cookie Bernstein. Used to be a cook in the Merchant Marine. He's really got his foot on the gas, and as the truck shoots past me I see Junior kind of slumped over in the bed of the truck—"

"Junior?"

"Junior Macready. Nice kid. Youngest guy on the crew. And he's covered with blood, see? And sort of clutching a hankie right *here*." Joseph slapped himself just above the bridge of his nose. "'Holy Mackerel,' I say to myself, 'that poor kid.' Little do I know! So I get up there finally, panting like a steam engine, and there's Lester and Stinky and Mulligan standing around—"

"What colorful mortal friends you've made—"

"And I forget all about Junior because there's this goddam crane, see, and what's dangling from it, fifteen feet up in the air? Guess. Just take a wild guess," said Joseph, pounding on the dashboard as his fury mounted. "Left! Left turn, Lewis! Jesus Christ on a Ry-Krisp, how could you miss it *again?*"

"You can always catch the streetcar to your burglary, you know," said Lewis. "I'm taking my wild guess now. Was it a certain oak sapling?"

"Except it wasn't a sapling any more," said Joseph. "It had grown into a great big artistically perfect tree, which *your boss* decided was just the thing for fairies to prance around under. So, this morning, right about when you were driving around this block for the umpteenth time, Max Reinhardt orders my buddies to dig up the oak tree and move it. Here! Park here. This is Mr. Goldfisch's spot, but he's visiting his aunt in Cucamonga."

"But what was all that business about Junior Macready being covered with blood?" said Lewis, as Joseph scrambled out of the car.

"I'm coming to that. Come on; if I don't get out of this lousy undershirt it's going to spontaneously combust," said Joseph, digging in his pockets for his key. Lewis exited the car reluctantly and followed him into the courtyard. It might have been any one of a thousand such places in Los Angeles: an oval of lawn with a single lamp pillar in the center, and, opening off the tiny common area, eight identical cottages, each with a hibiscus bush on either side of its front door.

"Excuse the mess," said Joseph, heading straight for the bathroom. Lewis perched on the edge of a chair in Joseph's tiny furnished parlor and looked around, as Joseph turned on the taps. There wasn't much of a mess actually; there wasn't room.

"How do you live in here?" said Lewis. Joseph shouted from the bathroom:

"Easy. I sleep in the bed and I shave in the bathroom. Mostly I eat in diners and coffee joints."

"But…it's so featureless. Don't you even have books, or pictures of your own?"

"I have couple of books," said Joseph. "Sentimental value, mostly. Look, Lewis, you know what happens the minute you start accumulating stuff."

There was a splash as he got into the tub and scrubbed vigorously. He went on:

"You get too used to a comfy chair, or a nice view, and you start thinking like a mortal. You get scared to let go of things. You put down roots someplace and, if you're lucky, the Company yanks you out and transfers you halfway around the world. If you're *not* lucky, you stay on for fifty or sixty years and watch all your mortal neighbors die, while the neighborhood goes to hell. Travel light, Lewis, and keep your mind on the job."

"And carry only memories?" said Lewis.

"Not if you can help it," Joseph replied. "They weigh more than ten years' worth of *National Geographic Magazine*, sometimes.

"Anyway, where was I?"

"So I go running up to the guys, who are standing around watching the tree like it was a public hanging, and I ask what's going on. Lester says, *Where you been, you missed all the excitement*, I say, *Some jackass wrecked my Ford,* he says, *Gee, that's too bad,* and I'm ready to grab him by the throat and choke him but Tex butts in and tells me how they dug down in a circle around this tree with picks and shovels, and then Stinky hooked the crane hoist around the trunk and they all stood back, and first it didn't want to come but then Stinky gave it a real good wrench and *pop,* it just jumped right out of the ground, ten feet straight up.

"Which was when this Mason jar came flying out of the roots and beaned Junior. Busted open and knocked him out cold. And the damn mortal points out the pieces of the Mason jar. I look, but there's no sign of the Tavernier Violet."

"Oh dear," said Lewis, as Joseph rose dripping from the tub and grabbed a towel.

"So there's this know-it-all mortal on the crew, we call him Doc, and he says how the jar must have been shoved down a gopher hole or something by a packrat, because they steal shiny things, like for example the big piece of costume jewelry that came flying out with the jar. *No kidding,* I say, wanting to sit down right there and bawl. And Doc says, *Oh yes, obviously the piece went missing from some Bowl performance or other back in the '20s.* He had it all doped out, see. *Can I have a look at it?* I query.

"*Oh,* says Mulligan, *we gave it to Junior when he came around. Told him as how since he'd got crowned, he needed some crown jewels.* It had gone right past me in the back of Cookie's truck. The gods look down and laugh." Joseph came out of the bathroom with a towel around his waist, and rummaged in a dresser drawer for underclothes. Lewis averted his eyes.

"How unfortunate. What did you do?"

"Planted the tree where Reinhardt wanted it," said Joseph. "What else could I do? Sweated blood until I saw Cookie coming back in his truck. No Junior with him; naturally we all crowded around and asked questions. The kid's fine, except for twenty stitches in his scalp and a concussion. Cookie dropped him off at his parents' house. He won't be back to work on this job. I found out where he lived so I could send a fruit basket."

"Thoughtful of you," said Lewis.

"I'm not sending the guy a fruit basket, I'm breaking into his house!" Joseph, decently clad in a pair of drawers, went to his closet and pulled it open.

"How many trenchcoats and fedoras do you own?" said Lewis, staring into the closet.

"Look, I'm a studio dick. A good operative dresses the part, right?" Joseph reached in and pulled out a black turtleneck sweater. "Here we go. Black shirt, black pants, black sneakers! If I have to burgle somebody's house, I'm going to do it right."

"I'm surprised you don't have a black mask," said Lewis.

"Good point," said Joseph, struck by the idea. "Should I maybe try to get one from Bert Wheeler's?"

"I don't think you can get there before they close," said Lewis. "Anyway, that was sarcasm."

"Cripes, I'm starving. You want to stop at a diner and get a couple of sandwiches before I drop you off?"

"I'll drop you off at your burglary, Joseph, but I'm not loaning you my car," said Lewis. "My case officer's very strict about how many automobiles I'm issued in any one fiscal period."

"Yeah, O.K., I know how that is. You can stick around and be my getaway driver, then."

"Joseph, I've got work to do." Lewis held up the folder of papers he had been clutching. "These have to be copied! They'll be destroyed in an archive fire in 2236, unless I have a good fake to substitute for them."

"2236?" Joseph bent down to tie one sneaker. "Heck, you've got plenty of time, then."

FOUR: TO TRUST THE OPPORTUNITY OF NIGHT...

In the end they got hamburger sandwiches wrapped in waxed paper at a stand on the Boulevard, and ate them on a side street below Franklin, a few blocks from Junior Macready's house.

"That's the stuff," said Joseph in satisfaction, tilting his pop bottle for a last swallow. He dropped it on the floor, wadded his sandwich wrapper into a ball and dropped that on the floor too, and sat straight. "O.K! 6700 Yucca. Let's drive by and case the joint."

The area just north of Hollywood Boulevard dated from the time the town had been a teetotalers' colony; it was green-lawn residential, with Eastlake and Craftsman homes set back from a street lined with jacarandas, and every back yard had an orange tree. Plenty of decorative gingerbread and trellises. Men were coming home to dinners; children were playing on the sidewalks, throwing long shadows in the slanting light.

"You're not going to try this until well after dark, I hope," said Lewis fretfully.

"Of course not. 6700! There it is. Make a left up here and park."

Lewis obeyed. They sat staring at 6700 Yucca Avenue. There was a long, long silence.

"I perceive problems," said Lewis at last.

"No kidding," said Joseph, disgruntled.

The house sat on the corner of Yucca and Whitley. It was a big, rambling Craftsman, covered in shingles painted a cheerful yellow. Other than a sprawl of climbing Herbert Hoover roses over the front porch, there wasn't a scrap of concealing vegetation anywhere on the house. Even the requisite citrus tree in the back yard was nowhere near an outer wall.

"Not one iota of lurking space, and all the windows and doors exposed to public view," said Lewis. "And...let's see...I'm picking up ten life forms from inside. Two of which seem to be dogs."

The front door opened. A mortal man emerged, middle-aged but powerfully built, and sat down in a rocking chair on the front porch. He opened out a newspaper and put his slippered feet up on the porch rail. After a moment a mastiff, carrying an immense beef bone, shouldered open the screen door and lay down beside the rocking chair. The dog set to work gnawing on the bone. The bone split with a *crack* that rang out distinctly in the evening air. Joseph shifted in his seat.

"That dog's got good teeth, huh?"

There was a frenzied barking from inside, and a cocker spaniel bounced itself against the screen door three times before bounding out at last, whereupon it raced madly from one end of the porch to the other. The mortal and the bigger dog ignored it. At last a little girl came out and grabbed the spaniel, dragging it back inside.

"A big strong dog and a little yappy dog," said Joseph, rubbing his chin. "And kids. Jeez."

"Is there any chance you got the address wrong?"

Joseph pointed silently to the mailbox, upon which was painted MACREADY. Lewis sighed.

Joseph crossed his arms and slouched back in his seat. Lewis leaned his elbows on the steering wheel and set his chin in his palms. Both men closed their eyes, listening, focusing in on the yellow house.

Cracking of bone. Rustling of newspaper pages being turned. Water running; the clatter of dishes being washed. Two mortal voices—young, female—raised over the sound of the water: *So then I told her she could keep her old roller skates. Gosh, did she get mad? I'll say she did, but...*

A click, a squeal, dance music coming over a radio—*the Paul Whiteman Orchestra, ladies and gentlemen!* Feet thundering across a hardwood floor, shrill voices in anger: *Gimme! Give'm back, you dirty bum! Ma! He took my Mickey Mouse!* A female voice cutting in: *Can't I get a moment's peace in this house? Mother, can't you make them understand that I am talking on the telephone?*

An older voice, female: *Now, boys, do you want me to take this up with your father?* Another radio switched on, with a higher, tinnier tone: four gunshots and a groan. *Stop shooting, boys; we've caught our jailbird. Thought you'd get away with it, didn't you, mug? Don't you know...*

Creaking, as stairs were climbed. *Junior, dear? Sit up, now; I've brought you a nice glass of grape juice. Oh, you barely touched that soup! Sorry, Ma; I kept spilling it. Thanks. Now, you boys stay out of Junior's room! Gee, you look like you been in the war! Beat it, pipsqueak. Say, what's this thing? Where'd you get a purple diamond?*

It ain't a diamond. It's a piece of fancy glass the guys stuck in my pocket. Some consolation prize, huh?

Can I have it? It'd make a swell hat for Saint Cornelius!

Both Lewis and Joseph opened their eyes and turned to each other, frowning in perplexity.

Sure. Just stop making so much darned noise. Okey-dokey! Oh, dear, this shirt was practically new, wasn't it? Maybe if I soak it with some White King...

"Saint Cornelius?"

Lewis accessed rapidly. "Cornelius the Centurion, pagan convert, first century. Also Pope Cornelius, third-century martyr."

"I know! What'd he mean, 'a hat for Saint Cornelius'?"

Lewis shrugged.

"As if this wasn't hard enough," muttered Joseph. "Now I'll have to break into a kid's room. Toys all over the place. Marbles. Jacks. Oh, this is going to be some picnic."

"If you can get inside at all," said Lewis, eyeing the mastiff on the porch.

The man on the porch read his paper until twilight, when he slapped at a mosquito, then rose abruptly and carried his paper indoors. The mastiff followed him. Soft evening fell, lilac-colored and unobtrusive.

There, a light went on in the front parlor; through the window the man could just be glimpsed, in an armchair beside the radio that played dance music. A light in the kitchen window, where the dishes were dried and put away; lights blooming yellow in the upper windows, where someone small was bathed, protesting loudly, and someone else was coached over his schoolwork, and a heated conversation was carried on concerning how stuck-up Mary Ellen Donaldson had become since her aunt had taken her on that trip to France. Someone else was reading a novel, by a pink-shaded lamp; someone else was listening to Cab Calloway in the dark, though the radio cast a dim golden halo on the wall behind it.

Lewis sighed.

"I envy the mortals, sometimes."

Joseph shrugged. He knew the feeling.

"If only they lasted," he said.

"Would their lives be so sweet, if they did?"

"They don't see what we see," said Joseph. "And, hell, we blink, and they're gone. This is what I was talking about! Seven more years, and Junior'll be sweating on an aircraft carrier in the Pacific. The kids'll grow up and go away. There'll be a condo block on this spot in fifty years, the gardens all gone, and you and I will be the only ones who remember these people."

"But we will," said Lewis.

"You think that's a good thing?" said Joseph. "We can't afford to, you know."

It grew late. One by one the upper lights went out; the man in the parlor got up, shut off the radio, and went through the house locking the doors and closing the windows. The immortals heard him climbing a flight of stairs, breathing hard. A light went on, briefly, as teeth were brushed; a light went out. Darkness.

They waited another hour, listening hard for the slowed heartbeats, the quiet breathing or snores that signified everyone slept. When it had been twenty minutes since the last car had passed on the street, Joseph yawned and stretched.

"I guess there's no point in putting it off," he said. "What do you figure? Roof approach? Chimney, maybe?"

"When did you get magic weight-loss powers?" said Lewis. Joseph gave him an aggrieved look.

"Listen, I can flatten myself out like a cockroach when I have to," he said, and got out of the car. "I don't suppose you could give me a hand with the streetlights?"

"I can try," said Lewis. "Best of luck, old man."

Joseph snorted and padded off into the night. Lewis looked at the two nearest streetlights, one halfway down the block and the other on the opposite corner. He bent his head and fixed his attention on the nearer one. He had never attempted this trick, and had no idea if he could really transmit in such a way as to interrupt the circuit.

*Come on, Lewis...*He scowled at the light, massaging the bridge of his nose, rubbing his temples, deep breathing, anything he could think of to focus. There! The light was flickering. Dimming. Yes! Down. Down, but not out...still, he could now make out the pale blue light of the waxing moon.

A faint thump sounded from the direction of the house. Was that Joseph, launching himself at the roof in hyperfunction? Lewis glanced over and saw Joseph poised on the chimney, looking down uncertainly. Joseph looked up, aghast, and Lewis realized that the streetlight had brightened again with his lapse of attention. He turned back immediately and dimmed it once more.

He kept his gaze riveted on the light, forcing himself to concentrate, emptying his mind of all other thoughts...except...Joseph would be covered in soot if he went down the chimney, wouldn't he? Greasy sandwich wrappers and sticky pop bottles were bad enough, but...of course, a mission was a mission, and nothing mattered but the work, and...all the same, maybe it would be best to spread some newspaper out over the upholstery...did he have any newspaper in the trunk? He didn't think he did...oh, wait, he had a road map some over-helpful service station attendant had pressed on him, the last time he'd gotten petrol...no, he was playing an American, mustn't call it that...

There was a crash from the house and a thunder of barking, and a split second later Joseph materialized by the car. He nearly yanked the door off in his haste to scramble in.

"Drive!"

"Wait!" Lewis tore open the glove box and felt around for the map.

"What are you *doing?*"

"You'll get soot all over everything—"

"I didn't go down the chimney!" Joseph threw himself in and pulled the door shut.

"Ow! Get off my arm—"

"Will you drive, for Christ's sake?"

"Did you get it?"

"No—" The barking was still going on, and lights had begun to go on in the house. Lewis started the car and they took off down Whitley, making a right at the Boulevard.

"Shall I circle back and drop you off at your place?" said Lewis hopefully.

"No! Drive around for a while," said Joseph, sounding furious. "We're going to have to go back."

"What happened?"

"Lousy chimney was blocked," said Joseph. "What's the matter with people? Why don't they hire a chimney sweep once in a while? Boy, are they going to get a surprise next time they try to light a fire in there. There must have been three dead crows blocking the flue."

"But you obviously got inside."

"Yeah, somebody left a bedroom window open. So I crawled down the side of the house and hung there a minute, checking it out. The smells were a dead giveaway: bubble gum, cedar pencils and goaty little kid sweat. *Bingo,* I said to myself, and kind of seeped down closer and scanned their breathing and brain rhythms. Two mortal children, males, both of 'em sound asleep. No dogs in the room.

"So I crawled in over the sill and looked around. Right there, on top of this desk, is this shrine made out of a shoebox, with a plaster figure of a saint in it. And guess what's stuck in a lump of plasticine on top of the statue's head."

"The Tavernier Violet," said Lewis. "Oh! It must be *Pope* Cornelius. The papal tiara, don't you see?"

"Who cares which stinking Cornelius it's supposed to be?" Joseph shouted. "It's sitting right next to one of those goddam clockwork monkeys with cymbals, O.K.? And just as I put out my hand, and I swear I didn't even touch the thing, just as I reach for the statue, Bobo the Chimp starts whaling away with the cymbals. Both kids sit up in bed, scream like a couple of bats, and a hundred and sixty pounds of mastiff comes charging down the hall. Exit Joseph, and how!"

"How unfortunate," said Lewis. 'What will you do?"

"I'll tell you what we'll do," said Joseph, attempting to calm himself. "We're going to go back there and get inside in broad daylight."

"We aren't," said Lewis firmly.

"No, this will work! Here's what we do. We stake out the place, see, and watch in the morning as everybody leaves, until there's nobody home but the lady of the house and Junior."

"And the two dogs."

"O.K., yes, the two dogs. And then you go up to the front door and ring the doorbell. Meanwhile, I'll be going around the back of the house. The mortal lady opens the door, you ask her if she'd be interested in buying a magazine subscription."

"I'll have to be shouting over the baying of the hounds," said Lewis. "Dogs never like me, you know. They can tell I'm a cyborg, somehow."

"That's the idea! They'll be crazy to get through the screen door so they can kill you, right? And the lady will be apologizing and trying to pull them back—"

"Trying?"

"And if Junior's awake it'll distract him, too, so nobody'll notice me going up the trellis under the kids' room, going in through the window, nabbing the rock and getting out of there, especially if I do it in hyperfunction!" said Joseph. "Problem solved. You tip your hat, thank the lady and exit, meeting me back at the car."

"Pausing only to pry a cocker spaniel off my leg."

"Jeepers, Lewis, be a sport about this, can't you? You're a *cyborg*. You can outrun the dogs."

FIVE: *O, I AM OUT OF BREATH IN THIS FOND CHASE...*

After a brief stop at the Orchid Apartments, wherein Lewis showered, shaved and put on a clean suit (thoughtfully tucking a can of red pepper into his pocket), they drove back to Yucca Avenue and parked halfway down the block, near enough to watch the front door. Lewis walked down to the Boulevard and returned with a copy of the *Citizen-News*, and, on climbing behind the wheel once more, opened the paper out, hoping to look as inconspicuous as possible.

At five-thirty the front door opened and the mortal man emerged, carrying a lunch pail.

"That's Macready Senior," said Joseph. "Works as a grip at Paramount. Off to catch the streetcar. One down."

At seven the door opened again and a young lady in a navy blue uniform emerged, carrying an armful of books.

"That's two," said Joseph. "Junior's sister, off to Immaculate Heart High."

At seven-fifteen the door opened again and a swarm of children emerged, the two girls in navy blue, the two little boys in salt-and-pepper corduroy trousers and white shirts.

"Three, four, five and six," said Joseph in satisfaction. "That's it. Off to school, kiddies."

But instead of parading off in the direction of the streetcar tracks, the children lined up expectantly by the mailbox.

"Perhaps they take the schoolbus?" said Lewis, folding up his paper.

"Crap!" Joseph sat bolt upright, staring at the older of the two boys. Lewis looked, then looked more closely.

"Oh," he murmured. The mortal child was clutching an open shoebox, converted to a shrine by means of stained-glass windows drawn in crayon, housing a small plaster statue.

"He's taking the damn thing to school!"

"Is that it?" Lewis intensified his focus. He made out the winking point of violet on the statue's head, just before a yellow schoolbus pulled up to the curb and blocked his view. "Yes, that's Pope Cornelius, all right, although he's had to make over a statue of Saint Jude; I don't suppose there are a lot of Saint Cornelius statues around. But his feast day is September 16, which is this Sunday, so—"

"Lewis, would you mind very much starting the car and following that bus?" said Joseph, slowly and carefully.

"There's no need for sarcasm," said Lewis, starting the car.

The schoolbus trundled along for some blocks, stopping often, difficult to shadow discreetly; but at last it pulled into a vast schoolyard just above Sunset. Lewis and Joseph pulled up and watched as the stream of children emerged from the bus and assembled in ranks before marching into the school.

"Cripes, the place looks like a fortress," said Joseph. "Circle around. Let's see if there are any windows."

Lewis obliged. He found a spot a block away to the east that provided them with a clear view of the eastern wall of the school: six windows, three on the first story and three on the second. In each was framed an identical classroom: four straight rows of desks occupied by thirty-six uniformed children. Only the ages of the inmates differed, room by room, with a certain slump noticeable in the shoulders of the oldest ones. Joseph and Lewis regarded them in silence.

"Then again, sometimes I don't envy mortals at all," said Lewis. "Slotted in like so many little machine parts. How can they bear it?"

Joseph shrugged. He pointed to the middle classroom on the first floor. There, on a table, was a veritable choir of plaster saints. Some were glued into abalone shells, some were mounted on pedestals made of painted tomato cans; there at the back was Saint Cornelius, with his violet crown.

"O.K., this isn't so bad," said Joseph. "We can come back here tonight and break into the place."

"You're going to desecrate a shrine?" said Lewis.

"What do you care? You were a Roman, not a Roman Catholic. It isn't like Saint Cornelius is going to lean down and pitch a thunderbolt at you."

"No, but the mortals believe in that sort of thing, and that can make a remarkable difference," said Lewis. "Besides, it's rather an endearing idea, don't you think? This whole little pantheon of minor saints, looking out for the welfare of humanity? For example, Pope Cornelius is the one you pray to to keep away earaches. I find that charming."

"You must have slept through the Reformation, huh?"

"No, I missed that century. I was Guest Services Director at New World One back then. Wouldn't it be nicer world, really, if the mortals had someone to watch over them?"

"Maybe, but all they have is us. Mind taking me back to my place so I can get changed for work? And, uh, giving me a lift to the Bowl, afterward?"

"Doesn't Mr. Mayer wonder where you've got to?"

"He thinks I'm visiting my mother in Altoona."

Theseus and Hippolyta came hand in hand across the great creaking trestle, leading the splendid if half-costumed wedding procession. Ignoring them, an electrician and his assistant went up and down ladders among the trees, installing the tiny flickering lights that would, on opening night, impersonate fireflies. The assistant stage manager counted out beats, over the faint whine of a Victrola playing Mendelssohn's "Wedding March" beside his chair. It creaked to a close just as the royal couple stepped onstage. He turned and flashed Reinhardt a thumbs-up.

"You see?" said Reinhardt, dabbing the sweat from his brow with a handkerchief. "It is perfectly timed, and nobody fell off."

"I do trust there will be a handrail of some sort, before performance?" said Theseus, with frosty *noblesse oblige.* He was being portrayed by John Lodge, a Boston aristocrat who had briefly condescended to the thespian life.

"But the point of the ramp is that it's just supposed to sort of hang there, like magic," protested the assistant director. Reinhardt looked back and forth between them until Lewis translated.

"A skilled actor is half acrobat," he said in response. "But if he is frightened, have the crew string up hand ropes. Black velvet ones."

Lewis repeated this in English, slightly edited, and the production manager threw up his hands in despair.

"Black velvet ropes? Where am I supposed to get those?"

"Theater supply wholesaler?" Lewis suggested. "Costume department?"

Miss Sibley, Lewis's immediate superior in the ranks of Reinhardt's assistants, fanned herself with a copy of the *Los Angeles Times.* She looked out at the hills beyond the Bowl and said doubtfully: "But in the actual performance, they'll have to come all the way down from up there, won't they? Carrying lit torches? My, that'll be dangerous, with all that dry brush."

"The Fire Department gave him a permit," said Lewis. "And he's going to time it again at Dress Rehearsal."

"Oh," she said, but not as though convinced.

The crowds of attendants filed onto the set, and lined up a little awkwardly on the turf. Weissberger turned to look at Reinhardt, who smiled and nodded. "Please," he said. "Go on."

The action of the play went forward—lovers forgiven, pomp and ceremony, and in came Bottom and his mates to present their play-within-the-play, *Pyramus and Thisbe.* Lewis leaned forward in his seat, in anticipation. He had seen some four hundred and seventy-three performances of *A Midsummer Night's Dream,* over the centuries, and *Pyramus and Thisbe* just got funnier every time he saw it.

The Prologue was spoken, the Wall spoke his piece. Enter Pyramus and Thisbe (Walter Connolly in rattling armor, Sterling Holloway in demure drag). The lovers swore to be true through the Wall's chink, and the fatal assignation at Ninny's Tomb was arranged. Exit Lovers and Wall; enter Lion and Moonshine, Moonshine being personified by Otis Harlan, best known later as the voice of Happy the Dwarf in *Snow White*. Enter Thisbe once more, Lion roars; Thisbe screams and flees, dropping Veil, which is promptly seized and rent by Lion. Exit Lion; enter Pyramus, leaping to conclusions and a death scene of epic awfulness. Shakespeare, perverting all his genius to write as badly as possible!

Reinhardt shifted in his seat. He stood and advanced a few steps down toward the stage. The suppressed giggles of the other actors fell silent at once.

"This is good," he said, "but I think it would be funnier if Thisbe is more bulky, more the big plowboy. Can you try it that way?" Lewis opened his mouth to translate, but the actor playing Quince (Frank Reicher) relayed the request first.

"But he isn't a plowboy, Professor Reinhardt," said Holloway. "Francis Flute is a bellows-mender." He mimed pumping a pair of bellows. "It says so in the script."

Reicher translated. Reinhardt frowned. He looked away, waving his hand.

"Then I would like to see you play it bigger. More the country bumpkin."

"I'll do my best," said Holloway. He squared his shoulders manfully.

"Please, go on, then," Reinhardt said. Under his breath he murmured, "It would have been so much funnier with W. C. Fields." He turned and climbed back to his seat. The actors watched him with a certain amount of resentment. Harlan sidled up to Holloway and thumped him on the shoulder.

"What the heck," Harlan piped cheerfully. "You can go have yourself some fun tonight and forget the old—"

Miss Sibley leaned toward Lewis, and unpursed her lips long

enough to whisper: "This is dreadful. Don't they realize the Professor is one of the giants of German romantic theater? The studios ought to have leaped at the chance to loan him their stars!"

Lewis looked sympathetic, but shrugged. "Plebeians, I suppose. It'll all work out on the night."

Six: Wherefore was I to this keen mockery born?...

The evening star was just visible when the Plymouth pulled up outside the school above Sunset. Joseph scrambled out of the car and closed its door. He had once again dressed in his all-black ensemble.

"Why don't you just circle the block a few times, O.K.?" he said. "Less conspicuous." Lewis sighed, shook his head, and pulled out from the curb.

He was on his fifth circumnavigation when he picked up the frantic transmission:

Lewis! Corner of Selma and Cherokee! Step on it!

Lewis, already headed down Selma, gunned the motor accordingly and a moment later drew level with Joseph, who vaulted into the passenger seat and pointed in the direction of a rapidly disappearing Model T. "After that guy!" Joseph shouted.

A thrilling car chase did not ensue, because the Model T proceeded up to the Boulevard and joined the slow procession of evening traffic in a westerly direction. Joseph did not, therefore, go into Action Cyborg mode and leap from the front seat of the Plymouth to the roof of the Model T and rip it open like so much paper, hauling his quarry out to deliver a lethal karate chop. Real cyborgs seldom get the chance to do that sort of thing, and never in front of several hundred mortal witnesses.

"What happened this time?" said Lewis, waiting for the STOP signal to swing down out of sight.

"It started out easy," said Joseph, peering ahead at the Model T, now separated from them by a slow-moving touring car. "Go! Go! Come on! Transom window in the second-floor boys' bathroom left open a crack. I got it open, squeezed though headfirst, ran downstairs to the kids' classroom. The shrine was right where it ought to be, all right, but somebody'd pinched the diamond."

"How do you know it was this person?" Lewis inquired, trying to pass the touring car.

"Because I switched to thermal vision, O.K.? And there were all these fading green and orange steps going up and down the aisles, and brighter steps going up to the table with the shrines, and a big red handprint around Saint Pope Cornelius and a thumbprint right in the middle of his face, and flaming red prints going away from the table again and out the classroom door!

"So I ran after them. They went all the way down the hall, and right there at the end was this big door with window panes. On the other side of it was this mortal, all lit up like Satan, locking the door and putting his keys in his pocket."

"Must be the school janitor," said Lewis.

"So I scrammed, and just as I was sticking my head out the bathroom window I saw the guy getting into his car."

"Oh, dear, he's probably headed for a pawnshop," said Lewis.

"Crap. Well, I know what we'll do. You rear-end the guy as hard as you can. I'll jump out—"

"Joseph, this car is Company property!"

"So are you."

"And I'm cheaper to repair!"

"Lewis, for Christ's sake—Right! Make a right! He's going up La Brea!"

Lewis cranked the wheel and they followed the Model T uphill as far as Franklin, where it pulled to the curb and parked. They cruised past it as a mortal emerged. But for his grubby overalls and undershirt, he might have been a Prussian officer or a headwaiter at some particularly snooty restaurant; he had an upright bearing and meticulously waxed moustaches.

Joseph, glaring at him as they passed, said: "That's the school janitor, all right."

"Oh, my gosh!" said Lewis. "That's not all he is! Don't you recognize him?"

"No."

"Access a record of male film stars for the years 1910 to 1925!"

Joseph obeyed, as Lewis took them up to La Brea Terrace and turned around. "Larry Montcalm? Jeepers, that was *Larry Montcalm?* He used to make three grand a week over at Selig Polyscope!"

"Lo, how the mighty are fallen," said Lewis. He pulled to the curb and parked, setting the hand brake, as Joseph stared at the mortal.

"I bet he's going to change his clothes and hock the diamond. Where's he going?"

They watched as Montcalm entered the vestibule of a brownstone on the corner. Joseph got out of the car. "You stay here."

"Gladly," said Lewis. Joseph strode down the street, looking determined, and vanished into the brownstone. A moment later he came running back uphill.

"Goddammit, he lives in the basement! Go down and park on Franklin."

Lewis groaned, but obeyed. By the time he had found a parking space, Joseph was ready to leap from the car in his agitation.

"Look at that! Could the basement windows be any more exposed? Right out on the sidewalk, for crying out loud! So much for a surreptitious entrance that way. Can you pick him up at all?"

"Sssh!" Lewis waved a hand distractedly, squeezing his eyes shut as he focused on the basement windows. Clinking, rattling, rustling, the sound of running water, a single mortal heartbeat..."He's alone, at least. Seems to be taking a bath."

"O.K.; I'll have to go in and knock on his door," said Joseph. "Though I don't look like a cop, in this getup...crumbs. *You* could pass for one, though. Look, why don't you go knock on his door and tell him you're a plainclothes cop—"

"What, from the Parochial School Patrol? How would anybody but us know he stole anything, at this point?"

"You could say you're a G-Man, and you've been tailing him on suspicion of being a Socialist or something—"

Lewis had several objections to this plan, and during the time they were bickering over alternate strategies the mortal finished his bath, got dressed and was humming to himself as he made noises suggestive of preparing a light meal.

"O.K.," said Joseph at last, "then you're going to have to drive me to a market where I can buy about ten boxes of Cracker Jack, because—"

"Wait! Was that his doorbell that just rang?"

They both focused on the basement. Yes; they heard footsteps crossing the floor, and then:

"Muriel, dearest! You're a little early; I'm afraid I was just sitting down to dine. Don't you look ravishing in that charming ensemble, though!"

It was a high voice with a peculiar throttled intonation, the sort best suited to cartoon characters. Martians in tennis shoes, perhaps.

"Well, that explains why his career didn't survive the Talkies," said Joseph.

"You look swell, yourself. Do you really like it?" said another mortal voice, female, not young, a little breathless. "I took the hem up a couple of inches, just like you said. And I made the hat myself, out of an old brocade cushion—"

"Delightful. Delightful. Yes, we'll be the sinecure of all eyes!" The male mortal sounded sly. "Particularly since...but where are my manners? May I offer you a plate of Campbell's?"

"Oh, no thanks, dear, I had a sandwich before I came over. I'm too nervous to eat much anyhow. Say, look at the right sleeve, here. Does it look like I got that stain out?"

"Why, it's like new! No one could tell, I assure you. And, under the circumstances, I doubt anyone will be looking at your *arm*, dear Muriel."

"Why, whatever do you mean, Lawrence?"

Joseph, who had been slouched down in the car seat, sat bolt upright. "Oh, no," he said.

"What?" said Lewis.

"All in good time, Muriel, all in good time. If you'll permit me—"

"Oh, sure, you go right ahead and finish your soup."

"I have this bad feeling about how Lawrence is planning to impress dear Muriel," said Joseph. Lewis intensified his focus and listened in. There was gallant small talk interspersed with the sound of soup being consumed, there were modest replies, there were the sounds of china being cleared away, and then:

"Oh! Lawrence, you shouldn't have!"

"Uh-oh," said Lewis.

"Nonsense. I saw this trifle, and I said to myself: 'That's the very thing for my Columbina!'"

"'Columbina'?" said Joseph.

All was made plain when, after fifteen more minutes of coy chatter, the mortals exited the building and came into view on the corner, where they looked both ways before crossing to Lawrence's Model T.

"Oh, *Harlequin* and Columbina," said Lewis. Joseph said something unprintable. Lawrence wore a diamond-patterned suit of blue and green, with a black domino mask; his lady friend wore a frilly skirt and jacket in a matching diamond pattern in purple and lavender. A mortal could not have made it out at that distance, but to cyborg vision it was painfully clear: there around her neck, on a chain, was a flashing violet light, brilliant as a movie starlet's eyes.

"Of all the lousy luck!" Joseph leaned forward and beat his forehead against the dashboard a few times.

"Stop that! You'll dent it. They're driving away, you know. Shouldn't we be following them?"

"Sure. Why not?" said Joseph listlessly.

Lewis started the car again and raced after the Model T. He followed it all the way to Highland and up past the Hollywood Bowl, by which time Joseph had recovered himself enough to be plotting again.

"O.K., all is not lost. The next time they pull up at a traffic signal, I'll leap out and grab the rock through the window. I'll run off into the bushes and up over the hill, you make a u-turn and pick me up again out on Mulholland—"

"What if they get my license number and call the police?"

"Then we'll ditch the car on Mulholland and you can report it as stolen—heads up, there's a traffic signal! Get ready!"

"Joseph, I've only had this car six months, and—"

"Dammit!" Joseph clutched his hair and pulled, in his frustration. Rather than stopping at the signal, the Model T had turned onto a side street that climbed steeply, paralleling Cahuenga. "No! Go after 'em!"

Lewis swerved to follow, neatly and narrowly missing an oncoming truck, whose driver shook his fist and pounded on the horn. The street climbed, and climbed; leveled out briefly and then climbed some more, throwing in a curve for good measure. A spectacular view of the Cahuenga Pass and the San Fernando Valley beyond opened out to the right, but there was no time to admire the scenery. As Lewis was shifting gears, Joseph pointed and yelled. "There!"

To their left, a number of cars were parked along the street, and the Model T was performing the profoundly chancy maneuver of turning around in a driveway just under a blind curve. Lewis slowed his car to watch as the Model T completed the turn safely and pulled in behind the other cars, from which other costumed mortals were emerging.

"It must be a studio party," said Lewis. "Look! There's Charlie Chase. And there's one of the Cherry Sisters, and Ralph Falconer... that's Richard Talmadge, he was a stuntman around the same time I was."

"Huh," said Joseph, looking thoughtfully up at the house to which the mortals were climbing. It sat at least eight flights of zigzagging stairs above the street, and was a sprawling, many-leveled Spanish-style place, with balconies and gardens. "Big house, lots of guests in masks, lots of booze flowing. I could crash it! I just need a costume."

"Where are you going to get a costume at this hour on a Friday night?"

Joseph snapped his fingers. "Last-Minute Lester's!"

"I beg your pardon?"

"A little Industry secret. He's on Curson Street. Let's go!"

As they were headed back downhill through the Cahuenga Pass, Joseph explained: "This guy worked in Wardrobe at most of the little studios. When a shoot wrapped, he used to take one or two of the costumes back to his place and forget to return them, you know what I mean? So he built up a collection. He pays for mothballs by renting out costumes to people in the know."

Fifteen minutes later they pulled up in front of a modest bungalow on a tree-lined street. Lewis waited in the car as Joseph went to the door; it was opened by a gaunt man cradling a small poodle in his arms. Joseph went inside.

Half an hour later Lewis looked into the rear-view mirror and beheld Joseph approaching the car. Startled, he turned around and stared out the window.

"God Apollo! What on earth—"

"It was all he had left tonight," said Joseph. "That a guy could wear, anyhow. Just shut up and let me in the car, O.K.?"

He wore a skin-tight black body suit, black pumps with spats, and white gloves. Lewis thought he might be impersonating Mickey Mouse, until noting the cane and bulky papier-mâché body under Joseph's arm.

"Mr. Peanut?"

"Yeah. Can we get this damn thing in the back seat? I'm not riding through the night wearing it."

Lewis got out and rolled down the window, but the giant peanut shell wouldn't go through; nor could he get the passenger seat tilted far enough forward to push it into the back.

"It's not going to fit in the boot, either," he said. "I'm afraid you'll have to put it on. Cheer up! It's not as though anyone will recognize you."

Muttering viciously to himself, Joseph lifted the peanut shell and struggled into it.

"Can you take his little top hat off?" Lewis asked. "Otherwise you'll have to ride sort of bent over."

"No, the damn hat is built in," said Joseph, a bit muffledly. He got his arms out through the appropriate holes at last. "Boy, this is some tight squeeze. At least I can see O.K. Well, fairly O.K. Where's the cane?" He spotted it on the grass and bent to pick it up. There was a sound richly evocative of cyborg flesh bursting through overstrained elasticized cotton-silk fabric. It was followed by a burst of profanity in Neolithic proto-Euskaran.

"Oh, dear," said Lewis.

"Does it show?" Joseph turned to and fro.

"No, you're all right—can you get the shell off again?"

Joseph peered down at himself. "Not without getting arrested."

He climbed awkwardly into the front seat, accompanied by more ominous sounds of fabric tearing. "Just drive, Lewis."

There were at least six traffic signals on the way back to the party, and Joseph shrank farther down into the seat at each stop, though Lewis merely smiled and waved at his fellow motorists when they stared. Not soon enough, they came back to the high winding street above which the house sat.

"My, they're in full swing," said Lewis, gazing up at the house. Every window was lit, and the sound of music and laughter floated forth.

"So much the better, huh?" said Joseph, groping for his cane. "Why don't you just let me off here, and park someplace close and wait? I'm not walking back to Morningside in this getup."

Lewis had to open the door for him, after which Joseph crawled out, straightened up and began his resolute climb of the first of the flights of steps. Lewis found a parking space halfway down the block below, and pulled in to wait.

It was dark, and quiet. The sloping lot on the other side of the street was dense with old trees, which filtered out traffic sounds from the Cahuenga Pass below. A single swaying bulb hung from a telegraph pole, halfway down the block, giving no particular competition to the crescent moon and stars. Lewis yawned. He settled himself into a more comfortable position and folded his arms.

"*Oh, weary night, oh long and tedious night/ Abate thy hours! Shine comforts from the East/ That I may back to Athens...*" he murmured to himself. Now, *that* would be pleasant. He'd liked Athens, when he'd been stationed there in the third century. There'd been a nice little wine-shop just off the School of Philosophy that had been a great place to relax with a scroll. Really quite a lot like California, at least in the quality of the light, that hot bright shimmer...

And of course there hadn't been any Wood Near Athens, more's the pity, unless you counted olive groves. Too thickly settled, even in the third century...there might have been a wood a league without the town in Theseus's day, but it wouldn't have resembled Shakespeare's English forest...rocky hills like Hollywood's, instead, with the same live oaks, and whatever the Mediterranean equivalent of sagebrush was... actually rather a lot like what Reinhardt had built, down the pass. Lewis wondered if he realized it?

He yawned again and let his primary consciousness fade to standard maintenance, while his secondary consciousness sorted through the day's work. He found it easy to forge Reinhardt's handwriting, but much more difficult to reproduce his sketches. Something to do with being a cyborg, perhaps. It was curious that Company operatives, though responsible for salvaging and preserving so much great art, seemed incapable of any creativity themselves...

Lewis was analyzing chromatic value in a watercolor study of the

Faery Court when he was roused to primary consciousness by lights flaring behind him. He peered into the rear-view mirror. A car was being started; someone leaving the party. Perhaps he ought to pull into the spot they had vacated?

As he was watching the other car's tail lights diminish down the hill and trying to decide whether to move, something hit the rear of the Plymouth with a *thump*. A second later Joseph had yanked the passenger door open and was frantically squeezing his costumed bulk into the seat.

"Go!" he shouted.

"Did you get it?"

"No. Follow that car!"

"But that wasn't Larry Montcalm—"

"I know! It was *another* thief!"

Lewis threw the Plymouth into neutral and coasted forward, starting the engine on the way down the hill. Joseph, gasping inside the papier-mâché peanut head, finally caught his breath enough to say—well, nothing that would edify the sensitive reader. When he had finished venting, however, he added:

"Arnaud Fletcher!"

"What, the gossip columnist?" They reached the bottom of the hill. The other car was nowhere in sight. Lewis, peering about uncertainly, switched to thermal vision and picked up the car's track—heading not down into Hollywood, but up Mulholland Drive. He followed.

"Yeah," said Joseph. "I was so close! No trouble getting in, at least once I'd got up all those damn stairs. I found a bathroom window open on ground level. Flushed the toilet and walked out bold as brass. Nobody even noticed. The gin was flowing free, let me tell you. All kinds of Industry old-timers there. Half the people who used to work at Edendale and box-lunch extras of DeMille's.

"They were pretty lively, for a bunch of has-beens; there was this big front room where they'd pushed all the furniture to the edges and rolled up the rugs, and they were dancing to Victrola records.

Which made it hell to get through the room, see, which I had to do because Harlequin and Columbina were doing the Lindy clear across on the other side. So I just sort of insinuated myself out on the dance floor and tapped some guy on the shoulder, and there I was Lindy-hopping with this dame dressed as Marie Antoinette when this dog came leaping in!"

"He cut in on you?" Lewis inquired, steering around a curve with a precipitous drop on one side.

"No, not a guy dressed as a dog; a real dog! A Saint Bernard!"

"Oh, dear. And I guess he wanted to rend you limb from limb?"

"No; this one couldn't tell I was a cyborg. He was a *happy* dog. He loved me. In the least dignified way imaginable, O.K.? Marie Antoinette broke away from me, just shrieking with laughter, which pretty much blew my plan of unobtrusively partner-swapping my way across the dance floor to Columbina's arms.

"There was this sideboard at one edge of the room with canapés and drinks and stuff, so I went over there with the dog still lurching all over me. I grabbed a martini for myself and dropped him a couple of deviled eggs; did he lose interest in me? Not a chance. He jumped up and tried to put his forelegs around my neck. Then he noticed my martini, and dove into it nose-first."

"He spilled your drink?"

"No, he drank it! The mutt was drunk! That was why he was so goddammed happy. You know what drunk dog breath smells like?"

"Please don't tell me." Lewis peered forward, straining to make out the fading heat trail that wound on ahead.

"So I set about three martinis on the floor for him and he ceased waxing amatory, thank the gods, just started lapping 'em up, and I looked around to see Harlequin Larry and Columbina Muriel retiring from the dance floor to a settee in a nice dark corner. I pushed through the crowd and worked my way along the wall, sort of over and around the furniture. I overheard all kinds of snippets of conversation that would make me a fortune, if I was inclined to blackmail somebody.

"In fact—" Joseph pounded his fists on the dashboard. "In fact, I remember Arnaud Fletcher talking about this other party that's going on tonight! That must be where the son-of-a-bitch is headed!"

"Well, where is it?" asked Lewis. A vista of Hollywood opened out to the left, a carpet of lights glittering as far as the sea; but up here was night and silence, and the occasional coyote blinking in the beam of the Plymouth's headlights.

"He didn't say! Except that it's at 'Jack's place,' wherever that is. Supposedly it's one wild party. 'Plenty of hot stuff, brother, and I do mean hot,' he said. He said it just like that, *insinuating*, you know?"

"I suppose he meant cocaine or something," said Lewis, as they came to the intersection of Outpost and Mulholland. Down or up? He focused and made out the tracks continuing up along Mulholland, though they were fading fast as the night air cooled them. He followed as fast as he dared.

"I guess. Or hookers. Anyway I managed to get over near the settee at last. It had been pushed up against a table and a couple of other pieces of furniture, so there was some space behind it, see? And I pretended to pass out and fall over, which nobody even noticed. In fact, there were already a couple of drunks snoring away in various corners back there. I crawled close up under the table until I was right behind Larry Montcalm and Muriel Whoever, and scanned 'em."

"That must have been a little difficult in a peanut costume," said Lewis, slowing the car as he studied the thermal track of his quarry. The other vehicle had left Mulholland and driven up a straight dirt track leading to a still higher elevation. Gingerly he urged the Plymouth forward.

"You're telling me, brother! But I thought I'd gotten lucky at last, because Larry had Muriel's feet in his lap and was rubbing her bunions, and she was lying back right above me in a sort of ecstatic state. I was able to rise up on my hands and sneak a peek; sure enough, neither of them noticed me. And there was the Tavernier Violet, hanging around the dame's neck on a dime-store chain—Say, watch out!"

"I'm sorry," said Lewis, through his teeth rather. "Plymouth doesn't equip their cars with mountain goat feet."

"Jeepers, what kind of idiot would build a house up here?" Joseph looked around. "See, if I hadn't been wearing the peanut suit I could have just hooked my cane through the chain, flipped the damn thing up and grabbed the stone, and been out one of the windows before anybody could yell. I wasn't any too sanguine about running blind down all those steps, though. Muriel was pretty far gone in bliss, so I figured I could try a little stealthy theft instead. I pulled off a glove with my teeth and got my finger and thumb on the catch, and managed to unfasten it.

"But right then somebody put on "The Charleston," and what did Muriel do but sit up squealing about how that's her favorite dance. She grabbed Larry by the hand and jumped out on the dance floor. I scrambled to my feet and—look out! Jesus, Lewis, you want to end up at the bottom of a cliff?"

"I don't think I can turn around here," said Lewis, gazing out into the black ravine that yawned before the Plymouth's front bumper.

"Come on, then," said Joseph, getting out of the car. Lewis set the hand brake and got out too. "Hey hup ho—"

Between them the two immortals lifted the car and walked in a half-circle. "So I jumped over the back of the couch," Joseph continued, *"just* in time to see the Tavernier Violet go bouncing off Muriel's chest onto the dance floor. She didn't notice it. I Charlestoned my way out into the madding throng, hoping to do a quick dip and grab it, but Larry (who didn't notice it'd fallen either) kicked it, in a burst of terpsichorean frenzy, and it went skating across the floor, trailing its chain, ping ping ping, in a series of bank shots off mortal feet, and ended up right under the nose of Mr. Arnaud Fletcher, who was dressed like Valentino in *The Sheik*, by the way."

"Just hold it there a moment, won't you?" Lewis climbed back in the car and shifted gears.

"Sure." Joseph held the car in place with one hand, then gave it a push as Lewis stepped on the gas. The car teetered for a moment and then climbed effortfully toward a still-narrower and more steep trail, with Joseph plodding alongside. "Where was I? So Arnaud Fletcher looked down, saw the rock at his feet. He stooped on it like a duck on a june bug, whammo, and stashed it in his robes. He exited the party, I exited in hot pursuit, slightly delayed because my big friend the Saint Bernard noticed me again and wanted to pitch some woo. By the time I found Fido another drink and got out the door, the damn mortal was at the bottom of the stairs and heading for his car."

"Er—" Lewis trod on the brake and leaned out the window. "I can't get up this goat path, I'm afraid. But I think we've found the other party, Joseph."

"What? Oh." Joseph looked up the trail. The moonlight was glinting off a number of automobiles, parked somewhat precariously on the side of the precipice. Beyond them rose something that looked remarkably like the dome of a mosque.

"Joseph," said Lewis, "Are those drumbeats?"

Joseph turned to listen, then shifted irritably inside the peanut suit until his ear was a little closer to the eye-holes.

"Yeah. They're darabukas," he said. "What have they got going up there, a Rudolph Valentino Memorial Lodge?"

"It smells like someone's barbequing a goat," said Lewis, wrinkling his nose.

"That's lamb. And cannabis. Great. O.K., I'm not going to try anything subtle this time. I'll march in there, find Fletcher, sock him, roll him and run for it. You'd better keep the engine running."

Lewis looked around. "Should I really wait right *here*? If I try to clear that rut at anything over five miles an hour, I'll break an axle."

"So it isn't the best spot for a quick getaway," Joseph admitted. Hastily he accessed a topographical map of the area, then transmitted a set of coordinates to Lewis. "There you go! See that ridge, right behind the dome thing? The hill drops down on the other side to Pacific View. You wait right below; I'll scram down the hill once I've got the rock, and we'll be away before the mortals can get their cars started."

"Oh, that's a much better idea," said Lewis, noting with relief that Pacific View was at least paved. "Good luck! I'm off."

"See you in the funny papers," said Joseph gloomily. Lewis let out the clutch, threw the Plymouth into neutral and braked his way down the hill until the front wheels were on solid pavement. He coasted down and around to the coordinates Joseph had sent him, and pulled up, carefully turning the front wheels into the curb.

Worriedly he scanned the Plymouth, checking for indications of metal fatigue or excessive automotive wear. Yes; he was going to have to take it in to have the wheels aligned. A lube job wouldn't do it any harm, either. The transmission seemed to be all right, which was miraculous, after that last climb, but perhaps he'd ask the mechanic to have a look at the clutch.

He sat there in the dark for a moment as a gnawing conviction grew that a twig had gotten stuck in the radiator grille on that last overgrown trail. At last he got out and walked around the front of the car. Yes; yes, there was one, wedged in firmly. Shaking his head, Lewis took out his penknife and became absorbed in working the twig out.

It took a great deal of care to avoid scratching the paint or puncturing the radiator, and so he was only dimly paying attention to the drumbeats that sounded on the night air, with the occasional drunken catcall.

He was polishing the headlights with his pocket handkerchief when the drums suddenly stopped. There was an outcry. Lewis craned his head back to look up the hill and saw a giant peanut plummeting toward him.

"Thank all the gods," he said, and ran around the car to get behind the wheel. As he rounded the fender, however, he was momentarily blinded by the lights of a car speeding down Pacific View toward him. He blinked away the afterimage as it passed; a convertible, and something oddly familiar about the driver...

Over the roar of the starting engine he heard the patter of feet as Joseph ran frantically toward the car, and felt the lurch as Joseph leaped on the running board.

"Follow that car!" Joseph bawled through the window, pointing after the convertible. "Again."

"But that wasn't Arnaud Fletcher." Lewis cranked the wheels away from the curb and stepped on the gas. Joseph clung to the passenger door.

"No! It's Sterling Holloway!"

"What?" Lewis replayed his glimpse of the passing car.

"Sterling Holloway!"

"*Thisbe* Sterling Holloway? What was *he* doing—"

"Lewis, shut up and drive!"

Lewis pursed his lips, and drove as fast as he dared with Joseph, screaming imprecations into the night, on the Plymouth's running board. The convertible sped ahead of them, around the curve and down the long hill that dropped to the floor of the Pass. Finally back on the long straightaway of Cahuenga, they began to close the gap. The taillights of the convertible had just begun to draw appreciably closer when Lewis heard the warning siren coming from behind them.

The traffic cop nearly wet himself laughing, but gave them a speeding ticket anyway.

SEVEN: *What, a play toward? I'll be an auditor...*

"We're lucky you didn't get us arrested," said Lewis, sullenly kicking at fragments of peanut costume.

"So I was a little sore," said Joseph, shouting from the bathroom. "It'll be O.K. anyhow. All you'll have to do is excuse yourself during the next rehearsal, run out to Holloway's car and search around for the rock. Easy."

"No, it won't be," said Lewis. He opened Joseph's kitchen cabinet and scowled at the contents. "I'm Mr. Reinhardt's translator, remember? *You* go search for the damned thing. Haven't you any Ovaltine?"

"What?"

"Ovaltine!"

"No. Make some cocoa or something."

"No, thank you. I still have to drive home."

"Here." Joseph strode out of the bathroom in his shorts, opened a drawer, dug out a bottle of single malt and poured a pair of shots into a coffee cup and a juice glass respectively. "Now it's breakfast. Look, I am a total innocent in this tribulation of cosmic proportions. Are you going to let me tell what happened or what?"

"Go on, then." Lewis had a sip of whiskey, breathed out fumes, and converted the sip to water and complex sugars.

"So there I was, sneaking up the trail toward the faux mosque or whatever it was," said Joseph. He downed his whiskey in a gulp. "I was hearing glasses clinking, mortals laughing, all kinds of stag-party hubbub. I couldn't hear Fletcher at first, until he came in loud and clear saying: *There! What do you think of that?*

"And this dame says in reply, *Oooh, Arnie, it's beautiful! Can I wear it?*

"Whereupon this third mortal chimes in, *Hell yeah! It can be the Eye of the Spider-God or something! We'll rewrite the script!* And he's answered by this fourth party who yells, *Who needs a script? We're doing this the good old-fashioned way!*"

"Oh, dear," said Lewis.

"You can say that again, brother," said Joseph from the bathroom, stropping his razor. "By this time, I was almost at this courtyard, all Moorish tiles, with the crazy house right ahead. Just then this door in the mosque opened, see, and out came these two guys dressed in burnooses. I scrammed up some steps to one side and hid, as much as I could, which wasn't much but neither of the mortals was looking my way. One of them was saying to the other one, *Aw, come on, be a sport. It'll be fun!*

"And I thought to myself, 'Isn't that the little guy who's playing Moonshine?'"

"Otis Harlan?"

"Yeah!"

"Otis *Happy the Dwarf* Harlan?"

"Look, who else has a voice like that? But then, the other mortal guy says: *No, no, I really don't think I'd better,* and instantly I knew it was Sterling Holloway because—well, who else has a voice like *that?* He says further, *I'm sure you meant well, but I didn't know it was this kind of party. Are you sure Jack knows about this?*

"And Harlan says, *Sure he does! You should see the parties he throws here! Look, stick around. You don't have to be in the movie. I'll introduce you to Maisie. She's a swell conversationalist.*" Joseph paused to shave his upper lip.

"Movie?" said Lewis.

"But Holloway just mumbled his regrets, and Harlan lowered his voice and started in about how he hoped Holloway was going to keep his lip buttoned about all this anyhow, on account of the Hays code. This was when I decided to try to get a peek into the garden, since that seemed to be where most of the noise was coming from. So I crept up the stairs and looked over the top and—what a scene, folks, what a scene!"

"What kind of scene?"

"It was another tiled terrace, O.K.? With a reflecting pool in the middle. And right below me was a wall sloping down in a sort of a ziggurat thing, and on the wall was this huge mosaic tile picture of a spider in a web. And this girl was leaning against it, as two guys in robes were putting fake manacles on her wrists, and they were all three giggling. She was stark naked except for some costume jewelry. I was looking straight down between her breasts and right there, looking back up at me, was the Tavernier Violet.

"The whole place was lit up bright as day with studio lights. There was a big old camera, and a director's chair, across the pool, and about fifteen guys and a handful of dames, everybody dressed in Arabian Nights getup. Over to one side there was a table with a punchbowl, and a hookah, and people lined up to take their turns at gin punch or marijuana, which would explain all the giggling.

"I spotted Fletcher, and a bunch of other studio folks, Barrymore included. 'Hah,' I said to myself, 'Hah, Mr. Profile, so this is another of your hideouts! Won't Mr. Mayer be interested to learn about *this!* If Mr. Mayer doesn't have a coronary arrest first.' Right then one of the sheiks finishes his cup of hooch, strides over to the director's chair, and plants himself in it. 'Holy Smoke!' I said to myself, 'It's Harold Lloyd!'"

"No!" Lewis was scandalized. "Not *Harold Lloyd!*"

"What, you're surprised? You hadn't heard he was a photography enthusiast?"

"*The Freshman* Harold Lloyd?"

"Yeah. Him. He sat himself down and yelled, *Ready on stage, everyone!* And everybody scrambled to their marks. Lloyd said, *O.K., the Loyal Sons of the Sheik and Screw-The-Talkies Productions presents Reel Two of 'The Sins of Old Babylon'! The sacrifice of the virgin to the Spider-God! The desert nomads have worked themselves into a frenzy of lust. Doris, you don't know what to expect. You're terrified, because you know what brutes men are, right? And here you are with them feasting their eyes on your fair white body. What do you imagine they'll do next, huh? Wait a minute, she's not fastened TO anything! You bunch of idiots! Cripes! Quick, somebody, get some rope!*

"And the girl yells, *Look, youse guys, either figure out what you're doing or get me a bathrobe!*

"And Fletcher himself came running up with a bathrobe and slipped it around her while this other son of the desert brought a piece of rope. He tied one end to the chain connecting Doris's manacles and threw the other one up at the top of the ziggurat, see, right by where I was hiding, and I could see he was trying to loop it over a water pipe sticking out there. So I backed down the steps as fast as I could, while he was scrambling up and tying off the rope. By this time nobody was in the courtyard. I could hear Holloway out in the drive, trying to get his car started.

"Then I heard Lloyd yell, *O.K.! Camera!* And somebody's clapperboard shut with a *clop,* and I heard the camera cranking away. I figured it was now or never, so I ran around the side of the hill. I couldn't see so well in the damn peanut head, so I lost a few seconds stumbling around trying to find a way to the pool terrace, and finally crawled through some bushes on my hands and knees. Suddenly I came out right behind one of the big spotlights.

"There, across the pool, was Doris the Virgin Sacrifice, batting her eyelashes and miming horror at Myron the Lecherous Spider-Priest, who was making a couple of half-hearted passes at her with a big wooden scimitar. As I watched, up strode Bill the Desert Chieftain, and stuck up one arm, and said, *No! We rode across many sand dunes to capture this beautiful slave! The Spider-God will not deny us our reward!* And he threw his robe open, and guess what?"

"I don't think I want to know," said Lewis.

"Yeah, well, I didn't either, but there it was for the whole world to see, and as Myron the Spider-Priest dropped his scimitar in feigned horror, guess what happened next?" Joseph slapped on after-shave.

"You mean they were shooting a pornographic film?" Lewis realized belatedly.

"So, since everybody's attention was pretty well riveted on the action, I figured I probably wouldn't get a better chance for a surprise attack. I took a running jump and cleared the pool, knocked Myron the Spider-Priest into the pool, shoved Bill the Desert Chieftain to one side, grabbed the Tavernier Violet, and ran like crazy for the far edge of the terrace. And jumped off."

"And the cameras were running the whole time?"

"Yeah. That's one stag film that'll make history. So there I was, rocketing down the hill pretty much on my back, and getting a little worried because it's quite a bit steeper than I'd thought it would be, and suddenly there's this tree coming at me. I threw myself sideways, but I swear this branch leaped out and hit my wrist."

"And you let go of the diamond," said Lewis.

"No! I had a death-grip on the damn thing, but I was clutching it by the chain. Which had broken when I yanked it off the dame's neck. And I was wearing those damn white Mickey Mouse mitts anyway, which made it harder to keep a grip. I had one of those slow-motion moments where I watched the rock go shooting away, like the chain was a whip snapping, and *katang!* It flicked out into the void of night. And dropped into the gulf of despair. And landed in the back seat of Sterling Holloway's car."

"What will you do now?"

"Do you know where the guy lives, by any chance?"

"No." Lewis rubbed his eyes. "And I'm not taking you on a desperate search, either. I've got to be at the Bowl at four this afternoon, and I haven't slept in forty-eight hours."

"Real cyborgs don't need sleep."

"This one does. Joseph, the dress rehearsal is tonight, for gods' sake."

"Dress rehearsal, huh? So Holloway's got to be there too! Keen. Now, what do you say we go get some flannel cakes at Musso and Frank's?" Joseph pulled on a clean shirt and beamed at Lewis's reflection in the mirror.

EIGHT: *THROUGH BOG, THROUGH BUSH, THROUGH BRAKE,*
   THROUGH BRIAR...

Lewis was still yawning as he made his way up from the Bowl parking lot, threading his way between the piers that supported the trestle. He didn't spot Joseph until he was seated beside Reinhardt, listening to the Los Angeles Philharmonic storm through Mendelssohn's

Overture. Joseph was crouched on the trestle, high above the scene, installing a series of black-painted two-by-fours along the trestle's edge and connecting them with lengths of black velvet rope. He winked and gave Lewis a thumbs-up.

Lewis nodded at him, briefly, and returned his attention to Reinhardt, who was watching the stage with furrowed brow. Theseus's court was hastily blocked out on the woodland set by standards and drapery, carried by sweating little boys in Moorish blackface and turbans. Theseus took center stage and declaimed about the slowness of the old moon waning, in tones that suggested he was just dying to take Hippolyta away to Martha's Vineyard for a post-nuptial bottle of bubbly.

The next scene, with the rival suitors, went badly. Olivia de Havilland was fiery and charming as Hermia, but neither Lysander nor Demetrius seemed to comprehend the meaning of their lines. Helena, entering late, had a good grasp of the role but couldn't project or make her gestures wide enough to suit Reinhardt. At his insistence, she spoke her entire soliloquy four times in succession, and by the end truly sounded despairing and heartsick.

Enter the clowns. Most of them, anyway.

"Wo ist Mondshein?" muttered Reinhardt, peering at the stage.

There's Holloway! Joseph transmitted. *I'll go ransack his car!* Lewis glanced up to see Joseph scrambling down the side of the trestle upside down, which so unnerved him that he stammered as he translated Reinhardt's question. The assistant director glared at the other comedians.

"He was just driving up as we went on," said Reicher, attempting to soothe Weissberger.

"Here I am!" Harlan came bustling onstage, out of breath but grinning. "Sorry, folks!" He took his place and elbowed Holloway, adding *sotto voce:* "You missed a swell party, and how!"

Their scene proceeded. Bottom, played by Connolly as a slightly pompous know-it-all, was just displaying his prowess in roaring as gently as any sucking dove, when a distinctly ungentle roar cut through the ether to Lewis.

WHERE IS IT???

Lewis flinched. Miss Sibley, seated behind him, leaned forward and put her hand on his shoulder.

"Are you all right, Mr. Kensington?"

Lewis nodded and waved his hand dismissively. "Just a little headache," he whispered, but braced himself.

THE GODDAM THING ISN'T HERE!

Are you sure it fell in the car? It didn't bounce out again? Perhaps you ought to go look in the bushes along Pacific View—

No. I saw it land! It fell in his sheik costume. He'd taken the robe off and thrown it on the floor of the back seat.

Is the robe there still?

No!

Then, I suppose he found it when he took the robe out.

Maybe. Why me? Oh, by all the frick-frackin' gods, why me? What would you do if you found a big purple diamond while you were getting rid of the evidence of a really embarrassing party?

Assume it had got there by mistake somehow? Stick it in my pocket?

Maybe. Yeah. Where's Holloway's pants?

In the changing tent? Lewis glanced involuntarily at the row of Army Surplus pavilions that had been set up as temporary costume and prop sheds. *But you can't go in there—*

Oh, I can't, can't I?

Lewis shivered and crossed his fingers, trying to concentrate on the rehearsal. They had made it as far as the Wood Near Athens now, Apollo be thanked. There was no more than a half hour to go until sunset. The sun had already fallen behind the high ridge to the west, though it still lit the face of Mount Hollywood with red slanting light. The Bowl valley had filled up with clear blue twilight, that had been unobtrusively deepening; now the electrician hit a switch. Winking fireflies lit up the forest on the stage.

One minor effect, and suddenly it all came together. The green gloom of the forest was haunted, living and breathing, a door into an eternal summer night. Lewis heard Miss Sibley catch her breath, clap her hands. He saw Reinhardt's shoulders relax a little.

"You see?" Reinhardt said quietly. "We always come back to this place."

The musicians had to be cued twice, but reprised the overture and set the scene. The shadows deepened. The principal danseuse flitted onstage in gauzy rags, a moth in the night; Puck emerged from the branches, the most disturbing little snub-nosed monster it would be possible to meet in a dark country lane, and shrieked his opening lines...

Lewis, I'm in a jam.

The spell broke. Lewis transmitted in real irritation: *Well, get yourself out of it!*

No, seriously.

You can't get into the changing tent, can you?

I did, actually. Crawled in under the back. I'm there now. Hiding behind the clothes rack. Just finished looking through Holloway's street clothes.

Well, was the diamond in his pocket?

No. That's not the problem, though. What the hell are all these greyhounds for?

What?

There are, like, six greyhounds tethered outside the tent door. They can tell I'm in here.

They're the hounds for Theseus's entrance in Act Four. You know: "My hounds are bred out of the Spartan kind/ So flew'd, so sanded—"

Lewis, never mind the damn—Huh? Shouldn't they be beagles, then?

You'd think so, but—

I could outrun a beagle, easy. Well, so what are the chances you can come down here and get the dog handler to take 'em for a walk, or something? They're, uh, starting to growl.

Why don't you simply crawl out the way you came?

Because there's some mortal standing behind the tent now, having a smoke. Besides, I think I know—HOLY MACKEREL!

Lewis shifted in his seat, listening for the baying of ravening greyhounds. He heard none, however; and, after a moment, ventured to transmit.

Are you still there, Joseph?

Yeah.

What's happening?

I'm looking at the Tavernier Violet.

Oh, good. Can I get back to my own mission, now?

I don't have it; I'm just looking at it. It's in a big fancy hat, on a wig head on the makeup table on the ladies' side of the tent. There's a couple mortal hairdressers sitting right next to it, gossiping. I just heard one of them say, "Wasn't that nice of Mr. Holloway, donating that piece of costume jewelry he found?" And the other one said, "It's such a perfect accent to the costume, too" See, the hat's all purple and gold.

Well then, why don't you grab it and run?

The goddam dogs are still outside. I'll just wait here. Sooner or later they'll step out for a break, right? Then I'll grab it. And, believe me, once it's in my hands, no mortal is going to be able to pry it out of my grip. I'll exit through the roof if I have to.

Good for you. I will now return to my regular programming.

Oh, ha ha.

Lewis relaxed and watched the play. Fairies pirouetted on the greensward, all silver and cellophane, leading the little mortal child round and round. Now came the dark host, goblins beckoning to entice him away to Oberon's court. Now the clash between moonlight and shadow, the unearthly custody quarrel. *This* part worked; Shakespeare's images, freed from print and grammar and the wooden incomprehension of the actors. Every mortal child knew there were things that fluttered and squeaked in the moonlight, and things that lurked in darkness where the trees came down to the fence line, and that it was perilous to venture out to play with them...Lewis felt a primal shiver.

Out came one pair of mortal lovers, and Lysander at least spoke with iron tongue. Reinhardt, listening, groaned quietly and shook his head. He got up and walked to the edge of the apron, signaling for the assistant director, and Lewis scrambled after him. Together, the three of them spent a fruitless five minutes trying to convey a sense of motivation to the young man, and finally retired to let Art take its course.

Lewis was murmuring a quiet prayer to the Muse Thalia when he picked up the growing crackle of Joseph's impatience.

Still down there, are you?

The clowns just left. Before that, one of the costume ladies was reading aloud from the latest issue of Silver Screen. *Helen Hayes's tips on making a marriage work. Don't any of these mortals ever need to use the bathroom, for crying out loud?*

How does Helen Hayes make her marriage work?

How should I know? I wasn't paying attention.

Lewis tuned him out and focused on the play. More lovers, more moonlight, more magic and misunderstanding. Where the actors were equal to their lines, or where the stagecraft carried it, things spun along beautifully; but there were some dismal halts.

Reinhardt began running his hands through his hair in agitation. He went onstage and remained there, with Lewis obliged to follow at his heel. He worked painfully through the staging of the four-way lovers' quarrel, with its overlapping dialogue ending in screams. Nor was he able to relax in the scenes between Bottom and Titania, for the ass's head had to be removed and refitted twice before Connolly was able to make his lines understood.

Great! The dogs have just been led away!

Good gods, are you still down there? Lewis had forgotten about Joseph.

Where else would I go? I'm going to grab the rock and run for it, Lewis—oh, crap. Here come a bunch of fairies and human bats. Jeez, there must be fifty extras lining up to change costumes. Isn't the damn play almost over?

There's still the torchlight procession to the Wedding March.

Oh, fine.

Puck got the magic flower business right at last, the mismatched lovers re-matched, and Theseus and Hippolyta came on with dogs and attendants to wake them. Bottom returned to his mates. A Happy Ending was decreed. There was a burst of subvocal cursing from the direction of the costume tent.

What's the trouble now?

The dame! Hippolyta! She's just had the headdress put on! No!

It's her costume for the Wedding Procession, Joseph.

No! There she goes! I'll never reach her, through this crowd! Where are they all going?

Up on the hill for the procession.

Up the hill, huh? In the dark? Hmmm.

Joseph, what are you going to do?

See you later, Lewis.

Wait! What—

Lewis heard a shrill scream from the direction of the costume tent, even as the crowd of actors straggled to the edge of the Bowl valley. He peered into the darkness beyond the lit stage, but saw only fathomless blackness until he switched to infrared. The night became a spectral green, through which the mortals walked in glowing scarlet silhouette. The men wore tights and tunics in a vaguely medieval-Venetian style, with immense bicorn hats like fans; the ladies wore hoop skirts with panniers, great unwieldy affairs, and tall headdresses of ostrich plumes. They reached the foot of the hill and one or two thoughtful ones switched on flashlights, looking for a path up.

There wasn't one. Lewis heard clearly the muttered complaints, and then the beam of someone's flashlight picked out the small flag Reinhardt had had planted, on the crest of the hill, to mark their starting point.

"We have to get up *there?* This is ridiculous!"

"It isn't as steep as it looks, Mr. Lodge—"

"There is a trail here, somewhere—" Lewis recognized the voice of the assistant director. "Professor Reinhardt chose this spot carefully—

the whole audience must be able to see you from their seats, you understand—"

"But in these costumes?"

"May I remind you this is Dress Rehearsal?"

"Somebody light one of the torches!"

"No! On your cue, if you please—Here, follow me—"

The great pulsing scarlet crowd began to seep uphill in a tentative sort of way, with a thread of mortals scrambling through the brush. And...flanking them to the right was a skulking figure in bluegreen, flickering with other colors as he stalked them.

Joseph, what are you doing?

I'm going to get the damn diamond. Whatever it takes.

But you can't—

Reinhardt, who had been making his way up from the stage, sat down beside Lewis and looked at his watch.

"I'm afraid they're a little late stepping off, Herr Professor," Lewis stammered. Reinhardt shrugged.

"This is why one has rehearsals," he said. Lewis looked back at the hillside. The mortals were nearly at the top of the ridge now, in a throng that glowed like a bed of live coals. The bluegreen figure could just be glimpsed some little distance down the ridge, advancing on them stealthily. It ran a few steps—halted—dodged around a bush and gained a few more yards. It was remarkably like watching wildlife footage of a wolf stalking a herd of sheep. Lewis felt an irrational urge to shout in warning.

The mortals wouldn't have heard him, though...

"Is everybody here?"

"Where are the torches? Not the electric torches, you idiot!"

"Mr. Weissberger, I can't see a thing—"

"Mr. Weissberger, I lost one of my slippers, I've got to go back and look for it—"

"Everyone, please, form up! Mr. Lodge, Signorina Braggiotti, this is your mark, here by the flag—will the rest of you please—"

"Mr. Weissberger, there's no path marked out—"

"We will simply walk downhill to the foot of the ramp," shouted Weissberger, rather V-ing his Ws in his stress. "It will not be a difficulty! Clyde, we will now distribute the torches!"

Beside Lewis, Reinhardt checked his watch again. Lewis bit his lower lip, watching as one unwary mortal strayed from the flock, going back down the way he had come. Looking for a lost slipper? Yes. He crouched, picked up something and balanced unsteadily on one foot as he pulled it on.

Oh, foolish mortal; for here came the bluegreen figure, slipping up behind the scarlet one. Bop! Lewis winced, as the scarlet figure collapsed and was dragged into a thicket. Colors shifted and flashed from within the thicket, and then the bluegreen figure emerged, having appropriated the mortal's costume. Absurd hat slightly askew, it scrambled up the hill to the end of the line that had formed, and grabbed a torch.

"The torches have now been distributed!" Weissberger's voice cracked. "On my signal, the torches will be lowered! Now!"

A figure at the front of the line suddenly glowed with a point of white heat. Squinting, Lewis made out the propmaster, who had lit a cigar.

"The torches will now be lit!" screamed Weissberger. The propmaster puffed his cigar to brightness and went hurriedly along the line of torches, dabbing its lit end on each of them in turn. One by one they flared alight. There was scattered applause from the benches all around Lewis. Reinhardt merely nodded in satisfaction.

"AND NOW!" Weissberger turned and spoke through a megaphone. "HERR PROFESSOR, WE ARE READY!"

Reinhardt waved his arms for the benefit of the conductor, who turned and raised his baton. The trumpet players sounded the fanfare, and the whole orchestra sailed into Mendelssohn's "Wedding March."

The procession stepped off. The long line of torches moved uncertainly through the night, with the assistant director and stage manager scuttling ahead through the sagebrush with flashlights, searching for a trail. Lewis watched the bluegreen figure at the end of the line craning its neck, studying the mortals ahead of it. It lowered its torch, crept off to one side, and then a stentorian voice called:

"Jeepers, look out! That's a rattlesnake!"

There were screams of alarm from the hillside. Torches wavered wildly, one or two were dropped and hastily retrieved, a bush caught fire and had to be beaten out. One actress, leaping out of the way of any reptile threat, overbalanced and fell backward into a spurge laurel. Her hoops collapsed around her like a Japanese lantern folding up, and her frantic legs were white-hot as they kicked the air, rapidly cooling to red. She had to be hauled upright by a pair of her fellow extras. Weissberger came charging back up the slope, ready to club any snakes he found with his flashlight, and vainly beat the bushes for a moment or two.

"What is happening?" Reinhardt stood, scowling. He shielded his eyes with his hand and peered out across the valley. Miss Sibley handed him a megaphone. "WEISSBERGER, WHY HAVE THEY STOPPED?" he bellowed, over the orchestra.

The assistant director went scrambling back, grabbed his megaphone from the propmaster, and called back: "IT WAS A SNAKE!"

"WAS ANYONE BITTEN?"

"NEIN, HERR PROFESSOR!"

"THEN PLEASE PROCEED!"

Weissberger turned and made desperate shooing motions at the milling actors. Altogether it was five minutes before the wavering line re-formed, and when it did, Lewis saw that the bluegreen figure had managed to advance halfway up the line of the procession.

By this time, however, the "Wedding March" had ended. The conductor turned and looked up at Reinhardt inquiringly.

"Play it again," said Reinhardt, forgetting to use the megaphone. Lewis waved his arms, semaphoring an encore. Once again the fanfare sounded, and once again the procession stepped off.

Dum dum dah *dum*dum *dum*dum *dah* diddly-*dah* diddly-*dah*—

The line of torches advanced in a tentative kind of way, bobbing along through the dark.

"Oh, my God, that's a coyote! And it's rabid! Run, everybody!"

There was immediate chaos on the hillside. Lewis saw the bluegreen figure dart out of line again, questing forward, but it collided and went down in a tangle of panicked mortals. There was a wild confusion of arms, legs, plumes, hoops and floppy hats. Some mortal gave an agonized yell.

"It bit me! Help! It bit me on the leg!"

"Where did it go?"

"There it is! You can see its glowing eyes!"

"I heard it growling!"

"Did it break the skin?"

"We must be near its den or something!"

"Hit it with a torch! They're afraid of fire!"

"Where is it?"

"Stop this at once! You will resume the line of march!"

"Listen, we were just attacked by a wild animal!"

"What? Where?"

"There it is? Shine your damn flashlight in that bush!"

A second of silence.

"Well? Where is it?"

"Well—well—it was crouching right there, a second ago!"

"I saw it too!"

"This is mass hysteria. Get into line, you idiots!"

"Say, do you want a punch in the mouth?"

"You can't talk that way to Americans!"

"You call yourselves actors? You will be fired!"

Someone took a swing at someone else, who dodged, but the blow kept coming and hit a third party, who dropped his torch and hit back, and another person was cracked across the shins with a flashlight, and it only got worse from there. Lewis cringed.

"They have stopped again," observed Reinhardt.

"Yes, I'm afraid they have," said Lewis.

"Why is this?" Reinhardt stood up and raised the megaphone. "IF YOU PLEASE! LET US CONTINUE!"

The orchestra faltered to a stop. Lewis saw the seething mass of pugilism halt, as though coming to its senses, and then grudgingly re-form the processional line. A couple of torches had to be relit. Several hats had to be located.

"WEISSBERGER?"

"THERE HAS BEEN A MOMENTARY DELAY!"

"WELL, WE WILL BEGIN THE MARCH AGAIN!"

"JAWOHL, HERR PROFES—WHAT DID YOU JUST CALL ME?"

The fanfare sounded yet again, and perhaps prevented further bloodshed, for the sullen line jolted forward and then, miraculously, kept on coming through the darkness. They were nearly over the last rise before the foot of the trestle now. Lewis, unable to look away, saw the bluegreen figure fall out and run slinking along the side, shoving to get further ahead. Further now still, ever closer to the front of the line where walked the tall stately figures of Theseus and Hippolyta, up until this point relatively untouched by the general mayhem.

"Hey! Who's pushing?"

"Stop that!"

"Well, aren't you the rude—"

"Say, what do you think you're doing?"

Here came the procession, onto the trestle at last: first Weissberger walking backwards (the propmaster had prudently decided to fall out and cross the parking lot underneath), one hand on the velvet rope to guide himself. Next came Theseus and Hippolyta, Mr. Lodge and Ms. Braggiotti, and now Lewis could make out the sparkle of their jewels—and, yes, there was the familiar glint of the Tavernier Violet, square in the center of Hippolyta's gold lamé turban.

They had come into the range of the spotlights at last and Lewis switched from infrared vision, but not before he caught a glimpse of the bluegreen figure hurtling forward through the line. The other members of the procession staggered and nearly fell, several dropped their torches over the side—they streamed down through the night like flaming comets—and there were more cries of anger and alarm.

What—no, you can't, not here! Lewis jumped to his feet involuntarily. Reinhardt turned his head to stare at Lewis and so missed seeing the bedraggled figure that thrust its way past the blackamoors holding Hippolyta's train. On it came, and Weissberger saw it now and raised his flashlight threateningly.

"You will get back to your appointed place!" he said.

Joseph dodged a blow from the flashlight, sprang upward, ripped the Tavernier Violet from Hippolyta's headdress, and narrowly missed having Theseus's scepter broken over his head by somersaulting off the edge of the trestle. Miss Braggiotti screamed and clutched at her head. Lewis bit his knuckles. He saw Joseph catch a beam halfway down and swing himself, apelike, to the inner framework, where he clambered to the ground and ran.

"What was that?" Reinhardt rose to his feet. "Are there monkeys in California?"

"Perhaps one escaped from a circus," said Lewis, for lack of anything better to say. The procession, thank all the gods, had recovered itself, and here came Weissberger down the ramp with his flashlight, grimly determined to lead them to the stage. Hippolyta's headdress was slightly askew, and missing its violet centerpiece, but she was otherwise unharmed. Lewis sank into his seat, vastly relieved.

As the final crashing chords of the "Wedding March" sounded, the procession stepped forth on stage and hit their respective marks.

"*Gott sei dank,*" murmured Reinhardt. Lodge faced front and declaimed:

"What the hell is going on? Miss Braggiotti was just assaulted!"

"It was some lunatic, masquerading as an actor," said Weissberger, who had seen the whole thing. "Please, madam, calm yourself. He probably just wanted an autograph. We will have him arrested if he comes near you again. And now, if you please, Herr Lodge, your line?"

Lodge harrumphed, but struck an attitude and began:

"Come now; what masques, what dances shall we have

To wear away this long age of three hours—"

"Hey!" Moonshine made an early entrance, waving his arms. "Hey, somebody's car is on fire back there!"

"Between our after-supper and bed-time—I beg your pardon?"

"What did he say?" Reinhardt asked, but an ominous red glow from beneath the trestle was making it plain now.

"One of you guys dropped a torch and it rolled under somebody's car!"

"Someone call the fire department!"

"Get the fire buckets!"

"It's not my car, is it?" John Lodge ran to the crowd that had assembled at the edge of the stage, peering vainly back at the conflagration.

No, thought Lewis, in sad resignation. *I'll just bet I know whose car it is.*

The fire engines had departed by the time Lewis made his weary way down Highland Avenue on foot. As he passed the American Legion Hall, a disheveled figure emerged from the bushes and fell into step beside him.

"Say...sorry about your car, Lewis."

Lewis considered socking him, and decided against it. He'd only drop Reinhardt's promptbook, and undoubtedly miss Joseph in any case.

NINE: *WILL IT PLEASE YOU TO SEE THE EPILOGUE...?*

Lewis adjusted the fit of his tuxedo jacket and frowned at himself in the mirror. However nicely his suits draped at the tailor's, by the time he put them on they always seemed to have expanded a size. He got out an old-fashioned leather hatbox, opened it, and drew out his black silk top hat. It was a veteran of opening nights going back as far as *Chu Chin Chow*, but still looked as smart as when he'd bought it in Oxford Street. Anything lasted, if you took proper care of it.

And what if he was reluctant to let go of things, especially memories? Memories were all an immortal could truly call his own. In the end, whatever the end might be, they were all he would have.

He set the hat on his head and tilted it back at a jaunty angle. All he needed now was a walking stick.

On his way to the umbrella stand, his glance fell on the promptbook. Reinhardt had taken Lewis's meticulously faked copy, and slipped it into his briefcase without so much as a second glance. Lewis would deliver the original to the Company's shipping depot in the morning, but for now...best to be cautious. He scooped it up in one hand, and with the other took down the framed print of *Love Among the Ruins* that concealed his wall safe. Having secured the promptbook, he rehung the print, looked at it wistfully a moment, and turned away. Time to go; he had a long walk to the Bowl.

As he stepped out on the sidewalk, however, Joseph's Ford came around the corner. Its left front fender was now green, its door was blue, and the left rear fender was a sort of a rust color. Joseph hit the horn twice, and threw Lewis a centurion's salute, grinning.

"Hey, Lewis, want a ride?"

"How thoughtful of you!" Lewis opened the door. Joseph reached over and swept a pair of tennis shoes and an empty Nehi bottle from the seat so he could get in.

"Hey, it's the least I could do, pal." He wore a suit that was clean and freshly pressed, if not exactly evening attire.

"Where's the Tavernier Violet?"

"In a pair of long johns at the back of my sock drawer," said Joseph. "Completely safe." He looked Lewis over and whistled. "Boy, you're dressed to kill! I didn't think people wore white tie and tails unless they could afford box seats, nowadays."

Lewis pulled out the pair of tickets he'd been given. "Section D, Row 9, Seats 14 and 16," he read aloud. "It's still an evening at the theater. One likes to uphold a certain standard, after all."

"Gotta change with the times, though, Lewis," said Joseph. He pulled away from the curb and stepped on the gas. "Otherwise, the mortals notice."

They left the Ford in the lower parking lot and made their way through the mortal crowds. The trestle bridge still stood, only slightly scorched in one area; the charred wreck of Lewis's car had been hauled away, and in its place a battery of klieg lights raked at the evening sky, sending white beams sweeping across.

Flashbulbs burst like actinic bubbles: Lewis turned his face to the cameras and glimpsed Reinhardt, posing in a tuxedo with Miss Sibley and the editor of the *Los Angeles Times*. Reporters were shouting questions in English, which Miss Sibley was answering.

Reinhardt was smiling, uneasy and uncomprehending. Looking at his eyes, Lewis knew he had already withdrawn from the alien soil, in fact from the mortal world, and was walking in spirit under the haunted trees. The Reichstag had burned, old Hindenburg was dead, and a petty politician whom no one had ever taken seriously had used fear to bully his democratic nation into a dictatorship, almost overnight. None of it made any sense. And Reinhardt was stranded here, in this crazy place, and could never go home again. Who wouldn't retreat into the Wood Near Athens?...

Lewis sighed. Joseph jostled his arm.

"Hey, there's a guy selling programs. You want one?"

The benches were wood weathered to silver, pale as marble in the lights, and rose in a semicircle like the marble seats in any theater in the classical world. The night air was Mediterranean-warm, smelled of pine trees, aromatic brush on the hills. You might almost imagine you were in Athens, if you closed your eyes; but only almost. The voices were all wrong.

Lewis opened his eyes, distracted by the mortal chatter of Southern California's cultural elite. Down in the boxes he saw furs and pearls, opera glasses, a few silk hats like his own; higher up, in the tiers that rose to the back of the house, were the people who had taken the streetcars to get here, who munched popcorn as they waited for the spectacle, or took stealthy nips of gin from pocket flasks. Most of them had never seen a Shakespeare play in their lives. What would they make of tonight's entertainment? Reinhardt's transplanted forest seemed dwarfed by the staggering towers of light from the klieg lamps, small and unreal, nearly transparent.

It got worse when the president of the California Festival Association came out to make a speech, going on at some length about the forward-looking citizens of California who, in partnership with the California State Chamber of Commerce, deeply and spiritually yearned to establish California in her rightful place as one of the leaders of the cultural and artistic world. Joseph chuckled and nudged Lewis.

"If only they knew," he said.

The lights went down at last. For a long moment there was only starlight, for the three-quarter moon had not yet risen above the hill to the east. Lewis crossed his fingers. *Click!* The fireflies lit, and a couple of carefully concealed can lights. There was the forest! Suddenly the trees were immense and ancient, suddenly the real world faded away and the dream was palpable. From the audience all around him Lewis heard the indrawn breath, one universal *oooh* of delight. He relaxed, leaning back.

All in all, it was a pleasant experience, though the painful parts were uncommonly painful. The lesser actors recited their lines with such flat lack of understanding they might have been reading from a Sears and Roebuck catalogue. The fairies twittered, Oberon overacted, Titania was shrill.

The mortals, however, didn't notice. Reinhardt's spell had worked, as effectively as the juice of the magic flower casting its glamour on the lovers' eyes. The two immortals looked around them, at the rapt audience. Joseph grinned and shrugged.

The wedding procession stepped off on cue, torches alight, and hit the stage squarely as the Wedding March ended. A bit of purple glass sparkled in Hippolyta's turban. Somewhere backstage, Felix Weissberger soaked his blistered hands in cold water and reflected that an afternoon's frenzied brush-cutting with a machete, marking out a path thereafter with clothesline, had been worth it.

Puck stood forth at last, smiling and untrustworthy.

"If we shadows have offended,
Think but this, and all is mended,
That you have but slumber'd here
While these visions did appear.
And this weak and idle theme,
No more yielding but a dream,
Gentles, do not reprehend:
If you pardon, we will mend.
Else the Puck a liar call.
So, good night unto you all.
Give me your hands, if we be friends,
And Robin shall restore amends."

Note-perfect. He bowed, scampered away into the trees, and the orchestra played Mendelssohn's closing music. The last four chords sounded; faded. The forest went dark.

The house lights came up abruptly, and Greater Los Angeles sat blinking on the benches. This was the moment when movie goers looked around for their hats and coats and brushed off spilled popcorn. That was what the audience did now, in deafening silence. And more silence. The moment dragged out interminably.

"Oh, for crying out loud," said Joseph in disgust. "'GIVE ME YOUR HANDS, IF WE BE FRIENDS!'"

He began to applaud, and Lewis joined in, and the gentry down in the boxes collected their wits and applauded too. The rest of the audience, those at least who were not already streaming for the exits in anticipation of a massive traffic jam in the Cahuenga Pass and Red Cars packed like sardine cans, finally realized that perhaps a sign of their appreciation was in order. There was some scattered applause.

Joseph and Lewis stayed in their seats until the crowd had ebbed away, as those few sensible locals did, and then strolled down at their leisure. Lewis glanced out at the Wood Near Athens, which had once again retreated into unreality. There was Max Reinhardt on the stage, shoulders sagging, staring up at the empty seats in dismay.

"Wait a minute," he told Joseph. He made his way through the boxes to the edge of the orchestra pit, and took off his hat.

"Herr Professor?"

Reinhardt turned his head. He looked as though he vaguely recognized Lewis.

"They really did enjoy it, you know. They're just not used to live theater."

"You think so?" Reinhardt's air of despondency did not lift.

"Wait till you see the morning papers! It'll be a smash hit. They'll have to add extra performances," promised Lewis.

"And how would you know that, young man?"

"Because you're a genius," said Lewis.

"Is America a good place in which to be a genius?"

"Well, of course it is."

Reinhardt looked out into the black void of Hollywood.

"I hope so,' he said bleakly.

TEN: BUT COME, YOUR BERGOMASK; LET YOUR EPILOGUE ALONE.

"Duh I entice yuh? Duh I speak yuh fair? Or rather duh I not in plainest truth tell yuh I duh not nor I cannot act?" recited Lewis in a monotone. Joseph snickered.

They were seated in a booth in Musso and Frank's, enjoying a late supper. Though it was near midnight, the place was crowded with the nocturnal denizens of show business: producers making pitches to studio executives, directors making pitches to producers, agents making pitches to directors, and actors begging their agents for work. Here and there a writer, lonely as a leper, sat brooding under the forest mural, over a fourth or fifth drink.

"I thought it was pretty neat, bad acting and all," said Joseph, loosening his tie. "Too bad the movie's going to be such a flopperola. Just as well Reinhardt can't know that in advance."

"People will still be watching it in a century's time," said Lewis. "I wish I could have told him that, at least."

Joseph shook his head. "You were pushing it, telling him as much as you did. You know the rules. Would they be able to handle it, if they knew as much as we do about the future? Hell no. 'Lord, what fools these mortals be.'"

"They aren't the only ones," said Lewis ruefully. A waiter appeared out of the shadows, bearing their cocktails on a tray. "Ah! And a perfect martini appeared, as if by magic. Thank you, Manuel."

The waiter withdrew. Joseph raised his scotch and soda.

"Here's to absent friends."

"Oh, gosh, if we drink to absent friends we'll be here all night," said Lewis.

"Good point. What'll we drink to, then? The rise of the Arts in Southern California? A bullet for Hitler? Good old Will Shakespeare?"

"To Max Reinhardt," said Lewis.

"There you go," said Joseph, and drank.

"*And so good night unto you all,*" said Lewis. He raised his martini. It caught the light from the booth lamp and shimmered frostily, bright as the moon's silver visage on a landscape of ephemeral sleep.

HOLLYWOOD IKONS

KAGE BAKER AND KATHLEEN BARTHOLOMEW

Before Kage died in 2010, this was one of the stories she told me to look at first. The notes went back ten or fifteen years—she was fascinated by ikons, and came up with the idea that they really could do "things" to the observer. The explanation ended up involving brain chemistry and classical mathematics.

   She was also very interested in WWII Hollywood at that time, and the two ideas got fused together in her research. And by the time I sat down to write this from Kage's handwritten notes and speculations, it was a lot easier to find a street-view of 1943 Los Angeles—Google is a great time machine. Kage had already assigned Joseph as the hero of this one, so all I had to do was channel her and connect the gold-limned dots. I hope you enjoy the result.

—K. B.

America! The New World!

Dr. Zeus Incorporated loved the place. We operatives who worked for the Company were as eager as any desperate immigrant to get there, too, especially after the U.S. got its feet under it.

   And one of the big reasons was chocolate.

Dr. Zeus is a vast, nearly omniscient cabal of scientists and business-men based in the twenty-fourth century. The scientists developed time travel (and guilty consciences); the businessmen used both of those to rescue select bits of the past for social good and amazing profits.

Now, you can only time travel one way, into the past. But if you can store or hide or just carry things long enough, they get to when you need them naturally. To handle *that* work, the Company applied neurochemical and mechanical enhancements to us, the operatives, making us into immortal cyborgs. We grab endangered plants, animals, art, and cultures back in the past and bring them into the future, just like ordinary mortals, for the benefit of mankind. And the enrichment of Dr. Zeus.

We're immune to illness, old age, most weapons and drugs. But in a lucky stroke, we're exquisitely sensitive to Theobromos. Chocolate. It's our only vice, as old Dr. Pretorius in *Bride of Frankenstein* declares. Dr. Zeus hates the fact that anything affects us, but for us who toil in the good Doctor's endless vineyards, it's our only buzz.

And the good old U.S. of A was the place to be, all right. Europe perfected chocolate to a high degree, but the United States made it available to the vulgar masses. And I've always been a pretty common sort of Joe. Whitman's, Blommer, Ghirardelli, Mars, Hershey's, Wil-bur's, Guittard, the Mast Brothers...you could find decent chocolate in any five and dime in America, right through the first half of the twentieth century.

Of course, just before that mid-century mark, a great big rock went crashing through happy storefront windows everywhere: World War II broke out. The United States rose to the challenge (eventually) and by 1942 they started rationing most things that made life interesting; nylons, rubber, shoes, cheese. Sugar. Gasoline. *Chocolate.*

My name is Joseph. I'm a Facilitator for Dr. Zeus—a fixer, the kind of clever guy who can manage to get a rare piece of art stored and maintained for a couple thousand years, until some rich fanatic can pay an obscene price for it. I was born 30,000 years ago in what would eventually be the Basque country of Spain, but I'm a thoroughly modern guy. The U.S. is my kind of place. I love the movies; I've got a closet full of fedoras and trench coats.

I was in L.A. as the Resident Field Facilitator in the 1940s. The war times, as war times always are, were rich and busy years for the Company. But as my local cover, I was also working a PI gig for MGM Studios in Culver City. Most of the time I was running as fast as I could, day and night. I was a victim of the war rationing: the local See's chocolate stores were down to being open one day a month. It was a damn good thing for most folks that Prohibition had been repealed, let me tell you. Me, I saved my chocolate ration coupons like everyone else, and hoarded the good stuff for free weekends.

May 1943 was warm and gray. It's always like that, springtime in Los Angeles. I've been in and out of the Basin since 1700 C.E., and even the Tongva back then complained about the Valley of the Smokes.

The nights were mighty dark that year, too, what with the occasional blackouts and the wartime light-reduction measures. The pleasure piers and the gambling ships down in Santa Monica were all dark—not that the party stopped, but it was a more subdued one. The ballroom at Lick Pier was very romantic with all the blackout curtains drawn; the Rosie Riveters liked to go there after their shifts and dance with any guy they could find. It was a hot scene at the Hollywood Canteen, too, but it was no good going there unless you were a man in uniform. The celebrities only danced with soldiers.

The great Battle of Los Angeles had been only six months prior, with rumors of Japanese planes and over 1,000 rounds of mortar ammunition shot by our own guys into Long Beach. Long Beach survived. No one was ever quite sure just what the hell was flying over the city that night, but all the light standards were promptly painted black on their seaward sides, and cars drove with only their parking lights on. Not that anyone usually had any gasoline.

I was living up in the Hollywood Hills then—I'd scored an apartment in a nice building above Highland, near the Bowl. A lot of small-time studio people lived there; the sort of folks who painted, and drove, and stood in for lighting checks, and hauled the wandering stars back on set when they got lost out in the wilds of Beverly Hills.

That last one was me. I'd heard about the place from a grateful hairdresser when I returned Van Johnson (sullen bastard that he was) to the set of *Madame Curie* early one morning. The place even had a garage, which would have been really nice if I'd still had a car, but Motor City was only making tanks these days. Luckily, the Red Car trolley line ran through the Cahuenga Pass, a half-block below my apartment building, and it could get me anywhere I needed to go to find whatever errant star I was hunting.

Easter 1943 was sort of drear and sad, what with the constant shortage of sugar, chocolate and young men. I was on assignment for MGM, keeping an eye on Spencer Tracy; with the war on, all MGM's stars had to present a super-respectable All-American lifestyle. Tracy's 1941 affair with Ingrid Bergman (another icy blonde who couldn't stand me) had segued right into his obsession with Kate Hepburn (another *redhead* who wanted me dead and buried in cowshit), but now he was spending Easter week with his Catholic wife.

The Red Car also ran straight out to Encino in the San Fernando Valley, where the Tracy family ranch was. Every morning I made the run out there, made sure Tracy wasn't hiding Easter eggs where he shouldn't, and phoned it in to the studio. With our senses, I could locate Tracy by his heartbeat from the Red Car stop, while having a cup of coffee three miles away. Things were quiet on the Company front, too, leaving me with nothing to facilitate. Which was fine with me.

So I was home at my ease on Tuesday, April 20, when Lewis returned from New York. Lewis is another old-timer operative, a Literature Specialist I'd known for close to 300 years. He was stationed in Hollywood, too. His specialty was twentieth-century fiction. His cover had been as a stunt double for Leslie Howard, until Howard got too old: we operatives don't age. The last several years Lewis had been rotating through gigs as a press secretary, assistant to assistant directors, continuity editor—scripts flowed through his hands, and the important ones stuck.

As far as I knew, he'd been chasing some manuscript on the East Coast. But his hysterical transmission was coming in from Hollywood and Franklin, only a half mile away, as clearly as if he was in my living room. Among the many nifty nanomachines that the cyborg process installed in our impermeable skulls was an ansible just a tick below the hydrogen line in the microwave frequencies. We could communicate instantly between any two points on the Earth, though most operatives kept it to an arm's length conversational distance... but Lewis's yelling and frenetic honking burst into my day off now pretty much simultaneously.

Joseph? Joseph, are you home? Lewis was obviously in a panic. And he was really laying it on with the horn, down in the street.

Yeah, I'm home, I'm right here! Quit the honking, Lewis, you're scaring the neighbors. I looked out my front window and saw a wonder: a gleaming green 1935 Ford Model B Woodie, parked facing the wrong way on Camrose, with the back seat crammed with luggage and what looked like a desk in the passenger seat.

Jeez, Lewis, is that you? Is that YOURS? I must have been broadcasting disbelief and envy, because he sounded pretty peeved when he answered.

Yes, it's me and yes, it's mine. I just drove home from the train station, but I can't stay there! Can I park here? Is there a place off the street? I need a place to stay—oh, it's just horrible—

By this time, I was out my front door and hurrying through the inner courtyard, down to the curb. The honking stopped as I came up to the car, but that was because Lewis was sitting there wringing his hands. And yeah—that was a desk in the passenger seat, legs in the air like a dead dog. The back seat had a steamer trunk in it, as well as several suitcases with Super Chief tags. Also a garment bag with a white silk scarf tying a pair of dress shoes to the handle, and a cardboard box full of bottles of colored ink and a quire of expensive note papers.

"What the hell is the matter with you?" I said, taking it all in. "You look like you're running away from home."

Lewis glared at me, but he was too upset to keep it up. "I've been in New York for the last two weeks on—assignment. You know." He glanced warily up at the windows of the two front apartments in my building. Not that anyone was watching.

"Yeah, right."

"And it all went perfectly, and I came home, and my train was even early; and then I got my car and drove home, and..." His eyes went perfectly round, the white showing all around his irises like a china doll's. "Oh, God! I had to leave, Joseph, I can't stay there—my apartment is infested with rats!"

I gotta say, I just stared. Rats were certainly not something the fastidious Angelino wanted in his apartment, but hey—it happened. Even to neurotically tidy guys like Lewis, who lived in elegant apartments down near Picfair. In Los Angeles in war time, the rats lived in the damned palm trees. They did pretty much as they pleased, since loose cats had a tendency to end up downtown in the Central Market, labeled as "Rabbit." But it couldn't have been the first time he'd encountered domestic vermin; like me, Lewis has walked forward through time on his own two feet for the last 2,000 years.

"You're scared of rats? What can I do, find you a cat?" I asked, leaning on his car roof.

"No, I'm not afraid of rats!" he said indignantly. "But I brought back several very valuable manuscripts, and they all need work, and I need a safe place to work on them while the landlord gets the rats out—and you should have seen the mess those damned things made of my parchment, and endpapers, and—and my camel hair brushes—!"

He pounded on the steering wheel, and for a minute I thought he was going to burst into tears. Not a sight I wanted my neighbors to see, especially if I was going to be putting him up while the rats got exterminated. And what else could I do, really? I *was* the Facilitator Field Rep for Los Angeles, and Lewis was not only an old comrade, he was a Literature Preservation Specialist—and obviously in the midst of a restoration project.

Also, (I couldn't help but consider) he had a 1935 Ford Model B, while I was on shank's mare for the duration of the present conflict. And Lewis always took excellent care of his cars...

"Of course, you can stay with me, Lewis!" I clapped him on the shoulder. "Listen, let's unload this stuff here in the front, it'll be easier to get it into my place. And you can park around back where my garage space is. Is this all you've got? Is there anything in the trunk?"

"Just the box of the manuscripts. I had to leave in such a hurry, I was afraid to put it down in the apartment..." He set the handbrake and climbed out. "I knew it would be safe if I locked it in the trunk, and I had to get my things out to bring here...it took three trips...!"

I went round to the passenger side and opened the door. "You brought your own desk, I see," I said diplomatically, and began to maneuver the thing out the opened door. It wasn't that heavy, especially for one us—we're a lot stronger than a mortal—but I couldn't quite see how Lewis had gotten it in there in the first place. It was resting upside down in the seat, with its delicate little clawed feet pressed up against the cloth of the ceiling. But I finally managed to get it slid out and put it on the sidewalk by Lewis's luggage. Didn't even scratch the paint.

The matching chair was in the back seat under the luggage. Of course.

Ultimately, he'd brought four suitcases, a garment bag, the trunk, the desk and chair, the box full of inks and paper, and another wooden box with a sound lid and a padlock. And three pillows. None of it was especially heavy, but my front door was narrow and behind two palm trees; getting that damned spindly desk around the trees and through the door was a pain. Lewis sat on my couch with his arms around the wooden crate of (presumably) valuable manuscripts, staring at me mournfully as I got the desk and the steamer trunk inside.

My place wasn't big, but it did have two bedrooms. Lewis's gear made a kind of sad pile in the middle of the smaller one—I'd never gotten around to really furnishing the room, and all it had was a rug and a secondhand Hoover in the corner. Lewis followed me in and looked around. The Hoover seemed to cheer him up.

"We'll get you a cot," I assured him. "And you can set up your desk under the window and have all the room you need."

Lewis finally put the crate down, and finally smiled, too.

"Thank you, Joseph," he said. "I—I really quite lost it back there. You have no idea what I've brought back with me, and the idea that it would all get rat-nibbled...well, it was just too much."

"Don't worry about it," I told him. "Now let's get your car in the garage—or, wait a second!" I snapped my fingers. I'd been waiting for this moment. "Listen, I've gotta go run out and do a bed check on Spencer Tracy, make sure he's home with the missus and the kids. Can I take your car? I can stop somewhere and bring back a cot and groceries, too. You can settle in and calm down."

Lewis just nodded and handed over his keys without a second thought. I knew then the book had to be something special. He was in that OCD trance that Preservers go into when they get their hands on some focus of their special obsessions—nothing mattered to him now but getting his habitat set up to house his prize. And Lewis was a guy who usually bargained for a lien on at least one of my limbs before he let me borrow his car!

This was going to work out just fine. He didn't even notice when I left him there with his desk and his books and his inks.

The ride out Ventura Boulevard to Encino was a pleasure jaunt in Lewis's Ford. I drove right past the front gate of the Tracy ranch, which was a lot easier than trying to triangulate on him from the train stop. I got close enough to see the palm trees and bougainvillea by the Spanish-style arcade of the front porch, and it was easy to locate Tracy and his family. I pinpointed him in the stables, with one mature female and one adolescent female: wife Louise and daughter Suzie. They were admiring a recently born foal from one of Tracy's polo ponies.

Well, that was certainly wholesome, familial and domestic-like. The ride back into Hollywood was relaxing too, with all the orange groves in the Valley apparently in bloom at once.... Nobody knew it yet (well, except me and my kind) but the first ever Smog Alert was due to settle down on Los Angeles this coming July. It would last for sweltering days. Ventura Boulevard would never smell this good again.

Since I had the car, I stopped at a secondhand store in Studio City and scored a wooden cot and some blankets. Then I went by the Ranch Market on Vine and picked up some staples for Lewis and me.

The Ranch Market was one of the first twenty-four-hour markets in Los Angeles. During the war, that meant it *might* be open at any hour, day or night. I got a bundle of their barbecued ribs, too, because you just never knew, these days, when they'd be available. They were worth waiting for, and there were always lines when the sweet smoke from the grills went drifting out the Market's open arched facade. It was nearly impossible to get roasts or chops or steaks with the war on. But, like every war I've lived through, there was always plenty of offal and bones. Liver and lights—and ribs—were easy to find.

And those ribs were the best I'd tasted since the *barbacoa* racks first went up in Tortuga and Port Royal—they brined 'em in seawater back then, and slathered them in rum and raw brown sugar. I think the Ranch Market did, too.

Anyway, I was caught up on duty and supplies when I got back to Camrose. I parked the Ford around the back, feeling very pleased with myself, and hauled all my booty up the long walk to my apartment.

"Hey, Lewis, I picked up dinner and some beer," I announced as I shouldered the front door open. "And a bed, too!"

Lewis wandered in, a book in his hands.

"There's a message for you on the credenza, Joseph," he said by way of greeting. His hair was sticking up every which way and his eyes had a manic glitter. Ah, the joys of work to a Preserver.... "And I reported in about my temporary change of address while I had someone's ear. And I used your phone and left your number and a *very* tart message for my landlord, too!"

"You probably didn't need to report you were here, as long as you're going ahead with your project. You brought your own link in your desk, didn't you?" I put the newspaper-wrapped bundle of ribs in the warmer on the stove top, and began unloading groceries.

"Yes, but I never get a live person on mine. And when I reported I was staying with you, Hermann Senex—remember him? I had no idea he was assigned to the West Coast now—anyway, he said it was just as well, because they had a new assignment for you and I would be helpful with it." He cocked his head and looked at me inquiringly.

"No idea, yet." I shook my head, putting a rye loaf in the bread box. "I'll call Hermann as soon as I'm done here and find out. Maybe someone suddenly wants comic books."

"I shouldn't think so," said Lewis. "I'm up to date on the full run of *Superman* through last month."

Wow. I'd have to ask him if I could take a look at those.

Lewis dithered about where to put the book while I set the kitchen table, and finally decided it would be safe on my coffee table.

"You're like a four-year-old with a new toy," I said.

"More than you know," he said. He fairly bounced in his chair with enthusiasm. "Do you know what I've got there?"

"Nope."

"It's the original manuscript of *The Little Prince* by Antoine de Saint-Exupéry! In French, with the original illustrations, the ones he did himself—he was in New York last month for the American edition's publication, and *I got it!*" Lewis practically slavered over the memory. "It took me months to produce the replacement. All those *naif* watercolors! I nabbed the original drawings, too, what he still had of them; the man is incredibly careless with his work! I've got most of the portfolio with me now. It'll all have to be stabilized before it can go into storage. Do you know, I found one of them crumpled up in the pocket of his coat, in a closet?"

The Little Prince was one of the great moral bedtime stories that baby Preservers got told, tucked into their little white beds in the nursery wards. St. Exupéry was one of the Good Mortals, see, and every fledgling Preserver loved that story. They all saw themselves, especially a sensitive guy like Lewis, as the valiant child taming foxes, defeating evil baobabs, and saving celestial roses.

"Sounds like a peach of an assignment, Lewis." I set a plate down in front of him, along with half of my small store of napkins and a hand towel. "Here, use extras—you're gonna want to keep your hands as clean as possible, right?"

"Are you joking? I'm going to *bathe* before I get to work on this!" he said indignantly.

However, at that point, the perfume of the ribs distracted both of us. For a while, there, my nifty little 1940s kitchenette sounded just like the ancestral cave in the Pyrenees where I'd had my first slice of smoked *pottok* brisket.

On our third round of ribs, though, the credenza in the living room started beeping. Lewis rolled his eyes over the bone he was delicately gnawing.

Your link, your call, he broadcast indistinctly.

Mortals can't hear our equipment's ultrasonic beeping, or see the higher-than-UV alarm lights flashing. For one of us, though, it's as bad as a migraine. I hurried over and slapped the thing quiet.

Facilitator Joseph here, I acknowledged.

Joseph, it's Hermann Senex at Beachwood Base. Got a moment?

It didn't matter if I did or not, of course, but Hermann was an informal sort of guy. He liked to keep it all on a friendly basis with us field operatives, and I appreciated that. He wasn't getting out much these days, because he was recruited 35,000 years ago in Germany from a mixed-race couple. The *Homo sap* neighbors had objected to his green eyes. Cro-Magnon and Neandertal parents endowed Hermann with a decidedly inhuman profile, a nose like Durante, and a complexion—between his swarthy Cro-Mag dad and his red-haired Neandertal mom—that screamed *miscegenation* to a twentieth-century American. When we could persuade him out for a beer now and then, we told people he was Rondo Hatton's stunt double.

Got an old case cropping up again for you, he sent. *You want the transmission first, or do you want to dredge it up yourself from your tertiary?*

Oh, give me the file reference, I replied resignedly. *There's always notes or some damned thing.*

So it came over in a tightly condensed transmission and I recognized the case at once. Oh, did I ever...I'd like to claim the memories surfaced with the scent of lotus and the taste of honey beer. No such luck; I got the records of my own reports, and the sensory recall of relentless heat, hot mud and an itchy wig. Honey beer had never tasted all that good, either. Still, I remembered:

Third Dynasty Egypt, and the Pharaoh Djoser was having a lot of trouble with his Pharaonic statuary and his pyramid tomb. The sculpture was awful and the pyramids kept falling down, slumping into lopsided mounds. Dr. Zeus was worried that the Egyptians might never get it right—and what might that do to recorded history? All history remembered was that it was all the idea of Djoser's architect, Imhotep.

The Company took a look at the representative art up at its own end of Time, and figured out what the secret was. The phenomenon of pareidolia had been at the root of it all, that tendency of the human brain to see faces in random patterns. The reaction in the fusiform and parahippocampal gyri could be deliberately evoked with the right curves and angles. The statues and wall paintings walked and talked to the Egyptian faithful: once they were painted the right way.

In its corporate paranoia, the Company decided it was their responsibility to make sure everything turned out right. They decided to impart the mathematical formulae as Truth from the Gods, and force the great Egyptian leap into greatness themselves. They'd given all the information to Imhotep, and launched the revolution in art and architecture that would shape Egypt for 3,000 years.

And I'd been Imhotep.

The formulae had turned up unexpectedly in Constantinople during the reign of Emperor Justinian, and been used to paint some really mind-altering ikons. A few mortal Byzantine artists died of strokes and heart attacks, brains burnt out by an ikon painter who didn't know what he was doing but could read a mathematical equation. One culture's Rapture is another's brain seizure. They'd given me several hard days, tracking the ikons down and getting them out of the way. They went into storage.

Aw, crumbs, Hermann. Is it time to deliver those things already?

Not exactly, he said. *We're kind of sending them out on a lend-lease deal. Someone in the current time is willing to pay literal tons of gold for them, but won't be able to hang on to them. Well, he doesn't know that, but—we do. We'll get them back in a few years and still have them for the twenty-fourth century deal.*

Like a gypsy horse, I said sourly.

Pretty much, Hermann agreed.

The Constantinople ikons, the Egyptian formulae for perfect portraits and flawless PR—I guess WWII was practically begging for something like that to resurface. Mickey Mouse couldn't handle all the propaganda.

Are we giving these bozos the scroll, too? I asked. *That's where the formulae are. It's the really dangerous bit. The ikons themselves will just kill mortals. The scroll can tell them how to make more.*

No, no, just the ikons! Hermann sounded shocked. *But the scroll may need preservation, and I thought Lewis could help with that.*

I consulted the assignment information further. *Okay, I see a list of possible sites where they might be. I'll start checking. Why aren't we sure where they are?*

Oh, it's been a while, I guess. So—everything good on this, Joseph?

Yeah, I think so. I'll check back with you when I've got them.

Great, said Hermann, in palpable relief. *Beachwood Base out.*

I could draw this out, but the memory still makes me fume.

Next morning, I left Lewis happily working away at his St. Exupéry and I sallied forth in his Ford to find the ikons. I quartered Los Angeles from the Valley to the Santa Monica Pier, and went through every stash and hideout address Hermann had left me. It took me two days. But the ikons weren't anywhere.

Finally I gave up and headed back to my apartment. I don't think Lewis noticed I'd been in, or out, or that I came back. But he noticed when I started yelling at Hermann over the credenza, and he came drifting into the living room to stare and eavesdrop.

They aren't anywhere you said they might be, Hermann. What's the trick here?

I'm sorry, Joseph. I really hoped you'd find them out there. But I have a note here for you, if you didn't, that this is a little complicated. They've been...misplaced. You're going to need to find them before you can deliver them. Hermann was apologetic as all hell about this. *Nobody knows exactly where they are. Somewhere in Hollywood, though.*

Not again! I howled.

Afraid so, Joseph. Well, Hermann sounded embarrassed now. *We've got a bit of a problem with the chain of custody. Somewhere along about 1750, we know the ikons came to the New World—but somehow the records never got converted to hard copy. We don't know where they ended up.*

Suddenly it was all clear to me. There'd been trouble like this before, with old operatives who got sloppy. And I knew which one it had to be....

This is part of that mess from New World One again, isn't it? I demanded. When that fat poseur Houbert closed down the base and packed out, and all those crates went missing! Isn't it?

Well, yes, though they weren't exactly missing, said Hermann placatingly. *We've got all the crates, and the numbers matched....*

But they were full of Mardi Gras costumes, Hermann! I yelled. Don't you remember? Paper hats! Party horns! Confetti and, and—fake gorilla tits!

Yes, yes, those were. But we know he had the ikons, and we're sure when they shipped out—even if not where, precisely. But we located the paperwork.

Great. I cracked my knuckles, imagining they were Houbert's.

It's not exactly organized, admitted Hermann. *But now we know where they aren't, because you went through all those. I'll have the rest of the paperwork in its boxes for you ready tomorrow. Actually, this is what I thought Lewis would be good at; this is a Literature Preservation problem if there ever was one. Good God, Joseph, we found a 200-year-old avocado in one carton.*

Crap. I thought furiously. *Well, it is pretty much Lewis's kind of thing, isn't it? But he's gonna just hate this. He's working on an original St. Exupéry manuscript right now!*

I know, and I really am sorry, Joseph. Poor Hermann sounded terrible—I mean, there was no way I was gonna say NO to this, but he was a good guy. He really did care. *It's Priority ASAP, but not Urgent. I think half of it is just that they want someone to do the scut work and get the ikons secured again. So Lewis can work on the files and the St. Exupéry, and you can do the footwork.*

Yeah. Okay. I can see how to handle this. Sorry, Hermann, I said. *This won't be too bad. We'll find the things and get 'em off to where ever they go next.*

I'll send the crates over tomorrow, then?

No, I said, remembering the Ford. *Save some money, I'll pick them up from you.*

Thank you, Joseph. I knew you'd figure this out. Beachwood Base out.

Lewis had been listening to all this with growing horror. And he was livid by the time Hermann and I signed off. Lewis had hated Houbert, the Administrator of New World One, with a deep and abiding loathing. Having to clean up more of the guy's snafus at this late date didn't exactly ease any of the old animosity. Especially not when all Lewis wanted to do was lock himself in a clean room with the St. Exupéry and gloat over the watercolors.

"Look, I promise you can split your time 50/50 between the manuscript and the files," I coaxed. "Even when you go back to your place, you can leave the ikon files here to work on, completely apart from the St. Exupéry, okay?"

He had to agree, of course. But I wanted at least some pale enthusiasm, to speed the job along. And I could see he was beginning to be taken with the chance to mete out some justice to Houbert....

Man, the State Department didn't have to work as hard as I did to get the Allies to cooperate! I should have gone into Government work.

When I got up next day, Lewis was already hard at work on the St. Exupéry. Which was good, because I was probably going to need his full skills and attention when I got the box of crap—pardon me, the famed Administrator Houbert's carefully preserved files—home from Hermann.

"Here." He handed me his house key and a slip of paper, along with a cup of something coffee-like. "That's my landlord's name. He lives in the back, on the bottom floor. He'll be expecting you later this morning to go over the extermination problem."

I looked down. "Linseed oil? China White? Ashes of Roses? *Gold leaf?* What, do you have to mix your own rat killer?"

"No, those are tints and a medium—as you know very well," said Lewis severely. "I need them for this job. Probably for the ikons, too. Oh, and there's an African violet on the kitchen windowsill; bring it along, please."

"You'll be back in a few days, for God's sake," I said. "And believe it or not, Lewis, I'm not running a hotel here."

"Well, there's no room for me at Beachwood Base, and that's not supposed to be used for general living quarters anyway," he said stubbornly. "And who knows how long it'll take for the exterminators to get rid of the rats? I'm not taking even Houbert's old cocktail napkins into a rat-infested apartment; more paper will just draw more rats!

"Besides," he added as I groused around finding my fedora, "you're almost out of coffee, *and* tea, *and* milk. And I left my ration book in the breadbox—if the rats haven't eaten it as well. So you'd better bring it, too."

"Arrgh," I said, or something along those lines, and went off into the gray morning.

Pulling out onto the sweep of Highland in the Ford, though, made up for a lot of exasperation with Lewis's nitpicking. I headed right down Highland and turned left on Franklin to find Beachwood, which was originally one of the canyon mouths below the Hollywood Reservoir. There were several housing developments up there, all following the example of the original Hollywoodland, it of the famous sign.

The sign read OLLYWOODLAND at the moment, since a drunken

caretaker, Albert Kothe, had plowed his truck into it a couple of years before. It would be a few years before the LAND was removed (or fell off; the stories would be conflicting) and the sign became the symbol of the whole sprawling imaginary world of the movies.

It wasn't lit up anymore, either, for fear of Japanese submarines seeing it across the flats of L.A. Also, because people stole the light bulbs and no one could afford to refurbish the sign just then. But the housing development was thriving, and long, skinny villages were growing up along the edges of all the hills.

The oldest and prettiest was Beachwood Village, a blend of cottages and mansionettes in the eponymous canyon. About halfway to the sign there was a pair of gatehouses, with no gate. They'd never had one, and no one had ever manned the little sentry boxes on the sides, either; people walked their dogs and sweethearts through them and marveled at the kitschy charm. The eastern arch had a tower rising above it, and the western one looked like a dollhouse.

Under the tower was Beachwood Base, installed on the sly by Dr. Zeus when the Hollywoodland development was built. It was a small and temporary base, scheduled to be replaced as soon as WWII ended and the Company could dig itself in at Catalina Island again. But right now, Catalina was overrun with the OSS training school, and Dr. Zeus was keeping a very low profile over there. So Hermann and a small crew coordinated everything from underneath Beachwood Village, and the rest of us operatives lived in rented rooms all over the L.A. Basin. Housing was tight in Los Angeles.

The Via portal was concealed in the hillside above and behind it. Hermann was waiting for me in the tiny foyer, with three big ferro-plastic packing crates. Someone had stenciled a bad wood-pattern on them, and stuck citrus fruit advertisements all over.

"Ave, Herman," I said, offering my forearm. The Old Ones prefer that manly style to modern limp hand shakes. We clasped arms—his hand ran pretty much from my wrist to my elbow.

"Joseph. Ave, ave, man, and thanks for taking this mess on for us," he said earnestly. He grinned—and that always made me grin too, because Hermann had the bath-towel incisors of the Neandertals, but with a Terry Thomas gap between them.

"That's Houbert's stash? Just three?" I asked in surprise.

"Those are all that matter, they've got the likeliest paperwork. I should have asked you how you were traveling, though. Did you take a cab?"

"Nope, borrowed Lewis's car," and I sent an image of the green Ford parked up above us. Hermann whistled appreciatively.

"Well, come in, Joseph, and let me get you some coffee or something."

That sounded unusually great. One of the advantages of holding down the fort in Beachwood Base was that Hermann and his gang got their supplies directly via Company channels. And everyone felt so bad about the plutonian posting, they sent along goodies whenever they could. No waiting in line at See's or Helm's for them; no Meatless Mondays or the gourmet joys of Roof Rabbit Ragout. While we field operatives drank Postum and used our tea bags three times each, Hermann ground Colombian beans fresh daily.

We spent some life-saving time with Hermann's excellent coffee and even-more-excellent coffee cake (all Neandertals are incredible bakers; I think it's the nose). Hermann printed out some lists for me. He'd found some indication of where some of the Mayan artifacts from New World One had ended up, too; which just might be a clue as to where the Byzantine goodies had gone.

Hermann always came through. That Neandertal thoroughness, and cheerful attention to duty—it was why there were so many of them, now hidden away in Company bases, where they kept the home fires burning for us less stable Homo sapiens types.

We got the crates down to the car, loaded them in and stood about for a little while, trading our admiration of Lewis's taste and luck in cars. I was figuring New York would take the Series this year, since they'd lost to St. Louis the year before and would have their dander up. Hermann was a man of the "anyone *but* those bastard Yankees" school of thought. We were just a couple of regular guys leaning on a car on a warm, gray afternoon...it's little scenarios like this that keep us keen and interested in life, you know?

I went back over the Cahuenga Pass and took a moving fix on Tracy, who was still at home being the good family man. I managed to score a tank of gas from a skeazy little station in Sherman Oaks—gas stations were rapidly turning into the new speakeasies—and took Sepulveda over and back down onto the West Side.

Lewis had an elegant little flat in a Spanish-style multi-unit on Packard near Hayworth. It was an elegant little neighborhood, too, full of tailored lawns and big sycamore trees. So it was quite a surprise to park in front of the place and see a rat sitting calmly in the driveway, cleaning its whiskers.

There was another one under the hedge lining the front walk. And there was audible skittering in the shrubs as I walked round to the back of the building. This wasn't a trap in the pantry problem; they were working up to Hamlin Town here.

The landlord, Mr. Hobson, was a withered but alert old guy in snappily pressed khakis. He looked like a New England shopkeeper as he opened his screen door to let me in. His apartment was clean and neat, and smelled like a New England general store, too. Cheese and crackers, oilcloth and pickles.

"So," I said, deciding to dispel any notion that I could be put off, "I'm representing Lewis Howard. I'm here to pick up some of his goods, and to inquire about an estimate of when the extermination will be done in his apartment."

"Dunno," said Hobson cautiously. "Rats can take some time, y'know. I'll probably have to do it myself—there's not enough chemicals OR exterminators to be had nowadays, it all goes to the Army."

"Well, let's face it, Mr. Hobson," I said. I waved a hand out toward the back lawn; there was a rat running along the edge of the drive-way. "This isn't a minor problem. You have Rat City thriving here."

He winced. "Yeah, they've gotten a little out of hand, all sudden-like. But I'm already laying out poison and traps, and it'll be all clear soon. Maybe a week? Maybe."

We argued a while—I wanted a guaranteed ETA and he wanted to stick Lewis with a rat-killing surcharge. I fixed him with my best ex-Inquisitor glare and intimated the Health Department might be called in to consult. I was pretty sure, from the scent in the air, that he was hoarding cheese; and I hinted that there were worse people I could consult than the Health Department.... He ended up rebating the rent, instead, though he couldn't promise a week's resolution. No problem, I needed Lewis longer than that for the job. We managed to compromise, and I gave him my card and number to call.

I showed him my note from Lewis, allowing me inside his place, and left him grumbling to himself and dragging out an enormous old compressor and a red can with a skull and crossbones painted on it. It didn't look good for the rats, or for the camellias along the drive, either.

I could hear rats, and smell them, too, as soon as I opened Lewis's door. That sweet-salt smell is unmistakable, and one of the nicer things about the twentieth century is the relative lack of it...and Lewis was right, they were everywhere. I found his ration book in the breadbox, but the bread was gone, of course. I gathered the other things he wanted and got out as soon as I could. The smell, the feeling of little beady eyes tracking me, the scritch of claws behind the furniture; I've lived and let live with our ratty friends over long centuries, but I'd really rather not.

As I left, I made a note to see if Lewis really did want a cat. Something elegant. Something blue-eyed, and long-haired, and bloodthirsty.

Lewis worked in a fine frenzy all week on the St. Exupéry. Saturday he set it aside, complaining bitterly, I might add, and got started on the three crates I had brought home. When I told him about Hobson and the rats, he just waved one hand at me and told me he trusted me implicitly.

Great. Now I was facilitating rats.

Sunday was Easter. To my surprise, Lewis was up before dawn, nattily dressed and walking up Highland with all the other dawn-risers.

"I like the lilies," he said. "And the quiet." Most of the attendees brought lilies to the Sunrise Service—Easter and canna and occasional sprays of candy-colored day lilies. Lewis denuded the front garden of my apartment court, and went up to the Bowl with an armful of cannas.

At least he came back in a good mood. It was a clear, bright Easter that year, the very best of spring weather in Los Angeles, and he set to on the crates from New World One with determination. I was relieved as hell, since I was beginning to wonder if I'd have to threaten him with rats.

When I checked in his room late that afternoon, he was surrounded by piles and piles of paper: but there was a weird order to them. They ranged against the walls like crumbling battlements, and then formed long curves centered on Lewis at his desk under the window.

"How's it coming, Lewis?" I asked.

Lewis looked around and waved a hand vaguely.

"It's all triage, so far," he said. "Based on how relevant the file is to your ikons; or if not, then to any art shipped from New World One; or if not, then any shipment with multiple headings that *include* art—and so on, and on. The farther away they are, the less relevant they are; the closer to me, the more."

"You look like the jewel in the lotus. Or Alice's caterpillar," I said.

"It's a fractal technique. I'm almost done with this part." He pointed at his cot. "Sit there and wait a few minutes, and then I should have something for you."

"Hey, that's great!" I sat down between a plastic box full of personnel room assignments and, yes, a pile of actual cocktail napkins. For the next forty-five minutes or so I watched as Lewis picked up files, scanned them, notated them and consigned them to various stacks: all at eye-flickering speed.

Finally Lewis tossed off the last file, dusted his hands, and swung round in his chair to beam at me.

"And the sorting is done!" he declared.

"Just like that? Lewis, you're a wonder! I didn't know it could be that simple!" I was really impressed, watching him was pretty amazing. "So what do you have for me?"

He indicated one of the curves that ran between his desk and the wall—a thin one with a doubled curve in it like a big cursive Q.

"This one's for you. Start at the wall end and go through every pile, and see what springs out at you," he ordered.

"What?"

"That's the line of greatest likelihood to tell us where the ikons got shipped." Lewis grinned evilly. "Did you think you were going to get out of this part, Joseph? Really?"

Well, yeah. I was a *Facilitator*. Which I guess he saw in my face, because he wagged a scolding finger at me.

"Come on, Facilitator. This requires your specialized brain, to see through all the twisty errors and subterfuges of lesser immortals!"

If this *were* a movie, I could show the next several days in classic Autumn Leaf calendar style—the daily pages floating off to join the piles of paper on the floor, a sea of time with the islands of pertinent paperwork rising from it. I could show you Lewis's triage in slo-mo, the pages floating with uncanny skill to land on their appropriate islands. And then I could show them all floating back off into our hands, in a nifty reverse reveal. There would be slow pans of empty coffee cups and eviscerated chocolate wrappers; cartons of Chinese food and bags of tacos. Of course, one of those tattered file sheets would eventually drift down against the green Army blanket on Lewis's cot, to reveal the location of the missing ikons. Voila!

It certainly happens that way in the movies, and for all I know it happens that way in real life. I don't know, I've never lived in real life.

Instead, we sorted paper for most of a week. We chased down names and locations and such-like clues on our credenzas, calling up a lot of operatives who were busy doing something else and were moderately annoyed to be questioned about possibly misfiling a shipment. (Like that never happened. Oh, man, the things that get lost even once they're in our hands!) I drove to a lot of quiet, unvisited places where crates from Dr. Zeus have a habit of getting stashed.

They were all washouts, though, and I had to go back to reading old reports and memos on where the stuff from New World One got shipped. None of the interesting stuff, like personnel files or treasure maps: just inventories, rosters, shipping orders; corrections to shipping orders, amendments to shipping orders. One thing we did finally ascertain: all the paperwork at least agreed that the ikons had come to Los Angeles.

I didn't even have any excuses to go check on Spencer Tracy; he'd moved back into town, to his usual hotel. It was all so damned boring!

"Portions of my cognitive software are shutting down," I complained to Lewis after about a week. "I'm not programmed for this."

"Think of it as forensics," said Lewis. He was working on the St. Exupéry illustrations again. "I always find it very satisfying."

"You're a Literary Preservationist! I'm an—an improvisational artist! I'm a PI, a gumshoe, a knight of the hard streets, man. I'm not designed to sort through all this bureaucratic crap!"

Lewis looked up at me. "You're always telling me you were designed to be flexible," he pointed out. "You can do anything I can do. It doesn't mean you have to enjoy it."

"You actually enjoy this?"

"Oh, my, yes," he sighed, and smoothed the edge of a page in a way that made me embarrassed to be looking. "You have no idea—the craving to set the text right, the need to make sure it will last. The satisfaction when you look down at perfection and know you made it happen—it's a totality of appetite and reward that approaches nirvana." He blushed. "I've always assumed it gets tied into our compulsive urges when we're training."

"Better than sex, huh," I said sourly.

"Oh, no!" he exclaimed. "A lot easier, though."

"Download your programming to me, then."

"It's specialized, customized, and personalized, Joseph," he said. "You know that. Your head would explode."

"I hate you, Lewis," I told him.

"Whatever gets you through this," he said, unperturbed. He glanced at the top paper in my stack, which was unmistakably a high-level memo. You could tell by the embossed red foil Kukulcan logo. "Isn't that a memo to Houbert?"

"Yeah. Like the other 7,264 I've looked at so far."

"Why's it dated three years *after* New World One closed?" he asked.

Good question. It was also upside down and hand-written in a scrawl that implied Houbert had been employing augmented chickens with epilepsy. Which was no problem for a Literature Preservationist like Lewis, which was why he was supposed to be doing this in the first place...

But it was a clue, a bona fide lead. The most I could get out of it, though, was someone sloppy inquiring where he ought to put something illegible. Obviously, it had been filed in the handiest open box when the last ones were shipping out to long-term storage. There was no answer or follow-up.

I finally tried calling up Houbert, who was running a neutral-ground casino in Monte Carlo, teaching vacationing Nazis and expat Europeans about real decadence. I never did get hold of the jerk, just got a one-word response from one of his latest sycophants.

Luckily for me, it was a name.

Slick Mick had been knocking around Los Angeles since the 1800s. His name was Micythos when he got here, but everyone—mortal and operative—had been calling him Slick Mick since about, oh, 1872. He arrived with the first wave of Yankees, when one more uncouth immigrant with no known ties or associates could settle down in the shadows of Los Angeles and start socking away goodies for the Company. Technically, Mick was a cultural anthropologist, and what did him in was Anthropologist's Disease: he went native.

It's impossible for one of us to go off the rails. It says so in the Company by-laws, I think. However, it's very possible for us to get... peculiar, especially with the OCD motivation built into the Preservers. If it gets bad enough, we get hauled in and reprogrammed; but if it doesn't interfere with our ability to do The Work, one of us can go on for centuries just getting weirder and weirder. Hence assholes like Houbert, and just plain crazy bums like Slick Mick.

If Mick had been mortal, he'd have been a drunk. As it was, he got his buzz off constantly eating chocolate, which left him in a permanently altered state. Mostly he was an errand boy and a messenger—like a homing pigeon. He could find his way anywhere he knew there was Theobromos. He behaved like a drunk, he looked and talked and smelled a lot like one, and he lived in the various hobo squats and leftover Hoovervilles downtown and on the edges of Griffith Park. It was easy to locate him, once we had the clue—a broad spectrum scan of the Basin on the operatives' frequencies only showed one transmission aberrant enough to be Slick Mick.

———— ✦ ————

Lewis and I piled into the Ford and set out in search of treasure. I had my entire stock of chocolate stuffed in a briefcase, to attract and bribe Mick. Lewis had all our combined coupons for chocolate and sugar—See's Candies was due to be open today.

I dropped Lewis off near Ivar and Hollywood, where a crowd was already assembling on the black and white tiles of the shop entrance. I went off to an empty lot on Franklin, below the boarded-up Japanese embassy building at the top of Orange. Mick's signal was a blurry light show in the front of my mind, leading me right to him.

He was lounging against a bit of broken wall, looking very content in the misty sunlight. Coveralls and a deformed straw hat made him look like one of Auntie Em's more depraved farm hands.

"Hey, Joseph," he greeted me. He had the rusty, dusty voice of an alky, though booze doesn't affect us much and Mick never actually imbibed. "Still babysitter to the stars?"

Only when I'm not on the job for the Doctor, I transmitted. I sat down carefully on the wall, briefcase across my knees. *And the word from the good Doctor is that you once took delivery of two or three Byzantine ikons from New World One.*

Probably, Mick allowed. *There was a lot of weird stuff came up from there when it closed down. Some of it, I just kept circulating through town, you know? Moving it from one place to another to keep it hidden....*

Yeah, sometimes you had to do that. Not every safe stash stays that way for a handy millennium; sometimes you need to move stuff every twenty years or so, just to keep it in the right area to be found on a given date. It was one of the main ways things got lost in the first place.

I clicked open the briefcase, and watched with interest as Mick's pupils expanded across his irises at the scent from within.

Whatcha got there, Joseph? God, even his transmission sounded hoarse!

Two and a quarter kilos of prime Theobromos, I said. *Most of it Guatemalan and Hershey's, mostly milk. A few almond bars. Six chocolate eggs. And about twelve ounces of malted milk balls.*

I thought Slick Mick would pass out just smelling it.

And it's all yours, Mick, briefcase and all, if you can remember where you put those three Greek ikons from New World One.

I swear, Mick's brain made gear-grinding noises as he sorted frantically through the chemical wreck of his memories. I was seriously considering advancing him just one Hershey bar, so his system wouldn't shut down from sheer frustration.

But Mick's brain wasn't a total mess yet. After about a quarter hour, while we both sat there in apparent silence, he suddenly straightened up.

I got it! I had to move them a few years ago, find a new place. They're in the Egyptian!

What, the Egyptian Theater? Are you sure you left them there, Mick? It's a pretty public space.

I'm positive! He was shaking with glee; that and the proximity of all that Theobromos. *Not in the lobby, in the back corridor where the toilets and the emergency exits are. I whitewashed 'em, and painted signs on 'em, and sneaked 'em in one afternoon—the little girl in the ticket booth thought I was just a maintenance man. Hey, you know what?*

What, Mick?

They still wear the kalasiri, them little girls at the theatre. Isn't that weird?

Mortals are like that, man, I said. *So—the ikons, they're hanging in that back corridor?*

Yes! Mick started to giggle. *They were really strange, too; gave me the willies somethin' awful. But now—one says* LADIES *and one says* GENTLEMEN *and one says* EXIT *I wanted to put* EGRESS *on it, 'cause the Egyptian is a fancy place, but it wouldn't fit.*

Mick's ruined mind shone in clear, transparent colors, as innocent of guile as a pile of broken bottles. He certainly believed the ikons were there; and by his peculiar logic, it made sense.

Mick, my man, you win the big prize. I closed the briefcase and handed it solemnly to him, and he clutched it to his chest like a warm blanket from the Sally Anns. He didn't really see me anymore after that. He was just sitting there inhaling the fragrance of the chocolate in his arms. Sometimes going crazy makes it easier to be happy.

...Joseph? Joseph? Can you come pick me up? I've got the goods! Lewis's transmission sounded breathless and triumphant.

On my way, Lewis. And I've got the goods, too! I was feeling pretty good myself. Because sometimes, just getting the job done is the best satisfaction of all.

Some people, though, even though they're powerfully augmented immortals, are doomed to live in china shops constantly invaded by bulls. I've often thought Lewis was one of those, and he sure as hell looked it when I picked him up round the corner from the See's shop a little later.

For one thing, he was clutching his market bag (promisingly lumpy, I saw) to his chest with a look altogether too much like Slick Mick's. His hair was falling in his eyes, one shoulder of his suit coat was torn open and he had a blooming black eye. Being one of us, it had to have been pretty recent to show at all. However, he was also grinning like the Cheshire Cat and practically levitated into the Ford when I pulled to the curb.

"What the hell happened to you?" I asked.

"There was a riot in the See's shop. I had to fight to keep my chocolate!" he said proudly. "But I did it!"

"Great. Hey, were they grandma types you defeated, Galahad?"

"Oh, ha ha—but, yes, there were some very combative older ladies there...."

"Well, here they come and they've got their umbrellas out, man!" I pointed at the furious posse hurrying down Ivar toward us, threw the Ford into reverse, and backed around the corner by the Burlesque Theater until I could gun it up Cahuenga and take off.

Lewis waved his hat (which looked like someone had stomped it) in farewell as we escaped.

"All right, you know where the ikons are!" he exulted, jamming the battered hat down on his head. "So what do we do next?"

"We're going to the movies, Lewis," I glanced at him. "With a stop to put away the goodies and get you a new coat. The secret of successful burglary is not to be noticed."

It was ridiculously easy after that, so easy that I was beginning to worry what would go wrong. Most of our work *is* relatively easy, actually—disasters are rare, and knowing the future in advance really makes the present simpler to get through. Still, there are mistakes (look at the snipe hunt we'd just been on) and things that required the brilliant improvisational skills of Facilitators like me.

But tonight was simple. Poor old Mick was years out of date— the usherettes no longer wore their Egyptian robes, but they'd never really looked like classic kalasiris anyway—more like Esmeralda the Dancing Gypsy. But the Egyptian was playing a great film, although no one in the audience but Lewis and I knew that *Casablanca* would be a deathless classic. And we'd both seen it dozens of times—but it *is* a classic, and we enjoyed it anyway. Between the newsreel—already pretty depressing in 1943—and the cartoon (*Der Fuehrer's Face*, an all-time favorite of mine), I went off to the men's room and had a few quiet moments to myself in the back corridors of the theatre. It might have been a little confusing for patrons coming after me with full bladders, because when I went back to my seat, the signs differentiating LADIES and GENTLEMEN were gone. They might have been found in the alley outside the exit door, if the door had still said EXIT. But it didn't.

As we strolled down the long court of the Egyptian, between the palms and sphinxes, I intoned, "Lewis, I think this is the beginning of a beautiful friendship."

"You say that every time we watch this film," sighed Lewis.

"Yeah, well, it's a good line."

When we walked back to where the car was parked on Las Palmas after the show, I ducked down the alley and got the three signs. And still nothing went wrong.

Lewis earned his keep as soon as we got them home, concocting something that smelled like a mentholated milk shake to clean the white wash off the edge of each sign. They were the right ones, the old colors shining like neon through the flat dull paint Slick Mick had used to hide them. You wouldn't think mere whitewash would do the trick, but...the Spanish once hid an entire golden altar from Captain Henry Morgan with a coat of white paint, and that bastard was hard to fool.

Lewis began a thorough cleaning as soon as we were sure, while I called in on the credenza to report that we had the ikons.

Great news, Joseph. Hermann congratulated me when he came on. *I figured all that was needed was a pair of old hands like you and Lewis. Stand by for delivery coordinates...*

There's always a weird wavering tone when some data dump comes over the credenza. I'm told it's not a real sound—ears and otic ganglia aren't involved, it's just an artifact of our neurons in response to the carrier wave that shoves the information into our cerebrums. All I know is, there's a hum like a distant howling, and then data coalesces out of it like a new memory.

This time it was two photographs—one of a house front, the other of a man's face—a telephone number and a name. The howl felt like it was running around my skull, morphing into nasty laughter.

I know this guy, Hermann. Not by this name, but—

There was an unhappy pause. *I know, Joseph. Everyone in town knows him, one way or another. But he's the agent for the party waiting for the ikons.*

Hermann—he's an agent for the Nazi Party!

I know, Joseph. Hermann sounded at least 60,000 years old now, and like he'd had a toothache the whole time. He went all formal on me then. *Facilitator Joseph, do you understand this assignment?*

Hermann Senex, I do. Joseph out.

And of course, I did understand it. I had just never imagined doing anything like this. We were supposed to be the good guys! But Dr. Zeus, in his infinite and omniscient wisdom, didn't choose sides. He played all sides against the future, for goals and reasons not obvious to we who slogged through the mud of Time. This time, there was apparently a great good reason for me to deliver mind-altering religious objects to the Nazis.

Like a student of American cinema didn't know where *that* was headed....

I knew this job was too easy.

When I told Lewis about it, he never even stopped in his careful cleaning of what I recognized as a martyr bishop. That ikon had frightened men to death, as I recalled.

"No." He shook his head. "No, I won't help you do that."

"I don't need your help," I said miserably. "I can wash off paint and deliver the things all by myself."

"No, you can't. You'll ruin them. And it's wrong." Lewis looked up at me. His face was calm, but his pulse was racing in fury. "This is against all our training, against everything we stand for."

Lewis held up the ikon. The face was nearly clear, and it set up that damned left-brain buzzing just like before. The things still worked.

"How can we hand these things over to the Nazis?" he demanded.

"Lewis, it's orders. The Doctor doesn't do things like this for, for—shallow reasons! And what can the Nazis do with them, anyway? They're just going to brain-burn anyone who looks at them!"

"Are you honestly saying you're just following orders?" Lewis was incredulous. Horrified. Well, so was I. "What if the Nazis learn to duplicate them? What if they use them on prisoners? What if they carry them before them into battle?"

I was groping desperately for an idea. Something Hermann had said—no, he'd *asked*..."He asked if I understood the assignment. That was all he said. He didn't say, *Do this thing,* he asked if I understood it! And I think we both do, Lewis. Don't we?"

Well, we had to tell ourselves *something*.

We stared at one another over the ikon. It stared into nothing and buzzed.

"Well, we have to give them the ikons. But I could change them," he said, half to himself. "Maybe we have to do *that*."

"Huh?" My, I was sharp today. I tried for more focus. "What?"

"I can paint new ones, duplicates, fakes. With errors. They won't do a damned thing. But Hitler and Himmler and all those asses in the Thule Society won't be able to tell that. They wouldn't know *Vril* if it bit them on the nose."

Something you need to know: we don't make art, we operatives. We know it, we appreciate it, but something in the process that makes us brilliant and immortal burns out most of our creativity. I've never known a Preserver who could paint better than a By-The-Numbers Kincaid. But we can copy like crazed Irish monks using quills made from angels' wings. We see every detail, we don't forget a thing, and our hand-eye coordination is, well, inhuman.

Lewis had been duplicating St. Exupéry's illustration from *The Little Prince* for weeks now. His forgeries would never be detected, the records showed that; and the originals would go on to some museum in the future.

Lewis read all this on my face, I suspect. It felt like it was a teletype running across my forehead, that's for sure.

"The Nazis will fall, eventually. We know that," he said. "Maybe we're meant to give them the fakes. Joseph, maybe we're meant to *help* them fall!"

Well, hell. Maybe we were. And even if we weren't, it was what we should have been doing. It was what we were, what we were made to do. I'd always prided myself on doing my best for the good of mankind and for the Company, whether mankind and the Company cared or not. Whether they knew it or not....

"I'm not an automaton, you know. I have morals. I'm flexible," I muttered. Lewis looked at me and raised one eyebrow.

"Do it," I said.

It took all the rest of that night, the next day, and into the night after that. Some of it I could do—even a Facilitator can wipe off white wash, like I said. And I could handle the scroll we found tucked into one of the frames, too. I'd dictated the original, and I spoke classical Greek better than Lewis. By the time I was done with it, it was useless. Dr. Zeus could store it anywhere, give it to anyone: all it would produce now would be a headache and writer's cramp.

Watching Lewis paint the fake ikons was a magic show. He had nearly everything he needed in his manuscript restoration kit; he made up a couple of washes from eggs and vinegar right in my kitchen. Maybe it was the heroism of the act—Lewis had an inclination towards heroics that I don't. Maybe it was that perfectionist thrill he'd been talking about. I don't know, maybe he just had an unfulfilled urge to be a forger. But even as he swore at the difficulties of tempera washes and trimmed his brushes to insane thinness, he was obviously having a great time. I was glad someone was.

If Dr. Z ever reviewed any of this, they'd just see Lewis restoring the ikons. Whether we were right or wrong to slip the Nazis fakes, we had to do this to finish the job either way. So everyone would live happily ever after—well, not the Nazis, but they weren't going to anyway. And you can't change history....

It was hard work. Not the reproduction of the shapes and colors—that was mere mechanics. But it took all Lewis's iron control as a

Preserver to keep from duplicating the damned effects of the ikonic formula. He had to start one of them over twice, when the face kept evoking that left-brain buzz.

When he was approaching the end of the project, Lewis sent me back to his place for a few esoteric chemicals—he said he could make a varnish that would accelerate the paint drying and make it look appropriately aged. And he needed new clothes. Since he was down to the picky details, I took the chance and got rid of the original ikons, too; I took them to Lewis's apartment, and left them leaning on the wall in his bedroom.

When I got back, he mixed up more Love Potion No. 9 right there in my sink, and gave the final polish to the ikons. I couldn't tell any difference, except these didn't make my brain buzz. But whatever the Nazis hoped these would have done, they sure as hell weren't gonna do it now.

I called the number, out in Beverly Hills, and exchanged mild insults with the butler. He finally conveyed my message to his master, and then his master's message to me, which was: "Tomorrow at 4 PM. Come to the back door."

I didn't offer to wear a carnation so they'd know me.

When it was done, I collected poor exhausted Lewis and took him home. There were no rats in evidence as we made our way up to his front door, and a strong smell of chlorine rose from the stones of the porch. Mr. Hobson, pottering among the camellias, gave us a "thumbs up" as we passed him.

The apartment smelled clean when we stepped in, and the carpet had that look of newly shampooed rugs. However, there was a surprise in the bedroom. The three ikons, leaning against the wall, were surrounded by a circle of dead rats.

I stopped Lewis from going right back out and murdering old Hobson, and sent him to make coffee. I got a broom and the can from the kitchen, and swept up the rodent Army of Darkness lying there grinning at the painted saints. And I looked at them closely as I dumped them.

When I took the trash can out to the back porch, I told Lewis, "The ikons killed your rats."

"What?" He stared.

"Yep. They all died of strokes and heart failure, like the guys I saw in Byzantium. Rats can recognize faces, like dogs do. That must have been enough for the effect to take hold in their brains. You've got a rat-proof apartment now, Lewis."

That cheered him up something grand. Me, too—it's nice when you can contrive some sort of benefit out of all the conspiracies and shadow plays that are an operative's working life. Even if it's just dead rats. Sometimes *because* it is.

Eventually, we hid the ikons again. But the Company doesn't know where, because they think the originals went to Germany. Where they were expected to end up, and where they specifically did no good for the Third Reich. And where they were eventually looted by the Russians. For whom they *also* worked no magic whatsoever....

We did that, Lewis and me. Our two bits toward making the world a better place: which is, after all, the whole point of Dr. Zeus. Right? Oh, I know that history can't be changed. But it can be lied to, and it's no better at identifying a fake than anyone else.

Those damned ikons were good for one thing, though. Maybe Lewis had managed to catch some of that lethal magic in the ikons after all, something only the mortals could see. I'd like to think he did. They still seemed to kill rats like a charm.

I've said it before and I'll say it again: Now, *that's* facilitating.

ABOUT THE AUTHOR

KAGE BAKER is the author of the twelve volumes of the Company series (*In The Garden of Iden*, *Sky Coyote*), following the historical adventures of time-traveling immortals. She also wrote a series of fantasy novels (*The Anvil of the World*, *The House of the Stag*, *The Bird of the River*), as well as one children's book, *The Hotel Under the Sand*, from Tachyon Publications. Baker was passionately involved in the theatre for most of her life, particularly in the area of historical recreation. Born in Hollywood, California, she spent the last seventeen years of her life in the legendary beach town of Pismo Beach. She died in 2011, at the age of fifty-eight, after a year-long battle with cancer. Her sister, Kathleen Bartholomew, is continuing to work on Baker's stories and novels from notes and instructions left in her estate; the most recent of these, "Hollywood Ikons," was written exclusively for this collection.